ON THE
Road
TO Ruin

Emily Tudor

For all the confused people in their twenties like me struggling with "the point" of all this. May we soon find an answer that makes the future feel a little less terrifying.

Recommended Reading Order

Hi! The book you are about to read is *technically* a spin-off from the other duet I have published. Now, it is not necessary to read *The Hart Sisters* duet prior to this one, but there are a few spoilers for those two books in this novel since it takes place after the events of that duet. However, if you do want to read it in the proper order, it can be found below!

<u>**Reading Order:**</u>
The Road Not Taken (Hart Sisters #1)
The Road Less Traveled By (Hart Sisters #2)
On the Road to Ruin (West Siblings #1)

Content Warnings

This book features on-page descriptions of grief, mentions of suicide, parental neglect, and mentions of an emotionally abusive relationship. Please proceed cautiously and protect your mental health. Call or chat 988.

Dicktionary

For those who want to skip the spicy parts, or those who want to skip straight to them. Whatever you prefer!

Chapter 13
Chapter 14
Chapter 16
Chapter 17
Chapter 21
Chapter 26
Chapter 31

Playlist

Denial — Judah & The Lion
Mess — Noah Kahan
Fresh Out The Slammer — Taylor Swift
Club Heaven — Nessa Barrett
Dirty Little Secret — The All-American Rejects
Run For The Hills — Tate McRae
New Romantics — Taylor Swift
Backseat Driver — asiris
Arm's Length — Sam Fender
She Always Takes It Black — Gregory Alan Isakov
Carlo's Song — Noah Kahan
GREENGREENGREEN — Chase Atlantic
Sex — The 1975
Bad Idea — Ariana Grande
Oh My — Alessi Rose
BIRDS OF A FEATHER — Billie Eilish
I NEVER EXISTED — Chase Atlantic
What You Need — The Weeknd
Silver Spoon — Erin LeCount
Scumbag — ROLE MODEL
TOO LATE — Chase Atlantic
Stuck With U — Ariana Grande & Justin Bieber
The Party & The After Party — The Weeknd

Augusta — Gracie Abrams

Everything Has Changed — Taylor Swift & Ed Sheeran

August — Flipturn

Fast Times — Sabrina Carpenter

Do I Wanna Know? — Arctic Monkeys

Cautious — Cassidi

Moonlight — Ariana Grande

But Daddy I Love Him — Taylor Swift

Francesca — Hozier

Sports Car — Tate McRae

Begin Again — Taylor Swift

Would That I — Hozier

Six Years Wiser — Harrison Boe

Mess Is Mine — Vance Joy

Leave Me Again — Kelsea Ballerini

You Are In Love — Taylor Swift

Catacombs — Krooked Kings

5 More Minutes — Sydney Rose

Autumn Leaves — Ed Sheeran

Carry You Home — Alex Warren

At The Beach, In Every Life — Gigi Perez

Isimo — Bleachers

Geronimo — Sheppard

Rollercoaster — Bleachers

"When Mum and Dad died, I thought I was going to die too. I was sure of it. But then I thought, what if I was already dead? But nobody else knew, and I was walking around dead. But everybody could see and hear me. That was dreadful. It only felt like dying because, actually, I was still alive—you have to be to feel that way. I wasn't dead. I was just really, really sad."

— Flora Wingrave, *The Haunting of Bly Manor*

"It is not time or opportunity that is to determine intimacy—it is disposition alone. Seven years would be insufficient to make some people acquainted with each other, and seven days are more than enough for others."

—— Jane Austen, *Sense and Sensibility*

Prologue

— DENIAL BY JUDAH & THE LION

Almost two years ago, I got a phone call that changed my life.

And it wasn't the good kind of life-changing call. Not even close. It was the call that would shift my entire world on its axis and if I had known that before I answered it, I never would have picked the phone up.

Almost two years ago, one of my brothers drove up to our family cabin, wrote letters for all of us he was leaving behind, and then left the earth by his own hand.

Ever since that day, I've been stuck in a hole—figuratively, not literally. It's the kind of hole that you try to climb out of, but eventually, your arms get tired of digging and your brain gets exhausted trying to think of new ways to leave, so you decide staying in it isn't the worst idea in the world.

It's been two years, and sometimes I still think he's going to walk through the door. It's been two years and I've officially stopped living my life. I don't know how to flip the switch and become how I was before this happened, but I don't know if I even want to go back to who I was before.

When Tobias was alive, I felt like a human being. Now... Now I have no idea who I am. I have no idea what to do. I'm stuck in a trap that won't let me go, but I'm the one who set it in the first place. I need to feel alive again. I need to feel *something* again, but all my emotions can only come out when my grief does.

I need to feel my brother around me again.

As I get out of my desk chair and march into my boss' office, I know quitting my job won't solve anything I'm feeling.

But at least it's a start.

Chapter One

— MESS BY NOAH KAHAN

"W ill you marry me?"

No, this is not happening. Have I crossed into some sort of alternate dimension? If so, how the fuck do I get out? "Gregory, I—"

"I knew you'd be shocked. I was going to wait until we went on our trip, but I couldn't." His smile beams as he's down on one knee in our foyer, and I'm silently figuring out how I can leave the house undetected.

I *was* going to come home, make dinner, and gear up for another night of wallowing in all my past decisions that have led me here, but it looks like those plans have been thrown for a loop. Fuck. My. Life. Only this would happen to me. "I-I don't know what to say."

"Well, one word and three letters might suffice." He nudges the ring box toward me, a giant glittering diamond sparkles on the end of it with some smaller ones on the gold band.

I don't know why I haven't said anything to him, but I know this isn't what I want. All it took was him proposing for me to finally understand that. The thought has been lingering in my head for a few months—that I wanted to break off our relationship—but we were too intertwined, and it felt like more of a hassle to do that. So I sucked it up and stayed, not wanting to prove my older brother right that I had made a huge mistake moving to Arizona with a guy I barely knew. *Fucking Tristan.* I wish I could blame my feelings on him, but I can't.

Gregory and I were never going to last because I don't think I ever truly loved him. He was comfortable. *I* was comfortable with him because he whisked me away from home and that's what I thought I needed when I met him. My reaction to what's happening is cementing that in my mind. *This isn't what I want.* "I don't think we should do this."

I watch his face fall as he lowers the ring. "Why not? It's the next step in our relationship. I thought this was what you wanted?"

"That's not a good enough reason to get married. We've never even talked about marriage. I-I can't do this." I bolt up the stairs, go to my closet, grab my duffel bag, and start throwing random clothes in it. As I'm ordering a car to the airport, Gregory spins me around to face him.

"What are you doing? Where are you going?"

"Pennsylvania, I think." I know for sure I'm headed there, but my mind is racing as I try to center myself after this horrible day. I quit my shitty job earlier. That's why I'm home so early, not because Gregory texted me he needed me. No, I was in the middle of quitting my dead-end, nine-to-five receptionist job I hated. Fleeing in the middle of a proposal was also not on my to-do list for today, but why not add another bullet point to the fucked up mess my life is?

How the hell did I get here? Not just Arizona, but life. How did I turn into the girl that followed her short-term boyfriend to another state, when I knew deep down it wasn't what I wanted? How did I turn into the girl that left her home to follow some man? I'm pathetic. I have no friends, no family, *nothing* here. Everyone I know and love is back in Pennsylvania living their best life, and why shouldn't I join them? "Look—"

"You're just going to leave? After all this, you're going to go?"

"Yes, that is how it works. I'm sorry, I—"

"After everything I've done for you, this is what you're doing? You're going to leave before we can actually start our future?" He throws his arms up, still looking at the expression on my face. "Get the hell out of here. We're over."

I turn to face him, his head buried in his hands. *Is it odd I don't feel bad?* "Obviously. A rejected proposal usually means the end of a relationship."

"God, you're such a bitch. You don't even care that you're breaking my heart, do you?" His eyes lock with mine, and suddenly the guilt trickles in. Only a little bit, but it's still there. He has rich parents, a bank account I'll never be able to earn half of if I tried, and a steady job as an assistant district attorney. His parents run the biggest law firm on this side of the country, yet he chose not to work for them until he has his inheritance money in his bank account when he turns twenty-eight. As if he doesn't have enough money already.

I have no job, no friends, no life, no relationship thanks to my own doing, and no idea where the hell I'm headed in the future. My life has quite literally fallen apart at the seams in the past two hours, and most of it is my own fault.

But it'll be fine. I'll get back on my feet because it's what I always do. I roll with the punches, and I don't take shit from anybody about it. "You deserve better than me. I'm sure you'll make some other girl very happy one day, that just won't be me. I have to go, my car is here." My voice is devoid of all emotion as I drag my bags down the stairs, taking one last look at the place that never felt like home to me.

"Teagen—"

I don't stick around to hear what he says before I'm throwing the door to the car open and making sure it's for me. He pulls navigation to the airport up while I try to book my flight online, finding the first available one back to Pennsylvania. I find a single seat, and grab it, not caring about the last minute price.

Before driving away, I hear Gregory smacking the window of the car. "Teagen, please. Can we just talk? My parents are going to be so disappointed."

My parents. Is that all he cares about? His parents' approval of our relationship and not the fact that I don't think we ever loved each other? Gregory was always nice to me. He was always a gentleman and the picture perfect boyfriend. He tipped well at restaurants and he was always nice to customer service workers, but that's about all he had going for him.

The only reason I agreed to move to Arizona with him was to stick it to my brother that I knew what I was doing. To prove I'm an adult, fully capable of making my own decisions. I thought when we got here everything would fall into place, but it never did. My brother was right, and that pisses me off.

In hindsight, Tristan meant well, but for once, I wanted to control my own decisions and prove to him and myself that I was making the right choice. All that fell apart when I realized I couldn't keep living like this—content.

I want to feel *alive* again. I've been chasing that feeling ever since Tobias died, but I'm not sure anything can fill that void. Our brother is dead and nothing will change that.

"Do you want me to leave?" the driver asks me through the rearview mirror.

"Please," I say, and he hitches the car into drive, leaving him standing on his driveway shouting something as he gets smaller in the rearview.

I thought moving to a new state and trying to start anew would do that for me, and it did at first, but as time went on, it dissipated again. All I've felt in the past year I've been here is lonely. Even with Gregory in the house, I always felt like I was alone. I miss my mom, Tobias, and the Hart sisters back in Pennsylvania. The West family used to have two parents and four children—my three brothers and me. Now it's just my mother, me, and my two remaining brothers—Theo and Tristan. Tobias and my father are gone forever. I've lost two people during two different parts of my life, and nothing can ever fill the void of their absences.

I don't want to face anybody when I go home. I'm a fucking mess, and crawling back to them when life on my own got too hard is embarrassing. I practically shoved down their throats that I could move to a new state by myself, because I was an adult and fully capable of making choices on my own. I told them they had to accept that, but in the end, they were right.

Maybe I'm not cut out for real life, and maybe I'll be alone forever because I'm cold, dead inside, and don't know how to fall in love with someone.

I couldn't fall in love with Gregory no matter how hard I tried. Every kiss, every touch, every glance at him felt flat and I don't think my body is capable of falling in love with anyone or anything.

My ride is now at the airport, and I thank him as I get out and run inside. My flight boards in an hour, and it's not so busy that I worry I might miss my flight. I get through security with no problem, and grab a water before sitting at my gate.

God, what am I doing? I have no plan from here. What do I do when I get to Pennsylvania? I can't tell Tristan I'm home because then he'll ask me a thousand different questions I don't feel like answering. I can't tell Bree because she'll tell her sister. I love that girl to death, but she can't keep a secret. If Bree tells Liv, Tristan will know by tonight. I can't go to my mom's because she'll berate me with questions too. Theo is in Vermont. And Tobias is dead.

Basically, I'm fucked. I have nobody else. No college or high school friends because girls think I'm too direct, and I've always had a hard time making friends.

Bree is the only exception to that. She's one of the most kind and caring people I've ever met. I started off being a fan of her YouTube channel, loving her videos and trusting her book recommendations with my life, until I met her and we fell into a friendship. No, actually, we didn't fall. We chose each other. I think I'm the only real person in her life besides her sister and Vince, and she's the same for me.

My one and only friend that I love with my whole heart. Tristan dating her sister in college was the best thing to ever happen to me.

Maybe if I go to her place and swear her to secrecy, my brother won't find out. If only I believed that, then I could, but somebody would tell Tristan and my family. I'm sure of it.

> **Teags: Hey. Are you home or on another trip?**

> **Bree: Vince took me on a vacation to get away from the vultures.**

> **Teags: Oh, good. You deserve it.**

> **Bree: Are you okay?**

> **Teags: Yeah, I'm fine. Just checking in. Love you!**

> **Bree: Love you too. Let's call soon, okay? I miss you.**

> **Teags: Will do. Tell Vince I say hi :)**

Vince is Bree's bodyguard turned boyfriend, and those two could not be more perfect for one another. They complete each other like two different phases of the moon, and I don't think I'm destined for what they have.

I'm destined to be the fun, crazy aunt who's always in the middle of a crisis. How fun. I'm going to die alone with nobody left to give a speech at my funeral. At twenty-four years old, I've officially fallen apart more times than I've been together.

My boarding group being announced lifts me from my fog, and as I get on the plane, I realize I'm officially in the middle of another life crisis, and it won't be ending anytime soon.

AFTER A FOUR AND a half hour flight next to a bunch of screaming children, I'm finally back on the East Coast, and I can breathe a little bit better already.

I get into my next car, the address already plugged in before the nice lady drives away from the airport. It's only about a twenty minute drive to where I'm going, and I silently pray I don't get kicked off of his porch.

Where I'm headed is risky. I don't even know why I plugged *his* address into the app, but my fingers did it anyway. I could've checked into a hotel or something, but I don't think I can handle being by myself for too long. I might go crazy. Plus, I already spent way too much money I don't have today.

It'll be fine. Just explain your situation to him, and he'll understand. He's a nice guy, and the fact that I've had a crush on him since I saw him a few years ago has nothing to do with it. Absolutely nothing, and that crush will never go anywhere because he'll never feel the same way, which is fine. I don't need him to.

I doubt my crush even exists anymore since I haven't seen him in a while. But as the car rolls up to his house, rain pelting the windows like a tsunami, I find myself feeling a little nervous. I thank the driver before I get out, shuffle toward his house and take a breath before I knock.

I feel a few drops of rain fall onto my face and I try to make myself look more put together, but I doubt it will work. I probably look like a fucking mess standing here on his porch. I'm still wearing the clothes I had on from work—a light gray blouse that might be see-through now, black slacks, and black flats because heels are the worst shoes ever.

A few seconds later, the door swings open and my stomach drops as I look at the man in front of me—black messy hair, golden skin that emphasizes his stunning features, and hazel eyes I could get lost in if I look for too long. He's not wearing a shirt, and his plaid checkered pants tell me he's getting ready for bed soon. *Shit.* I forgot how late it is. I hope he doesn't have a girl over.

Dominic Graves might be the only person my body will ever react to, and I will never be able to have him because he's best friends with my brother.

Guess that crush hasn't left yet.

His eyes sweep over the state of me, and before he can say anything, I do. "I didn't have anywhere else to go. Can I come in?"

Eyebrows still pinched together, Dom wordlessly moves to the side, silently inviting me in. I go to grab my duffel bag from my side, but he reaches out and takes it before I can, while I follow him into the living room.

He shuts the door, and only then do I allow myself to look at his abs that are practically on display. *Good god, pull yourself together.*

"Tha—"

"What the hell are you doing here?"

I don't really want to get into *that* right now, so I go with the next best option. "Please don't tell anyone I'm back in Pennsylvania."

Chapter Two

— FRESH OUT THE SLAMMER BY TAYLOR SWIFT

"Harry, all I'm asking is for you to feed my fish while I'm out of town. Why are you making it such a big deal?"

He chuckles across the line. *Dick.* "I wasn't aware you had any pets. Especially tiny ones that float. Exactly how many fish do you have?"

"Three! And they're awesome, so stop making fun of me," I jest as I throw a few more outfits into my suitcase. "Fish are real pets, and I'm tired of all your stupid jokes."

"Fine. I'll feed your stupid fish. But if one of them dies, it's not my fault."

I stop what I'm doing when he says that. "You better not kill my fish, or I'll pull something worse on you, Harrison."

"I'll try my best," Harry sighs across the line. "So, where the hell are you off to this time?"

"My parents are making me go to a few locations across the country so I can meet with some investors so we can start franchising in different states. It's only for a few weeks, but it's what I have to do to prove to them I can handle myself when it comes to the family business." All I've been doing since I got out of college was trying to prove to them I'll behave myself while working for them, but all they've let me do since I graduated is bitch work. I was basically a glorified mailman running around to different branches in Pennsylvania delivering things. Yet another way my parents made me prove myself to them. I didn't complain once while in my previous position, and now they're making me prove myself again with this cross-country trip.

On top of that, they keep reminding me I should be grateful. Grateful for the money they've given me and the job security I'll have for life, but all I feel is resentment. I didn't ask for that money, and sometimes I wish I never took it.

"You sound thrilled, Dommy."

Yeah, thrilled. I'm absolutely thrilled I get to travel across the country and attend fancy business meetings for my parents, when I really want nothing to do with the family business that my parents have always cared more about than their kids.

I'm the youngest of three, and my siblings are already in their spots at Graves Jewelry, while I'm still here having to prove myself to my parents. None of my siblings had to do anything like this in order to start working for the company, but of course, as the wild child, I have to go the extra mile to make my parents trust me. Never mind the fact that I was in the top five percent of my class. Never mind the grades and the accolades I got in college. The only thing they care about is keeping the family name at the highest of standards, and I don't fit whatever they want our image to be.

I'm the family embarrassment. The child that likes to party, drink, and do other unsavory things, or so they say. Just because I like taking the edge off sometimes doesn't mean I'm incapable of being a professional.

But my parents won't change their minds, and I've been prepped for my role in the company my entire life. I've always known the only reason they had three kids was so they could hand off the business to us. Graves Jewelry is the fourth child in my family, and they've always been the favorite.

It's bad enough they're hanging the money they so nicely gifted me over my head, but this life is all I've ever known. Things could be worse. People have it so much harder than I have, but I'm still drowning in the weight of my parents' expectations of me when I don't even want this job. If I was strong enough, I'd say fuck them and the company, but I'm not. This has always been my path and there's nothing I can do to change it.

"Dom? Did I lose you?" Harry asks over the line.

"No, and it's fine. I'm as thrilled as I can be. I've known this was going to be my path my whole life."

"For someone who has known this was his end goal, you sure haven't mentioned it to your close friends at all. Any time we asked you about your family back in college, you changed the subject."

I roll my eyes as I throw more clothes into my suitcase. "Yeah, and you guys never pressed."

"Dude, I'm just saying."

"Yeah, I know. Maybe one day you'll get me drunk enough and we'll have some sort of feelings session, but until then, you get to hear me complain."

Harry laughs. "Great. Just what I want to hear."

"I aim to please, Har." I hear a knock at the door. "I got to go. My food is here."

"Well, I'll see you when you get back then?"

"Yup."

"Have a good trip, D."

"Thanks, dude," I say as I hang up the phone and toss it onto my bed.

It's fucking late, and I didn't have time to eat today since I had back-to-back meetings and had to come home and start packing. I've been putting all of this off because I'm not looking forward to driving across the country for weeks on my own, so I'm in a time crunch now.

And I forgot to eat dinner.

And lunch because I was in a fucking meeting that could have been an email.

I jog down my stairs, and as I swing my door open, the girl on the other side of it is not who I'm expecting. It's not my food.

It's my best friend's little sister—Teagen West. I have to say, she is not who I expected to see this late at night, and part of me wants to call her brother once I find out what she's doing here. She's standing on my porch, a bag attached to her hand, and her knuckles are white from how hard she's holding onto it.

She's wearing something that looks like she came directly from her office—the one in Arizona. What the hell is she doing back here? And why is she at my door and not Tristan's?

"I didn't have anywhere else to go. Can I come in?"

Uh, what? She definitely has a million other places to go. Her brother's place. Bree's house, her best friend. I should be last on the list of places she should go, and I know they didn't turn her away, so she clearly came here first.

I say nothing as I move to the side and invite her in. She looks...different. Disheveled, almost. I'm used to seeing her looking murderous all the time, but instead of her usual expression, she looks defeated.

Did something happen in Arizona?

I grab her suitcase from her, offering some help so she can get inside and warm up. She follows me into my living room as I shut the door. I *really* wish I had grabbed a shirt before this, because standing half-naked in my living room while my best friend's little sister stares at me is kind of uncomfortable.

"Tha—"

I cut her off, wanting answers as to why she's at my house so late. "What the hell are you doing here?"

"Please don't tell anyone I'm back in Pennsylvania."

"Why the hell not?" I ask, still confused. She's being weirdly cryptic.

"It's complicated."

"So, explain it to me," I say. There's another knock on my door. "That's gotta be my dinner this time."

"Your what?"

I open my door and sure enough, a small bag sits on my porch, and a car is pulling out of my driveway. *Thank fuck.* I'm starving.

I turn around, Teags still standing rigidly in the same spot, and I pass her on my way to the kitchen. "Come here and we'll talk. How long has it been since you've eaten anything?"

"Since before I got proposed to."

Huh? "Since what?"

She leans against the island in my kitchen as I open the bag and pull out a few trays. I grab two plates from my cabinet and split my dinner in half. Normally, I would sit down, throw some show on and eat this all myself, but she has caused a rift in my plans.

I take a bite of my sushi roll before I ask her again what she's doing here. "What's going on? I thought you lived in Arizona with your boyfriend."

"Well, I did. Until a few hours ago when he proposed and I said no and fled the state."

"Yeah, you've mentioned the proposal already. I don't understand why you're back here."

"It's complicated, and I can't go to Tristan about it because I don't want to have that conversation with him. Bree is out of the state, so this was my last option."

"What about your mom?" Tabitha West is a true gift to the world. Anyone who's close to the West family knows that.

"My mom would tell Tristan. Or she would parent me about my life choices, and I can't go back to that house. I can't."

I sigh heavily as I take another bite. *Fuck, this is good sushi.* "Okay."

"I just need to stay here for a few days and then I'll be out of your hair."

I'm about to tell her about my trip, but her phone rings and interrupts our conversation. She looks at it, declines, and then puts it on the counter. A few seconds later, it rings again and she does the same thing. That happens about ten more times as I try to keep eating.

The twelfth time she silences it, I say something. "Do you need to get that?"

"No, it's fine."

It rings again. "Answer your fucking phone so we can talk. Someone is obviously worried about you."

She starts to laugh. I've never heard her voice so high-pitched. "Trust me, he isn't worried about me." Then she finally picks up the phone, and all I hear on the other line is yelling.

I try to stay out of it and not eavesdrop, but he's *screaming* through the phone. I didn't think that shy fucker had it in him. Granted, I've never met him, but him not ever wanting to be around her family is very telling of who he is. Her boyfriend never impressed Tristan or anyone close to her, and that's all I needed to know about this guy.

"I'll get my stuff at some point, okay? Just calm the fuck down," Teags yells at him as her eyes flit to my face, probably uncomfortable having this conversation in front of me.

More yelling ensues, so I exit to my living room so she can have some privacy. I can still hear everything from my couch, but I pretend to stare at my phone, not reading a single thing from the article I clicked on.

"I just left Arizona. Hours ago, I was shuffling around your house and shoving my shit into bags. I get that you want to move on to please Mommy and Daddy, but I can't just come back. I need some fucking space from your high expectations. They practically suffocated me. Give me a few weeks, and I'll come grab my shit."

I hear a pause, her angered breathing coming from the kitchen.

"Don't you fucking touch anything of mine. You can move it, but don't throw it out." She pauses to take a breath. "Please."

I try to read my article again, but the only thing occupying my mind is the girl in my kitchen. Why did she leave him? Was it the proposal or something else? Why is he being such a dick to her? What the fuck is going on?

"Tell your parents to go fuck themselves then. I'm not their puppet, and I'm certainly not yours anymore. You and your family can't fit me into a box anymore. Goodbye," she says as I hear her phone slam onto the countertop.

She comes out to the living room, her eyes full of rage, and plops down onto the other side of the couch. She huffs a few times before continuing to eat, rather angrily, I might add. I've never seen someone eat sushi so pissed before.

"Do you want to talk about it?" I ask a few minutes later.

"No."

"Okay."

We're quiet for a few more minutes as the two of us sit in an awkward silence. This is weird—her being here. The two of us have always floated around one another, and the only time we've been alone before now was when I drove her home from her brother's wedding. She got drunk, and I took her home because Tristan asked me to, and we barely said anything on the drive. She curled into herself, her shoes in her lap, and I had to help her inside because she could barely stand.

I didn't want to ask what was going on with her, and she didn't want to talk about it either, so we didn't. Much like now, the two of us are pretending like things are fine when we both know they're not.

"I won't be here for a few weeks. I'm going on a cross country trip for work, so you're going to have to find somewhere else to stay. I can hold you hostage until I leave, but—"

She turns to me. "If you're leaving, let me watch your house for you. As a thank you."

"No."

She looks around, clearly frazzled. "But your fish could die."

"Harry is going to feed them for me."

"Then can I go with you? I need to pick up my stuff from Arizona anyway."

I shake my head. There's no way I'm getting involved in whatever shitshow she left in Arizona. For one, Tristan would kill me, and that's not a road I want to go down. He's super fucking protective of his only biological sister, and I don't need his wrath on me.

I have enough pressure on me with my parents breathing down my neck. I don't need to add anything else to that weight.

"No. I don't even need to tell you why that's a bad idea. Can't you go to a hotel or something?"

I swear I see tears spring into her eyes, but as soon as I notice them, they're gone. "No. I can't be alone or I'll go crazy. I've been by myself for too long, and I can't handle it anymore."

She just got out of a year long relationship, so what the hell does that mean?

"You really want to come with me on a trip across the country for a few weeks?" I've never had someone—let alone a girl—want to willingly hang out with me for an extended period of time. Nobody I know would ever voluntarily do this with me, but maybe the company would be nice. Maybe Teagen West traveling with me on the road is exactly what I need before my life becomes dull, uninteresting, and sad. Working for my parents sounds closer to a death sentence more and more everyday, especially with all the fucking rules they're forcing me to follow.

No drinking, no smoking, no fucking, and I'm not supposed to do anything to tarnish the family image. So basically, I can't have any fun.

"It sounds better than sulking about how my life has fallen apart in the span of twelve hours. What do you say? Want to help a girl out and help her pack up the life she fled?" She holds out her hand, her body radiating confidence.

But those eyes... Those eyes show how scared she really is. I can see the fear she has, and it almost feels like it mimics my own. She said earlier Gregory trapped her in a box, and now he can't anymore. If I had the balls to do it, I'd tell my parents they should fuck off. That I never wanted to be a part of the family business. That I want to figure out my own path away from them.

I've never been able to do that. To keep them happy, I have to play their stupid games, and go to their stupid events, despite wanting nothing to do with them.

This was always my siblings' paths, but it never felt like mine.

You might say I'm the black sheep of my family, and that has never felt more true. Especially now that I'm succumbing to their expectations of me.

"Fine, but what's in it for me?"

"A lifetime filled with good karma for helping out someone in need?"

"No, if I'm lying to my best friend—"

She scoffs. "Tristan is your best friend? He told me Harry was—"

"*If I'm lying to my best friend,* then I need something in return." I think for a second, but nothing comes to mind. "You owe me, and I'll figure out what at some point."

"Fine. I guess that's only fair." She yawns, and I see her body start to droop. She's probably exhausted from whatever day she had.

I get up off the couch and hold my hand out to her. "Now, let me show you to your room so you can sleep the day off."

She nods her head but declines my hand as she gets up and drags her bags up my stairs.

Chapter Three

— CLUB HEAVEN BY NESSA BARRETT

DOM SHUTS THE DOOR behind him, and when I'm alone with my thoughts again, I already feel the need to be doing something. So, I open my suitcase, grab my stuff, and head for a shower.

I need to wash today off of me, and long, hot showers always make me feel better.

I'm excited to go across the country with him because then I won't have to think about the utter disappointment my family is going to feel when they realize I'm back in Pennsylvania. Tristan will brag about how he was right, and my mom will once again be walking on eggshells around me, waiting for me to fall apart about my failed relationship and life.

She should know I never do that in front of them.

I grab my phone and shuffle my playlist, needing some music to drown out all the thoughts I'm having at the moment.

My relationship failed. But was it ever going to last in the first place? Probably not.

I quit my job and now have no stable income. Well, at least I'm not attached to someone I know I'd never love.

I have no idea where my future is headed. Who needs a plan? Plans never work out the way one wants them to.

My brother is dead, and he's not coming back. God, I miss him. I really fucking miss him.

I turn the shower on to the hottest setting, step in, and as soon as the hot water hits my body, I break.

I've become really good at crying in the shower. This way, nobody can hear the sounds of my sobs as water cascades all around me. It's easier like this. Nobody has to worry about me because I can get all my emotions out now, and shove the rest down.

It's foolproof.

My music plays from the playlist Tobias and I made when he was still here, and his favorite song comes on.

That makes me cry even harder because sometimes when I play this song, I imagine him walking through the door, hugging me and telling me it was all a bad dream. I imagine his smile lighting up our household again, and everyone crying tears of joy that he's back. For a split second, I see it all play out in my head.

And then I remember sitting in the front row at his funeral. I remember watching my mom and Tristan tearfully read eulogies about him. I remember people I barely knew coming up to me, telling stories about him, and saying how sorry they were. How they couldn't imagine losing someone like Tobias at such a young age. How they couldn't fathom what my family was going through.

I was twenty-two years old when my brother Tobias took his life. Now I'm twenty-four, and nothing makes sense.

It all feels surreal. I remember the day I got the call when my mom found out. I could barely hear what she was saying through the phone, so I dropped everything and rushed back home from my job.

I found her on the floor of his room, clutching one of his blankets. She was in shambles. Tears running from her eyes, face looking like she was in physical pain, and her body curled in on herself. I could barely decipher what she was saying.

Then I heard it. Those nine words that linger in my mind every single day.

"Your brother is dead. He took his own life."

I didn't believe her. I didn't know which brother she was talking about and I couldn't bear to ask which one it was. Then she told me the police were here. That they found Tobias at the cabin. That he was gone.

God, of all the memories that stay in my mind, those never fucking leave.

I once had three older brothers: Tristan, Tobias, and Theo. Now, I only have two. All three of them will always have a sister, but I'll never have three brothers again, I'll only ever have two. Tobias will never have a sister ever again because he's gone. I'm only a sister to him in the past tense.

I listen to this playlist whenever I feel like bashing my head into a mirror. Sometimes, it helps. Other times, it makes things worse because I can't feel him in the music. Tobias and I bonded over music. He was constantly showing me new artists and songs he thought I would like, and in a way, he molded my taste in music from a young age.

He lives on in my head through the playlists we made together, and through his favorite songs he used to sing in the car while I rolled my eyes at him.

I regret doing that now—rolling my eyes at him when all he was trying to do was get me to sing with him. I never did. I thought it was lame, or some other stupid reason I can't remember now. I'm not a great singer, and I never understood singing when you couldn't hold a pitch.

Now, I'd give anything for one more song with him in his car. Any amount of money, any time, *anything* for one more song. But I can't because he's dead. He's gone. And he's never coming back.

He's only a memory now.

I keep playing these songs over and over, hoping they'll keep his memory alive in my head, and it's usually hit or miss. Sometimes I remember exact memories, and other times, I can't feel him at all.

Can he hear the music I play wherever he is? Does he know I'm always thinking of him when I press play?

I don't know how to fix the part of me that thinks this is all a nightmare. That one day he'll shake me awake, smile down at me, and put on a vinyl to make me feel better.

Two weeks ago, I heard a new song on the radio that I liked, and I went to send it to him in our messages when I remembered he was gone.

I had to pull over and sit on the edge of the highway while I cried.

Then I unlocked my phone and saw every message I sent him when I found out he was gone. All of them went unanswered. I texted him over two hundred times the day he died, hoping for an answer. I wanted the police to be wrong. I wanted him to tell me it wasn't true.

I called him the same amount of times, wanting to hear his voice in his voicemail message. Every time I heard his voice come up, a little part of me hoped he was getting my messages.

But then reality punched me in the face and I realized I had to call Tristan and tell him that our brother was dead. I had to call Theo, too, because I knew our mom couldn't. She could barely speak. She cried so hard she passed out on Tobias's floor. I had to drag her to her room and tuck her into bed so she'd be comfortable.

I could barely utter the words before I broke down. Tristan had never heard me cry that bad before, not even when our dad died—granted, I was a lot younger when that happened. Tristan hung up on me as I sobbed into the phone, and then I pulled myself together enough to call Theo. Theo yelled at me, saying this was a sick joke, and I was a liar. Tears were pouring down my face and one of my brothers hung up on me while the other told me I was a liar.

They've apologized profusely since, but it still hurts thinking about that day. I get that we all react differently to news that sweeps you off your feet, but I was all alone in Pennsylvania. Tristan was living his life in California, and Theo was in South Carolina. Neither of them were in state when my other brother died—I was all alone with my mother. And I had to carry us both until they could get back here.

It was the hardest time in my entire life, and it's still not over yet. It's been almost two years, and the pain hasn't lessened. None of us have been okay since that day everything changed. We went from four siblings down to three.

Sometimes I think healing is complete and utter bullshit. Time heals all wounds, everyone says, but I don't see how that's possible.

The ache to see my brother again gets heavier every single day. Sometimes I get worried it might swallow me whole. That I'll be meaner and more closed off than I am already when the grief overcomes me—when the grief wins, if it hasn't already.

I'm a blunt person. I can't help it. Maybe my dad dying had that effect on me, or something. I don't know why I'm like this—cold and unattached. It's easiest for me, and somehow I attached myself to Gregory, but I never fully finished the stitch. I knew I'd run in the end. I knew this was going to be the outcome in the back of my head, but I had something to prove by being in a relationship with him.

I had to prove I was loveable despite everyone knowing love is the most embarrassing emotion I can feel. I had to prove I was an adult capable of making my own decisions despite everyone else's opinions.

But I never loved Gregory. He was a placeholder—a person I used to show everyone else I was capable of certain things. I feel bad doing that to him, I do. I feel shitty using him like I did, and maybe part of me loved him in the beginning.

I don't really know what love feels like. Sure, it's described in all the romance novels I read, but I don't think I've ever felt anything close to what they did. I don't think I'm wired that way—to love someone. To be *in* love with someone.

All the love I felt as a kid died when my father did. It took me a long time to feel something again, and I think Tobias dying kicked all my lost feelings back up.

That's my explanation for why I can't stop crying. It's not because of my grief, no, it's just all the emotions I shoved down throughout the years bubbling up.

I was so young when my dad died, but I knew what it meant. Everyone explained it to me and said they were sorry for having to teach me about the topic at such a young age. I didn't understand why they were apologizing. I thought it made me stronger for being ahead of the curve on the topic of death.

When my dad died, I cried a few times. Mostly when everyone else was crying so I wouldn't seem heartless.

But when Tobias died, a river of tears poured out of me, and it still hasn't stopped.

I miss him. I miss my brother so fucking much some days that my chest hurts. I still call him sometimes to hear his voice. I don't know how many times this past year I've called him and I'm waiting for the day his number goes to someone else and they tell me to stop.

I finish my shower and sobfest, and as I'm getting dressed, I find myself rummaging through my duffel bag, hoping a familiar white envelope comes into view.

But it never does.

Did I leave it in Arizona? Did I forget to grab it?

Fuck, I'm the stupidest person on the planet. I flee the fucking house without the one thing that matters more than anything to me.

I swipe my phone to Gregory's contact, knowing he probably won't answer me now, but hoping that he honors my wish. He knows how important that letter is to me, and I'd like to think he's capable of being an understanding person even though I ran out on him mere hours ago.

> **Teags: Please don't touch anything of mine. I'll come pick it up soon.**

I'm such a fucking idiot. I'm delusional if I thought this was all a good idea. First, I ran from my engagement because I didn't love my boyfriend I moved in with on a whim. Then, instead of going back home to see my mom, I ran to Dom's house to hide. Now, I'm crying because my life is falling apart at the seams even though I was the one who made it unravel in the first place.

It's all my fault. I'm the only one to blame for the past few months, and I have to live with the consequences of my own choices. I thought I was smarter than this. I thought I was capable of making my own decisions about my life, but clearly, I was wrong.

The weight of my own failure is punching me in the fucking face, and I'm letting it.

Not being able to find the energy to get up, I lay on the floor, and cry myself to sleep.

Chapter Four

— DIRTY LITTLE SECRET BY THE ALL-AMERICAN REJECTS

THE FACT THAT I'M harboring Teags as a fugitive doesn't stop me from getting my morning workout in.

I've never had company that lasted longer than one night, so knowing she is across the hall sleeping is throwing me off-guard.

I quietly walk down to my kitchen so I can make a protein shake like I usually do, but when I shove the banana into the blender, I realize if I turn it on, I might wake her up. And based on how exhausted she looked last night, she needs to rest.

I don't know what the hell happened in Arizona—besides the proposal. What I do know is I saw a different version of Teags last night. Gone was the girl who pushed my buttons every time she saw me at some party or holiday at Tristan's house. In her place is someone different. She looked tired, worn out, and unlike her usual self.

She was always so passionate about anything and everything. When she speaks, you can't help but listen. Even though I rolled my eyes at most things she said—especially when her quips were directed towards me—I still paid attention when she had something to say.

Stop thinking about her, I think to myself. I need to fucking focus. It's all my parents have wanted me to do lately, but she's thrown a wrench into my plans.

Not wanting to wake her up, I take my blender outside on my deck and plug it into one of the outlets. I start it up, flinching when it turns on because everything feels so much louder when you have someone you're trying not to wake up. I swear that's a real thing. Why does every bang, bump, and noise echo a thousand times louder when you're trying to be quiet?

I take all my shit back inside before I down my protein shake, shove my headphones into my ears, and start my run. Yesterday was leg day at the gym, but today is cardio. Since it's a nice day out, I'm going to take full advantage and run a few more miles than I normally do.

For some reason, I'm feeling more on edge this morning than I usually am. And since I can't fuck away these anxious feelings, I do the only thing I can and exercise them out of my body.

Two hours later, I'm stepping out of my shower and ready to start my day.

I throw on some jeans and a plain shirt before I head downstairs to make breakfast. I'm a firm believer breakfast can make or break your day. I don't usually skip any meals, but any time I skip breakfast, my day goes to shit.

So, as I prepare a simple egg sandwich, I crack two eggs because I'm sure the girl upstairs is starving. It's weird having her here—my house feels smaller knowing someone else is in it, but I like it. The company is nice after having been alone for so long. I talk to my friends basically every day, but it's different than physically seeing them.

Tristan has his own life with Liv—which they deserve.

Harry has a girlfriend and a kickass job he loves.

Ethan is living his dream and shooting a movie on location. I have no fucking idea where he even is.

And I'm slowly crumbling as I await my shitty life of working for my parents' company—the life I've been tailored for since I was little.

That's partly why I'm enjoying Teags's company, even if it did throw me off at first.

As if she sensed I was thinking about her, I hear her walk down the stairs, and when she comes into the kitchen, she doesn't spare me a glance.

She sits herself down where she was last night, and I continue to make breakfast, glancing between her and the eggs every few seconds.

She looks more exhausted than yesterday—her eyes are red and puffy. *Has she been crying*?

From what Tristan has told me, his sister never cries. Or, she hates crying and emotions? I honestly can't remember exactly what he said, but I'm not going to pry her about it. She'd probably threaten to stab me with a fork if I started asking her about her feelings.

So, I decide on a different route.

"We're hitting a few places on the road. First, Chicago. My parents have yet to franchise the store there since we have lots of competitors, so they're counting on me to push that across the finish line. Then we'll hit Oklahoma City. I have no idea why they want a store there, but I do what I'm told. Then, we're going to California."

"And before California is when we're detouring to Arizona, right?"

I stare at her before I take a bite. "Yes."

She sighs heavily but tries to mask it with a bite of her sandwich. I can tell she's nervous about all this. She tries to keep her walls up around everyone, but in the past day, I've seen more of who she really is behind the mask she keeps up.

"So, if we're packing up your entire life in Arizona, we're going to need a truck. This trip should take a few weeks, so pack accordingly."

"Well, considering I only have a duffel bag full of random clothes I shoved into it, that won't be a problem."

I lean against the island of my kitchen. "How many outfits did you bring?"

She looks at me, a confused expression on her face. "What kind of question is that?"

"You didn't plan ahead?"

She scoffs. "No, I didn't plan ahead as I was rummaging around in my closet trying to get away from Gregory and his fucking ring."

Shit, I shouldn't have asked. "That's fine. I'll take you shopping before we leave so you can at least have some proper clothes."

"That's not necessary—"

I cut her off and she rolls her eyes at me. "You'll need some new clothes anyway for the events you're going to accompany me to after we get back."

Her eyes are bulging out of her head as my surprise catches her off guard. The idea came to my mind while I was running this morning. It's bad enough I hate the events my parents always make me go to, but recently they've been setting me up with women I'd rather not spend my time with—heiresses. And other rich socialites that are of appropriate social status to be seen with me. I couldn't hate it more.

It's not that there's anything wrong with them, I just can't find it in me to make small talk and act like everything they say is the most interesting thing I've ever heard.

"What did you say?"

"It's how you'll pay me back after I take you on this trip."

"By hanging on your arm at events that I don't and will never belong in?"

"I find you more interesting than the girls my parents set me up with. If you're with me, they can't do that. It's a win-win."

"Sounds like a win-lose."

I tilt my head at her. "It's only a few of them until they get off my back. You'll get free clothes, food, and booze out of it." I reach my hand across the island at her. "What do you say?"

She thinks it over for a few seconds, and I know I've won when she looks down at my hand and back up at me. "Fine. I'll help." She points her finger at me. "But if you try to get me to wear big, poofy dresses, then you've got another thing coming, Dominic."

Oh, the full name. I must be on her bad side, again. "You can wear as much black as you please. After all, we'd match. It's my favorite color too."

Another eye roll. "Why do your parents care about your image so much?"

"Who the fuck knows?" I do. I know why. It's because to the public, we have to look like a normal family with parents who love their kids. A typical family dynamic that has never been ours. Behind closed doors, we couldn't be further from that. I wasn't even raised by my parents. I was raised by the nannies that lived in our house because our parents were too busy building their empire over taking care of their kids.

My siblings and I couldn't be further apart, but in public, we all act like the perfect little family.

"So, how are we going to get a truck?" she asks me, while poking at her bagel.

"Ethan has one. I'm going to ask him if I can borrow it while he's shooting on location. If he says yes, we'll trade cars when we meet him wherever he is now."

"Gotcha."

I throw my plate in the sink and wash it off before I turn back to her. "Are you done?" I ask, even though she's barely touched it.

"Yeah," she says as she pushes the plate toward me. "So when do we leave?"

"In a few days, but I'm taking you shopping later."

"But—"

"The sooner you stop fighting me about this, the better."

She rolls her eyes at me before she jumps out of her chair, and a few seconds later, her door slams.

Even with her anger, it feels nice to have some sound in this house again.

Dom: Hey, where the hell are you filming again?

Ethan: For the last time, I'm not giving you any hot actresses phone number.

Dom: That's not why I texted you.

Dom: I need to borrow your truck, and I'll leave one of my cars with you while I do.

Ethan: Why?

Dom: I'll explain more when I see you.

Ethan: If you give me one of your cars, I want the Ferrari Spider.

Dom: Deal.

Ethan: Just tell me when you need the truck and I'll send you my address.

Dom: Thanks, man.

Chapter Five

— RUN FOR THE HILLS BY TATE MCRAE

So, it turns out that living with a man you've had a crush on for years isn't the easiest thing in the world. When I walked down the stairs and saw Dom making breakfast, his tattooed arms on full display and his hair still wet from a shower, I almost started drooling.

I'm officially broken.

As I sit in the passenger seat of his car, my thighs humming as he speeds into the mall, I know I'm fucked.

What is it about his mere presence that has always made me feel something? And what do I have to do to turn it off? Smack him? Fuck him? Never see him ever again? Though, the last two aren't an option. He'll always be in Tristan's life, so avoiding him or fucking him won't work.

"Teags?"

I shift my head to his and notice he's halfway out of the car. "What?"

"Are you coming or do I have to drag you into the mall kicking and screaming?"

Ugh. I hate shopping, but I do need new clothes. Half of the shit I grabbed was work attire, and I'd rather peel my face off than wear another blouse ever again.

Just as I'm getting out of the car, my phone rings.

When I take it out of my pocket, it's Tristan. *Fuck*. He can't know that I'm back here, right? There's no way he figured it out.

I've never been so scared to pick up a phone call before. Well, except maybe one other time, but I didn't know I should've been scared before I answered it.

I swallow and my breath gets caught in my dry throat as I answer. "Hey, what's up?"

"Why the fuck did you turn your location off?" my brother yells across the line.

"Tristan, you know where I am. Why do you need my location to be on at all times?"

He sighs on the other side of the line, and even though I'm not looking at him, I can feel Dom's eyes on me.

"You know why." My brother's voice lowers across the line.

"It's pointless. You and Theo don't need to know that I'm at the fucking grocery store in Arizona."

"Can you please turn it back on?"

"No. I'm tired of you always watching me like a hawk, even from miles away," I snap at him, and I immediately regret saying what I did. I know he worries about me because Tobias turned his off before he did what he did. I know he's afraid it will happen again. But I wouldn't do that—not after it's already happened once. I've seen firsthand what that does to people, and the thought of making my family feel how I did after Tobias died makes me sick with worry. "I didn't mean that, Tris."

"I know, but I'll back off."

"Thank you," I whisper. "I have to go."

"I'll see you, Sis. Don't be a stranger."

"Bye." As I hang up, I feel Dom shove me from behind.

"Are you ready to go shopping?" He smirks from beside me now, and I have to stop myself from rolling my eyes.

"Let's get this over with."

"Ugh," I say as I shimmy out of another outfit. I hate this. Why do none of these stores have normal fucking clothes? And why is shopping for jeans so humbling?

I went up two sizes, and for some reason, it still feels like they don't fit. I also can't bear to look at the price tags because there's no way I can afford this since I quit my job.

Basically, I'm fucked.

"Are you alright in there?" Dom asks as he knocks on the door of my fitting room.

"No," I tell him. "Can you grab me another pair of these but a size up?" I say as I hand him the black jeans I tried on.

"Sure."

As he's doing that, I try on a few more shirts, and to my surprise, I end up liking a few. After he brings them back and they fit, I end up with three pairs of jeans, some black flared leggings, and a few different shirts. It's going to be decently warm where we're going, so I grabbed clothes according to the weather.

But as I step out of the dressing room, I remember that I need new underwear and bras, and Dominic is standing right in front of me.

"Anything else you need?"

"Uh, yeah, but you don't have to—"

He grabs the clothes from out of my hands, and effectively shuts me up. "Get whatever you need. I'm here to carry things, follow you around, and pay."

Well, that's nice of him—

Wait, pay?

"You're not buying me all of this."

He nudges my shoulder with his. "Yes, I am. It's only fair since you're helping me out. And you quit your job, remember?"

"I don't need your charity," I say as I walk over to the selection of bras and underwear.

"Consider it a bonus, then."

I huff as I sift through the thongs, all too aware of Dom looking over my shoulder as I browse.

"Do you mind?" I ask him.

"What?"

God, he's so fucking oblivious. "I need a little privacy."

"Oh, please. It's underwear. I've seen it before, many times, in fact. Though, most of the time, I am taking it off with my teeth, so—"

Before I can stop what I'm doing, I take one of the thongs I was just looking at and shove it into his mouth.

He mumbles a few things at me as I look at him.

"Are you done?"

He raises his eyebrows at me before I grab the underwear back from him. "Oh, come on. I'm trying to lighten the mood. You're horrible at this, you know."

"Horrible at what?"

"Shopping. It's supposed to be fun, but you look like I'm holding you hostage inside the store."

"It's awkward shopping as if we're old friends and it's weird that you're about to buy me underwear."

"It's not that weird."

I tilt my head at him. "Oh, do you do this often then? Maybe with all the women whose panties you ruin after ripping them off with your teeth."

"Well, no. I've never taken anyone I've fucked to buy clothes. It's too serious for my liking."

"Then why are you doing it for me?" I ask, my voice low as if I didn't really want to ask the question. I secretly do want to know, though.

"You're Tristan's sister, so it's not as weird," he says, looking at me as I hold the thong that was in his mouth. "Don't get me wrong, it's still fucking awkward, but you're helping me out. This is a mutually beneficial agreement. A contract, if you will."

"Well, then I guess I'll be buying these since I've ruined them with your mouth."

Dom only winks at me before he grabs it from my hands. "Great choice."

And now all I can think about is wearing them in front of him before he rips them off—

No. No. *Do not go there.*

He heads for the register, so I grab a few more pieces and follow behind him. When we get up there, the lady behind the counter looks between Dom and I.

"Did you find everything you were looking for?"

"Yes, thank you," Dom says as he pulls his card out of his wallet. His Amex *Black Card.*

What the actual fuck? How much money does he have?

"Your girlfriend has wonderful taste," the woman says as she folds up the clothes I picked out.

I don't know why that word is stuck in my brain. She called me his girlfriend.

"Oh, I'm not—"

He cuts me off as he throws his arm around me. "She does, doesn't she?"

Oh my fucking God, what is going on?

I smile nervously as I wait for this alternate universe to disappear. There is no way in any timeline where I would be known as Dominic Graves's girlfriend. As we walk out of the store, I bring it up.

"What the hell was that?"

He only smirks at me. "What?"

"You know what." I nudge his arm that carries my bags for me. "You let that woman think we were dating."

"It was good practice for the future. At these events, you'll be my girlfriend. And you have to be convincing enough so my parents believe the charade and back off."

Oh, fuck. I never thought of it like that. I assumed I'd be the arm candy that didn't have to speak to anyone. That's how it was at Gregory's events, but if I'm going to convince his family that I'm his serious girlfriend, I'm going to have to get really good at acting.

I don't know if I'm going to be able to do this. I don't think I could do this without falling more and more into Dom. I already think he's the hottest man I've ever laid my eyes on, but knowing it's fake for him and not me would be an unsteady line I don't want to deal with. It's not like I want some lovey-dovey relationship with him. I just think he's the most beautiful person I've ever seen. It's purely lust driven, I'm sure of it.

But I don't think I could survive him reciprocating those feelings—even if they are fake.

"So, you'll still do it?" he asks as he throws the bags in the back seat of his car. *When did we get outside?*

God, I need to pull myself together.

I need Dom to take me to Arizona so I can grab my stuff, and I think this trip across the country will do me some good. It'll give me some space from both here and who I was in Arizona, and maybe then I'll start to feel like myself again.

Maybe this trip is exactly what I need to feel my brother alongside me again. After all, he was the sibling who loved to travel and discover new things. So, maybe this trip will give me a new perspective that I hadn't seen before. And maybe then, Tobias will come back to me.

"Yes, I'll still do it."

"Yes, I'll still do it."

Chapter Six

— NEW ROMANTICS BY TAYLOR SWIFT

"Teags, it's time to get up," I hear someone say before a loud *pop* filters the room.

That gets me right up, and when I open my eyes and see Dom standing in front of my bed with a confetti cannon in his hand, I realize this is how he's decided to wake me up on the first official day of our trip.

"Nothing like a fucking heart attack to get me up," I say as I swing my legs off the side of my bed.

"Well, aren't you a ray of sunshine in the morning," he replies with a giant smile on his face.

"Why are you so happy this fucking early?" I'll never understand people who prefer the mornings. Mornings are for sleeping in, having coffee, and slowly waking up. I can't fucking function without caffeine. It was part of the reason Gregory never woke up next to me most days. He always went to the office early on account of having a lot of work to do, but in reality, I know he hated waking up next to someone as grumpy as I am in the mornings.

"Look, I went back and forth about a fun way to kick off our trip, and this seemed like the best option."

"Yes, but I need my—"

"Your coffee is on your fucking table. Look to your right."

So, I do, and sure enough, a full mug sits on top of a coaster. I take a sip, and it's the exact way I make mine—black. No cream and no sugar.

"I assume you take your coffee straight up. You fit that vibe," he says as he cleans up the confetti mess he made. "But if you need cream or sugar, it's in the kitchen."

"No, this is perfect," I say quietly as I take another sip.

"Sorry, what was that?" he asks with a smirk.

"You heard me. I'm not repeating myself."

"Fine," he says as he throws the pile of confetti that he cleaned up at me. "Get dressed. We're leaving in an hour."

"Yes, sir," I joke as I get up from my bed and head to the bathroom.

As I set my coffee cup down and turn to close the door, I notice Dom still standing in my room, staring at me. *What is he doing?*

"Did you need something else?"

He shakes out his haze when he hears my voice. "No, sorry. I'll start packing the car."

SHE SHUTS HER BATHROOM door and I'm still frozen to my spot.

"Yes, sir."

Those two words out of her mouth had me thinking about things I would never think about when it comes to Tristan's little sister.

I need to get fucking laid. That's all I'm chalking the weird feeling up to—the fact that I haven't had sex in months. I've been wound way too tight lately, and as those words came out of her mouth, I had thoughts that I haven't had since I stopped having sex.

Like pushing her back onto the bed and shoving my—

No. I can't think about this right now. Not now. Not *ever.*

I shake all of those feelings out, and as I'm walking down the stairs with my last suitcase in hand, my front door opens, and in walks Tristan and Harry.

Tristan, as in Teags's brother.

Teags, the girl who's using my guest room shower, right now. As in the girl who's supposed to be in Arizona like her brother thinks she is.

"What the hell are you guys doing here so early?" I ask them, wondering if it's possible to get them the fuck out of my house in record time.

"We've come to send you off, Dom. Aren't you going to miss us for a month while you're traveling the country?" Tristan asks as he sits on my sofa.

"Oh, please, he'll probably find someone to keep him company on the road and forget all about us, Tris," Harry says as he looks at the bags I have stacked in front of my door.

What the fuck is going on? Did the universe send my worst nightmare to ruin my life before I'm supposed to go on a trip?

"Guys, I have to leave soon, so thanks for stopping by, but I have to go," I say as I try to usher them out of the door.

"Dom, where do you keep your fish food?" Harry asks me, and I forget that he's the one that's going to be feeding my fish while I'm gone.

"I left you a detailed note on the fridge for anything and everything you could need."

"A detailed note? Who are you and what have you done with the real Dominic Graves?"

I laugh at his assumption. "I'm still here, Tristan."

"No, you're not. Not only have you hidden your entire life from us for years, but you failed to tell me that you had a pet."

"Pets," Harry corrects him. "He has a few fish."

"Yeah, and they're all named after *Rick and Morty* characters," I tell them.

"Wait, is the shower running?" Tristan asks as he ascends my stairs. "Do you have a girl over?"

Yes, but not in the way you think. "Yes, and you two clowns need to get the fuck out before you embarrass her." Ew. I hate the fact that I insinuated that I slept with Teags right in front of Tristan. Granted, he doesn't know his sister is currently using my shower, but I do.

It just feels wrong.

"Aw, Dom..." Harry says as he puts his hand to his heart. "You've become soft."

"Shut the fuck up."

"Come on, Dom. You never used to care when we saw girls come out of your room in college. How is this any different?" Tristan asks me, still on the steps leading up to the second floor.

It's different because your little sister is up there hiding from you. And if he were to see her coming out of the guest room of *my* house, I think he'd kill me.

Scratch that, I know he'd kill me.

He doesn't know she's back. He doesn't know about the agreement we made to help one another out, and he never fucking will. As far as I'm concerned, once this contract between Teags and I is over, we'll never speak of it again.

"It's different because I'm a grown ass man. I have a house, a job, and I'm taking shit more seriously," I say as I grab my bag and open the door. "Now, if you'll excuse me, I have to pack up my car."

"Fine. We'll get out of your hair, Dom," Harry says as he follows me out.

"Was she at least good in bed? You deserve some good sex before you have to be celibate for a month while you're on the road." Tristan asks, and I have to hold back my gag.

No, Tristan, your sister was not good in bed. I wouldn't know because I haven't slept with her. "It was great."

Harry gives me a hug before he puts one of my bags in the trunk for me, and Tristan slaps me on the back before he leaves.

"I'm proud of you, man. I know you don't talk about your parents much, but when I look at you now, I see a good man."

I scoff at him. "Well, what did you see when you looked at me before?"

"Someone who was desperate to stand out in a crowd. And I knew the entire time that it wasn't actually you."

"Wow, how intuitive. Did Livvy tell you that?" Olivia Hart was the best thing to happen to Tristan and the rest of us in college. She not only infiltrated Tristan's life, but between her drool-worthy baked goods and overall vibe, she cemented herself as the fifth member of our group in college.

He rolls his eyes at me. *God, is that a West family thing?* "Maybe, but she's right."

"Whatever. Enjoy Pennsylvania, assholes. I'll see you when I get back."

"See ya, Dom. Have fun and take lots of pictures," Harry jokes as he gets into his car.

"See you soon, man."

"Sounds good, Tristan."

Then I watch as they both drive out of sight with the sun just starting to rise into the sky. God, that was way too fucking close. At least now, the two of us will be traveling where nobody knows who we are. On the road, I don't have to worry about the possibility of Tristan seeing me and his sister together.

The fact that he was still this close to knowing that Teags was the one using my shower still has me on edge. But I can't go for a run this morning because we have to fucking leave.

So, I'm going to have to deal with the fucking anxiety and pent-up energy by shoving it down and pretending that it doesn't exist.

"Hey—"

I jump at her voice before I grab her by the arm and shove her inside. I kick the door closed with my foot. I know Tristan isn't around anymore, but for some reason, I feel better knowing she's behind closed doors and away from the public eye.

"What the fuck, Dom?"

"Your brother was here."

Her eyes practically bulge out of her head. "What? When? Why?"

"A few minutes ago. Him and Harry wanted to say goodbye to me before I left. They, uh, heard you using the shower."

"Oh fuck," is all she says.

"Yeah, fuck."

"What did you say to them?"

"I told them you were some girl I fucked last night."

I swear she stops breathing, but she masks her expression so quickly that I can't decipher it. "Oh, well, good thinking. It's not suspicious, right?"

"No. It's what everyone expects of me." And I hate it. I hate that everyone assumes I'm some guy who loves to fuck and never wants to commit.

Sure, I *was* like that, especially in college. It was hard to focus on more than one thing at once for me, and relationships never mattered in the grand scheme of things back then. I was there to do my work, get good grades, and have enough fun to last me a lifetime.

It didn't work. Well, most of it. I got the grades my parents were happy with—nearly perfect. But I didn't think I could balance my grades, a relationship, and everything else that comes with growing up while you're in college.

So, I did what I knew I could handle, and I slept around.

It was fine, I guess. Unfulfilling as fuck when people realized that I didn't do relationships. More and more people came up to me to have that one night. It's all I'm good for, and since my parents won't get off my back about setting me up with dates, it's all I'll ever be good enough for.

Just one night is all I'll ever get.

"Are you ready to go?" I ask her, and for some reason that statement feels weighted, as if it carries so much more than the meaning itself.

"Yeah, I'm ready. I'll go grab my bags."

"Okay, I'll meet you at the car."

And by the time we're on the road, I know that this trip is either going to bring Teags and I closer together, or the two of us are on the way to ruining our lives.

I silently hope for the former as I turn down my street and my house goes out of sight.

Chapter Seven

Ohio

— BACKSEAT DRIVER BY ASIRIS

It's really fucking weird being around Dom this much. I've had a crush on him for as long as I can remember and this is the most time I've spent in his personal space, except when he drove me home after Liv and Tristan's wedding. Dom walked in on an extremely personal conversation between my brother and I yelling at each other about my life choices, and then Tristan barked orders at me and Dom drove me home because I was way too drunk.

"Can you walk or do I need to carry you up to your place?" he asks me as *I sigh in his passenger seat.*

"I can do it myself."

And then I'm pretty sure he walked me to my door and then left. I was really drunk, so I only remember tiny flashes after the beautiful ceremony Liv and Tristan had. I vaguely remember talking to Nico—Vince's business partner and my friend—for a bit, but other than that the only thing I really recall is being pissed at my brother. That's where all this animosity between us started. He tried to dictate my life choices, and I kept yelling at him, stating that I could make my own decisions.

Turns out, he was right, and I should've listened to him in the beginning.

But hindsight is a fucking bitch, and I stand by my actions. That's one of the main reasons I came running to Dom's house when I came back. I knew Tristan would try to parent me and rub it in my face that he was right, and I couldn't deal with that.

I also didn't want to admit that the longest relationship I've ever had failed miserably because I'm too afraid of loving someone that doesn't make me feel anything.

So, I ran back to what I knew. I ran back to the safety and comfort that Pennsylvania brings, except I couldn't face my family. I couldn't face admitting that I made the wrong decision when they all told me that a year ago.

"Here's the game plan. We're headed to Ohio first to switch cars with Ethan. He's there filming for his next movie. I'm leaving my car with him, and that way we'll have a bigger vehicle to grab all your stuff in."

"Sounds good," I say as my arm hangs out the window.

"Then, Chicago. We'll spend a few days there, then hit the road to Oklahoma City. Repeat that a few more times and then eventually we'll be back home. Hotel reservations are already booked, and I even changed them to all have two beds so you're comfortable."

"Thank you." I'd sleep on the floor before sleeping in the same bed as Dom. I don't sleep well in the same bed with people. Every time Gregory and I slept in the same bed, he always complained about how I'd latch onto him during the night and he always had to push me off.

I'm not a cuddly person. I'm not some sort of teddy bear that needs affection at all times.

But it is nice to be held, sometimes. To be wanted.

Since seeking comfort isn't something I do naturally when I'm awake, I end up clinging to someone subconsciously when my body is most at ease—when I'm sleeping.

And I *still* got rejected.

I'm starting to second guess why I ever thought Gregory and I would work out. All the signs were there, I just didn't want to read them.

God, I'm a fucking idiot. An idiot who has no idea what's going to happen after this road trip detour is done. Because when Dom and I get back, and all the events he needs me to go to are over, what do I do then?

Maybe I'll ask Bree if she needs an assistant. That I could do. Not only would it allow me to work with books, I'd also be able to work with my best friend all day. That sounds like a dream.

Or maybe I could put my business degree to good use and open up a small business like I always dreamed of doing.

Nope.

Never in a million years could I have the courage to do that, but for the rest of the way to Ohio, I imagine my life and what it can look like if I have the guts to do what my heart truly wants.

Hope is always a dangerous thing for a girl like me, and I should quit thinking about it before the idea turns into something more, something dangerous.

By the time we pull into Ethan's place a few hours later, I've scrubbed the idea from my brain completely. Sure, I have a degree, but I have no clue what it would actually take to start my own business.

"Wow, this is nice," I say as he parks the car in the driveway. Dom drove one of his fancy ass cars, and I'm assuming it's because Ethan wants to borrow it. Tristan kept bugging Dom before I left to drive one of his cars, and now I see why. Not only are they expensive, but they *look* sexy. And feeling the hum of the engine underneath my body has made me have to look up very specific keywords for my next book.

"Stay in the car," Dom says as Ethan walks out of his place. It's a quaint house on a decently quiet street. I wonder what he's filming here, but knowing how the industry works, he probably can't tell us.

"Why? I want to stretch my legs, and I'm going to have to get out anyway," I say as I open the door.

Surprise laces Ethan's features as he looks between us.

"Oh, what the hell did you do?"

I TOLD HER TO stay in the fucking car.

I was going to distract Ethan with some bullshit so I could sneak Teags into his truck before he noticed, but of course she had to fight me like she always does. I get that she doesn't like being told what to do, but for someone trying to stay under the radar, she's pretty shitty at it.

Teags speaks before I can explain.

"Don't tell Tristan that you saw me here," she stammers. "Please."

"Did you kidnap her?" he asks, his head shifting between us as if he's watching a tennis match. "Teagen, blink twice if you need help."

I look over at her to see if she's going to blink, but she only continues to stare at Ethan, her head cocked to the side.

"Huh, maybe I should ask Dom that question instead," Ethan says. Tristan's sister is a fucking spitfire, and even though she's younger than all of us, we're all a little scared of her. Everyone besides Tristan.

Though, she's not scary anymore. Since she popped up on my doorstep, we've slowly become acquainted with one another. She may act all scary with her black outfits, black hair, and constant attitude, but deep down underneath those glasses of hers, she has a heart.

"So, what's going on here, then? Or am I going to have to wait a few days until someone explains it?"

"Well, Arizona didn't work out, and I ran out of my old house like it was on fire after turning down a proposal. And since I didn't feel like going home or going to Tristan's house to have him brag in my face about how he was right, I ran to Dom's house instead. I've made myself a fugitive so I can pack up my old life, move back to Pennsylvania, and then worry about what to do. Dom is only helping me out since we're driving right past Arizona on his road trip."

"Okay…" Ethan doesn't seem convinced, but she is telling the truth.

"My life is falling apart, Ethan. And I don't have the mental power to hear my brother brag about how he knew this was coming. I don't want my mom to look at me with her sad eyes when I walk back home and have to live in the same house Tobias used to inhabit. Theo and Bree are both traveling, so Dom was my only option."

Hearing her say she didn't want to go back to the house Tobias used to live in hits me in the chest. I didn't know she was still hurting so much, but I understand not wanting to be back there. I can't imagine what it feels like being any of the West siblings and having to walk back into their childhood home.

Well, Teags is already doing better than Tristan did. Immediately after the funeral, he ran away and bought a whole ass apartment because he couldn't bear to step foot back in that house. Those two really are more alike than they think. I bet that's why they butt heads all the time.

"Okay. I won't tell him. As long as you two get back in one piece."

"We'll be fine, Ethan. We made a deal and since I'm helping her with this, she's going to help get my parents off my back about settling down."

He only laughs at us. "Oh, so it's a mutually exclusive agreement."

"Exactly," Teags says as she softly shuts my car door. *At least she didn't slam it.* "Now, I'm going to move all our shit to the truck. Can I have the keys?"

"Sure," he says as he throws them to her.

"Dom, pop the trunk," she says and I do.

Before I go over to help her, Ethan rushes me, grabs my forearm, and drags me to the side where she can't hear us.

"What the fuck are you doing?"

I roll my eyes at him. "I'm helping her out. She showed up on my doorstep the other night. What the hell was I supposed to do? Leave her out in the rain?"

"Tristan is going to kill you."

"Only if he finds out," I smirk at him. "You better keep your mouth shut. I mean it."

"I will, but only because of what Teags said." He looks me up and down. "And you're sure about doing this? Aren't you on this trip for like over a month or something?"

"Yes, I'm sure. I'm being a nice guy by helping her grab her shit from her ex's house, and if he tries to do something stupid, I'll be there to help her." I don't trust the fucker. Not after I heard him yelling at her over the phone the night she came back to Pennsylvania.

"You're never this nice, D. Just don't do anything stupid while you're stuck in a car with her. Tristan will kill you if you corrupt his little sister."

"If she corrupts me first, then it's not my fault, though, right?" I smirk because I'm a fucking asshole. I forgot how fun it was to stress my friends out. It annoys me that nobody ever trusts me when I tell them why I'm doing something. They always see me as someone who doesn't take my life seriously, but I would never knowingly do something stupid without a reason for it.

"I hope you know what you're doing."

I look over at Teags who's putting the last suitcase in the car.

"It'll be fine." I look at him. "I'll bring your truck back in a few weeks, and don't wreck my fucking car or you're paying for it."

"Trust me, I won't."

"Good," I say. "Now, if you'll excuse me, we have to leave soon."

"Good luck."

"Thanks." *I'm gonna need it.*

Chapter Eight

— ARM'S LENGTH BY SAM FENDER

AFTER MY PHONE RINGS for the fifth time in five minutes, I decide to answer it.

"Gregory, what the hell do you want?"

"When the fuck are you coming to get your stuff?"

I sigh heavily and remove my phone from my ear as he continues to yell at me. It's only been a week. I don't know why he's so up in arms about all this. I don't even have that much stuff at home—mostly clothes that I'll never wear again and books.

I couldn't care less about anything but the letter from my brother, and all of the physical music I left behind. If he touched any of that, I don't know what I'll do, but it won't be pretty.

After I look at Dom and see him unimpressed with my conversation, I sigh.

"Do you want me to talk to him?"

I shake my head. "No. It'll make things worse," I say as I put the phone back to my ear.

"You've embarrassed me. I've had to pretend like everything's fine when people at work ask me about you, and I hate lying to them. Plus, my parents are already trying to hook me up with people because I've been going to events by myself."

"Gregory, I'm so sorry you've had to deal with all of this, but can you stop fucking yelling at me? I'm on the way to you."

I hear Dom laugh and try to cover it with a cough.

"Do you realize what you've done by rejecting my proposal? I had it all laid out for us and you ruined everything."

I sigh heavily, again. I understand how he feels, I do. I did run out on him, but he never noticed how I wasn't myself in Arizona. He never cared when I would come to bed late at night after he was asleep. He never noticed that my eyes were always red-rimmed and puffy after I showered.

All of these things I hid, but he still didn't see me. Nobody really sees me anymore. Sometimes it feels like I'm a ghost floating in and out of everyone's lives. Ever since Tobias died, I can't remember the last time I felt truly like myself.

And that's why I said no to Gregory. That's why I'm now on this road trip with Dom because maybe, just maybe, I can find that part of myself I lost. Maybe I'll be reminded who I used to be and can find her again.

"Teagen? Are you even fucking listening to me?"

"No, I'm not. All you're doing is yelling at me and telling me how I ruined your life. I've had enough. I will let you know when I'm five minutes from your house, but other than that, stop fucking calling me. I'll be out of your life soon. Goodbye," I say as I hang up, not wanting to hear whatever bullshit he has to tell me.

I sigh heavily before I throw my phone into the cupholder and sulk.

"Well, that was dramatic."

"Dom, I've had enough, seriously—"

"Damn, Teags," he says as he pokes me in the arm. "I was trying to make you feel better."

"It would make me feel better if I could throw my phone out the window." But I can't. Because it has all my music on it and if I can't talk to Bree over the next few weeks, I might go crazy.

Then Dom starts to laugh.

"What's so funny?"

"I don't know what you saw in that guy."

Me either. I think I saw him as an escape. An escape route from my former life where my brother and father were dead and I was slowly losing who I was.

"He seems like an asshole, and based on the conversation I heard you and Tristan have at his wedding, he thought the same thing I did."

Sometimes I forget that he heard all that. The two of us didn't say a word about it when he drove me home. "I get it, Dom. Tristan was right all along."

"I'm not saying that—"

"Well, then what are you saying?"

He shrugs. "I never imagined you with someone so uninvested in your life. Not only was he never around, but you never talked about him. Usually when you talk about the things you're interested in, you talk with your hands. You're just more animated, I guess."

"How the hell do you know that?"

"Have you ever seen you and Bree talk about books? That's literally what happens every single time. You both are really fucking loud."

Oh. I guess that makes sense. It surprised me that he knew that. Dom and I aren't friends. We're not even acquainted. He's someone I know through my brother and that's all it will ever be.

"I still don't get why you were with him."

"It was okay at first," I tell him. And that's not a lie. I did like him. I thought he was cute when he walked up to me and started reciting facts about the painting I was looking at. He asked me for my number and I gave it to him because it was something I would never have done before.

Then we started texting and then we went out a few times and it wasn't bad. It was fine. He was good company before I started to retreat. When we moved in together it all went downhill.

"What happened then?" Dom asks me.

I want to say nothing. I want to keep it all in like I usually do, but he feels safe. He would never tell Tristan, at least I don't think so. In this truck and on this trip, I feel like I can trust him. "He used to give me all these little paper cuts. One day he would comment on my outfit and I'd go change to appease him. Another day he would raise his voice at me, about something I didn't do, and I'd apologize profusely until he would calm down. All these things added up over time and I noticed how unhappy I became, how stationary I was."

He says nothing as I continue.

"I'm not sure why I stayed. I think I got to a point where running felt like more work than staying. So, I fell into a routine and stayed in it until one day I decided I had enough. I quit my job, came home, and I walked in and Gregory was on one knee. It wasn't what I wanted. I looked around that day and realized that my life wasn't mine. It was all his, and I was just a guest star in his story. Somewhere along the way, I stopped living. I was existing around him and in my life."

I hear him sigh as he looks at me. "I relate to that, in a way."

"You do?"

"Yeah. It's how I feel working for my parents."

I think he's going to elaborate, but he doesn't. And as we keep driving toward Chicago, I hope that this trip will fix the parts of me that feel broken because I don't know how much longer I can live like this.

I can't be half out of the door in my own life, but that's all my life has felt like lately, and if I have to claw my way out, then so be it.

Chapter Nine

Chicago

— SHE ALWAYS TAKES IT BLACK BY GREGORY ALAN ISAKOV

Dom parks at the hotel and I all but leap out of the car to stretch my legs. Granted, it was only a few hours from Ohio, but my ass is asleep.

"I'll go check us in if you want to grab a cart and put our luggage on it."

"I can do that," I say as I look up at the big ass hotel he booked. I've never stayed somewhere this fancy, and I know Bree told me Dom's family is loaded, but actually seeing it is way different.

I'm not used to luxury, but I'm definitely not going to complain if one of these rooms has a tub with jets. Since I brought my Kindle with me, a nice bubble bath would be perfect with a glass of champagne before bed. God, that sounds perfect.

We walk into the hotel and he turns and heads for the front desk before I go to grab a cart. A man stops me when I try to grab one.

"What car is yours, madam?"

Madam? Shit, this place is really fucking fancy. "Uh, the truck over there." I point to Ethan's truck.

"Wonderful. We'll get your bags and bring them up to your room."

Before I can say anything he walks away, two other people in suits follow him and head to our car.

I guess I don't have to do anything, so I go and sit down on one of the many couches in the lobby. There's even a fucking fountain surrounded by water, and the color scheme for this place is gold and black.

I don't think I can even afford to breathe in this place.

I pull my phone out and take a picture, wishing I could show Bree, but knowing I can't yet. I need to document this. I'll never be in a hotel this nice ever again, so I might as well soak it up while I can.

"Teags?"

I turn and see Dom standing behind me. "Yes?"

"Ready to head up?"

I get up and palm his chest. "Yes, I am."

The two of us head to the elevator and step inside. When he presses the button for the thirtieth floor, I almost have a heart attack.

"What?" he asks.

"Nothing. Just never stayed on a floor with such a high number."

"It's not the penthouse. It's just a big hotel, I promise."

I can see his tattoos creeping through his shirt as he pulls his phone out and starts typing. The elevator dings and I follow him to wherever our room is. He unlocks it and I notice our bags are already in the room.

How the hell did they get up here so fast?

Whatever. I'm just excited to have a bed all to myself and get some good sleep—oh my god.

"Dom," I say as I smack him. He's still looking at his phone. "Dominic!"

"What?"

"I thought you said you changed all of the reservations?"

"I did," he says, but when he looks up and sees one single bed like I saw, he sighs. "Fuck. They told me it was all set at the desk. I can go down and ask them to change rooms or something."

"It's fine," I say as I start to unpack my suitcases. I'm too tired to deal with this, and switching rooms sounds like way too much work.

"No, I'm going down there right now, and—"

I stop him before he can leave. "Stop."

"I'm not going to sleep with my best friend's little sister." I tilt my head at him at what he's insinuating. "You know what I meant."

"You mean to tell me that you've never slept in the same bed with another girl?"

"Usually there isn't much sleep happening when someone is in bed with me," he says quietly, as if he's ashamed or something.

"Look, I don't mind if you don't. I'll build a pillow wall between us so we each have our own side, okay?"

"It really wouldn't be much to change it, I can go down right now and—"

I shake my head. "It's not worth the trouble, and all I want to do is take a shower and go to sleep. Doesn't that sound nice?"

"Yeah, it does. You go first and I'll order us some room service. I assume you're hungry?"

I nod my head.

"Does a burger sound good?"

"Yes, it does." I smile, and as I shut the door on the bathroom and notice a tub separate from a shower, I smile even wider.

This trip might be exactly the break I needed.

SLEEPING IN THE SAME bed as your friend's little sister is weird. Especially when I wouldn't consider us to be friends.

We're more like road-trip companions.

After an awkward dinner, the two of us crawled into bed exhausted from all the driving we've done today. And now, I can't sleep. I have a meeting tomorrow with some investors and for some reason, I'm nervous.

I don't get fucking nervous, but I am right now. And the only reason that's true is because of all the stipulations my parents have me under. They thought that instead of flying, I should drive. They wanted me to think long and hard on this trip about why I belong in the family business—as if it hasn't been the path I've been on my entire life.

God, I'm tired of it already. I've barely started this road I'm on and I already want off of it.

When I wake up tomorrow, I have to represent the family business, and I'm not looking forward to it.

I look at Teags beyond the pillow line she made us, and see the steady rise and fall of her chest as she sleeps. At least one of us is getting good rest.

This isn't at all how I envisioned this trip going, but somehow I know it's already been more fun than if I had done this alone. So, I'm grateful that she showed up at my doorstep and took me up on my offer. It's going to be a lot more fun with her here, even though I still have to work.

I think the two of us need one another on this trip. I need her to make me feel less lonely and out of my head thinking about my parents and their expectations of me. And she needs me to kick Gregory's ass if we get to Arizona and he starts yelling at her like he was on the phone earlier.

I've never met him, and I'm not looking forward to it. Every conversation I've overheard with him has made me like him less and less. I don't like the way he treats her, and based on what she said earlier, this yelling has happened before.

I don't like it. Not one fucking bit.

And I'll kick his ass if I have to—if she wants me to. Tristan would be okay with it too. He didn't like the fucker either.

Wanting to get some sleep for tomorrow, I flip onto my side and close my eyes, hoping that sleep will come soon and I won't wake up in a shit mood tomorrow.

I'M IN A SHIT mood.

I knew I would be, but actually waking up with the weight of this existential dread on my chest is not what I wanted.

My alarm continues blaring, and I race to turn it off because I don't want to wake Teags up. It's really fucking early, and the girl not only hates mornings, but she doesn't take kindly to being woken up without caffeine.

Which I don't have, but when I notice that her arm is thrown over my chest and one of her legs is intertwined with mine, I freeze.

How the hell did we get to be like this?

I'm a pretty still sleeper. I don't move around much. As soon as I get comfortable, I'm dead asleep and I usually wake up in the same position.

So, I'm betting that our wall of pillows being destroyed is all on her.

I don't mind it, per se, it actually feels kind of nice, but trying to get her off of me is going to be the challenge of the century.

Her hair is spread out all over the place, the black curls branching out like the roots of a tree on her pillow. Well, on *my* pillow. Her head is basically attached to my shoulder and as I try to slowly slide out of bed to take a shower, her body follows mine.

Shit.

I would love nothing more than to stay in bed all fucking day, but I can't skip all of these meetings.

So, I grab her arm and lift it ever so slightly before I slide out as quickly as I can. I stand as still as I can, taking her in and hoping I didn't wake her up. After a few seconds, she's still asleep and I let out a breath, knowing she would have thrown something at me if I woke her up this early with no coffee.

Before I walk away, I notice a flash of black ink peeking out from underneath her pajamas. Does she have a tattoo? Or maybe she has a few hidden ones? I know Tristan has one—he got it for Liv while they were apart. I was surprised when he showed up at my place a few days after Liv dropped off the face of the earth. He asked me to go with him to get a tattoo, so I took him to my usual place. I could tell he felt like shit, and if this was what he needed to do, I'd do it.

I'm a good fucking friend to the boys. If they need me, I'll drop anything for them. And when Tristan came back after Tobias died, I was by his side. He'd have done the same for me. That's what I love about the guys. We're there for each other when we know we need to be.

I have tattoos up and down my arms, and a few on my legs and thighs, so I took Tristan to the only place I trusted and watched as he sat in the chair, clearly still upset about Liv, and got tattooed.

I don't know why I assumed that Teags wouldn't have any, but it appears hers aren't visible as much as mine are. Thankfully, my suit covers it all.

I head over to the desk where the phone sits before I press the number to order some room service.

"Can you have three cups of black coffee sent up to my room? No rush."

"Yes, we can do that. It'll be around fifteen minutes."

"Tell them to let themselves in and leave it on the table."

"Sounds good, Mr. Graves."

I hang up and then grab my suit from where it hangs in the closet. I ironed it last night while Teags was in the shower, so it should look okay.

Normally, I get my shit dry-cleaned, but since I'm traveling, that's not an option.

As I step into the shower, the hot water cascading down onto me, I feel more awake.

Twenty minutes later when I step out and fix my fucking hair, I hear footsteps padding around the room. It's either my hostage waking up or room service.

When I exit the bathroom, I adjust the cufflinks on my arms before I see Teags sitting up in bed, a scowl on her face as she scrolls through something on her phone. It's probably a book. I swear I've never seen anyone read as much as she does. Except Bree and Liv, but Liv writes more than she reads these days, according to Tristan.

But what else is there to do on a road trip? Nothing, I guess.

"Good morning, Hostage."

I swear I see her eyes roll even in the dim light. "God, I hope I don't get Stockholm syndrome."

I smirk. "You never know. I'd say I'm a good captor compared to some of the ones I've seen in movies."

That earns me another eye roll. I should keep track of how many times I can get her to do that. I feel like it would be a fun game while on the road. "What are you up to today besides this meeting or whatever?"

"Well, besides the meetings, I have a lunch with one of the investors. He's a family friend." I fucking despise that man, but to my surprise, he told my parents a lunch with me after this all-day affair would help to seal the deal. So, in their words, I can't skip this fucking lunch.

Yay fucking me. All I'm doing all day is sucking up to these corporate fuckers. Just like I'll be doing for the rest of my life as the head of franchising for Graves Jewelry.

"Sounds like fun."

"Not really," I say as I fix the collar of my shirt.

"Well, the kind of fun that makes you want to take a pencil and stab your eyeballs out." She smiles at me, and I swear this girl could kill me in her sleep if she really wanted to.

"If that's your idea of fun, I'm worried about what you're doing today."

She sighs heavily. "Well, I'm going to explore the city. I've never been here before, so I might find a cute coffee shop or something. And maybe I'll visit a bookstore while I'm here. I have options."

The thought of her exploring the city of Chicago by herself scares me, even though I know she can handle herself. Well, to an extent. I don't think anyone would willingly approach her based on her facial expressions most of the time—pissed off—but you never know. Someone could stab her with a needle and she'd be gone in seconds. "You're going to explore Chicago by yourself?"

"Uh, yes? That is where we are, right?" She gets out of bed and drags the curtains back.

"Do you have pepper spray or something?"

She tilts her head at me. "Yes, and a knife. I carry them at all times, Dominic. Stop worrying about me and go to your stupid meeting."

"I want you checking in with me on the hour, every hour."

"That's ridiculous."

I throw my arms out. "Do you know how much crime there is in Chicago?" She shakes her head at me. "A fuck ton! Chicago is like number one in the country for violent crimes."

"Maybe I'll get lucky."

My mouth drops open. "Do you have a fucking death wish?"

She throws her arms out at me. "It was a fucking joke, Dom. I'll be careful and I'll text you when I'm back in the room. I won't be out for long, I just can't sit in this hotel room all day."

I run a hand through my hair, no doubt messing it up, but not fucking caring. "Fine."

"Now, shoo. And thanks for the coffee."

"Feel free to order breakfast too. I wasn't sure what you would like," I tell her, grabbing my phone to order a car to pick me up. I don't know why I expected some sort of good luck text from my parents, but there isn't one. I almost thought they cared about me for a second, but how could I forget that they only care about the success of the company. And if I do well today, I'm sure there's a phone call in my future.

Maybe a pencil to the eye won't be so bad...

I grab my briefcase, throwing a bunch of the papers I prepared at home in it and click it shut. I can feel Teags watching me the entire time, and as I step out of the room, I slam one of the keycards on the table for her.

"Keycard is on the table. Don't fucking lose it."

"Thanks," is all I hear as the door shuts and my day begins.

Chapter Ten

— CARLO'S SONG BY NOAH KAHAN

THE BELL JINGLES AS I enter a small coffee shop. I told Dom I was going to do some exploring, but mostly I needed to get the hell out of the hotel room. I thought coming on this trip across the country with him would help get me out of my own head about things.

It hasn't worked. Granted, we're only at our first stop, but maybe my expectations were too high.

The ache feels stronger for some reason. I don't know what's wrong with me. I don't know why I can't just be normal. I somehow feel things, but at the same time, nothing at all. I don't understand myself most of the time.

I order my usual and sit down in one of the open chairs while I wait for my food. People fill up the space around me, hustling and bustling with laptops out, books open, and conversations being had between friends or colleagues.

I'm in a room full of people, yet somehow I still feel alone.

My name is called and I grab my coffee and croissant before I sit back down and pull my book out. I try to read, but my usual escape into dark romance novels isn't working.

I'm broken. The wires that connect my body, mind, and heart together are crossed, and I don't know how to fix it. I want to escape. I wish I could escape all the weird feelings I'm having, but it seems that they all want to bubble up right now.

I knew I couldn't run forever. I knew they'd come up and I'd have to deal with it, but I hoped I had more time. The last thing I want to do is start crying and not be able to stop before I head back to the hotel and Dom sees me.

That actually sounds like my worst nightmare.

Wanting to banish the tears, I whip my phone out and call my brother. He answers on the fourth ring. "I didn't disturb you, did I?"

"You're never a disturbance," Theo says from across the line. "What's up? It's the middle of the day, aren't you supposed to be at work?"

Shit. "I took a few days off. I was feeling a little under the weather."

"Are you okay?"

"Yup. Fine. Just wanted to call and check in. It's been a while since we talked." *And I miss you.* Theo knows that, but he never makes me say it.

"Well, Vermont has proven to be the hardest search ever. I swear our brother was some sort of psychopath in another life. Good thing he didn't become a serial killer or something. He'd be way too good at it."

I chuckle at the thought of Tobias becoming a serial killer. He was always really into puzzles and codes and shit, but he could barely kill spiders. The guy was too soft for the world, and eventually, the world took him back.

Too soon. Way too soon.

"Still hunting for his reason for sending you back to where we spent our childhood? Come on, Theo, I thought you were better at this," I joke, as he scoffs at me.

"Oh, I've found some clues here, don't you worry. And there's a reason he gave this to me and not you. You're terrible at solving things like this."

"It's not how my brain works, and Tobias knew that."

"Yeah, he did."

Tears start flooding my eyes. *Do not cry. Don't cry or you won't stop, and you can't deal with this right now. Not today. Not ever.*

I'll never get over using past tense words when talking about Tobias. Was. Knew. Did. In another life, but not this one.

"So, what else has been going on?" I ask, needing to banish the tightness in my throat.

Theo launches into this giant spiel about how he's been living in our old vacation house up there. He's been slowly going through some stuff that was left behind, and he even said he's made some new friends up there. I get the feeling there's something else he's not telling me, but I don't press. All of us remaining West siblings are on our own journeys trying to figure out our grief. Tristan ran back here and went full caretaker mode, I chose to run to Arizona, and Tobias sent Theo on his remaining bucket list stops.

We all have a small piece of him because of the letters he left us before leaving forever, but we're all trying to sort through our grief. I'm sure Theo is glad to be back in Vermont. Both he and Tobias always bugged my mom about when we would go back, but after my dad died, we never did.

I think there were too many memories of our family being whole in that house—just like the cabin. Those two places are where we got to be in our own little bubble, but it popped when our dad died.

Our bubble grew bit by bit as we all healed, or tried to heal, from that. We finally felt as whole as we could, but with a small part missing.

Our bubble popped again when Tobias died, never to be created again.

"That sounds nice, Theo. I'm excited for you."

"Me too," he says as he shuffles around. "But I have to go. I'm, uh, meeting a friend for lunch."

Why did he say it like that? "See you soon, hopefully?"

"I'll be back home at some point, but you're in Arizona, so—"

"Right. Maybe I'll venture back up to Penn. Just tell me when you're coming back, okay?"

"Got it. I love you, Teags."

"Yup. Love you, too." I hang up my phone and throw it into my small backpack before I lean back in my chair.

I play with the rips in my jeans before the bad thoughts start to invade my head again, so I grab my phone and text my best friend. She answers immediately.

Teags: Hey, what are you up to right now?

Bree: I have to film this sponsored thing, but what's up?

Teags: Oh, nothing. I don't want to disturb you.

Bree: You're not a disturbance.

Teags: Can we call at some point?

Bree: Of course. Is everything okay?

Teags: Yeah, I just miss you is all.

Bree: I miss you too. We can schedule a reading date later?

Teags: Sounds good.

I hate feeling like a burden to people, and I know she would never say that about me, but sometimes I feel like a bother. So instead of shoving my emotions at them and feeling like a pain in the ass, I shove them further down. My legs shake under the table as I try the last thing that usually works to get rid of the bad thoughts.

Music always helps. Something about the lyrics to certain songs that showcase exactly how I feel helps my body calm down. I grab my headphones from my bag and turn them on, throwing them over my ears and as I hover over my usual playlist, I swipe down and click the one Tobias and I made.

I grab my coffee, throw out my other shit, and head onto the sidewalk, music blaring from my headphones as I pass by people going about their day.

Chicago is a beautiful place—the Windy City as it's been coined. There's something so comforting about being underneath these tall fucking buildings. It puts things into perspective. I'm so small, so unimportant compared to all of the lives that are bustling around me. Each building is filled with thousands of people, some probably going through something similar to me.

But they're just people like I am. Everyone is living their own lives with their own shit weighing them down, yet we still have to go to work, take care of ourselves, protect the planet, donate when we can and more. It's fucking exhausting sometimes.

I'm glad I got to talk to Theo, and part of me wishes I could call Tristan or my mom, but I don't want them to know what I'm doing. I don't want them to worry because they have enough on their plates without my quarter life crisis interrupting their own grief.

I'm the youngest in my family. I've carried them through tough times when Tristan—the oldest—was gone. But now, I feel disconnected from them. Tristan is busy creating his own life with Liv—the life he rightfully deserves. Theo is busy traveling the country and reconnecting with Tobias on his journey. My mom started these classes at the town center to get out of the house more, and her daily social media updates show that she's trying her best to put herself out there again.

Everyone is moving forward, or trying to, but I'm stuck in the quicksand of my grief. Not being able to feel my brother around is causing me to sink further and further into it, with nobody in my family here to pull me out. Maybe I should let it take me. Maybe I should sink into the sand and let it swallow me whole.

I don't know if I started feeling this way after Tobias, or if that's who I am. I'm the black sheep of my family, I always knew that. I'm rough around the edges. I'm not as nice as my siblings. I'm not as sweet as my mom is, and I barely remember my dad to figure out what traits I inherited from him.

I'm a mess. I'm an outsider in my own family, and since I'm the youngest, there's a good chance that everyone is going to die before me and I'm going to be left alone to mourn all of them. Nobody will be left to speak at my funeral. There will be empty chairs in the front reserved for my family, but nobody will take that space up.

A song comes on that I haven't heard in months, and it stops me in my tracks.

He used to love this one.

Can he see me where I am? Can he see me walking around this city trying to connect to him? Is he disappointed that I don't feel him? Especially if he's right here. What if he's been by my side this entire time, and I'm the problem?

I wonder if he sees that my hair has grown longer than I usually let it. I wonder if he sees me wearing glasses and doesn't recognize me. I wonder so many things about my brother wherever he is, but no matter how many songs I play and listen to, I feel nothing.

If I could play these songs to make him come back, I'd never turn them off.

I wander into a small park and sit on an empty rock, needing a moment off of my feet that suddenly feel like jelly.

I grab the ends of my hair and brush through them. It's mostly split ends by now, and normally I'd get it cut, but part of me can't bear to put it back to how it was before. To how I looked when he died.

I don't recognize that version of myself. She feels so different from who I am now, and if I tried to get myself to look how I did before, I know it won't help the ache that resides in my chest. I know that a haircut won't bring Tobias back, but I've been growing my hair out anyway.

And any time I've cried in the past few months, my hair and glasses have helped to cover my puffy eyes. Gregory never noticed after my showers that tears were streaming down my face. One time, I was sniffling so hard that he turned the television up and went to sleep. He never bothered asking, and I don't know if it's because he knew I wasn't a crier, or maybe he thought I had allergies.

I didn't.

I was sad. Really fucking sad, and I tried to hide it as best I could from my own boyfriend. From my family. From my best friends.

I've been lying to my family for months by pretending I'm fine, and part of me feels bad about it, but the other part is in full self preservation mode.

Another song plays, and nothing happens. No feelings of Tobias, no memories pop up into my head, and a single tear falls from my eye.

I'm going to forget him. I'm going to forget every small detail about the way his smile used to light up the room. The way his hair moved in the wind. The way he leaned against the tree in our yard while he watched me sit on the tire swing.

I can see it all in my head now, not fully, and that thought cracks my chest open. I don't remember my own dad, and now I'm going to forget what my older brother looked like. I wish I had his note in front of me. If I did, maybe I could see him more clearly.

I turn my music off and shove my headphones off before I grab my phone and dial another number. It rings and rings until the voicemail box comes in.

"This is Tobias West. Not East, North, or South. Leave a message at the—"

Hearing his voice always sucks the air out of me. "I can't feel you yet. But I hope you know I'm waiting. I assume you're with Theo right now, guiding him on his journey. I know you can't be in two places at once, but I could use some help from my big brother. So, if you have time, please come find me, wherever you are."

I press end on the call and turn my phone off.

And like a dam breaking, the tears finally fall.

THE TEARS DIDN'T STOP for two hours. I had to run out of that park because I figured me sitting on a rock and crying probably looked batshit crazy to any bystanders.

I roam around for another hour, I think, and as soon as I'm around the corner from the hotel, I turn my phone back on.

Shit, when did it get to be past seven? I can't remember what time Dom said his meeting would be done, but I assume it'll be late.

I know how wrong I am when I step inside the hotel and see Dom yelling at the front desk.

"What do you mean you have no idea when she left? Don't any of the cameras work in this place?"

"Sir, I'm sorry, but the system—"

"I don't give a fuck about the system. Reboot it, goddammit! My girlfriend isn't answering her phone and I'm worried sick. So, you better do something, or my lawyer will be—"

Before this goes further, I walk up to the desk and place my hand on Dom's bicep, ignoring what he said and how it made my stomach flip. "Hey."

"Is this her?"

Dom doesn't say a word as he grabs my arm and drags me to the elevator, his eyes flaring with how pissed off he is. *Probably shouldn't have turned my phone off...*

"D—" I open my mouth to apologize, but he cuts me off.

"Not a fucking word."

The elevator ride is silent, and when we get into the room, he backs me into the door as soon as we enter.

"Where the hell were you?"

"I was out exploring the city like I told you earlier. I couldn't stay in the hotel room all day." *Because I was feeling really in my head, and I needed out. It didn't help. I feel worse than before, but I can't tell you about it because you'll look at me with pity because my brother is dead.* Nobody looks at you the same after you have a death in your family, especially when you're young.

It's worse when tragedy strikes twice. The looks get worse. They get sadder, more empathetic, as if I'm going to break if they say the wrong thing.

I've been treated with kid gloves ever since my dad died, and it was worse after Tobias. Sure, I'm older now, but the looks stay the same. The tragedy is all that everyone remembers about my life, and nothing else seems to permeate into their minds. So their faces stay the same, the condolences get longer, and the hugs squeeze my body a little tighter. They always say how they hate doing this for a second time.

I hate it. Sure, I feel like absolute garbage, but I'm still a human being. I'm not going to break like glass if someone yells at me or treats me like normal. I prefer it, in fact.

"Why didn't you answer me? I called like fifteen times." His breath is hot on my face, and I know he's only freaking out about this because he feels responsible for me while we're on this trip.

Both of his arms are caging me into the door, and I feel bad for making him worry, but he's not my parent. He doesn't control me.

"I turned my phone off." My stomach is bottoming out, as if I'm on a rollercoaster, but I try to breathe through whatever's going on in my body. "Were you worried about me, Dommy?"

"Yes. I thought you got kidnapped or something, but then I realized if that happened they would've returned you."

"Is that so?" I tilt my head at him.

"Knowing you, you would threaten to chop the fucker's balls off. He was probably scared shitless of you." He reaches out and pushes my glasses up my face. The small contact makes my breathing uneven. "Though the glasses make you less petrifying."

"Are you scared of me?"

"Do you want me to be scared of you?"

"Maybe."

His eyes move to the ground before they come back up to my face. Tingles spread from my toes to my neck with that one look from him. *Get it together.* I only notice now that he's still wearing his suit, a watch that probably cost more than my entire life, and a chain that sparkles underneath his neck.

Neither of us threatens to move from whatever power trip we're having, and I love seeing this side of him. He sounded unhinged when he was yelling at that poor guy at the front desk. I've never seen him lose his cool like that, and I hate to say it turned me on.

Gregory couldn't turn me on, if ever, but one short look at Dom has my entire body pulsating. I hope he can't feel it or else I'll have to book a flight back to Pennsylvania on account of being too embarrassed to be in the same room and car with him for a few more weeks.

"You called me your girlfriend in the lobby." It comes out before I can stop it. Those two words have been hanging in my head since I heard him say that.

His lips lift into a smirk. "If I called you my friend, it wouldn't have packed the same punch."

"Is that what we are? Friends?" I ask, feeling a bit too brave right now.

"The two of us will never be friends. We're just helping one another out on the road, right?"

I swallow hard, my throat suddenly feeling dry. *Must be because of all the crying.* Sure, let's go with that. "Right."

He looks at me for a few more seconds before he pushes off the door and heads into the bathroom. As soon as I hear the shower turn on, I know it's going to be an awkward night, so I grab my headphones and my book, and escape into another fictional world that's better than this one.

Chapter Eleven

Dominic

— GREENGREENGREEN BY CHASE ATLANTIC

After I toss and turn for the one hundredth time, I decide that sleep is probably not coming to me tonight.

I look over at Teags on her side of the bed, one singular pillow sits between the two of us, and I wonder if she's awake.

Her hair is spread out on her pillow like it always is. I see her chest rise and fall in a steady rhythm, and I'm glad all my tossing didn't wake her up. When she got back here after her impromptu stroll, she looked exhausted. I'm glad she's getting some rest.

But now, whenever I close my eyes, I can't stop seeing her red-rimmed eyes from earlier. She had to have been crying, right? Why else do people's eyes get red? Allergies? Eye surgery? I have no fucking clue.

I can't stop seeing her face when I got her back up to the room. And I didn't ask why. *Why didn't I ask her?* God, am I the world's biggest asshole?

No, I'm not. We don't talk about shit like that. That's not who we are to one another. I actually don't think that there's a label for basically kidnapping your best friend's little sister and helping her pack up her life.

I'm just Dom. And she's Teags. That's it.

My phone buzzing on the side table gets me right up, and I don't bother checking who it is before I answer it.

"Hello?"

"Dominic." The frozen sound of my mother's voice comes through my phone.

I sigh heavily before I get out of bed—quietly so as to not disturb my hostage—as I head for the bathroom. I'm already dreading this conversation. I should've known after my meeting today that my parents would call to check in. It's late though. I hoped that they would leave me alone while on the road, but as usual, they only call when it works for them. I'm hoping the investors I met with brought them good news because if this trip starts out bad, it would probably only get worse.

"Mother."

"I spoke with John earlier. He said the meeting went well."

My parents were never ones to beat around the bush. Every time they call, it's never social. It's always business.

I can't remember the last time they called me to wish me a happy birthday. Or the last time they showed up for something important—like my college graduation. Not even a single text. I only got an email from them talking about my role at the company.

"And?" I ask.

"They've agreed to invest in another location."

"That's wonderful news," I say, my tone of voice not matching the words coming out of my mouth.

"If you continue like this for the rest of the trip, there are bright things on the horizon for you at Graves Jewelry, Dominic."

"Is that all?"

"Yes. Your father and I are very proud of all you're doing to prove your worth to the company."

To the company. Not to them. It's never them. It's always about what's good for the fucking company. "Good night."

I hang up the phone, slamming it down on the counter, as I try my best to shake off the feelings that always seem to float up when my parents talk to me.

Here I am, proving my worth to them, when I don't even care about the company or any of it. I've always wanted out, but somehow I always get sucked back in. I don't see any other options for me besides the family business. And at least this way, I can get some experience if I do end up going a different direction in the future.

Fuck, I hope so. If I end up working for my family my whole life, I don't even want to imagine what that would be like. But it sounds fucking terrible.

God, I'm so fucking tense. Not being able to drink or fuck has been messing with my head lately. I can't seem to ever relax. My jaw is always tense, my shoulders always bunched, and I have a headache that hasn't gone away for months.

There's no way that I'm sleeping now, but I head back to bed anyway.

I quietly step out of the bathroom and head back to bed. As soon as I get settled on my side, I hear a voice.

"Is everything alright?"

"Sorry if I woke you up," I say, flipping over onto my back so she can hear me better.

"You didn't." Her voice is uncharacteristically soft. If I didn't know she was lying right next to me, I don't think I would've heard her.

"I could've sworn you were asleep earlier."

"Are you watching me sleep, Graves?" I can hear the smile in her voice.

"N-No, I—"

"I was joking," she says as she flips off of her side. The two of us are now lying the same way, looking at the same ceiling, and the only thing that separates us is a single pillow. "So, who was on the other side of the phone that pissed you off so much?"

"Do you actually care or are you just pretending?"

She takes a few seconds to answer, and I'm worried that I pissed her off. I shouldn't have said that. I don't even know why I—

"Well, if I'm sharing a bed and a car with you, then talking is pretty much all we've got."

I stifle a laugh. "I guess you're right, but I don't want to bore you to death with my family troubles."

"Well, I'm the queen of family problems, so if you want an outside opinion, I can try and help."

I want to ask her what that means, but if I'm not going to give anything, I doubt she would either.

"I mean, if you don't want to talk, then we can continue to not sleep and stare at the ceiling, I really don't mind—"

"My mother called. She wanted to let me know that the meeting I had earlier went well and the investors I met with are going to help build a location here."

"That's good, right?

I sigh heavily. "I guess, but... I don't know. Any time my parents talk to me, I always feel rattled. My mother has a way of making me feel like the smallest person on the planet."

The silence after I say that is staggering, and I can only hear the two of us breathing quietly. It's kind of helping my stress levels though. In a weird way, talking about all this in the darkness feels a lot easier than keeping it all bottled up.

"I understand that," she whispers, and it's freaking me out that she's speaking so softly. She's always so assured and confident in everything she says, but now the way she talks feels muffled. It's not like her at all, and I kind of miss the Teags that snaps at me because she knows she can.

"What do you mean by that?"

"Nothing, I—" She starts to flip over, but I lean over the pillow barrier and grab her arm.

"You were crying earlier, so I assume something's been on your mind all day."

"You noticed." It's not a question, more like a surprise that comes off of her lips.

"I basically cornered you against the door," I say, still holding onto her arm. I let her go before I speak again. "Your eyes were red. Swollen too."

Her hand rubs the spot I was touching on her arm as she leans against the headboard, making herself more comfortable. I wasn't holding her that tight. At least, I hope I wasn't.

"Did I hurt you?"

She shakes her head, and before I think she's not going to elaborate more on what we were formally talking about, she does.

"Tristan," is all she says.

I know she's not a fan of words, but I think I can gauge what she means. The night I drove her home from the wedding, I walked into a pretty heavy conversation they were having in the middle of the West house.

From what I gathered while I was washing my hands is that Tristan was trying to control Teags and the decisions she was making. Mostly, the decision about moving to Arizona. Which very clearly backfired since she's with me to grab all her shit from her house after showing up at my doorstep in the middle of the night.

"Got it," I say. The two of us are speaking, but we're not really talking. Words are coming out of our mouths and we both moderately understand what the other is saying, but it's surface level stuff.

"I have an idea," she says, turning to me. "Let's get high."

"What?" She has officially caught me off guard. "Right now?"

"Yeah, why not?"

"Because... Because it's like one in the morning, and we have to leave tomorrow."

"Oh, come on, live a little. We're on vacation."

I smack her arm. "No, we're not. I'm on a business trip and you're my stowaway."

"Hey, I'm a willing participant in this," she says. "Come on, let's do it."

"We're not getting high."

"HOLY SHIT, I'M SO glad I brought this with me," I say as I laugh at the face Teags is making. Sure, per my parents' rules, I'm not supposed to be doing this, but they're not here. And my tolerance is so high this isn't even going to do anything.

"I've never been high before, this is crazy," she says, dragging out every syllable in that sentence.

I laugh some more. I've never had this much fun getting high—not even with the guys. We used to do this once a week so we could all blow off some steam, but usually Tristan and Harry opted out during baseball season. The night would usually end with all of us falling asleep on various pieces of furniture in our living room.

Well, our old living room.

"Wait, you've never been high? Like ever?" I ask her.

"Nope," she says, a smile on her face. "But I like it. It's fun."

"Ugh!" I swipe my hand down my face. "Your brother can never find out about this. I'm basically corrupting you."

"No talking about my brother anymore. What Tristan doesn't know won't hurt him. He can't boss me around. I'm twenty-four years old, and can make my own decisions."

"I know."

She moves a little closer to me and puts her hand out. "Then let's keep this a secret between us, okay?"

"Deal," I say as I shake her hand.

"God, your hands are so soft," she says as she brings our joined hands up to her face. "Look at those veins too. I like how you can still see them under your tattoos."

"What are you doing?" I ask, her eyes still popping out of her head as she examines my hand. She grabs my other hand and does the same thing.

"You know…" She takes another hit. "I've had a crush on you for years, Dom. So the fact that I'm touching you right now is mind-boggling."

I start to laugh. Is she being serious? She's had a crush on me for years, she said? How the fuck did I miss that? Is this some sort of joke? "What did you say?"

"What?" she asks, letting go of my hands as her eyes start to droop. "Oh my God, I'm so tired."

And before I can say anything else, she slumps over onto her pillow and falls asleep.

I stifle a laugh before I see how she's sleeping. She looks like she's doing some sort of yoga pose, so as I waft the smell out of our room through the window, I move all of the shit off of our bed and lay her down underneath the covers.

I would be worried she's going to wake up and bite my head off, but with how high she was, I don't think that's something that will happen tonight.

I have to say, corrupting Teags is kind of fun, but again, I can't mention any of this to her brother when we're back and I'll have to pretend like this trip together didn't happen.

All of these little moments between us on the road are ours, and it feels weird knowing we'll have secrets between us when we're back home. Though experiencing her high was hilarious. I'm not sure if what she said was true or not, but I doubt she was being serious.

Plus, I would have noticed if she had a crush on me, or *has* one. I know what it looks like when someone is into me, and she doesn't look at me that way.

Nobody has ever looked at me for anything more than one night, and with the way my life is going, nobody ever will.

Chapter Twelve

— SEX BY THE 1975

Dom wakes me up by jumping on the bed.

"You are such a man child," I grumble into the pillow I placed in between us, but somehow during the night it fell onto the floor. "Leave me alone."

"We have to go. Get the hell up and get a move on. Oklahoma awaits," he tells me as he jumps off of the bed and starts packing up his suitcase.

"Wonderful."

"There's a coffee waiting for you on the bathroom sink."

That makes me perk up, but my eyes are still closed. It's going to take a fuck ton of coffee to get them open after whatever happened last night. "Why did you leave it there?"

"It's your shower coffee. You know, kill two birds with one stone and caffeinate while you're in the shower. It's a win-win."

"You might be the weirdest person I've ever met," I say as I finally open my eyes and look at him. He somehow looks even better in the daylight.

"That's not what you said last night."

"What are you talking about?" I ask him. I remember the two of us speaking last night, but the memories of what we talked about are fuzzy. "What the hell happened last night?"

"I corrupted you and the two of us got high," he says as he runs a hand through his hair, his muscles practically bursting from beneath his short-sleeved shirt.

"Oh." I vaguely remember mentioning that. I thought it would be a good idea. When he walked out of the bathroom last night, I could *feel* the weight of the call he took in the room.

So I thought it would help, and I guess it did. He looks more like his normal self this morning, and I hear him clear his throat before I come out of my haze.

"I take it you don't remember what you said to me last night."

What the hell is he talking about? "Uh, no. I assume I said a lot of stupid shit. What did I say?"

"You said you had a crush on me." He shifts awkwardly where he stands. "Is that true?"

Oh, fuck me. "No." I laugh it off. "Of course that's not true." That's not technically a lie. I wouldn't call it a crush, it's more lust-driven. And nothing will ever happen between us anyway. It's wishful thinking, if you will.

He smirks back at me. "I figured. I just wanted to double check." He clears his throat, a thick blanket of silence coating the room. "Uh, are you going to shower or what?"

"Yeah, sorry," I say as I head to the bathroom, grab my coffee, and step into a hot shower, hoping that this combination is enough to make me wake up.

WE'RE TWO HOURS INTO our drive, and apparently my plan of getting high last night didn't actually help. Dom looks tense as he drives, his arm out the window as the sun beats down on our truck. His jaw hasn't relaxed since an hour ago, his shoulders haven't come down, and his knuckles are white against the steering wheel. What the hell could have happened in the past hour that's made him so tense?

I take my headphones out of my ears and turn to him.

"You know, your brooding is ruining my music."

"I didn't know music could be ruined."

"It's one of my hobbies, and you *can* actually ruin hobbies. Especially with whatever vibe you have going on." Silence fills the car. "And you're not even listening to music, right now? Are you a serial killer or something?"

"No, I just didn't feel like listening to anything."

"That's fucking weird, dude. Not even a podcast?"

He shrugs at me as I roll my eyes.

"Oh, so you don't have any hobbies? Everyone has them, you should try it sometime. Maybe it'll make your knuckles less white." I gesture to his hand around the steering wheel.

He loosens his grip after I point it out. "I have hobbies."

"Like what?" I ask as I shift in my seat, my hair whipping in my face from the windows being down.

"Drinking, smoking, working, and fucking."

My heart skips a beat at the last word. I'm no stranger to swearing, but for some reason when he says shit like that, it carries a bigger weight.

I take a breath before I respond. "Fucking is not a hobby, Dominic. Neither is working."

"Well, you're clearly not fucking correctly. Gregory must not have known what to do with his dick. And I haven't been—"

He stops himself from saying whatever he was about to. "Haven't been what?"

"Nothing."

"Oh, come on, Dommy. It can't be that bad. Just tell me." I poke his arm.

"Why do you want to know so bad?" he quips back, but I'm not backing down.

"Because talking is better than silence, so what were you going to say?"

"Why don't you like the silence?"

Because silence reminds me that I'm alone. That Tobias is dead. That I'm unlovable. "Stop changing the subject, what were—"

"I haven't had sex in a while per my parents request to be more focused on my job."

My eyes widen of their own violation. Dominic Graves telling me that he hasn't had sex in a while is a huge surprise, considering I've overheard Tristan in college talking about Dom and all his escapades.

"Oh, well—"

"Just forget I said anything," he says as he cracks his neck and looks anywhere but in my direction. Is he embarrassed?

"Gregory and I haven't had sex in months." I don't know why I blurted out information about my dry spell to Dom of all people, but maybe it'll make him feel better about his situation.

"Oh."

"Yeah, so, it looks like we're in the same boat." I try to laugh off the awkwardness I feel about talking about sex with Dominic fucking Graves.

"Speak for yourself, I'm doing fine."

A laugh comes out before I stop it. "We got high last night and it was the happiest I've seen you on this trip so far. Clearly, you're not doing fine."

"Just drop it, okay?"

"Fine."

I turn back in my seat as I throw my headphones back on and swipe to put an audiobook on. I'm in the middle of this mafia book someone recommended to Bree on her channel. She put one line that was super out of context in her video, and I immediately went to download it.

I read it a few weeks ago, and now I'm listening to the audiobook. The narrators are great, and I've been dying to hear this one smut scene in spoken word. The two main characters are in an arranged marriage, and this particular chapter has them having really hot hate sex.

They agree it's a one-time thing, but obviously, it doesn't stay that way.

It takes a second for the book to load, probably because we're in the middle of fucking nowhere, so I stare out the window and away from Dom as he continues to drive.

A few minutes later, it still hasn't loaded so I check the app and notice that it's playing on my phone.

But my noise-canceling headphones weren't connected. So, Dom probably heard the chapter out loud.

Fuck. My. Life.

I slowly take my headphones off. Maybe he won't say anything if I don't bring it up? I clear my throat as I look at my phone, and drag my book back to where I left off.

"No, please, keep it going. I was interested in where his tongue was about to go."

I see a smirk on his face as I slap him on the arm. "Shut up."

"I didn't know those were the kind of things you were into. I mean, I knew you were a little crazy, but I wasn't expecting you to be into those types of books."

I roll my eyes. "And what does that mean, Dominic?"

"Oh, shit, the full name."

I don't say anything.

"Look, I didn't mean it in a bad way. I wasn't expecting to hear what I did coming out of your phone."

"And what did you hear?"

He adjusts how he's sitting. Maybe I should offer to drive soon. He's been driving the entire way. His back must hurt or something. "A very detailed description of a guy eating his wife's pussy. And he sounded *starved*."

He says that with a tone I've never heard before. Wait. There's no way. Is he turned on? Oh, God, this is even worse than I thought. I'm usually capable of reading these books with a fully straight face in public, but when he says that I try to hide the blush that creeps up my face.

"That's what happens when you get between a mafia guy and his wife. They tend to be possessive—in the books, at least."

"And you're into that? Possessiveness and threatening to kill a guy for how he looks at you?"

I sigh heavily. It's always so hard to explain this to people who don't read. "It's a psychological thing. I like being inside the mind of people who don't see just black and white. The world has so many shades of gray to it, and it's interesting seeing people navigate these fucked up situations. And it makes me feel like I have some control over my life, especially when I feel like I've been spinning out the past few years."

His eyes soften as he looks over at me, his gaze searching mine for something. "I can understand that."

"Good. Now, don't judge people for what they read. It's rude."

"I won't if you turn that audiobook back on."

What? He wants to keep listening to it? Right now? Together? That feels way too intimate for such a small setting we're in. Ethan's truck is tiny and I've never listened to smut with someone before. "Are you sure?"

"Yeah, Teags. Put it back on."

So, I do. And we both listen for a few chapters. It's not as awkward as I thought it would be, but I'm way too hyper aware of Dom and all of his movements. Any time he runs a hand through his hair, or adjusts how he sits, I notice it. He's all I can see in my mind as I listen to the characters. I'm so fucked. I clearly still feel *something* for him.

It's only lust though. It's always been that and nothing more. Maybe if I just fucked him out of my system, then—

Wait. That's it.

"Dom," I say as I turn to face him.

"Teags," he mocks me, but glances at where I sit in the passenger seat.

"We should make a pact while we're on the road together."

"A pact? Like what?"

I take a breath before I say this, feeling bolder than I ever have. "A sex one."

He slams on the breaks as he pulls over to the side of the road and parks the car. "What the fuck did you say?"

"Clearly, you heard me if this was your reaction." I motion to the truck. "What's wrong with you?"

"You're the one talking about sex the day after you told me you have a crush on me."

My hands cover my eyes. "Oh my God, I told you that wasn't true. We're both adults here."

"Yes, and you're also my best friend's little sister."

"Stop talking about my brother," I yell, not wanting the mention of Tristan to ruin my confidence. "Look, you're stressed out. I'm in the middle of a life crisis and the worst dry spell to ever exist. I thought it would be a good idea."

"A good idea doesn't involve me fucking my best—"

"I get it, I'm Tristan's little sister. But I'm also a grown ass woman with needs, and you're a grown ass man with needs too. It would only be while we're on the road, and since neither of us has feelings, it would be easy to stop it when we get home." My throat goes dry at the end of the sentence, but he doesn't notice. I don't have feelings for him, not relationship ones, at least. I could do no strings attached, and I know he can too.

He's quiet for a few minutes and before I think he's actually considering it, he puts the car back into drive.

"No."

"But—"

"No, Teags."

I sigh heavily as I turn to face the window, put my headphones on, and don't play any music.

Chapter Thirteen

Oklahoma City

— BAD IDEA BY ARIANA GRANDE

I'M SITTING IN MY bed at the hotel—there's two in this hotel room, thank you Oklahoma—debating on whether or not I want to text my family group chat. Since I've been on the road, I've been missing my family a bit more than I normally am. When I was in Arizona, I could keep myself busy. I'd go book shopping, on walks, and Gregory always had some sort of dinner we had to attend. So I never really let myself miss them because I knew where they were.

I miss my mom. I want to ask her what the hell I should do, but at the same time, I don't want her pity. I don't want her to look at me and see another child that she failed.

No, I can figure this out myself. I have to.

Instead of doing something I might regret, I grab my phone and load up the audiobook I started. Dom and I finished the other one on the road after he broke the silence I was giving him. I haven't read this book before, but it's a mafia series I saw a bunch of people raving about online.

Therefore, it's the perfect book to distract me from all of my current troubles. There's nothing better than getting lost in a fictional universe for a little while.

There's something so comforting to me about losing myself in the dark and morally gray area of characters. It makes me feel better when some of them can describe exactly how I'm thinking sometimes.

The world isn't black and white. It never will be. For me, I do what I think is right and I'm pretty unapologetic about it. But I'd never do something to intentionally hurt someone. That's where these books and I differ.

Some of these men kill people for looking at their wives the wrong way—granted, the people they kill are usually horrible people—but it seems like an over exaggeration.

Though, I do kick my feet when it happens. It's hot. Sue me. I guess that's what happens when you grow up without a father figure—my taste in books is a giant calling card for my daddy issues.

Which is fine, I guess. That explains why Gregory never liked experimenting sexually. He was a little too vanilla for my tastes. I liked to experiment, to try new things, but he never did. When we had sex, it used to take me what felt like ages to get turned on.

Like I said, I'm not cut out for the cute and lovey dovey bullshit.

I like to be fucked, and if I can't get that in real life, at least I can live vicariously through the books I read.

I shove my headphones on even though Dom is still at his meeting, just in case he comes back and a smut scene is playing like it did in the car the other day. It was embarrassing, but considering the other scenes in that book, it was probably the tamest one he could have heard.

It could be hours or minutes, but eventually, I hear the door open and slam shut, and as I take my headphones off, Dom comes into full view.

Looking stressed out and hot as fuck.

His gaze alone could cut me in half with how lethal it looks. *What the hell happened at his meeting?*

He's not wearing his suit jacket—he threw it on the bed when he came in—his white sleeves are rolled up, revealing his tattoos. And his tie is loosened and hanging down his neck.

"What happened?"

He only gazes at me, continuing to loosen his tie until it's completely off. "What are you doing?"

He looks over at my bed where my phone and headphones rest on the sheets. "Nothing. Why do you look like you're ready to kill someone? Was your meeting that bad?"

"No. It was fine," is all he offers me.

I can practically see the veins bulging from his arms because of how tight his fists are clenched. Fine. He doesn't have to tell me anything. I don't even know why I asked or cared in the first place.

Probably because you're getting closer to him.

Instead of pressing him on it, I return to my audiobook. "Whatever."

"What are you listening to this time, Teags?"

Wanting to fuck with him a little bit, I answer. "The main male character just shoved his cock into her mouth. So, if you'll excuse me."

His jaw only clenches as he unbuttons his shirt. I see a peek of ink as I try to avert my eyes but fail miserably before he turns and heads for the bathroom. I hear the shower turn on a few seconds later and I know he's probably going to be in there for a while.

One thing I've learned about him on this trip is that he takes long ass showers. Longer than me even.

I wonder why he asked me about my audiobook. And even so, I wonder why he turned down my offer for sex while on this road trip. Clearly he could use some release. Or even better, he could need it to make the meetings he's going to more tolerable. If he's going to be like this for the rest of the trip, I don't know if I can handle being in his proximity.

I'm no ray of sunshine, but he was always fun. Now, he's annoyed and pissed off most of the time.

I start to settle into my next read, and a few minutes into it, I hear something crash in the bathroom. It didn't sound too bad—I can't tell if the shower is on yet—but when I hear another sound, I hop up from the bed, and head for the door, pressing my ear against it. All it takes is another pound on the wall for me to burst in, trying to see if he's hurt or injured, but it's the exact opposite.

The shower is on, he's inside of it, water cascading down his tattooed body, arm stretched out to the wall, his hand wrapped around his dick.

I look away immediately, feeling like a fucking idiot, and before I can leave before he spots me, he speaks.

"What are you doing here?"

"I-I thought you were hurt. There was banging on the wall. I-I... I thought you fell or something."

"Or something," he says as he grabs his towel, turning the shower off. "Sorry to worry you."

"Uh, it's okay. I'm glad you're okay."

"What else are you thinking about right now?" he asks me, not having moved from where he was getting out of the shower.

"How can you tell what I'm thinking?"

"You're making that same face you did in the car earlier." I grab my hair with my hands, smoothing my split ends in between my fingers. "Oh, so that's what you're thinking about then."

I sigh heavily. "I didn't like being shut down so easily. You didn't even let me explain myself."

He waves his hand out. "Explain then."

I'm surprised he even wants to listen to me after how quickly he tabled our discussion earlier. "It could just be while we're on the road. I help you out with your...stress and you help me figure out what I like during sex."

His eyebrows shoot up. I knew he wasn't expecting me to say that, but it's true.

"It would be another one of our mutually beneficial agreements we seem to like so much."

"Oh, so now we have a thing, huh?"

I can't help but laugh. "I guess so."

"So, I take it Gregory didn't really like experimenting with you then."

I shake my head. "When we did have sex it was fine, but I always wanted more, and he never wanted to try anything. I want to find out what I like for the future, and this trip sort of fell into our laps, so I figured the worst you could say was no and we never talk about this again. You'll bring me to Arizona, we'll finish out the rest of our deal, and everything will go back to normal."

His face twitches ever so slightly, and if I wasn't staring at him, I would have missed it.

"And since there are no feelings on either end, it would be perfect."

His eyebrows shoot up again, and it could be a few seconds or a few minutes before either of us speaks.

"Deal."

My eyebrows shoot up. "Really?"

"What can I say?" he sighs heavily. "Mutually beneficial agreements are a specialty for us. I'll teach you what you like during sex, and we can have some fun together."

"Well, good," I say, a smile coming off of my face. "When did you want to start?"

"Since we skipped about a thousand steps, how about now?"

"Now?"

"Might as well make use of the little time we have," he says, taking a long look up and down my body. "What do you want to try first? What's been at the forefront of your mind that he was too scared to try with you?"

My breathing starts to pick up, and I wish I could blame some of it on the steam, but I can't. It's just how my body seems to react to him, especially when sex is the topic of conversation.

"He never wanted to be too rough. I think he was afraid I would break."

"You want to try it rough?"

"No sex yet, Dom," I tell him. "Baby steps."

"Whatever you say goes."

"But maybe we start with a rough blowjob?"

"Is that what you want?"

I nod.

"Words, Teags. Say out loud what you want from me and I'll do the same for you. That is how this works, you know."

I take a deep breath, gathering all of my courage before I say the next words out of my mouth. "I want you to fuck my mouth. Roughly, Dom," I say as he turns the shower back on, steam starting to surround us again from how hot the water is. "Please."

He doesn't blink, only heats my body with his stare as he speaks. "Get over here and get in the shower, clothes on, on your knees."

I waste no time before I listen to his instructions, and as soon as I'm ready how he wants me, he drops his towel and gets into the shower with me.

Thank God the shower is big enough for two people or else this would be far more difficult. I see the appeal of shower sex, but I was never sure I would like it. Though reading about it in books is fun. Like I said, most things are more fun when they're fictional.

"It won't be sweet," he reminds me. "Are you sure?"

Fuck. "I'm sure. I don't like sweet," I say as I look up to him. "Can I?" He nods his head before my hand wraps around his shaft. His head falls back as I stroke his dick, the warm water helping to lubricate my hand.

He shoves my hand off of him. "Open your mouth and let me fuck that pretty face."

God, I feel myself pulsate at that one sentence. After what feels like years of thinking my vagina is broken, it's nice to know it can still get aroused.

"I'm not going to ask again. Open your fucking mouth."

I comply and he wastes no time before he shoves his cock to the back of my throat. The water is still falling around us, but the only thing I'm focused on is making Dominic Graves come down my throat.

Or on my body. Either way, mission fucking accomplished.

"God, you look so beautiful taking me down your throat," he says as he pulls out and thrusts back in again. It burns a little since I can't quite take all of him comfortably, but I'm doing the best I can with what little control I have.

I should've known he likes to be in control, but what he doesn't know is that in the bedroom, I like relinquishing mine. He doesn't know I'm as turned on as he is right now.

I reach my hand up to cup his balls, and as I do, his right arm flies out as he anchors himself to the wall of the shower.

He's still fucking my face, his dick reaching all the way to the back of my throat, and I can only sit here and steal touches of him. My right hand is massaging his balls, and my left hand is exploring his body that's covered in tattoos. I knew he had the ones down his arms, but he also has a few on his thighs, back, and down his torso.

I hollow my cheeks out, wanting to drive him a little crazier with some more suction.

"Jesus, Teags, just like that, baby."

I try not to think too hard about that word he just used, but it leaves my mind as soon as it enters because of how mercilessly Dom is fucking my mouth. I've never seen him so out of control before, and I can tell he's unleashing at least a few weeks of tension on my face right now.

And fuck, it feels so good.

"Do you need your shirt on or can I rip it?" he asks, looking down at me where I sit, his dick still stuffed in my mouth. "Actually, don't answer that."

He stops thrusting into my mouth, so I take over before he reaches down and rips my shirt off of my body. I wasn't wearing a bra either since I've just been sitting in the hotel room all day, so my boobs spill out of where he ripped it.

"Much fucking better. Now, I know what to cum on."

"You owe me a new shirt, Dominic."

His hand comes down and cups my chin. "Don't worry, baby, I'll buy you however many shirts you want."

"You fucking better—" I can't finish my sentence because he shoves his cock back into my mouth.

"You know, I don't know why I was against this originally." His hand comes to my wet hair. "I prefer you with your mouth full, Teagen."

The use of my full name is driving me insane. It's the *way* he says it, dripping with lust like the fucking devil himself.

After a few more thrusts, I can tell he's close, so I reach up to cup him again, and in an instant, he pulls out of my mouth, and releases himself onto my boobs.

"Fuck," he grits out, his hand wrapped around his dick as he covers my chest. "That's it, take it all, Teags. Fuck look at you all covered in my cum."

I take a second to get my bearings, my body on fire as I come down from the high I was just on. I stand from where I was kneeling, my knees killing me because the tile on this shower floor is not comfortable. "Now, get out. I need to clean up."

"This was my fucking shower you invaded," he says, a lazy smile on his face.

"So? You made a mess that I have to clean up," I say as I shove him out of the shower, already trying to get my shorts off. They're sticking to my legs as I drag them down my body, fully aware of Dom still staring at me.

He complies, though a little confused still, as he grabs a towel from the rack and starts to dry off.

"Oh, and Dom?"

He turns to look at me as he raises his eyebrows.

"You could've come down my throat. I would've been good and swallowed."

I see him throw his head back as I turn around and laugh to myself, stunned at the sound that just came out of my mouth.

Temporary, this is only temporary.

Chapter Fourteen

— OH MY BY ALESSI ROSE

An hour ago, I had the best orgasm I've ever had.

And it was with Teagen fucking West, right after she walked into the bathroom and heard me moaning and groaning.

Did I walk into an alternate timeline or something?

Jesus, I can't stop fucking thinking about the way her mouth took my dick. It's driving me fucking insane.

That wasn't what I was expecting when I got back here after the meeting from hell. It went fine, just like the last one, but I was so fucking bored talking about the numbers from our other locations. I hated what I was doing. I hated the persona I had to put on to make the appropriate impression, and when I left that meeting, I was pissed off.

Now, I can't fucking sleep. I'm laying and staring at the ceiling of our hotel room, thinking about the girl in the bed next to me and how she gave me the best blowjob I've ever had.

And I've had a lot of them. I slept around a lot in college, and plenty of girls have done what Teags did earlier. With her, it was different. It felt explosive, and not even when I came all over her chest. It was like that the entire time—especially when she gave me an attitude. My dick has never been so fucking hard, and even thinking about it now has it twitching in my boxers.

God, I need to get it together.

I've never been so confused before. Normally, things like that never came with anything else, but Teags is sitting ten feet from me.

Never in my life have I been so confused by an orgasm. I know I'm helping her figure out her own likes and dislikes with sex, but I didn't think one orgasm could confuse me this much. It's just while we're on the road. It's temporary, yet I cannot stop fucking thinking about it.

I sigh heavily before I turn to face her bed, noticing that her eyes are also open. God, the two of us might drive each other crazy before this trip is over just by how similar we seem to be. I've learned a lot about her during our time together, and it's not even close to being over.

I can't tell if my newfound information about her is a good or a bad thing, but I can't say that I hate it. It's nice to learn about what's underneath the layer she shows to the world.

Though it was nice to see her confidence back when we were in the shower. She looked a lot different than the girl who showed up on my porch.

Maybe we both have Stockholm syndrome?

"Can't sleep?" I ask her.

"Nope."

An idea crosses my mind, and before I can stop, I grab my phone and open an app I haven't used in a while.

"Hey, have you ever read anything by Jane Austen?" I ask her.

"Uhh, yeah. A while ago." I hear her shuffle on her bed. "Austen is more Liv's territory."

Based on what I've heard Teags reading and the picture of Jane Austen on the quiz website, that tracks.

"Why?" she asks me, confused as to this topic of discussion so late at night.

I show her my phone. "Do you want to match your personality to a Jane Austen heroine?"

"I'm not going to take an internet quiz with you in the middle of the night."

I shift so I'm more comfortable on my bed. "Why not? We can't sleep, so maybe we should find out which character best matches us." I click on the quiz. "Here, I'll go first."

I swipe through the questions, picking what best matches my personality, until I get stuck.

"What do you see me as? A lawyer, a guidance counselor, an author, a doctor, an accountant, or a social worker?"

"Why the hell are you asking me?"

"Because I can't figure it out and I need to know what Jane Austen heroine I am."

I hear her laugh quietly to herself, as if she doesn't want me to hear. "I'd say a guidance counselor."

"Really?" That's not what I was expecting her to say. "Why?"

She shifts so she's facing me completely, her legs crossed underneath her. Now that my eyes are adjusted, I can see her better. Her fucking tiny white tank top and matching shorts is all I can focus on, and my head goes right back to her kneeling in front of me mere hours ago.

Her voice pulls me out of my haze. "Well, you act like an ass most of the time, but I've heard you give my brother and Liv good advice. Plus, you were there for Tristan when he was dealing with Tobias. That speaks volumes to me about who you are even if you act like a dick the other fifty percent of the time."

Wow. I've never had anyone describe me like that before. Is that how she really sees me or is this just for the quiz?

"Oh," I say, running a hand through my hair. "Thanks."

"What other questions are there?"

"The next one is what I look for in a romantic partner," I tell her, suddenly feeling awkward.

"And what did you pick?"

"Adventure, but that's not really what I look for, I guess."

"What's the real answer?"

Why do you want to know so badly? I refrain from saying that because in the cover of night, we're having a real conversation for the first time. All of our walls are down—well, mine are. I'm not sure if hers are, but I feel like I can tell her anything right now. "Someone who wants me for who I am. Not the money I have, not the business I'm in, but just me."

I don't add how most people have only wanted me for sex in the past because digging into my insecurities isn't something I want to do at the moment. I also don't add that I don't tell people about my family because once they know, I see dollar signs shine in their eyes.

She doesn't say anything as I clear my throat and swipe to the next question.

"If I had a dog, what kind of dog do you think I'd have?"

"As opposed to three fish?" she quips, and I laugh.

"Why the fuck does everyone make fun of my fish? They're great pets!"

"They're great pets for six year olds who won them at the fair, Dom. You're a grown ass man."

I guess she has a point, but I happen to like taking care of them. "I got Elinor from Sense and Sensibility."

Teags only laughs when I say that.

"Is that bad?"

"Well, what does it say?"

I read through what the quiz says, and it actually hit the nail right on the head about who I am and how I view myself.

"You hold yourself to high standards and act practically. Hiding beneath all of this, however, is a deep sensitivity for those you love and depend on you. Sometimes, you desire to let loose and pursue your own dreams, but you never do, in fear that everything would collapse around you."

Damn, whoever made this practically crawled inside of my brain.

"Uh, nothing."

"Oh, come on, tell me."

I shove open my comforter. "Come over here and find out."

"Absolutely not."

"If you want to know, then get your ass over here."

"Dominic—"

"We shared a bed in Chicago, and a few hours ago my dick was shoved down your throat. Stop being weird and come here."

I hear her sigh before she gets up and plops herself down on my bed, her legs shifting underneath the blankets near mine.

Fuck, I'm not even touching her and already I want to be closer. It's the dry spell though. I'm sure this will pass how it always does—swiftly.

"Do you do this often? Take random quizzes at night when you can't sleep?"

"Sometimes."

"And does it help?" she asks as she gets comfortable. Her foot brushes against mine, and even though she has a sock on, I can feel the burn where the contact was.

"Not always. Most of the time it makes me laugh and then I get up and workout no matter what time it is."

"Can I do one?"

"Sure," I say as I hand her my phone. "Which one are you thinking?"

She scrolls down the giant list that's up on my phone before landing on one about Danny DeVito. I only laugh as she starts the quiz.

"What? He's a great actor."

"I guess you just don't seem like the type to be his biggest fan."

She smacks me in the arm after I say that. "What the hell does that mean?"

In the cover of night, I look into her eyes more than I should. Her glasses are off and I can see them more clearly. Her eyes are sparkling into the phone, and I notice she has small flecks of green in the brown of her eyes.

The first question is similar to the last one I took—which career she wants—and to my surprise, she picks a business owner.

She swipes to the next question, answering it before I had time to look at all the choices. "Don't go too fast. It's a common quiz courtesy to let your partner pick an answer too."

"I didn't know quizzes came with so many rules."

"I knew you were going to pick the Mad Hatter though. You're predictable."

She smacks my chest this time, her eyes lingering a bit too long on one of my tattoos.

She goes through the rest, and I criticize her choices for all of them. Some of them are no surprise, but others I find myself wanting to ask why she specifically chose that one instead of a different one.

"The Hulk? Really?"

"I'm sorry. Who's the one taking this? Oh, right, me. Keep your opinions to yourself." She slumps down further into one of my pillows. "And I understand him. He gets super angry and smashes a bunch of shit. Sometimes, I wish I could do that."

Understandable, I guess.

She answers the final questions and her character ends up being the Lorax. The fucker who has a hard-on for the environment.

"I can't tell if that's a good thing or a bad thing," she says as she snorts because of how hard she's laughing. She covers her mouth immediately, and that only causes me to start laughing. I cannot believe that sound came out of her mouth.

"What the hell was that?"

"It happens when I laugh too hard," she says as it happens again. "Fucking hell! Make it stop."

I stop from telling her that I don't mind hearing her laugh.

I also stop from thinking about how lonely this trip would've been if she had not been on it with me.

God, what the fuck is happening to me?

"I have a proposition for you."

That shuts her right up. "A proposition?"

I nod.

"What sort of proposition?"

I reach my hand over to cup her face, she pulls away from me at first probably because she can't see me too well. But when her cheek settles in the palm of my hand, I know I've got her. "Let me return the favor."

Her eyes widen, her pupils dilating as they fill with lust. I know she knows what I'm referencing.

"What?" she whispers.

"Let me return the favor from earlier." My thumb moves back and forth on her face. "You surprised me earlier, now this is me doing it to you. Is being surprised with sex on your list of things to try while we're on the road?"

"It's okay, I—" She's getting all flustered all of a sudden, and she tries to pull back from me. Based on how both of her nipples are pebbled under her shirt, I know she's turned on. It's so goddamn easy for me to tell. She might hide so many parts of herself, but I see how she looks at me.

"Cat got your tongue?" I ask her.

"I-I don't..."

"Don't what, Teags?"

"I don't... get aroused easily. Gregory used to use lots of lube when we did have sex."

"Hmm," is all I say.

"We shouldn't be talking about this. Just forget it," she says as she tries to get out of bed. I grab her wrist and pull her back toward me.

"Hmm," I hum again.

"I-I can't even believe we're having this conversation."

"Hmm."

"Why the fuck do you keep saying that?" she asks me, already out of breath and I've barely even touched her. *Oh, this is going to be so much fun.*

"It's just interesting, is all."

"What's interesting?"

"You said you don't get aroused easily," I let my lips brush against her neck, feeling her pulse race underneath her soft skin. "But I can smell your arousal from here."

"Dom," she whispers.

"And it's driving me fucking crazy."

Both of us are breathing heavily, and God, have I fucking missed this. I've missed making someone feel good.

"I'm not..."

"Well, let's see shall we?" I say as I get up and drag her by her feet down the bed. She yelps and I kiss my way up her legs until I get to her pussy.

She has a wet spot right through her shorts, and she was trying to tell me she doesn't get aroused easily? Seems pretty fucking easy to me.

"Can I?"

"Dom..."

"Yes, Teags? Tell me what you fucking want from me."

Her mind clashes with how her pussy feels because I can see her go through about ten different emotions before she speaks again. "Touch me."

Fuck yes. I drag her shorts down her body, and the little fucking minx isn't wearing any underwear. "You're a bad fucking girl, Teags."

"W-why?" she asks as my mouth comes closer to her center.

"You're not wearing underwear," I say as I thrust two fingers into her. Fucking hell, she's so tight. Her pussy is squeezing my fucking fingers, but when I bring them out to show her, they're slick and covered in her arousal.

Just the way I fucking like it.

I put both of my fingers in my mouth, and just one taste has me fucked up. She tastes like the most intoxicating drug. I've only had one hit and I think I'm going to be addicted for the rest of my fucking life. My brain should be screaming at me to stop doing this, but the only thing I'm focused on is making her feel good. That's all I can seem to care about at the moment.

"I guess you were wrong. You're not the problem, Teags. Gregory was. At least that's what it seems like to me down here, but maybe I need a different perspective." I swipe my tongue through her, and she shivers beneath me. "Give me two minutes."

"For what?" she asks, her voice dripping with lust. She sounds like the devil on my fucking shoulder, and even though I know I should not be doing this, I couldn't give less of a fuck.

"To make you scream, baby," I say as I grab my phone and set a timer.

"You're not seriously going to time this," she says as she runs a hand through her hair, some strands sticking to her face because of how hot it is. "You must think quite highly of yourself."

"I'm a little rusty, but I think I can do it."

She rolls her eyes at me. "If you don't, you owe me something."

Always a fucking competition with this girl. "Fine."

"Great, I'm seeing a—"

The girl is half naked in front of me and she's trying to have a full on conversation. "Are you going to start it for me, baby?" The term slips out of my mouth like it did earlier and I can't stop it.

That shuts her right up. "Yes." She lifts my phone up and presses it, and when my tongue swipes through her soaked pussy, her legs lift off of the bed. I turn my attention on her clit, her hips bucking in my face when I bite down on it slightly.

"You like it rough like earlier in the shower, don't you?"

One of her hands finds my hair as she drags my head back to her center. "Fuck, keep going, please."

I snake my hand up to her mouth, thrusting two fingers inside so she closes her lips around them. "I don't need any help, but why don't you get my fingers wet for me?"

She complies and when I thrust them into her, my tongue biting and sucking on her clit, I hear her moan into the pillow next to her.

Music to my fucking ears, that is.

I move my fingers a little faster, knowing she likes it rougher than most. She took my dick like a fucking champ earlier—better than most girls do when I face fuck them—and just thinking about that while my fingers and mouth are buried in her pussy is turning me on.

Returning the favor might not be enough for me, but we're taking it slow tonight, and I respect that.

"Like that, Teags? Do you like how my fingers fuck you?"

Her only answer is a moan, and when I feel her pussy start to clench around me, I know I have her right where I want her.

"Dom," is all she says as her orgasm builds, and I suddenly hate how her fucking eyes are closed.

"Open those eyes and focus on me, baby."

She complies and when her lust-filled eyes hit mine and my thumb connects with her clit, rubbing circles around it. She looks fucking ethereal like this and I can't get enough of the sight in front of me. Watching her unravel in the cover of the darkness is just what I needed to see. Even though I didn't plan for this to happen tonight, I'm not mad about it.

What my parents don't know about won't fucking kill them. How even are they supposed to keep track if I'm behaving myself on the road?

"Come on, Teags. Coat my fucking fingers."

And then she explodes, her hips buck against my fingers as I keep fucking her with them while she comes all over my hand.

"Give me all of it. I want every moan, every sound, everything."

"Fuck," is all she can say, her pussy clenching hard around my fingers before she comes down a few seconds later. I've already stopped the timer, and I think I could beat my time if this happens again.

She's breathing heavily into the pillow, her body limp from how exhausted she is.

Perfect. Just how it should be.

"A minute and a half," I say as I look down at her on the bed. She's a fucking sight, this girl. And as her gaze clashes with mine, I take the fingers that were just inside of her and lick them clean.

She might act like she's cold and mean, but she tastes so fucking sweet.

"I expected less time, but good for you," she mumbles, almost incoherently. Even flushed and exhausted from an orgasm, she's still talking back to me.

I flop on my bed next to her and after a few seconds of heavy breathing, she moves to get up, but I'm quicker.

My hand grabs her arm and I drag her back into my bed, my arms around her as she eventually falls asleep a few seconds later.

If I'm not careful, I could ruin everything on this trip—my job, my relationship with Tristan if he ever found out about this, and my fucking sanity.

God help me, I don't really fucking care.

Chapter Fifteen

— BIRDS OF A FEATHER BY BILLIE EILISH

I WAKE TO AN empty bed.

And it's not like I'm disappointed or anything, but after the night we had, it kind of stings. I know he has a few meetings today, but I at least thought he would wake me up so I could have some coffee.

Though, why would he?

It's just sex. It's just another mutually beneficial agreement on the road, and Dom is a great partner to try all this out with. We both agreed to it, and it's basically a win-win, but for some reason, I feel like another shoe is about to drop on my head.

Fuck, did he touch me. Though, that feels like too small of a word. He *ignited* something inside of me and I don't remember a time I was that wet and needy. With Gregory, I was bone fucking dry—so much so that I thought my body was broken.

It turns out I'm not the problem, it was just who I was with. Dom is the hottest piece of forbidden fruit and we happen to be traveling across the country together.

A knock at the door stops my spiral, and I pull the covers up above my chest before I tell whoever it is to come in. I assume it's room service or something. Dom would walk right in and housekeeping isn't coming until tomorrow.

A woman wheels a cart in and parks it by the front of the room.

"I think you have the wrong room," I tell her as nicely as I can. "I didn't order anything." I was thinking about getting some coffee, but I had yet to pick up the phone.

"Mr. Graves left for the day and he told us to come up with this at nine a.m.," she tells me. "There's a note for you on here."

Oh. "Thank you," I say as she smiles at me and leaves.

I grab my phone, my mouth watering at the array of things on the table before I snap a few pictures. I feel like that's all I've been doing on this trip since these places we stay at are so fucking fancy. I'm never going to get any opportunity like this again, so I have to document everything that I can. I also have been doing that more—taking pictures so I can remember things. My memory sucks sometimes.

My phone buzzes as I swipe my camera away.

Dom: Good morning. Did you get my gift?

I can't help the smile from coming through on my face. I send him one of the pictures I took a few seconds ago.

Teags: Yes, thank you.

Dom: I figured you needed some sustenance and coffee. You didn't yell at the person who came in did you? I know you get feral before you have your coffee.

Teags: Feral is aggressive, and no, I was very nice.

Dom: Save some for me? I'd love to have some breakfast in bed later.

Teags: I'm making no promises.

Dom: Did you see the note?

Shit. I forgot the lady said something about that too. I sift through all of the dishes before I find a small card with writing on it. Again, a smile pops through my face and my body starts to get hot.

Teags: You're sure about this?

Dom: I wrote the note, didn't I?

Dom: And maybe I didn't get enough of a taste last night.

Teags: Dominic…

Dom: Save the full name for when you're screaming it later.

Teags: Don't you have a meeting to get to?

> **Dom: I can sext and talk business at the same time, Teags. I'm a wonderful multitasker.**

> **Teags: Concentrate, idiot. I'll be here for you later.**

> **Dom: Fine. Enjoy breakfast, Teags.**

> **Teags: Thank you for sending it.**

God, the way I feel about this man right now should be considered illegal. Getting into this while on the road probably isn't the best idea I've ever had.

But I can't find it in me to care. Not only did I just run away from a life I couldn't bear to live in for another second, but this trip is all about finding myself again. I'm chasing the feeling of truly being alive because for so long I've coasted through my life. I got comfortable, and I never again want to live my life like that again. When I left Arizona, I barely recognized myself—I still don't—but maybe this trip will hold the key to finding myself again.

Maybe some hot, dirty sex with Dom will help me realize what I need in a partner—someone dominating, not too vanilla, and someone who I trust enough to relinquish my control to. If anyone can help realize that, it's him, but I know he would never be in it for the long haul.

It helps that he's not a relationship kind of guy. He'll have no strings attached to me when this is over and I firmly believe I can keep my heart from falling for him. My crush has always been lust, not love, and scratching this itch will be just what it needs to hopefully fizzle out at the end of this deal between the two of us.

I've found myself in another mutually beneficial agreement, and it couldn't be more perfect.

I have zero expectations for this thing with Dom and that's how it will remain. I quite literally broke up with Gregory a few weeks ago, so I don't think a full-on relationship would be good for me, right now. Dom not only steers clear from them, but I think I will be for the time being. I gave a sliver of my heart to Gregory—the tiniest amount—and I still couldn't love him. Maybe I could have if I opened up and let him really see me, but I didn't want to. It's how I've always been—shielded, guarded with my heart. I'm not sure how to fully give myself to someone, and since I'm twenty-four years old, I don't think it will ever happen.

Plus, love doesn't exist for me. I'm not a warm person. I don't like when people touch me, and most people steer clear of girls like me. I'm cold, unattached, and indifferent to most things.

Like I've said before, I'm going to be the fun, single aunt and that's fine by me.

As I sample some of the side dishes—hashbrowns, bacon, the works—my phone rings, and being the idiot that I am, I pick it up assuming it's Dom.

It's not.

Bree's face shines at me from across my screen before I see her face drop.

"Teags, where the hell are you? That doesn't look like your house in Arizona."

Shit. "Uhh," is all I can say. My brain has frozen and I can't think of a lie to tell her. I also hate lying to my best friend, and I know she's probably worried sick, so before she calls Vince and Nico to track me down, I tell her the truth. "I'm in Oklahoma."

"The musical, right? You're in a production of the musical *Oklahoma* because there's no way you're in the state of Oklahoma when you live in Arizona." I see panic lace her features. "Vince, can you come here, please?"

"Bree, I'm fine, I swear."

Her face pinches at me, her fingers twisting the bracelet that always rests on her wrist. "That is exactly what someone would make you say!"

Vince comes into the phone and stares at me, a blank look on his face. "Where the hell are you? Tristan freaked out and called me when you turned your location off."

Vince has gone full bodyguard mode and I expected nothing less from him. Even though he's not Bree's bodyguard anymore—he traded that title for boyfriend—he still can't turn it off after all these years. He and his best friend Nico have their own business together, and while Vince handles the protection side of things, Nico does more of the security side, amongst other things.

"Please don't tell me you and Nico tracked me," I roll my eyes.

He shakes his head. "No, well, at least I didn't. Tristan calmed down, but he's still worried sick about you."

I sigh heavily, knowing that's probably the case. "He needs to learn to give me some fucking space to breathe."

"I know, Teags, but can you blame him?" Bree says. "Just promise me you're okay."

"I'm okay, Bree. I..." I trail off, unsure of wanting to say the next words out of my mouth. "I'm on a road trip with Dom."

Both of their eyes bulge out at me, surprise lacing their features.

"Dom? As in Dominic Graves?" Bree smiles at me and I can already tell what she's thinking. She knows about my stupid crush on Dom and I guarantee Vince knows about it too.

"Tristan's friend? The son of the jewelers?"

"That's the one," I say, my voice shooting up a few octaves as I take another bite of my pancakes.

"Teags, what the hell are you doing?" Vince asks me.

My best friend's mouth is fully open as she stares at me through the screen. "How the hell did you manage to be with Dom on a road trip?"

And then for the next hour, I explain my entire situation with Gregory, the last-minute flight I took back to Pennsylvania, and how I ended up on his doorstep. Both of their faces are full of shock, confusion, and giddiness—at least from Bree.

"Oh my God, this is the craziest thing you've ever done." She smiles at me.

"You're telling me, girl. I've never made so many rash decisions back to back in my entire life. I feel like I'm going crazy," I tell her.

She looks over at Vince before she speaks. "Baby, can you give us a minute?"

"Sure, angel." He presses a kiss to her forehead before he leaves the frame. "Don't do anything too stupid, Teags."

"No promises, Vincey," I joke back with him.

After a few short beats of silence, she speaks again. "Are you sure you're okay?"

I want to lie so bad. It would be so easy to tell her I'm fine. To say that for the first time in a while, I feel confident in the path I'm headed on, but I can't lie to her. Bree is the only person on the planet who truly sees me for who I am. She's not only my best friend, but she's the sister I never had, and lying to her would make my bones ache.

"I'm not, Bree."

"Do you want to talk about it?"

I don't really want to dive into every one of my insecurities, but I start with an easy one. "I made a mistake moving to Arizona."

She sighs at me, her eyes full of sincerity as she looks at me through my phone. "It's okay."

I shake my head. "No, it's not. I ran. I ran from it all just like Tristan did and he tried to warn me about it, but I didn't listen. I fucked up."

"You wouldn't be a human without fucking up every once in a while."

"I know, but I still fucked up. I can't get the year back that I wasted in Arizona with Gregory, and lately I've been feeling..."

She must sense my hesitation because she coaxes me a bit. "Feeling what?"

"Empty," is all I can say. "I feel like a skeleton walking around in a body."

She sniffles and I see a tear fall down her face. "I know the feeling, and I'm sorry I can't help more from here."

"Don't apologize, your presence is helpful enough. I'll be home in a few weeks anyway."

"Thank fucking God. I miss you, you freak."

I laugh, smiling to myself that I have a person on this planet who misses me when I'm not near. How rich am I to have found someone as wonderful as Bree Hart? "I miss you too. I'm sorry for scaring you, but I will keep you updated on the road. It actually feels good knowing you know about all this. I've been going crazy trying to keep this a secret."

"I bet, especially since you're in such close proximity with a certain someone." She pumps her eyebrows at me a few times and I almost gag.

"It's just a crush and it's not important. We're travel companions, for now." I didn't tell her about the pact we have while we're on the road. I'm taking this one thing at a time, and the last thing I need is for Tristan to find out about any of this—especially that. "And by the way, please don't—"

"My lips are sealed and so are Vince's. Although, he might have told Nico already."

I roll my eyes. *Of course he did.* Those two are as attached at the hip as Bree and I are—though Vince would never admit it. "I'll handle Nico."

"Sounds good to me, babe. Now, I'd love to chat all day, but I have a video to film."

"Ugh, thank fuck. I've been rewatching all your videos when my eyes get tired of reading. I need some new content to binge while I'm in the car."

"You'll enjoy my next video." She smiles at me. "I'm ranking under-rated dark romance novels I've read."

"I could cry right now," I say as I put my hands to my chest.

"We'll talk soon, okay? And if you get lonely, I'm always available for you."

"I know, Bree. I know," I say a bit quieter. "See you soon."

"I love you to the moon, Teags."

I smile at my best friend through the phone. "And back, Bree."

Chapter Sixteen

— I NEVER EXISTED BY CHASE ATLANTIC

Dom: This meeting is never ending.

Teags: Aren't these meetings important? Shouldn't you be paying attention?

Dom: Yes, but I can't stop thinking about what you taste like.

Teags: Really?

Dom: Did I sound like I was joking?

Dom: Are you going to be ready for me when I get back to the hotel?

Teags: Do you want me to be?

Dom: Yes.

> **Dom: And wear those panties you put in my mouth when I took you shopping. I wanna shove them in yours later when I'm making you scream.**

> **Teags: As long as you rip them off with your teeth, then we have a deal.**

> **Dom: Fuck, baby, you're killing me.**

> **Teags: Touché, asshole.**

AFTER I STOP AT the store to buy some condoms, I practically rush up to the hotel room where I know Teags is waiting for me.

Part of me should feel like a horrible piece of shit for being this excited to fuck Teagen West of all people. I'm sure I'll pay for this later, but it's only while we're on the road.

I finally open the door to the room, and when I get inside, I see her.

She's laying in bed reading, but her eyes meet mine instantly. And I don't dare move because the room got a thousand degrees hotter and I swear if I move, I might get struck by lightning.

She still has time to back out of this. She can say one word and I'll head to the bathroom, shower today off, and go to sleep.

But all she does is whisper.

"Are you going to come over here or what?"

"Take your pants off and come to the edge of the bed." I know she likes it rougher than most, and I know she loves when I boss her around—no matter how much attitude she gives me. If anything, her throwing it back to me gets my dick hard.

She complies, and as she shuffles to the edge of the bed, I start to take my cufflinks off, along with the tie off that's cutting my air off. My shirt is off in seconds, and I watch her look at all the tattoos on my chest and arms, her eyes widening ever so slightly.

She gets to the end of her bed, sits on her heels, and folds her hands in front of her.

I slowly step over to her, press a kiss to her forehead before I run both of my hands down her arms.

"Good job, baby."

"Dom, please," is all she can say. "I've been waiting all fucking day."

I bring my lips to her neck, softly biting and sucking because I'm going to take my fucking time with her. "Patience, I'm getting you ready for me."

"I'm soaked already," she tells me.

"Oh, really? I think that took me less time than the other night." I smirk against her lips. "Lie back."

And she complies like the good girl she is.

"I know you like it rough, but what else do you like?" When it comes to sex, I'm a giver. Making other people moan and feel pleasure is my favorite fucking thing on the planet, and it turns me on knowing I'm about to hear her scream into my mouth while I fuck her.

When I look down at her and she can't meet my eyes, I stop what I'm doing.

"Teags? Did you hear me?"

She nods.

"Let me hear that voice. Don't get all shy on me now." I lean down and nip at her ear. "I love hearing you talk back to me."

"I do like it rough, but other than that, I don't really know. Gregory never wanted to experiment or try anything other than a few basic positions."

God, he sounds like one boring motherfucker. Or maybe he was jealous his girlfriend was cooler, funnier, and hotter than him. I totally get it, some guys can't handle that.

I'm not some guy though.

I want her to understand it's okay asking for the things she likes, especially in the bedroom. And maybe after all this is done with me, she'll have a little more confidence with sex after her ex tried to make her feel stupid for wanting to try different things.

I know a lot of things aren't for everyone, but I've always said I'll try anything once. How else will I know if I like it or not? He must not have done that, and part of me wants to punch him in the face for making her feel bad about asking to try new things.

"Well, maybe we can try some things so you'll know what you like in the future. Since this is an on the road thing, I'm your partner in this. I'm not going to make this weird. Sex is supposed to be fun for both people, and I'll never judge you for asking to try something with me."

She smiles softly underneath me, and before she can give me an answer, I rip her shirt off of her body. The tiny tank top she always wears to bed is shredded on the floor, and as I look down at her only in the red fucking thong she shoved into my mouth weeks ago, I swear I could start drooling.

"Is that okay with you?" I ask, needing her to say the words.

"Yes, it's okay with me."

"Good." I smirk as I take her in beneath me. "Now, do you want to start this by making love, having sex, or fucking?"

"Well, what's the difference?" she asks, a hint of something in her tone.

"Making love means I'll whisper sweet nothings into your ear as you take me slowly and sensually."

Her breathing starts to pick up and it's taking everything in me not to skip this conversation and bury myself inside of her immediately.

"I'm not sure I'm a making love kind of girl," she reiterates, her tone breezy, but her pebbled nipples are telling me all I need to know. God, she looks so beautiful underneath me, and as I take her in, I can feel my cock pressing against my pants. "What's next?"

"If we have sex, it's no strings attached, and I fuck you like I'm never going to see you again." Just like I did to all the girls in college, but that I'm not going to say out loud.

"Well, that doesn't work either," she reminds me.

"Of course it doesn't," I say. "There will always be strings with us." Not only is her brother one of my best friends, that's one string, but there's a second one that has tangled itself around us while we've been on this trip.

I'm so close to her. I'm so fucking close I could capture her mouth in mine. It's taking every last shred of control not to snap and take her before we can even finish this conversation. There's something so captivating about her, and it continues to draw me in until I'm going to get bitten or something worse.

The next words she says come out in a low, tight whisper, only for me to hear. I can tell she's as turned on as I am, and the thought makes a smile bloom across my face. She needs me as bad as I need her, and once this thread between us snaps, it's going to feel so fucking good giving in.

"What's the last option?"

My hand goes around her neck, and her head rises for me to have the best access I can as I give it a soft squeeze. Her pupils have exploded. I can barely see her brown eyes underneath, and she's looking at me as if I hold the key to the universe in the palm of my hands. She's a fucking sight to behold, and as I look at her, I feel like I've just discovered the eighth wonder of the world.

"If we fuck, then I'll give you everything you need. I'll make you scream my name until your throat gives out, until the people in the rooms next to us know who I am. When I fuck you, I'll treat you like the slut I know you are, like the girl you try to hide from everyone else."

"Dom," she breathes out, my hand loosening around her neck as her breathing speeds up, her pulse following suit. "Don't make promises you can't keep. You might not be able to handle all the things I want to try."

"Oh, baby, trust me. I'll handle you all night long with my hands, tongue, fingers, and cock. Any way that you beg for it, you'll get, and I'll erase every bad orgasm your past boys have given you and replace it with ones that make your toes curl when you fantasize about it tomorrow."

"Dom." She squirms underneath me.

"Just say the word and I'll get on my knees and worship you all night long," I say as I press a kiss to her neck, then up her jaw, then behind her ear before she whispers three beautiful words.

"Fuck me, Dom."

"You want me to fuck you, baby?" I ask again, the build-up to sex often being my favorite part. I'm going to savor every fucking moment of this.

"Dom—"

"The appropriate response is yes, sir."

Her pulse picks up underneath my hand, and I can't help but smile.

"Say it. Tell me you understand what we're about to do."

"Yes, sir, I understand."

My cock jerks against my pants, and I've never heard those words sound so fucking sweet until now.

"Good," I say as I kneel in front of her and spread her legs. "Pull your panties to the side for me."

And before she can even say anything, my mouth is on her sweet cunt, and I get a taste of what I had the other night. Her arousal is already dripping all over my face, and as she moans and groans, her nails digging into her thighs from where she holds her thong, I keep going.

"Dom, oh my—" She doesn't get to finish speaking because I throw her legs around my shoulders, slide her panties off with my teeth, and shove them into her mouth.

"Be quiet for me," I say as I undo my belt, slide my pants off and throw a condom on my aching cock. I know I promised her we'd try some new stuff, but I already feel out of control, even though I only had a small taste.

I need to be inside of her or I might go crazy.

I flip her around, a small yelp coming from her stuffed mouth as her beautiful ass rests against my body. She is a fucking sight in front of me, and as she looks behind at me, her eyes hooded, her pussy dripping for me, I wrap her hair around my fist.

"Is this how you want to be fucked, Teags? You want me to throw you around and tell you what to do?"

She nods, her eyes not moving from mine, her red thong still stuffed in her mouth.

"You're being such a good girl for me," I say as I run my hand up and down her back, teasing her center with my cock. "Are you ready?"

She nods again, her breathing getting faster as I slide into her. I bet she's going crazy not talking back to me, but tonight is me seeing if she likes being submissive. This is our first day of trying new things, and in my opinion, it's going rather well.

As soon as I start sliding in and out of her, she gets down on her forearms even further, my dick hitting a deeper spot than it was before. I alternate my pace, going between fast and slow just to drive her fucking crazy before I grab her hair in my fist again.

I pull her hair so her head comes back toward me, still fucking her as I bring her ear up to my mouth.

"Your pussy is taking my cock so well," I say as I turn us toward the mirror in the room. "Look at what happens when you listen to me. Look at how fucking perfect you look when you take it."

Muffled groans are all I hear as we watch each other in the mirror, my eyes not straying from the look on her face as I grip her hair tighter in my hand. The only other sounds heard throughout the room are the ones we're making.

"Can you get back down on the bed for me?" I ask as she nods, and I throw her onto the pillows, her thong falling out of her mouth.

"Dom," she says as I stop what I'm doing.

"Are you okay?"

"Yes, sir, I am." My cock jerks inside of her and she tilts her head at me.

"Can you fucking blame me?"

Another eye roll before she opens her mouth. "Can you, um..." she trails off as she starts to get shy on me again.

"If you want something from me, just ask," I tell her, my hand cupping her jaw. "This is an open, safe place to discuss things we want to try. So, go ahead."

"I want you to tie my hands up with my thong."

My eyes widen as I realize what she's asking. "Really?"

"Yes, sir."

"Then put your head back on the pillows and give me your hands, baby," I say as she complies and I slide back into her, a moan coming from the both of us.

I reach over and grab her hands in mine, the thong twisting around her wrists as I tighten it as much as I can so she can't move them.

"Is that okay?"

"It's perfect," she says, already out of breath and I've barely moved. She likes this. There's not a doubt in my mind that Teags likes to be tied up. Her pussy is clenching around my dick, and just by the way she's shoving into my hips is telling me she wants me to move.

And what she wants, she gets—at least while we're on the road.

So, I slam into her, not giving a single fuck about the noise of the bed shaking, or how much of a mess we're making because she has officially discovered something she likes with me, and even though she was shy about it at first, she voiced it.

I love being able to pull pleasure out of her, and I was worried this entire pact on the road would feel a bit too transactional for my liking, but it hasn't. In a way, it almost feels natural between us, and I think it's because of how similar we are.

And the fact that we know this is a means to an end. We're just having fun on this trip, nothing more and nothing less.

"Dom, please," she moans into the pillows. "More."

"Shut up and take it," I say as I pick up my pace.

Her hands are clawing at the thong, and she's practically begging to touch me, but my greedy little thing isn't allowed to. My cock is slamming into her, yet she's still begging for more.

"Good girls come first, Teags," I tell her as she clenches around me again. "Be good for me and coat my fucking cock."

"Don't stop," she begs.

"I'd never dream of it," I say as I grip her hair in my fist again, pulling a little harder. She screams as I feel her start to come, my release not far from hers. She's moaning and groaning and clenching around me so fucking hard that I keep thrusting, chasing my own release inside of her for the first time in who knows how long.

Fuck, I forgot how good this felt. I forgot how good making someone else scream felt for me.

"Let me fill you up, baby," I say as I start to come. "Fuck, Teags."

I have to reach out and put one of my hands against the headboard because of how strong my orgasm is. My entire body feels shaky as I come down and pull my dick out of her.

I press a kiss to her back before I untie the thong so she can get more comfortable on the bed. She moves around as I get up and discard the condom in the trash.

I slump against the bed as I slide my underwear back on. I'm too fucking out of breath for my liking. What the fuck is happening to me? I'm in great shape since all I've done is work out since I stopped using other outlets for my stress, but how is sex one time with her like this? I can barely feel my fucking legs and I'm sweating and panting like a goddamn dog.

"Are you okay?" she asks as she slides up to where I'm sitting on the edge of the bed, her body languid and her voice dreamy as she copies my positioning.

"I'm okay," I tell her. "How about you? Did you like what we did?"

I feel like a goddamn idiot for asking, but I'm curious to see if she learned anything new about herself today.

"I did." She smiles to herself as her cheeks turn red. "I enjoyed being tied up more than I thought I would."

"Really?" I shove her with my elbow.

"Mhm." She pushes me back. "I knew I liked reading about it but it was a thousand times better than I thought it would be."

"Good to know." I throw her a wink as I pinch one of her nipples. "Now go shower and I'll join you after I order dinner for us."

"Dom, it's—"

My hand goes to her throat immediately as I cut off what she was saying. "Those aren't the right words."

Her eyes lock on my arm that squeezes her neck a tiny bit more before she whispers what I want to hear.

"Yes, sir."

I press a kiss to her cheek before whispering in her ear. "Good girl."

"Fuck," she whispers as she throws her head back as soon as I reach for the phone

"For someone who rolls her eyes and tries to act all scary, you're surprisingly good at submitting to me."

"What can I say"—she swings open the bathroom door—"I'm a wonderful listener when I want to be."

As I hear the shower turn on, the only thoughts I have are about the girl in the other room, and I can't help but think this was a terrible fucking idea. Those thoughts quickly leave my mind as I open the door to the shower and see her smile back at me.

It's just sex, I remind myself.

That's all it will ever be.

Chapter Seventeen

— WHAT YOU NEED BY THE WEEKND

"Teags," I hear him whisper as I start to wake up.

I mumble something incoherent I'm sure, and as I open my eyes, all I see is darkness. Am I having a nightmare or something? I swear I just opened my eyes.

"Is it still dark out?" I say as I feel something press against my lips, a soft cloth over my eyes. "What time is it?"

"I blindfolded you with my tie," he whispers against my lips. "You were moaning and groaning all over me this morning."

"I was?" I say as my breaths get a bit shorter.

I feel him start to pull the blanket off of me. "You were. And now we both have a problem."

"And what's that?"

"Well, my cock is aching because of all those noises you were making, and the hotel is probably going to charge me because of how much of a mess we're going to make of these sheets again." He starts to kiss up and down my body, and everything feels heightened because I can't fucking see him.

"Is that going to be expensive?" I ask, my body heating with every small movement he makes on top of me. It's impossible for me to remain calm anytime Dom is near me—especially when it's like this. He and I are being vulnerable with one another despite our no strings attached agreement, and I like seeing him like this way too much. Well, even though I can't see him at the moment.

We fucked for the first time yesterday after his meeting. And then we showered together and he sat me down on the small bench in there and fingered me until I coated his fingers. Then we had dinner, watched a movie, and I think I fell asleep on top of him.

But I guess he didn't bother moving me back to my bed if I was practically on top of him this morning.

I'd dive more into what that means, but I don't have time before he's slipping my shorts off of my body, and I hear foil ripping as my breathing gets heavier. He lifts my legs onto his shoulders as he slides into me, the two of us moaning as he finally gets inside of me.

"Shit, you feel so fucking good."

"Dom, I'm a little sore," I tell him as I try to even out my breathing.

"Fuck, baby, I'm sorry," he drags his hand through my hair. "I'll be gentle. I promise."

I feel a smirk turn up my lips. "Well, not too gentle."

"That's my girl," he says as he picks up his pace, lifting my hips up so he can hit deeper, and fuck, being blindfolded is really making me miss seeing what's going on. But I'll say, all of my other senses are heightened, and he feels so fucking good as he slides in and out of me.

"Choke me," I say as he stops, probably surprised by what I said. "Please."

"Since you asked so nicely." His hand comes around my throat, squeezing the perfect amount as he continues to fuck me as rough as he did last night.

I love that he doesn't see me as something breakable. I love how he knows I can handle the things I'm asking for. Gregory never even wanted to try, and the fact that Dom is a willing partner on this road trip makes it so much better.

I don't feel like a fool asking for what I want during sex. I feel powerful and more confident than I ever thought I could be in the bedroom. I know it's only been like two days, but I can already feel the changes in myself.

"God, look how soaked you are for me," he says as he rolls his hips against me. "Were you dreaming of me while you were moaning and groaning all over me this morning?"

"Yes," I whisper, even though I don't really remember. As soon as I woke up, I forgot what I had been dreaming about.

"Take that blindfold off," he says to me. "I want you to see what we look like."

I comply, and seeing him go in and out of me is a sight I'm never going to forget.

"Dom?" I ask as he loosens his hold on my neck, my eyes tracing the tattoos that cover his body. "Can I get on top?"

He only smirks as he flips me around, his back hitting the pillows as I sit on top of his thighs, looking down at him as he lays beneath me.

"I'm yours to do with as you please," he tells me, his arms coming to my ass as he squeezes it.

I only roll my eyes as I grab his cock and line it up to my center as I slowly slide onto it, his eyes rolling to the back of his head as I fully sit.

"You feel good, baby," I say to him as I start to move, only for a phone call to interrupt what we were doing. "That's not mine."

"Fuck," he says as he reaches for his phone, and as I start to get off of him so he can take it, he sets my hips back down. "Don't stop, Teags."

"What?"

And then he answers the fucking phone. "Ethan, you better not have crashed my fucking car."

I widen my eyes at him before I start to fuck with him, trying to make it so he's struggling to talk. I roll my hips as I slowly bounce on top of him, his face pinching as he tries to concentrate on what Ethan is saying on the other line.

"What do you want?" he asks him. "I'm a little busy at the moment."

"That's the understatement of the century," I say as Dom smacks my ass and I pick my pace up, grabbing the headboard as I steady myself and watch his face pinch with how turned on he is.

"Oh, nothing," Dom says. "And your truck is fine. You didn't have to call just to check in, dude."

"I want both of your hands on me, Dom," I whisper as I lean closer to him. "Please touch me."

"Yes everything is fine, Ethan. I really have to get going." The last few words are incoherent, Dom throwing his phone to the side before he takes over. He starts to match my pace, both of his hands running all over my body as the two of us quickly fall into our own lust. We're chasing our orgasms and as soon as mine hits, I let it melt all over me as he takes over and fucks me until his eventually comes.

By the time I climb off of him and lay next to him, the two of us are panting, and I'm smiling so hard I can barely feel my face.

"This was the best idea I've ever had."

"Wow, don't brag too much," he jokes with me.

"Oh, come on," I say as I turn to face him. "Just admit I'm right."

He sighs heavily before he takes the condom off of his still semi-hard cock. "You were right, this was a wonderful idea," he says as he leans into my boobs, grabbing one of my nipples in his teeth. "And you are already getting better at asking for what you want."

"Was that a compliment?"

"Yes it was," he says, pinching my other nipple in his fingers. "God, I'd love to paint these beautiful tits of yours, Teags."

"In your dreams," I tell him as I get up and head for another shower. "Now, let me return the favor for yesterday in the shower."

And as he rushes out of bed and towards me, he grabs my legs and hoists me up, carrying me to the shower as a laugh bubbles out of me before I can stop it.

This might have been a terrible idea, but at least I'm getting some good sex out of it. And I'm having fun for the first time in a long time. That in and of itself is a fucking miracle.

This trip was exactly what I needed, it's just an added bonus I get to have sex and experiment with the guy I'm not supposed to be doing this with.

— SILVER SPOON BY ERIN LECOUNT

WE'RE PACKING UP THE truck, and for some reason, I either need to throw up or I need to smoke some more of the weed Dom brought with him.

We have officially hit the point in our road trip where we're on our way to Arizona. Arizona, as in the place I ran from mere weeks ago with nothing but a small suitcase and a bookbag. Not only did I run from the longest romantic relationship I had, I also ran from a fucking proposal.

Gregory hasn't stopped blowing my phone up since this adventure started—if I can even call it that. It's certainly felt like one so far, but I've officially silenced my notifications from him because I can't handle being yelled at about how terrible of a person I am.

I already know how terrible of a person, sister, and friend I am, and I don't need him reminding me about it every fifteen fucking minutes.

"Teags?" Dom's hand comes to my arm. "Are you okay?"

Somehow that simple touch from him has calmed some of my nerves, but I still feel on edge for some reason. Maybe it's the fact that I'm fucking one of my brother's best friends, or maybe it's the impending doom that's going to come when I have to face my ex again, or maybe it's the grief from my brother's death creeping up on me.

More than likely, it's all of it. I don't want to go back to this place that never felt like home. I was a prisoner of my own devices in Arizona. I chose to move there with him, so it's my own fault. I fucking ran from the place where Tobias's memory lingers because I didn't think I could handle all the emotions I was feeling.

I still can't. I don't feel things well. I run from my emotions and pretend like they don't exist until I'm listening to a song in the shower and the dam breaks. I either feel nothing or I feel everything. I much prefer feeling nothing. It hurts a lot less.

"Teags?" Dom grabs my face in his hands and looks at me. He *really* looks at me. I wonder if he can see the struggle going on in my head or if I still hide things well.

"I'm okay. Sorry, I'm not looking forward to this part of the trip," I tell him as he shuts the tailgate.

"I'll be with you the entire time, baby." There's that goddamn nickname again. Does he mean that or is this another thing we're doing on the road? "Are you scared of him?"

The question confuses me. "Scared of him?"

"Has he put his hands on you?"

Oh. "No. He isn't that kind of guy. He much prefers using his words to cut deep. He is a lawyer, after all."

Dom's eyes narrow at me. "Still seems like a piece of shit," he says as he rounds the truck to open my door for me. And five minutes later, we're on the road and listening to my most recent audiobook.

I roll my window down, suddenly needing some air because as we get closer to Arizona, my heart beats faster and I'm worried about how Gregory is going to react. He's not a fighter by any means, but he still scares me. His messages have been incessant since I left, and I'm really not looking forward to facing him again.

I understand I ran from his proposal, but we never would have made one another happy. If anything, I did us both a favor. I'm hoping once I grab all my shit, he'll leave me alone, but I could be hoping for something that will never happen.

I'm also worried about the letter. If he did something to it, I might kill him, and then Dom and I would really be bonded for life. That letter is the last piece of him I'll ever have, and I'm still kicking myself for leaving it behind.

An hour into the drive, I turn my audiobook off. I was barely listening to it because I can't stop thinking about how fucked my life has become in a matter of weeks.

"I know you hate talking about feelings and shit, but this car has been too tense for the past hour. Did I not make you come enough this morning?"

Leave it to Dom to break the ice by talking about sex.

"No amount of orgasms can help my anxiety right now."

"Then let's talk about it. What are you afraid of?"

Are we really going to do this? "It's fine. We don't have to talk about this."

"What else are we going to do now that you turned the book off? I'm pretty sure some smut was coming up, and I won't mention how rude that was of you to edge me like that. My dick has been hard for half an hour."

I can't stop the laugh from coming out. "My condolences," I joke. "Just because we're fucking while we're on the road, that doesn't mean we have to do feelings too. I know you're not that kind of guy, and I'm not that kind of girl, so it's fine. I'll be fine."

I've become way too good at gaslighting myself.

"I can be whatever kind of guy you need me to be. If you need me to listen, I can do that. I'm not a complete psychopath, you know. I do have feelings, believe it or not, and you've helped calm some of those down on this trip. Let me return the favor."

"You seem to be quite good at that." His brows pull together. "Returning the favor."

That only causes a smirk to form on his lips.

After a few beats of silence, the words seem to pour out of me. "Did you know Tobias left us all letters before he..." I trail off, not wanting to say it.

"Tristan told me about it, yeah."

"When I fled Arizona, I forgot mine, and I'm worried Gregory did something to it."

"Like what?"

"Ripped it to shreds, threw it out, recycled it, burned it, take your pick. It's really the only thing I'm coming back for. I don't need my clothes, or my shoes. I'm only going back for the letter, my books, and my records."

None of the clothes I wore to work ever felt like mine. It almost feels like I was playing dress up the entire time I was down here. I wasn't myself, and I don't know how it took me this long to realize it.

When I look back on the girl that made the decision to move to Arizona, all I see is someone weighed down by grief. All I remember is feeling so goddamn much that I needed to escape it or it might have drowned me.

Well, I escaped, and it turns out grief is something you can't outrun. It hangs at your side, over your head, and it lingers in the air around you until you acknowledge it. Even then, it doesn't just go away. It sits on your chest and punches you in the gut every time you hear, see, or think about something involving your dead brother.

"It wasn't home," Dom whispers. "At least not to you."

"No, it wasn't."

"Having a home is underrated. I've never had one and I'd be stupid to think I could find one or break the cycle in the future."

"What does that mean?" Based on the past few weeks, I can tell he's strained from his parents. For one, he never talks about his family, and every time his parents called him since we got on the road, he's always tense after. I recognize his disdain for his parents because it's how Liv and Bree felt about theirs too. Bree always told me she felt like she was walking on eggshells around them, and Liv was ignored her entire life.

"My parents are pieces of shit. And despite the fact that I'm doing all of this for their company, I know they couldn't care less about me."

"That's hopeful, Dom."

"It's hard to have hope when your parents only see you as a body to mold to take over the company when they can no longer run things."

I turn in my seat to face him more. "What do you mean?"

"Nothing." His hand tenses around the steering wheel.

"You're not just a body. I mean, you have a great one." He laughs. "But that's not all you are."

"I don't need your pity compliments."

"It's not pity. It's the truth. Yeah, you're an asshole sometimes, but it's a front. Because underneath the jokes and the other shit, you're smart, kind, and you let your best friend's sister tag along on your cross-country trip when you could have taken me home. You let me stay at your house while I sorted my shit out, and you're a decent human being who cares about his friends."

His hand loosens around the wheel. "You think so?"

"I know so, Dom."

"Well, if we're going to do this, then you're not so tough either."

"Oh, really?" I jest. He may think he knows me, but he doesn't.

"Yeah, Teags. That exterior you put up to keep people out, to scare people away? It doesn't work. You've got a secret soft side and no matter how much shit you give to other people, I've seen it. You can't hide from me—at least not well. I see your red eyes. I see how things get to you. You don't have to hide your feelings because those are what make you a human. You've had a rough few years—which is downplaying it—and you're allowed to break apart and not know how to fit yourself back together."

I take a deep breath as his words sink in. He's right, of course. I push people away. I don't make friends easily because most people think I'm scary or too rough around the edges. I have Bree, but she's always been different. She has always been the exception, Liv too. I have no friends from college because I never got too close to anyone. It was always easier for me to hang out on the outside of things and never show anyone who I am beneath the surface.

"I know I can do all that. It doesn't mean I like it."

He only laughs. "Nobody likes crying, screaming, or being angry at the world. It's just something we all have to deal with when shit hits the fan." He turns to look at me. "But don't forget that you have people to talk to."

"Does that include you?" The question slips out before I can stop it.

"I guess it does." He smirks. "At least while we're on the road, right?"

Right because after this is over, we're going to pretend nothing happened. Our mutually beneficial agreement will come to a close and Tristan will never find out about any of it.

"Right," I agree as I play with the ends of my hair, a weird pit forming in my stomach. "What did you mean earlier by you being just a body to your parents?"

He cracks his neck before he speaks. "They were never around when I was young. I have two siblings and all three of us were raised by nannies for our entire childhoods. They weren't really parents, more like distant relatives who we saw once a month when they came home from the office. They never celebrated holidays with us. Every year on my birthday,

I get a card with no signatures on it which I'm sure one of their assistants went out to get because I can guarantee they will never remember our birthdays."

God, that sounds horrible. First the Hart sisters' parents and now his. What the fuck is up with people having kids and being shitty parents to them after they chose to have them? It makes no fucking sense to me. Why bring a child into the world if you're not going to love it with everything you have?

It hits me how privileged I am to have grown up in the home I did. Not only did I have two amazing parents who loved me, but I also have three siblings whom I love more than most people on the planet. Tobias isn't around anymore, but I'll never take the love he had for me as his sister for granted.

"As far as I'm concerned, the only family I have is the one I found in college with your brother. I know he gives me shit most of the time because I can be an asshole, but I know if I needed him, he'd drop anything for me. The same with the rest of the guys."

"Well, you all dropped everything for him when Tobias died. He tells me all the time how you guys saved his life."

Dom shakes his head. "That was all him and probably Liv too. We shouldn't get all the credit."

"Don't sell yourself short." I reach over and grab his hand. "I know we're a means to an end, but you'll always have a seat at Tristan's table. He loves all you guys so much and I wish I had a relationship like you guys do—platonically, of course."

"You have Bree, though."

I nod. "Of course, but I didn't have the typical college experience where I was supposed to find my people like my brother said I would. All college brought me was a crippling fear that I'm a terrible person and a dead brother. After Tobias died, I stopped caring about a lot of things, and the friends I did make in college faded away because I was too busy drowning in grief to go out and party every night."

The truck gets silent and I feel him squeeze my hand. I forgot our hands were intertwined, and as I try to pull away, he moves our joined hands to the top of my thigh as he caresses small circles over my skin.

"Partying is overrated anyway," he whispers to try and make me feel better. I notice he parks the truck, and I didn't even realize he was stopping to get gas because I was too busy focusing on his hand on my thigh. "I'll be right back. Do you want a snack or something?"

"I'm okay," I say as my phone starts to ring. When I look down and Nico's face pops up on my screen, I laugh.

"That's not Gregory is it?"

"No, it's just Nico."

"Make it quick," is all Dom says as he slams the truck door.

I roll my eyes, brushing off the fact that he might be jealous, but I doubt it. Plus, it's Nico—we would *never* cross that line. Not only would Vince kill him, but that's not who we are to one another. We share some commonalities in our lives, and through that, we've become closer. He feels like another annoying big brother to me, and I love what our relationship has morphed into since I've known him for a few years.

"What's up?" I say as I answer. "I'm kind of busy."

"Busy traveling across the country with Graves? Yeah, I heard. Vince told me, and what I've been wondering is why you didn't seem to want to mention that."

"What I do in my free time isn't your problem."

"It is when your location is off. Teags, I know we've only been friends for a little while, but you should know how panicked I was until Vince told me what was going on. I thought you were—"

"I'm fine," I say in a softer voice. I'm mentally kicking myself because I didn't even *think* about Nico when I did that. All I wanted was space from my brother and his constant check-ins. But with Nico, it's different.

He probably thought I was in danger, and I hate that I made him so worried. "I needed some space from my brother. I'm sorry, I didn't mean to remind you of all that. I wasn't really thinking."

"A text would be nice next time. Don't make me break laws to find you ever again, okay?"

"I'm sorry," I say again. We have some similar trauma and have bonded over the fact that we've both lost siblings. Though, it's worse for him because his sister has never been confirmed dead—she's just gone. Vanished as if she were never on the earth in the first place. But not many people know that about him, and it's never been my story to tell. "Feel free to track me as you see fit, Nico."

"It's not just for *your* protection. I do it for Liv and Bree too. Everyone close to me. You know that."

I want to tell him again that it's not his fault, but he worries about getting close to people because of what happened to his sister. The two of us have been good for one another these past two years, and Nico has always been someone I reach out to when things get really dark. When I was in Arizona and didn't want to call and worry my siblings or Bree, Nico was always the person I dialed.

"So, how is this trip across the country? Are you feeling alive again or more suffocated from being in a car with Dom?"

"I hope you know I'm rolling my eyes at you, right now," I tell him.

"I can feel it from across the country. And you still don't scare me."

"Whatever. Is that all you needed?" I ask as Dom climbs back into the truck, an annoyed look on his face. "We're getting back on the road."

"Just wanted to check in. Don't do anything I wouldn't do."

"Okay, so what you're saying is that I can call a swat team to Gregory's house if he pisses me off? Can I get verbal permission that you would do that?"

And with my stupid question, he hangs up.

"You ready?" Dom asks me, a hint of annoyance in his voice.

I nod, and for the rest of the ride to the hotel, the only speaking that's done is from the audiobook I put back on because I can't stand the silence.

Chapter Eighteen

Dominic

Arizona

— SCUMBAG BY ROLE MODEL

Teags and I have not spoken since she got off the phone with Nico earlier. Her audiobook is the only noise that floats between us, and I try to loosen my grip around the steering wheel. *Try* being the keyword. I can't have the rest of this trip being as awkward as it is now.

It might just be a feeling I'm having, but something changed in this car after she hung up the phone with Nico.

Why do those two converse so much? Why did she seem happy when she noticed it was him calling? I guess I should feel better that she has someone that makes her look like that when the phone rings—Gregory made her face pinch and twist in disgust before she silenced his notifications.

Why does it piss me off so much that she smiled while talking to him? I could see her face in the side mirror while she talked to him. She looked... relieved, almost.

Why does that make my blood boil so much?

We're nothing but fuck buddies while we're on this trip. We're a temporary fix for one another while we each sort out our shit. Teags is packing her life up and moving home, and I'm starting my journey in the company I've been destined for my entire life. The two of us are a means to an end to one another.

I can't help the anger that bubbles up before I shove it down. What the hell is wrong with me? Before I let it fester for the remainder of the drive, I open my mouth to ask her about it, only she beats me to it.

"Why are you being so weird?" she asks me as she turns to face me while I drive.

"I'm not being weird," I deflect. "How was your chat with Nico?"

She scoffs at me. "Is that what all this brooding has been about?"

I shrug my shoulders at her. "I was just wondering what you two talked about. I remember you two being chatty at Tristan's wedding, but I didn't know you stayed in touch so much."

She takes her glasses off and pinches the bridge of her nose, and I swear I hear her mumble something under her breath.

"Forget it," I say, not wanting to piss her off even more.

"Nico and I are friends. He understands what I've been going through more than most can. We chat sometimes, that's all. He called to ask how the trip was going."

"So, Bree and Vince told him about what we're doing?"

"He's Nico. He doesn't need anyone to tell him anything." She smiles to herself. "But we're friends."

"It doesn't matter what you two are. If you're something, that's okay." I don't want her to think I was jealous or something because I wasn't. Just curious, is all.

"Friends, Dom. Men and women can be platonic, you know."

"Not in my experience," I say quietly.

"What?"

Oh, nothing. I've never had a woman want to be my friend before without wanting something from me so I have no idea how to be platonic with someone of the opposite gender.

"Nothing," I say as I pull into the hotel parking lot.

I park the truck, the heavy silence looming over both of our heads before she gets out and goes to grab our bags.

One night stands are all I've ever been used to because I knew my parents were going to meddle in that part of my life from a young age. It's how they got together—my parents. They were set up by my grandparents to keep the family business running.

Relationships in my family are nothing but a business transaction, and I guess I'm already following in their footsteps because isn't that what we are? They'd be so proud if they saw me. Maybe I'm more like my parents than I thought.

"Are you going to help me or what?"

"Sorry," I say as I get and head to the tailgate.

The two of us make it up to the room after getting all checked in, and all I want to do is eat something. It took us sixteen hours to get here from Oklahoma City, and I swear my body is exhausted after all this driving I've been doing. I don't think I'll need to go on a road trip ever again at this rate. I've done enough driving to last an entire lifetime.

"I'll order us some room service while you shower," I tell Teags.

"Okay," she tells me as she grabs her stuff and softly shuts the bathroom door. She's been weird ever since we got up here. It's like she's antsy, or something. I know we were in the car for a long time, so maybe her legs are restless and she needs to stretch them out.

I knock on the door.

"What?"

"You don't have to open the door, but if you want to take a long shower, I grabbed your phone so you can listen to music. It was a long drive, so stretch your legs, okay?"

The door creaks open ever so slightly and she looks up at me, her glasses discarded, and I can see her eyes already wet with tears. She says nothing as she reaches for her phone. When she looks down at it, her face falls. "You queued my playlist already?"

I nod.

"Thanks," she whispers before the door shuts in my face.

I don't know what else I expected, but as I lay down on my bed, my phone starts buzzing, and I pick it up without checking who it is. When three familiar faces fill the screen, I smile.

I missed these fuckers.

"Dom! Where the hell have you been? You haven't responded to a single one of my messages with a useless meme. I was starting to think you were stranded in the middle of the desert somewhere," Harry tells me.

"How are my fish, you dumbass?"

"Oh shit," Tristan says with a laugh.

"Tristan, start recording or something," Ethan says to me and my alarm bells are going off that something happened to my fish. "We're going to want to remember this for the future."

"Okay, so, don't kill me," Harry says as he runs a hand through his hair.

"If you flushed my fish, Harrison, I'm going to fly back to Pennsylvania for an hour just to kick your ass."

"Technically, *he* didn't do anything to your fish..." Tristan trails off, still laughing.

"That's true! *I* didn't do anything," Harry says. "But hypothetically speaking, one of your fish might have taken a bite out of another one."

My body jerks up. "What the fuck did you say?"

"Look, I was trying to clean the tank with the instructions you left me, and I must have skipped over the part where it said to not put them all in the same space," Harry tells me. "It took me dismantling the tank to notice that the three of them can't get into the other parts of the tank."

"What happened, Harrison?"

"I put Morty and Rick in the same bowl and Rick took a bite out of Morty."

Ethan and Tristan are laughing, mostly out of pity for Harrison because they know I'm going to kick his ass when I get back to Pennsylvania.

"Don't you know you're not supposed to put beta fish in the same tank? How's Summer?"

"Whole," Ethan jokes before I shoot him a glare. "Sorry."

"So, my fish is dead? You killed my fish?"

Harry only nods, and I gotta say, he looks super guilty. It's not really his fault. I've put them in the same space before while cleaning their tank, and nothing has happened. Maybe Morty just did something to piss Rick off.

"I'll get you another fish, I swear. I'll do whatever it takes—"

I cut off his anxious rambling. "Just don't kill any more of my pets, okay?" I feel way too exhausted to deal with this right now, and I'm sad about the fact that one of my fish died while I was gone. Today has been the weirdest day ever.

"You good, Dom?" Tristan asks me. "You look... different."

"Gee, thanks," I joke. "Just tired, I think. I'll be back to normal soon."

"Are your parents still hounding you while you're on the road?" Ethan asks, knowing there's more on the road than my parents and their expectations.

"Yes, as usual, but I'll be fine. Just have to get through it, you know?"

"That's not a life, Dom," Tristan tells me, the weight of the rest of his sentence lingering in the air. Everyone knows I'm going to be unhappy for the rest of my life. I had my fun in college and now it's time to buckle down and start the life I've been prepped for since I was a kid.

I hear the shower turn off, and my heart starts to race because even though Tristan won't be able to see her, I still worry about what could happen if he finds out about Teags coming on this trip with me.

He would murder me, for one. Then he would revive me just to make it hurt more than the first time.

"Look, can we talk about my future at a later date? I want to shower and get ready for bed. I have a huge meeting tomorrow."

The boys nod at me, and as I hang up the phone, Teags walks out of the bathroom, her hair wet, glasses back on, and wearing tiny fucking pajamas as usual.

My dick is rock hard in seconds.

"You didn't have to hang up just because I came out," she tells me as she sits on her bed.

"Your brother was on the phone," I say. "Him and the rest of the guys."

"Oh," is all she says. "What did he say? Does he look okay?"

I know lying to her family must be hard. I don't know how she hasn't gone crazy all this time we've been traveling. Not only did she come back home, but she told nobody that she did. She's like a ghost, and with a family as close as hers is, I know she's going crazy lying to all of them.

"He looked okay," I tell her. "My fish on the other hand..."

"What happened to your fish?"

"One of them killed the other one."

"Oh. I'm sorry. I know you cared for them," she says, her voice sincere.

"Thanks," I tell her, not wanting to move off of my bed. My limbs feel tired. Hell, every breath feels like it takes an insane amount of effort. I feel like I'm drowning in my own body, as if I'm walking around like a zombie in the fucking apocalypse.

I shouldn't be this exhausted at the age of twenty-seven. I shouldn't be waking up every day with the weight on my chest getting heavier and heavier. Shouldn't life be easier than this?

"Are you okay?" Teags asks as I open my eyes and see her on the edge of my bed. *When did she get over here?* Her hand reaches out and touches my leg, the contact making the weight disappear off of my body in an instant.

"I'm fine," I tell her.

"You sound like me when I'm lying." She smirks, a sad look in her eyes. "Can I be honest for a second?"

Hearing those words coming out of her mouth makes me sit up. "Of course you can."

She rubs her hands together before they trail up her body, her hands as restless as her legs were earlier. I guess that shower didn't help as much as I thought it would. I stop her movements by threading both of her hands in mine and placing them on my thighs.

"Teags," is all I say before she finally looks at me.

"I'm scared."

Teagen West is scared. I never thought I'd see the fucking day where she admitted that out loud.

"What if he did something to my letter? What if I'll never have that piece of my brother again because of the decision I made a few weeks ago?"

"Then I'll kill him so you don't go down for it. How does that sound?"

She unthreads her hand from mine just to smack me. "I'm serious, Dom!"

I tuck a piece of hair behind her ear. "I wasn't kidding. I know how much that would gut you, and the fucker doesn't deserve to breathe air ever again if he makes you feel like that." Hell, I'd bankrupt his family's law firm just for all the shit he's already done. I researched him one night when I couldn't sleep, and his family is worth a pretty penny on the West Coast. They're the biggest law firm in the Southwest, and Gregory works for the state of Arizona.

And yet, I could still drain the fuck out of them. I could do it for fun, and I wouldn't lose any sleep knowing his life would be ruined.

That's the one thing I do like about my last name—most people know not to fuck with my family. We're not just jewelers, even though most people know us as such. We invest in other businesses across the country and there's an entire separate division of the company that only focuses on that.

We've bankrupt competitors before. We've done shady shit, but that's why we're still on top. My family will do whatever they need to in order to keep the business afloat—legal or not.

"I don't think I'm going to be able to sleep tonight," she tells me. "I just want to get this over with. I want to move on from this shitty chapter of my life."

"And you will, baby," I tell her as I press a kiss to her hand.

"But what if—"

I know she's going to keep on rambling, so I grab her face with my hands and bring her lips to mine. She's surprised at first—mostly because I've never voluntarily kissed her before.

And now I know why.

Her lips are soft as they mold with mine, and as she straddles me, wanting to get more comfortable, I deepen the kiss because I need more. Never in my life have I needed to kiss someone this badly. Never in my life have I wanted to spend hours just kissing someone.

This is dangerous. Teagen West is *dangerous* to me.

Kissing was always a no go when I fucked girls back in college. And even if I did, I only did it to get to the other part of the night quicker. It was always a means to an end.

But with Teags? With *her*? God, I think I could spend hours losing myself in her mouth like I am now. I want to absorb every small moan she makes. I want to kiss her until we're both out of breath—until all we know is the way each other breathes. My dick is throbbing as I feel her on top of me.

I slip my tongue into her mouth, my hand now around her throat as I squeeze and a gasp comes out of her mouth. She tries to throw her head back, but I keep her tethered to my mouth, not wanting her to stray too far from me.

"Feel better?" I ask her in between kisses, my teeth grabbing her bottom lip in mine as I somehow pull away from her.

She's breathing heavily, so she doesn't answer me immediately.

Instead of hearing a verbal answer, I simply open the covers on the other side of my bed, grab her ass, and flip her around so she's on her back.

"Get comfy and order whatever you want. I'm going to shower and we're going to watch a movie."

I see her smile come back as I shut the bathroom door, and when I'm out twenty minutes later, I notice *American Psycho* queued up on the television.

"Really?"

Her eyes stray to the area my towel is currently covering before I snap and her eyes come back to mine. "What? This is one of my comfort movies."

"This is your idea of comfort?"

"Yes." She smirks before she opens the sheets on the other side of our bed. "Now, come join me before I eat all of your food."

So I do, and for the first time in my entire life, I sit in bed with a girl, eat good food, and she passes out halfway into the movie right over my lap. I put all of our plates on the cart room service brought and as I get comfortable in bed, I shuffle Teags around, careful as to not wake her up, and her body molds against mine as she sleeps.

As I run my hand through her hair, I realize how truly fucked I am. I've never had a serious relationship, but all of this shit Teags and I are doing on this trip? It feels like the closest I've ever been to one, and that terrifies the fuck out of me.

Chapter Nineteen

— TOO LATE BY CHASE ATLANTIC

Nico: Good luck today. Don't do anything stupid unless he does it first.

Teags: Are you talking about Dom or Gregory?

Nico: Whichever.

Nico: Just grab your shit and get out.

Teags: That's the plan, thanks. I'll call you if I need assistance.

Nico: I'm sure Dom would love that.

Teags: Can you fuck off?

Nico: Never.

> **Nico: But if you need a bomb or something for his house, I know a guy.**

> **Teags: Is the guy you?**

> **Nico: No. How stupid do you think I am?**

I STIFLE ANOTHER LAUGH that threatens to come out of my mouth. Nico might be annoying sometimes, but he always knows how to make me laugh.

"What's so funny over there?" Dom asks, his tone clipped.

"Nico's threatening to bomb Gregory's house."

I swear I see his lips curl up. "Oh. Well, that I would be okay with."

Of course he would.

"Turn left," I tell him, the area way too familiar for my liking. When I left, I knew I would have to come back, but being in this area again is making me feel itchy. I'm starting to be unsure of myself again. I know I made the right choice, but part of me can't help feeling like an asshole for how I went about it all.

But then again, Gregory is to blame. He's the one who got down on his stupid fucking knee and bombarded me in the middle of his entryway. I had just quit my job, and all I wanted to do when I got back was to make a plan of how I was going to get the fuck out of Arizona.

Well, I guess he made it easier for me. It was more a spur of the moment decision to hop on a plane and I wouldn't have done that if he hadn't proposed.

As Dom pulls onto Gregory's street, I swear my heart is going to beat out of my chest. I don't know why the fuck I'm so nervous. I'm just grabbing a few things I left that I care about. Most of the life I had here is staying behind because that wasn't really me living it. It was a different version of myself I slipped into and couldn't get out of.

I never want to go back to being the woman I was when I lived here, but I don't know if I can get back to who I was before. I don't know if it's possible because of how fucking sad and angry I feel all the time.

Why did I hold on as long as I did? Was I trying to hold onto my brother or the one semblance of control I had over my own life? I bet it was that. Ever since Tobias died, I've felt like I was spinning out of control. My entire world crashed and burned that day, and every day since, I needed something to ground me. Having a choice over my decisions and my life worked for a bit, but now I'm so unsure of everything I do.

I guess it was like everything else in my life—a placeholder.

"It's the white one."

Dom pulls up to it and parks the truck next to the curb, and I make no move to get out.

"He knows you're coming right?"

I nod.

"Do you want me to go in with you?" Dom offers.

"No, it's okay. I don't have much to grab."

He reaches across the center console and grabs my hand. "I can tell you're nervous, and it's okay. In a few hours, this will all be a distant memory."

I nod because he's right. I don't know why I can't breathe properly. Is the air thinner down here and I only just noticed?

Am I ready to close this chapter of my life? Yes, but there's a different part of me who has no idea what's coming next after this trip. I'm going to have to move back in with my mom until I figure something out because I'm sure after this arrangement with Dom is over, he's going to kick me to the curb.

But moving back into my childhood home sounds like the worst idea ever—especially since there will always be things missing from that house.

I take a big deep breath, trying to take in as much air as I open the door.

Before I get out fully, Dom's hand that's still in mine pulls me back before his lips meet mine in a quick kiss.

"If I hear one raised voice, I'm coming in, okay?"

I somehow nod through the shock I feel as I get out of the car. Did he know he just kissed me or was it subconscious of him to do that?

What the fuck has my life turned into?

I knock on my old front door and as Gregory swings it open, I have a feeling in my gut that today is going to end horribly. Vince always says to listen to your gut, and mine is swirling so bad I feel like I need to throw up.

"Well, come on in," he says, his tone laced with malice.

I walk into the house and I'm suddenly hit with a wave of nostalgia from the last time I was here. As long as Gregory doesn't get on his knee, I'll be fine, I think.

"All your stuff is where you left it, you know, when you fled after breaking my heart."

I'm sure his heart is broken. I'm sure whoever's panties are on the floor in the living room is keeping him in good company while his heart heals because those aren't mine.

"I just need a few minutes," I tell him and he waves me off.

I take that as my cue to head upstairs to my old room, and when I find Tobias' note in my side table, I can breathe a little better. I open it and read it again to make sure he didn't mark it or anything, and he didn't. Thank goodness because if he had done something to this, I would have killed him and not felt an ounce of remorse.

All I have left to grab is my record player, all my accompanying vinyls and cassette tapes, and some of my books. Thankfully, I mostly read on my Kindle down here, because lugging a bunch of books back and forth would be terrible. I don't work out enough for that.

I head into the other room where I stored all my stuff only to find the room empty. Gregory and I had two extra bedrooms in this house. One of them was his office and the place where he spent most of his day when he got home from work. The other was my sanctuary. It was where I went when I couldn't sleep or wanted some time for myself, and now, it's empty. What the fuck did he do with all of my stuff?

"Gregory?" I yell, my heart starting to race again. Where are all the vinyls Tobias bought me for every birthday? Where are the ones I stole from the basement that my Dad liked to listen to? Where the *fuck* are my books?

"What?" he asks as he strolls into the room.

I wave my hands around at the empty room. "Where's my stuff?"

"Well, you only seemed worried about the letter from Trevor, so I thought the rest was fair game." He smirks.

"His name was Tobias," I tell him as I step forward. Anger is coming off of my body in waves. "What the fuck did you do?"

"Do you know how much some of those vinyls and cassette tapes are worth? It was nice making a bit of money to spite you since you humiliated me when you left. My parents had to scramble to find someone to accompany me to all the events we had on the schedule."

Is he expecting me to feel bad for him? "Well, thank god for Mommy and Daddy. I'm sorry you had to deal with that, but I had actual problems going on."

"All you did was cry about your dead brother. Well, guess what Teags? Crying about him isn't going to bring him back."

Oh, so he did notice? He noticed all those nights when I would cry myself to sleep, my red and puffy eyes, every single night, he noticed. He just didn't give a fuck. I don't bother staying around to hear whatever else he has to say before I race down the stairs and see a box of my books by the door.

"I couldn't get any money for those, so you can have them," I swear I can hear him smiling behind me. "But your vinyls and tapes are long gone, Teagen. Sorry if you wanted those, but I wanted a wife, so I guess we both can't get what we want."

"How fucking dare you—" I don't have time to finish my sentence before I feel a presence by my side that takes ahold of my hand.

"What's going on here?"

I'm seething, but I feel better now that he's here. Gregory acts so high and mighty while we're alone, but whenever we were in public for events, he was the nicest guy ever.

"Who is this, your brother or something?"

He has literally met my entire family before. Tristan and him shook hands and he can't tell this isn't him. How the fuck is he so good at his job? Maybe since he's up everyone's asses everyday, his brain doesn't work outside of that.

"It doesn't matter who I am," Dom tells him before he looks at me. "What happened?"

"My vinyls and cassette tapes are gone. He sold them." Gregory only laughs before Dom can ask me anything else. "Is something funny?"

"Of course," he laughs. "Another knight in shining armor to save you from yourself, Teagen. Does he know how much of a bitch you are yet or do I need to make him realize?"

"Stop," I threaten. Dom is the least of his worries if he calls me a bitch again.

"Baby, it's okay," Dom tells me, a smirk on his face as he looks down at me. That goddamn nickname is making my stomach flip, and I don't know how much more of it I can handle. "He sold all of your stuff?"

I nod, unsure of what Dom is going to do.

"Baby? Seriously? I thought you hated pet names," Gregory tells him as he stands on the stairs.

"Maybe with you." Dom takes a step forward, still holding onto my hand. "You're Gregory Asher, right? Parents are Karen and Mark?"

Gregory narrows his eyes as Dom speaks. "Y-Yes. How do you know that?"

"It doesn't matter, but it will if you call her a bitch again. What did you do with her stuff or am I going to need to beat it out of you?"

"I call it how I see it, buddy. She's the one who ran out on me and our life here. I'd say that's a pretty bitch move, wouldn't you?"

Is he trying to get Dom to agree with him? "I'd say you were suffocating me here and that's why I left, but everyone is entitled to their own opinions."

"Good one," Dom says as he squeezes my hand. "Now, her stuff, Gregory."

"It's gone. I sold it all. Every vinyl, every cassette tape, and even that fancy record player."

A tear falls from my eyes as I think about all the music I'm never going to have because of what he did. All the vinyls my dad played when we were younger while we all danced around in the backyard are gone. All the vinyls Tobias and I went shopping for when we hung out and geeked out about music are gone. All my cassette tapes my Dad left me are gone too. Tobias bought me that record player just before he died.

Every shred of connectivity I had to my Dad and Tobias are gone—at least the physical versions. Of course I have all the music on streaming, but it's not the same. They never touched my phone to play the music. My phone can't remember as they placed the needle down, or put the vinyl on the track.

Another tear escapes and I wipe it away as my mind filters back into the conversation.

"Teags, do you remember everything you had here? All the names and shit?" Dom asks me and I nod.

I always have copies on my phone of the albums I have on vinyl and cassette, but most places don't make cassette tapes anymore. Those were more of a collectible, but it's the thought that counted. I had them because they tethered me to the people I lost, and even though I couldn't play the tapes, I still felt the energy they gave off. It always helped to jog my memory of my father. I can barely remember him. Most of the memories I have of him are fuzzy, but when those songs played, I could see him a bit clearer.

Now they're all gone.

"Good," is all he says before he raises his fist, and punches Gregory in the face. He falls off of the step, disoriented as he lays on the floor on his back. I grab the box, knowing we're probably going to get the fuck out of here after this. Dom raises his fist again and punches him one more time.

"The first one was because you're a dick. The second one was for how you treated Teags, and this," he says as another punch hits Gregory in the stomach, "that was to remind you to leave her alone. No more calls or messages. Consider this your only warning or I will ruin you even more than I plan to."

What the hell is he getting at? I know his family has a lot of sway in things, but Gregory's does too. I wouldn't want him getting wrapped up with him just because he pissed me off.

"Ready?" he asks me as he grabs the box from me.

"Almost," I say before I raise my leg and kick Gregory in the shin. "Now I am."

"That's my girl," is all Dom says as he grabs my hand where he holds the box. I shut the door behind us with a laugh as we rush to the truck. Dom throws the box in the back seat as he opens my door for me.

By the time he gets into the car, Gregory is watching the two of us from the door, a pissed off look on his face. I throw him my middle finger as I buckle my seat belt and Dom drives away.

A few minutes into the drive, we both burst out laughing. Nothing about it was funny, but I think the two of us are hopped up on adrenaline. I'm still extremely pissed off, and I'm sure I'll cry about my music and record player later, but for right now, I need to laugh.

What the hell did I ever see in that guy?

"He looked like he was going to piss himself when I walked in." Dom smiles at me.

I could see that. Gregory is a very clean-cut, haircut once a month kind of guy. He doesn't get tattoos or eat take out because his parents would scold him, and he has the energy of someone who peaked in high school. Dom is the complete opposite. Tattoos run all across his body, his black hair is always all over the place unless he has a meeting, and his face looks stone-cold, but he's not as scary once you get to know him.

"I bet he's calling Mommy and Daddy to tell them what happened."

"Yeah, well, I know his name and he doesn't know mine. I'll have his parents' company ruined by the end of the week," he jokes. At least, I think it's a joke.

"You're not serious, are you?"

He looks over at me, his face as serious as he sounds and I'm about to tell him to stay out of it before he starts laughing. "Of course not."

I smack his bicep as I laugh, before I notice he's not on the route to California like we planned on.

"Where are we going?"

"We're taking a detour, is that okay?"

"Well, I was promised an adventure, Dom."

"Then buckle up, baby, because that's what you're going to get." He smiles over at me before his hand lands on my thigh and squeezes it.

And even though I'm still pissed off about my stuff being gone, somehow in this truck, Dom makes me feel better with a simple touch.

I'm so fucking screwed because my feelings that were once lust have now turned into something more, and I know I can't do anything about them.

Chapter Twenty

Las Vegas

"Are you sure you want to do this?" Dom asks me for the twentieth time as we get out of the car.

"Yes, I'm sure," I tell him as I look up and stare at the walk-ins welcome sign of the tattoo parlor. "Why are you so nervous? You're the one with a thousand tattoos. This is going to be a cakewalk for you, Dommy."

I swear I can feel him roll his eyes from behind me.

"Oh, baby, I can handle it," he says as he snakes an arm around my waist. "But I worry I'm corrupting you on this trip. First, I got you high, and now we're getting tattoos."

I turn around to face him, his eyes already focused on mine and my breath catches in my throat. God, he is so beautiful and I know what his lips taste like. Not only that, but he saw how frustrated and sad I was after my encounter with Gregory, and he's taken me to Vegas to cheer me up.

Dominic Graves has driven me to Las Vegas and he's probably going to corrupt me even further. I can't say I'm too broken up about this predicament I'm in, but I worry for my heart at the end of all this.

"You and I both know I can handle it," I whisper, wanting to fuck with him a little more.

I'm in Las Vegas with Dominic Graves and he's going to show me a good time, or whatever he said on the drive here. I've never been here before, but I have heard the clubs here are next level, and I've never been to a club before. I didn't go during college because I didn't have any friends, but I've always been curious as to what the atmosphere feels like.

If there's good music and dancing, I'll be okay, but first, Dom and I are getting tattoos. I've been wanting to get another one for a while, and Dom seems like the perfect person to get one with.

And he offered to pay for it, but I'm already keeping a tab of how much I need to pay him back. I hate when people spend money on me, and just because Dom is rich, that doesn't mean it feels any better.

I only have one tattoo, and it's lyrics from my Dad's favorite song. He always used to sing it, whistle it around the house, and he always told my mom that song perfectly described how he felt about his family.

The song being "Everything I Do, I Do It For You."

The world took him too soon, and this tattoo I'm going to get is something I can remember Tobias by. I might not have either of them anymore, but these tattoos will remind me how they're always with me.

They will always be a part of me even though they're gone, and that has to be enough.

When we walk into the parlor, I notice that it's empty, which makes me a little nervous.

"Where the hell is everybody?" It took us five hours to get here, and another two hours were spent at the hotel freshening up. It's dark as fuck out because the sun has already set, and I thought Vegas was the city where night life thrived, so where the hell is everybody?

A guy walks out of the back and looks at the two of us, and my stomach drops to my feet. Are we not allowed in here or something? The sign didn't say they were closed.

"Are you Dominic?" the guy asks us, and he nods.

"That's me." Dom smiles at him before he puts his card on the counter. "Thanks for closing the place down. It's more comfortable for me and my girl this way."

I'm sorry, what did he say?

"No problem, man. What are you two thinking about getting?"

I'm still stuck on what he said before. "Did you—"

"Rent out the place for a few hours so you'd be comfortable getting a tattoo for your dead brother? Yeah, I did, Teags. Is that a problem?"

I shake my head, too stunned at his admission that words can no longer form.

"Good. Now, do you want to go first?"

I nod and then I show the guy what I want and where. Dom does the same, but he annoys me because he hasn't shown me what he's getting yet. I don't know why he's keeping it a secret. I'm going to see it at some point.

While the guy goes to get our stuff ready, we sit down on the couch and fill out the normal paperwork. I want to ask him so badly about all the things he's done for me on this trip, but I also don't want it to stop. He's calling me a nickname outside of the bedroom. I woke up the other day curled into his chest and he was running his hand through my hair. I didn't dare move and make him think I was awake.

When I used to float into Gregory's body in the middle of the night, he would simply push me off and wake me up. When I did it with Dom, he embraced me and lulled me back to sleep with his hand through my hair. He didn't know I was awake, but the action made me both giddy and terrified. Giddy because for a split second it felt like he was my freaking boyfriend, and terrified because of how natural it was and how much I liked it.

Or maybe this is all practice for the second part of this agreement and he's faking all this so it's more natural when the time comes. I could gaslight myself into believing that, but the tiny part of my heart that still has hope thinks that maybe he and I could become something other than road trip companions.

Instead of breaking my own heart by asking all of that, I decide on a different route. "How much are you paying this guy to keep his shop closed while we're here?"

"Not much," he shrugs as he signs his name on the sheet.

"A number, Dom."

He only looks up at me, face as normal as it can be as he mutters a number. "Ten thousand."

"Dollars?" There's no fucking way.

"What?" he says, not understanding why I'm freaking out. "I support small businesses, Teags."

I roll my eyes as I sign my name. "You spent ten thousand dollars so I would feel comfortable here?"

"Of course I did."

If I wasn't already sitting down, I would need to. I swear my legs would have given out if I was standing up.

Before I have a chance to ask him why he did all that for me, the guy comes back and escorts us to the tattoo chair. I go first, of course, and I'm lying down because I decided to put my tattoo behind my ear.

"How's that placement?" he asks me as I get up and go to the mirror to see it. My only other tattoo is on my hip because my dad used to pick me up and when I was little and when we danced, he would tap my hip as he swung me around while the music played.

This placement seems right for Tobias' memorial tattoo.

"It's perfect," I say as I lie back down. I hear the buzzing of the tattoo needle and I feel Dom's hand on my thigh as he begins. I hate that I feel tears brimming while I think about what this tattoo means. I hate that I still feel empty after all this searching for my brother. I hate that I can't stop thinking about what all of this shit with Dom means.

But for right now, I let one tear fall as I remember my brother and the love for music we once shared. Music will always be ours, and anytime I put my headphones on, I'll remember the tattoo behind my ear and remind myself that Tobias is not only in music, but he's also with me even when I can't feel him.

Maybe if I say it enough, I'll believe it.

And twenty minutes later after the guy sanitizes everything again, Dom is laying down on his stomach getting his very muscular back tattooed. Well, the back of his shoulder, I guess. At least this position allows me to see it.

"You ready?" the guy asks him.

"Teags, hold my hand."

I roll my eyes at him. "You're not serious."

"Of course I am." His arm fiddles around for my hand and eventually I succumb and hold his stupid hand. "Now I'm ready."

The needle starts, and I watch as the guy fills in an anchor tattoo on Dom's back. I have to stop myself from drooling because no matter how many times I see his muscles, it's never enough. I'm a sucker for arm veins, muscles and all that, and he has all of that plus a million tattoos that cover his entire body.

Dom is like my own fantasy come to life, and I'm unsure of how anyone else can compare to him in the bedroom and now out of it if he keeps doing all this nice shit for me.

It takes about half an hour for the guy to finish Dom's and in total it took an hour for this guy to tattoo the both of us. And Dom paid ten thousand dollars for it.

"Thank you," I say to the man when we leave.

"Come back any time," he says and I'm sure he means that because Dom paid an ungodly amount of money for two fairly simple tattoos.

"Where to next?" Dom asks me.

"Well, we are in Vegas..." I say and he catches what I mean immediately. He pulls his phone out, types a few things into his keyboard, and within a few seconds, he's grabbing my hand and pulling me forward.

"We're not getting a car back to the hotel?" I ask and he shakes his head.

"I'll protect you from anything unsavory, and I thought we could both use some air outside of a car." He pulls me closer to him. "Want to check out the club next to the hotel?"

"Of course I do, but I think I need to change."

"There's a place on the way where we can get you something. Just enjoy this walk with me, Teags."

I enjoy everything when I'm with you.

Woah. Where the fuck did that come from?

I shake my head out of those thoughts and instead think about how nice it feels to not be inside of a vehicle. The two of us have been cramped inside Ethan's truck for this entire trip, and it does feel nice walking. I used to go on a lot of walks back in Arizona when the sun would set because Gregory was always too busy working to go with me.

I still wonder why I stayed for so long. I regret not leaving sooner. I regret wasting parts of my life with him when I could have been focusing on making myself feel less like shit.

"Why did you decide on that placement?" he asks me. "Not many people get tattoos behind their ears."

"It's where my headphones go, therefore it's where my music goes."

"It looks good. Tattoos suit you," he compliments me and I swear I'm blushing. Thank God it's dark out because if he saw my face, he would probably run for the hills.

"Thanks. I've been meaning to get more, but I can never decide what to get." I look over at him, tattoos covering his body and I wonder how he decided on the ones he got. I'm super indecisive when it comes to tattoos, piercings, and all that, but it seems like he gets whatever he wants.

But when he wears his suits to his meetings, they're always covered. I wonder if that's part of his parents stipulations.

"What does that symbol mean anyways?"

"It's a tie. When it's written out on sheet music, two notes with the same pitch are played as a single note. It reminds me of how Tobias and I bonded over music." I hesitantly reach up to touch my new tattoo behind my ear, and I smile. Tobias would have loved it.

"And the one on your hip? What does that one represent?"

"It was my Dad's favorite song." I don't tell him how I can barely remember my father. I don't tell him how I used to sit in my basement and watch old home videos from when he was still alive just to hear what his laugh sounded like because I couldn't remember. That's actually how I found out he used to dance with me in his arms—I watched it on a video because my mom used to record everything.

"Oh," is all he says.

"I'd ask what all of yours mean, but I think you have too many for me to do that," I joke, trying to shift the subject onto a happier one.

"Ask me about the one I just got then," he smirks, goading me into asking.

"Why did you get an anchor tattoo, Dom?"

"It's a reminder to remain grounded even if I feel like I'm being held down by other things."

"Do you feel like you're being held down?" The question slips out before I can stop it. I find that happening a lot when I'm around him. He makes my guard come down, and I don't have to tiptoe around him as much as I used to with Gregory.

"Yeah, I do. By my parents and the life I don't really want."

"Then why don't you do something else? Why do they dictate every-thing?"

He only looks over at me, the bright lights of Vegas shining above us and I know he's not going to answer my question.

Then he kisses me. It's so quick that it barely registered in my mind, but I felt it. I felt him on my lips even for that small moment.

"What was that for?" I whisper.

He shrugs at me before I feel him open a door behind me. *When did we get to this shop?* "I did it because I wanted to. Because my parents may dictate most things about my life, but they're not here, and if I want to kiss you, I will. How does that sound to you?"

I can't stop my smile from coming off of my face. "That sounds like a good choice. I'm glad you made it for yourself."

And then he kisses me again. "Good. Now, go pick out something pretty and we can get to the club."

"Oh, what, you're not going to shut this place down so I can shop in peace?" I joke.

"Excuse me—"

I smack him before I start perusing the racks, feeling the weight of his stare on me the entire time.

The giddiness in my body, the pep in my step, and the butterflies in my stomach are all telling me I'm screwed.

But whatever version of myself I am right now is telling me to enjoy this while it lasts, so that's what I'm going to do. I'm going to enjoy feeling like I'm in a relationship with Dominic Graves even though I know when this trip is over, everything will go back to the way it's supposed to be.

Even if I might be ruined in the process.

Chapter Twenty-One

Dominic

— THE PARTY AND THE AFTER PARTY BY THE WEEKND

I've never been one to regret my choices, but I'm starting to regret this one.

Teags is trying to kill me in the red mini dress I bought her to go clubbing in. Not only does she look fucking amazing in it, but I'm not the only one whose been noticing. I swear every pair of eyes is on her and I want to rip them out of their sockets.

I'm not even sure where this protective asshole instinct has come from, but something changed after Arizona. Teags was gutted when she found out what Gregory did, and I didn't think twice about this detour so I could cheer her up. I wanted to do it, so I did. I don't regret it because seeing that smile back on her face? Seeing her light up as the music hits her body? It's unreal. Teagen West is unreal, and she's unraveling me by the minute.

She looks ethereal as the lights flash inside of the club, her body swaying to the beat of the music as she lets loose and dances. Music is playing but I can't understand the lyrics because she is the only thing that has my full attention.

Different girls have tried to come up to me but they quickly lose interest when they realize I'm not paying attention to a single word they're saying. I'm nursing my fucking drink because I cannot pry my eyes off of her. She looks otherworldly as the lights flash around this place and accentuate every fucking curve on her body.

I know she and I have been trying some new shit while we're on the road, but I wonder how she'd feel if I pulled her off of the dance floor and fucked her where someone might see us. I'm not sure if she's into anything like that, but I can barely handle myself right now.

Some guy tries to dance up on her, but as soon as she feels him behind her, she turns around and sticks her hand in his face. He leaves as soon as I stand up, and then her eyes are back on me, heat spreading all over my body. The past few days have been a fucking whirlwind, and I know we're having fun on the road, but this girl dancing in front of me is driving me fucking mad, and I think she knows it.

The song switches and she motions for me to come over to her, so I take my drink and head over to her. I swear this girl could make me do anything in the state I am right now. If she asked me to crawl across the floor to get to her, I'd get on my knees right now.

I throw the rest of my drink back before I set my glass to the side, wanting both of my hands to be free if I'm allowed to touch her. It seems like she's calling the shots right now, and I'm going to let her.

I lean down to her ear, peppering small kisses to her neck and behind her ear. "Can I touch you?"

She nods, throwing her head back against my chest as she keeps dancing against me.

"Fuck, you feel good," is all I can say as my hands travel lower and lower.

She wastes no time before she grabs my hand and leads me off of the dance floor, her mouth on mine as soon as we're in a place with less people. This corner of the club is dark, but there's still a ton of people around us, and I couldn't give less of a fuck. Her mouth is on mine and I can feel the air leaving my lungs as she grabs onto my shirt, unbuttoning the first few so she can grab onto something.

"It seems like you want something from me," I say between kisses. She has me shoved against the wall, and if we get caught, we're totally getting kicked out or better yet arrested, but that only makes my dick even harder.

"I want you to be a good boy and get me off with your fingers before you drag me out of here and fuck me in our hotel room."

I throw my head back, feeling like I got struck by lightning. I might be the luckiest man alive, but karma is absolutely going to bite me in the ass for about a thousand different reasons.

I hate that I don't fucking care though.

"Are you going to be good for me?" she whispers as she looks up at me, her big fucking eyes full of need and I'm the only person who can help.

"I'll be such a good boy for you, baby," I say as my hand finds her center, only to find out she's not wearing any underwear. "You've been bare for me all night?"

She shrugs. "Maybe."

"You're driving me fucking crazy," I say as I soak my fingers with her pussy, thrusting two of them inside of her. "Take my fucking fingers and hide those moans from everyone else in here. Those are only for me, aren't they?"

She's squirming against me, and I turn her around, her back against the wall so she can steady herself. This girl is unraveling every morsel of control I've tried to have, and this little detour we took is turning out to be the best fucking idea I've ever had.

"Shit," she says as my thumb finds her clit, my fingers still working her tight fucking pussy, and I can feel her start to clench around me. "Dom."

"Does this turn you on, Teags? Knowing anyone could catch me fucking you with my fingers right now? Do you want someone to catch us like this?"

"Please make me come," is all she can say, her pussy tightening around my fingers. "Please."

She's still in charge, so I follow orders and lift her leg up onto my arm, needing to hit deeper than I have been and as soon as I hear her about to moan, I cover her mouth.

"Eyes on me, baby. I'm the one making you feel this. Don't you fuck-ing dare look at anyone else." She nods as I coax the rest of her orgasm out of her, her body going limp as soon as she finishes. Her eyes flutter a little, but I grab her face with my other hand. "Eyes."

She lifts her head just in time to see me lick the remnants of her orgasm off of my fingers, and fuck, she tastes like the deadliest fucking sin for me. I need *more*. I lean down to her, a small whisper coming through my ears.

"Now you're going to fuck me until I can't walk." Her eyes find mine before she kisses me again. "Is that understood?"

"Yes, baby, that's understood." She barely has time to respond before I throw her over my shoulder, pulling her dress down so it covers her, before I speed walk out of the club and head for our room.

There's no way either of us are sleeping tonight.

"YOU MIGHT HAVE BEEN in charge down there," I say as I throw her onto the bed. "But now it's my turn."

"God, yes," is all she says as she adjusts herself on the king sized bed in our room. "Fucking use me however you'd like."

"Is that what you want?" I say as I slide my belt out of my pants, threading it back into the loop as I wait for her answer. "I'll give you anything you ask me for, but you have to be sure it's what you want."

She takes a second to think before she gets on her knees, crawls toward me on the bed, and starts to unbutton my pants. "While I liked being in charge," is all she says as she takes my dick in her hands, "I much prefer you telling me what to do while I listen like the good submissive brat you know I am."

My fingers find her chin as I get her eyes on me. "Then suck, Teags."

"Yes, sir," is all she says before her mouth is on my cock and I'm grabbing the rails of the bed with my hands. She bobs her head up and down my dick while one of my hands finds her hair, grabbing it around my fist so it's not in her way.

"Let me fuck that pretty mouth of yours," I say as she stops and holds her mouth open just how I want her to. "Such a good fucking girl," I tell her as I fuck her mouth, knowing she can take it. Her eyes start to get watery and as I pull out of her mouth, I grab the belt I discarded.

"How do you want me?" she asks as she starts to slip her dress off of her shoulders, but before she can I grab her legs and drag her towards me.

"Keep the dress on and lift it over your ass," I tell her as she watches me unbutton the rest of my shirt, throwing it off of me. "And then get on your knees for me, baby."

I smack her ass as she flips over, crawling toward the middle of the bed before she lifts her dress how I told her to and I stroke my cock while I watch her listen so well to my directions. I roll a condom over my throbbing cock before I finally get onto the bed, the belt in one of my hands as I get my dick wet with her already soaked pussy.

"You feel like a fucking dream," I say as I thrust into her in one go. "God, Teags, you were driving me crazy dancing down at the club."

"I was trying to," she tells me, looking back at me with a smile on her face. "And I think you liked being called a good boy when we were down there."

My dick flexes inside of her when she says that, her smile growing bigger as she realizes she was right. It's not that I liked it, but it was the way she said it that really killed me. This girl could call me anything she wants and I'd give in to her.

I grab the belt and fasten it around her neck, tightening it with one hand, my other grabbing her ass, lightly smacking it and hearing her moan.

"How does this feel?" I ask her, but all I can feel is how tightly she's strangling my cock right now. "Baby?"

"I need you to move," is all she says, her voice light and raspy. "Please, I need you to fuck me."

I lean toward her ear, the belt tightening under my grip. "Tell me." I trail my other hand down her back, goosebumps spreading down her body as she shakes underneath me. "Did you ever ask him to do this to you?"

"Dom—"

I smack her ass again, needing an answer to my question.

"Yes," she whispers. "Once I did."

"And I'm guessing he turned you down."

She nods as best she can. What a fucking idiot.

"God, he was too vanilla for you," is all I can say. "Or maybe he didn't know how to handle someone like you, Teags."

I start thrusting in and out of her, slowly at first to give her a small taste of what's coming.

"What does that mean?"

I tighten the belt as I quicken my pace. "You're a fucking firecracker, Teags. You're hot." Thrust. "Stubborn." Another thrust. "Fucking opinionated." Another. "And I think you intimidated him." I quicken my pace. "But luckily for you, I know how to handle you."

"I don't need to be handled," she says, her voice getting quieter by the minute.

"No, you need to be fucked. Isn't that right?" I say as I pound into her, my control loosening by the fucking minute. I need to mark her. I want her to feel me every time she sits down over the next few days. I want to cover her in my fucking cum until she forgets every bad thing Gregory told her about herself. "You're taking my cock so well, baby."

The only sounds I can hear are her moaning into the bed as she arches even more, my cock hitting deeper and harder, before I feel her legs start to shake.

"The only way you get to come is if you scream my name."

I swear I hear an incoherent yes sir before the only sounds I can hear are her ass slapping against me as I continue the pace she seems to love so much, my name sounding like a fucking prayer coming off of her lips with the way she's chanting it.

"Give me all of it. Fuck," I say as I fall off of the cliff, my orgasm taking over so much so that I can barely fucking see as I cry out her name. By the time we're both sated, I pull out of her, loosen the belt around her neck, and dispose of the condom. She's practically half asleep as I drag her out of bed and into my arms, turning the shower on so we can both feel clean before we go to sleep.

"Dom," she mumbles into my arms as she struggles to stand up.

"I'll hold you up, don't worry," I say as the warm water hits our skin, the two of us letting out a collective sigh as we breathe in the steam. I sit her down on the small bench in the shower as I look at her neck. It's a little red, but I don't think it's going to bruise. "How are you feeling?"

She only smiles at me. "I feel fucking amazing."

I can't help but crack a smile at her answer. "That's good, baby."

"Seeing you all," she waves her hand at me, "dominating is the world's biggest turn on. Pun intended, I guess."

"Well, down in the club was probably the hottest thing I've ever seen," I tell her, pressing a wet kiss to her mouth. "You're fucking sexy when you're telling me how to get you off."

She laughs to herself as she adjusts how she's sitting. "My ass hurts."

"I'll massage it," I say as I stand her up, her arms coming around my neck as she latches onto me.

"Can you wash my body for me? I don't think my arms or legs work anymore."

I'd do fucking anything for you if you ask me. "Of course," I say as I grab the loofah and lather it up, not liking how my heart seems to beat faster when she's around me like this, so I try to remind myself that she and I are a means to an end.

But like a moth to a flame, her body finds mine in bed as soon as we're out of the shower and dressed. She falls asleep as soon as her head hits the pillow, and I spend the entire night trying to ignore the feelings stirring deep in my chest, and eventually sleep consumes me.

I dream of her the entire time.

Chapter Twenty-Two

California

— AUGUSTA BY GRACIE ABRAMS

As I explore the beach and boardwalk around the hotel, I try to take my mind off of everything that has gone on while on the road.

It's not working, but it sure is fun pretending like it is.

For one, I ran from a proposal and my old life that was going nowhere. Then I ran right to my brother's best friend's house where he basically hid me hostage. Now I'm on the last stop of our road trip, and I have feelings for him. Actual, real-life, romantic feelings for him.

This trip brought us closer together—way closer—and I think I might be the only one feeling conflicted about what the hell has been happening on this trip.

We were fucking. Just messing around so we could let off some steam and have good sex, but it morphed into so much more for me. With every nickname that's slipped from his mouth, with every little thing he's done to make me happy and comfortable, my heart has been slowly falling more into him. And I like it. I think that's the most embarrassing part for me.

I like when he calls me baby. I like driving around aimlessly with him across the country. I enjoy his company because he gives me as much shit as I give him. He can match my energy more than anyone else can, and I like it.

I'm having feelings—*real* feelings for a guy. I don't know if I'm going to be able to survive this predicament I'm in if I have to pretend to be his girlfriend in front of his parents.

Though, I wouldn't be pretending, but I'm sure he would be.

God, my head is a mess, and I know exactly who to call when I need advice or someone to listen to my stupid problems.

She answers on the third ring, and I've never been so happy to hear my best friend's voice.

"Thank goodness you called," Bree says over the line. "I had to hear from Nico that you were headed to Arizona."

"Sorry for not calling. There's been a lot going on," I say as I sit on a nearby bench. "I'm prepared to give you a full update."

"You know I'm not one to pry."

I sigh heavily, loving my best friend more than words can express. "And I love you for that, but I need some advice for once. My head feels like a scrambled egg."

"Then let's try and unscramble it. What's going on?"

As the ocean air blows through my hair, I take a deep breath and finally say the words out loud.

"Dom and I have been fucking while we're on the road, and I think my dumb feelings have morphed into something I've never felt before."

"You two have had sex? I need details immediately." Bree's silent for a few seconds as I let her take in that information. "Are you in love with him? Is that what you're saying?"

"I don't know. That's what I can't figure out." I run my hand down my face. "I've never felt like this before. Not with Gregory or anyone else, and I'm terrified. I'm having actual feelings for once and I don't know how to navigate all of this. We agreed to it being only while we're on the road, but when we stop all of this, I don't know what I'll feel."

"It's difficult the first time, that's for sure." She's quiet again before I hear her laugh under her breath. "I can't believe this is real. I can't say I'm shocked, but I kind of am."

"How did you know you were in love with Vince?" I ask, wanting to know if she understands my mixed feelings about all this. On one hand, I could see myself being with Dom. I like being around him and not just because of the sex.

But my brother would kill the both of us, I'm sure. And what if I start to feel how I did with Gregory after a few months or a year? What if I'm broken and can never love anyone or anything ever again? What if I never feel alive again? And what if I've fucked myself since all I've done is make fun of love my entire life?

I thought it was embarrassing, but now that I'm feeling it, I'm starting to disagree with that statement I once made.

"I knew I loved Vince because he made even the normal moments some of the best. One time, he cut my strawberries and hung around chatting with me in the kitchen all night, and it was the best night of my life." She chuckles under her breath at the memory. "I think love is finding someone who can make the mundane moments most people take for granted meaningful. At least for me, that's what love looks like. I wanted to feel safe, and Vince does that and more to keep me out of my head and in the present. I never want to retreat to a different reality when I'm with him."

"That's beautiful." I'm so glad she found him. The girl deserves the best life possible after all she's been through.

"What do you think love looks like for you? Do you have an idea of that at least? I know you hate the emotion, but if you had to say what it looked like for you, what would it be?"

"I don't think I know what it looks like." I shake my head as if she can see me.

"Just imagine it, Teags. Imagine what love would look like for you."

"But—"

"Humor me, okay? I know you think love is embarrassing. All I'm asking is that you imagine it."

Imagine it. Okay, I can do that. I love escaping reality inside of the books I read, so this should be easy right? I close my eyes and try to clear my mind, letting the sound of the waves around me sink into the background.

"Love isn't quiet for me. In my head, it feels loud. It feels like standing on a rooftop screaming your lungs out because you want everyone to know you're feeling something. It's driving fast with the windows down so my hair can whip all over the place. Love to me feels *loud*. It's someone kissing me in front of their friends because they want to show they love me in front of everyone. It's not a secret. It's loud and reckless and—"

I cut myself off because when I'm describing all of this, I see Dom's eyes looking back at me in my mind.

Oh, I am *so* fucked.

"Is that how you feel with him?" she asks, and I can already tell she's smirking across the line.

"Oh, fuck."

"Don't freak out when I can't slap you back to reality. Just take a few breaths."

"Bree, this cannot be happening. I *just* got out of a relationship. I literally just got all of my stuff back from Gregory's house while on this road trip. I cannot be falling from one shitty relationship into another this quickly. How the fuck do I get rid of these feelings? Is there like an off button, or something?"

Bree only laughs as I look around, panicked. This can't be possible, right? I sound insane. I can't believe I'm on the phone with my best friend talking about how I'm in love with my brother's best friend after I just turned down a proposal.

What kind of alternate reality have I walked into and how the fuck do I get out of it?

"Take a few breaths," she reminds me, and I do. It only makes me feel a little better. "I need to mention the fact that you were mentally checked out of your last relationship for months, babe. Even I could tell just from our phone calls. So, it's okay that you're having these feelings now. In fact, since this is the first time you're feeling this, I think it's perfectly acceptable. And even if I didn't, it's your life, Teags. Wasn't that the whole point of why you moved to Arizona? To make your own choices? Maybe you're scared of all this because you finally have control back and it's terrifying you."

Damn. Is she right? Do I have my control back?

If I think about it for a second, she's right. Not only has this trip helped me get some distance from everything, but Dom has allowed me to call some of the shots in and out of the bedroom. He hasn't tried to stifle me, he's only listened to me, made me laugh, and gone along with all the stupid shit I recommend for us to do.

I wanted to get another tattoo, so we did. I wanted to go to the club, so we did. He's letting me try new things when we have sex, and he lets me take control, not minding when I boss him around.

And even when we get back and have to pretend to be dating, I'm sure he'll let me set the boundaries for the two of us.

How did I not realize this before?

"Oh my..." I say, the realization hitting me in the face like a ton of bricks.

"Is that Teags?" I hear Vince say. "Has she seen the news?"

"What are you talking about, baby?" Bree asks him as I sit and stare out into the ocean, the sun starting to lower in the sky. Dom did say his meeting was going to take longer than normal since this investor guy is a hardass, but I didn't think I was here for that long.

I guess time spent with the people you love really does make time fly, even if over the phone.

"What is Vince talking about? Did something happen?"

"I'm putting you on speaker." I hear a click and then she speaks again. "What's going on?"

And then another voice filters through the phone. "Your boy's company tanked."

Nico? "How can that be possible when we're literally on the road for his job?"

"I'm sending the article to you," Nico tells me. "I bet Gregory is pissed."

Oh, Gregory's company. That makes more sense.

"What happened?" Bree asks, just as confused as I am.

"Look, angel," Vince says at the same time as I click the article. My mouth drops open as I read the entire thing, my eyes widened in shock.

"His family was embezzling from clients? They were charging for time they didn't actually bill? How the fuck did someone find that out?"

"I have no idea, but I bet your boy had something to do with it," Nico chides, and I scoff. There's no way. For one, he couldn't have done it that quickly, and when would he have had time to do that? We've been so busy between Vegas and driving to California that we've barely had time to do anything.

"Your boy? Did I miss something?" Vince asks and I hear Bree laugh.

"I'll update you later, baby. Can I, Teags?"

"As long as none of you tell my brother, then spill away, Bree."

My stomach hasn't returned to normal because I remembered a conversation after we left Arizona. Dom made a joke about destroying Gregory's company, but he told me he was kidding.

What if he actually made good on his promise? How does that make me feel?

Thank God I don't have to think about that because there's no way he actually did it.

My phone buzzes as I'm about to tell them about that, and when I look down, I smile unconsciously at my phone.

Again, I am *so* fucked.

Dom: Where are you?

Teags: Boardwalk.

Dom: Send me your location. I'll meet you there.

I do as I'm told, and as my mind filters back into the conversation the three of them are having, I realize I didn't hear a word of what they said.

"I missed all of that, but I have to go. Dom's looking for me."

"Oh, is he now?" Nico jokes.

"Stop," Bree tells him. "Teags, think about what we talked about and trust your gut. I love you to the moon, girl."

"And back. Thank you for always answering when I call."

"Thank *you* for calling, babe. I'll see you soon," she says.

"Make good choices," Vince says before I hang up.

I stay at the bench, and Dom finds me a few minutes later, his suit replaced with shorts, a linen button-up shirt, and sneakers. I can see his thigh and leg tattoos way clearer, and my mouth starts to water of its own volition.

He's so fucking sexy, it pisses me off.

And one of the thigh tattoos is a fucking dragon that goes all around his leg. It's quite literally the hottest thing I've ever seen.

"Hey," he says as he leans down and presses a kiss to my lips. The gesture was unexpected, and my stomach flips again. My feelings are betraying me. If I tried to stand up, I don't know if I could. "How long have you been down here?"

"A few hours, I think. I kind of lost track of time."

"Are you hungry? Do you want to grab some food and take a walk on the beach or something?" He runs a hand through his messy hair, and I suddenly have the urge to do the same, but I don't. "The office I was in had a beautiful view of the water, and it took everything in me not to cut the meeting short so I could spend some time with you and actually have some fun while we're here."

Am I reading into things too much or could he feel the same way about me that I do about him? God, I'm so fucking confused. This is all fake, right? This is all practice for when we have to be a couple in front of people who think we're dating. At least that's what my brain is telling me.

"I'm not too hungry, but maybe we could walk on the beach?"

"Sure," he says as he guides me over to the entrance to the sand, his hand on my lower back. I'm way too aware of this beautiful man next to me, and it's driving me insane.

Before we get fully on to the sand, he leans down and grabs my shoes from my feet, holding them in his hands so I don't have to.

"So, your meeting went well?" I ask, trying to get my thought spiral to stop. The question I really want to ask him is on the tip of my tongue, but I can't get it out.

"As well as expected. I'm sure my parents will be getting a call soon to find out if it's a yes or a no, but I don't want to talk about that."

"Oh, that's okay." He grabs my hand in his. "What are you doing?"

"Holding your hand. Is that okay?" he asks.

No, I should say, but I don't. I can't because I like the feel of his hand in mine way too much.

"It's okay."

And the two of us walk up and down the beach for however long, just taking in the sounds of the ocean and the bustle of people around us until we get to this break in the beach. I'm about to turn around and go back to where there's people, but Dom pulls me back and the two of us stand facing the moonlight, hands joined between us.

"What did you do today?"

"Nothing, really. I talked to Bree before you found me, but I mostly wandered around with my headphones on."

"What do you think about when you do that? I've noticed you do that in every city we've been to, but I didn't want to pry. I assumed you needed space or something."

"Can we sit?" I ask, my legs feeling jittery again. I don't know if it's him, this conversation, or what, but I feel like I can barely stand.

"Sure," he says as he plops our shoes in front of him.

I take a deep breath before the words come tumbling out. "I do it because it makes me feel connected to Tobias. I've been searching for him everywhere we've stopped, but I can't feel him. Even if I listen to the songs we used to dissect, I feel nothing, and it scares me."

"Oh," he says, a calmness to his tone. "I know music was your and Tobias's thing, but I didn't know the rest."

"I can't feel him when I listen to our songs and I worry I'm going to forget him like I did with my dad. He died when I was so young, and I can barely remember what he sounded like." I look over at him, feeling cracked open but *safe*. Because when he looks back at me, it's not with judgment or pity. He's simply listening to me talk, and that's all I could ask of him. "That might happen with Tobias if I'm not careful."

"You could never forget him. Just like he'll never forget you. You'll always be his sister, and someday, you'll see each other again."

"You believe in that kind of thing?"

He simply shrugs. "No, but I have hope that the people we love can talk to us even when they're not here anymore." He squeezes my hand in his. "And I bet your dad and Tobias are really proud of who you've become over the past two years. If they could see you now, they'd be proud of how sharp, snappy, outspoken, and strong you are despite all you've been through."

"Is that how you see me? Strong, snappy, and outspoken? Because I think some people would use the words cold and bitchy," I joke, trying to lighten the mood.

"Don't call yourself that. Do you even realize what you've been through? Do you realize how fucking strong you are or do I need to convince you?"

I shrug, unsure of what to say.

"Your family has been through things I can't even imagine. The grief, fuck, it would have killed me if I was in your situation, yet here you are"—he gestures to me—"still standing despite everything that's been thrown your way. Why do you downplay that? Why do you downplay your emotions as if they don't matter? Because they do. If you want to cry, cry. If you want to fucking scream, then do it. You deserve to let it all out in whatever way you want to without others judging you for it. They didn't live it. You did."

I let what he's saying sink in. My stomach flips, my hands are shaking—which I'm sure he can feel—and I let a tear fall. "You know, technically, I'm not standing."

That only causes him to laugh as he leans over and wipes the tear from my eye. "You've always got a comeback, don't you?"

"Well, I am snappy, according to some." I smile to myself. "Thank you. I needed to hear that, I think."

"You're welcome. Now"—he stands up and brings me with him—"let's go skinny dipping and live on the edge for once."

"You want me to get naked in public? Isn't that a felony?"

"You're safe with me, baby. Let's have some well-deserved fun," he says as he unbuttons his shirt. "What do you say?"

"Is the water cold?"

"You'll get used to it. I'll heat you up if I need to." He winks at me and I smack his arm as I laugh.

"Fine," I say as I pull my shirt off. His eyes go straight to my boobs, and I smack him again.

"What? You expect me not to stare at you when you look like that? I thought you enjoyed it when I gawked at you."

"I do, but we're on a very public beach, so, let's go," I say as we strip the rest of our clothes. Before I can back out, he throws me over his shoulder and runs into the water.

He drops me into the water, and as I go under, I think that this is what love feels like for me. It's running into cold water, knowing it's going to sting a little, but when you adjust to the temperature, it feels comfortable and normal.

Dom makes me feel like I could run full force into the water. He makes me want to do that with him by my side, but I'm sure after this is over, we'll go our separate ways and this will all just be memories the two of us share.

Unfortunately, my brain has become used to him and his proximity since we've been on this trip. The temperature between us has settled, and I've become comfortable being around him, kissing him, and knowing where the birthmark is on his back. I've memorized every inch of him, and that's not something my brain will ever forget.

The two of us are simply killing time together while we're on the road trip, and when we get back, I'm going to have to fight like hell to choose a direction on the road we're on.

We've reached a fork in the road. One side being that we keep pretending and when we get back, maybe something will come of the two of us. The other side being we go our separate ways and forget that this all happened.

And as we float against one another in the water, my legs wrapped around him, my head against his chest listening to his heartbeat, I know for sure that I don't want to make a decision. I simply want to stay in this moment with him forever.

But we're killing time until that moment comes, and I wish there was a way this could end without something getting ruined—whether it be my heart or my relationship with my brother. I'm sure Tristan would kill the both of us if we tell him about this excursion we've taken.

Whatever road we go down doesn't end well, and I'm not prepared for any of it. Though my heart has been broken so many times before, I'm sure it could handle cracking a little more before it breaks.

Or maybe this will be the final thing to break it in half.

Chapter Twenty-Three

Dominic

Somewhere In The Midwest

— EVERYTHING HAS CHANGED BY TAYLOR SWIFT FT. ED SHEERAN

THIS ROAD TRIP HAS turned out to be more fun than I expected.

When I first imagined driving across the country all by myself, going to endless meetings to show my parents I could fit into my spot at the company, I thought I would end up driving into the ocean.

But with her along for the ride, it's been so much different. Not only have I laughed more than I knew I would have, but I've smiled, had good sex, smoked good weed, and it's been nothing short of memorable. Fuck my parents, honestly. What they don't know and will never find out about won't kill them.

And I may have destroyed an asshole's company along the way too. He deserved worse, honestly, and it pisses me off that I didn't get to see his face when everything went down. All it took was a few phone calls. Those were the easiest calls I've made in my entire life, and I did it all for a girl currently sitting quietly in the passenger seat of the truck.

If it were up to me, she would never know what I did for her because what I did meant nothing. I keep telling myself that, but in my mind, I know why I did it. Deep down, I knew exactly what I was doing when I pressed the call button.

And I don't regret what I did because he fucked with the wrong person.

How dare he sell all of her stuff? If he *really* knew her, he would know how much those records meant to her. He's a piece of shit and he got what was coming to him. I just sped up the karma that was eventually headed his way.

But back to the girl in my passenger seat. She's been quiet on this entire drive back, and the thing I can't pinpoint is why she's not speaking or really doing anything. Normally, she's easy to read, but right now, I can't seem to figure her out.

"Are you okay?" The question slips out before I mean it too. I can't stand feeling awkward with her. After all we've been through on this trip together, you would think talking about real shit would be the easiest thing for us, but it's not.

"Yeah," is all she says, and I can tell she's lying.

"Are you worried about the next part of our deal?"

"No," she says, finally turning her knees toward me in the passenger seat. "But if you're going to force me to talk, then I'm putting music on."

"Fine by me," I say with a smirk. "And I'm not forcing you to talk, but the air in this car is far too dense for my liking and we still have like seven hours of driving."

Teags scrolls on her phone before she finds a playlist suitable to start playing and before I know it, she's fully turned to face me.

"So, what's the plan when we get back?"

"The plan?" I ask, confused.

"Yeah because I'm currently homeless but Bree knows about everything we've been doing, so I could probably stay with her—"

"Woah, woah, woah. Bree knows *everything*?" Has she told her about our on the road pact too? Am I going to be totally fucked when I get home? Is Tristan going to be standing outside of my house with a baseball bat waiting for me to get home with his sister in my passenger seat?

"She's not going to tell my brothers." She looks away from me. "But Vince and Nico know too."

"Okay." I pull the car over. "How the fuck do they know and why?"

"Wow, and people call me dramatic."

"Teagen."

Her eyebrows shoot up. "Oh, fuck, not the full name."

"Spill."

"Nico tracked my location and I told him because I had to. He was worried, and due to things you don't know and I can't tell you about, I told him what was going on. I've been updating him since he called me. And Vince knows because Bree knows. If she can't tell her sister or Tristan, then she can tell Vince."

I sigh heavily, hating that people know this and it's all going to get blown out of proportion when I get back. This could end horribly, and I'm already not looking forward to Tristan punching me in the face when it does.

Or worse.

And I know Vince and Nico are going to want to talk to me too. Those two are nosy and protective of the girls. Rightfully so, especially after everything Bree has been through, but they're going to ask me a thousand dumb questions that I'm going to have to thoroughly answer when we get back.

I can't *wait* for that conversation.

"Fine, but did you tell Bree about..." I trail off because she already knows where I'm headed.

Her cheeks flush and I have the answer I was looking for.

"She's my best friend. You wouldn't believe the things we talk about."

"Yeah, I bet," I say as I lean back in my seat.

"Okay, now let's go," she says as she reaches over and turns my signal on for me.

I grab her hips and set her back down in her seat. "No."

"No?"

"Stop worrying about being homeless. You'll be staying with me for the time being."

Her eyes widen in shock as if she wasn't expecting me to say that. "Is that a joke cause it's not very funny."

"No, I'm not joking. On one hand, if we're going to convince my parents we're actually dating, it would make the most sense to have you live with me for a little while."

"Are you worried about them dropping by?"

"No, but I can never be too careful," I say, running a hand through my hair. "On the other hand, I like having you around. This trip was a lot better because you were on it, and maybe I'm a selfish son of a bitch, but I wouldn't mind having you in my space for a little longer, especially since your part of the deal is only just beginning."

Her lips part and I almost think she's going to say something, but she continues to stare at me.

"Does that sound okay to you? I figured you could sleep in the guest bedroom and you can stay as long as you need to until you get back on your feet."

She's frozen like a statue in my passenger seat before she launches into me, her arms around my neck as she melts into me as much as the seatbelt will let her.

"Thank you," she says into my neck, and when she pulls back, her eyes are glassy. "That sounds perfect. I promise I won't overstay my welcome."

"Overstay as much as you want, Teags."

Eyes still locked on me, she whispers so low I almost can't make it out. "I assume our pact is over when we get home."

"Well, yeah, it was only an on the road thing, right?"

She nods her head so fast I feel like I should be offended. "Yeah, yes, of course."

I smile, but I certainly don't feel that great. My stomach feels like it fell to my feet, and I really don't want to unpack that. There's no way these are feelings... right? I've never really had those for anybody before, but I know I've never felt how I feel with Teags with anyone else before. But I'm sure that's a purely platonic thing. Yeah, we've fucked a few times, but that was it. There are no feelings involved on my end.

I turn my signal on, and it takes about twenty more minutes for either of us to say anything.

"So, what do these events look like? I'm trying to mentally prepare myself."

"Well, they're really just a bunch of mingling. Sometimes, there are auctions and random shit to raise money for, but most of it is networking and showing off to other business men and women. My parents like to make it a family affair, but nobody can ever show up with an empty arm. Most of the time, they would set me up with someone for the night, but I'm getting really tired of that—"

"Hence, where I come in," she says before she lightly punches my arm. "I will try my best to say nothing, look pretentious, and see if I can steal some of Bree's dresses to wear."

I shake my head at her. "I'll take you shopping when we get back. I'll buy you a few things my parents will deem up to their standards."

"Oh, okay. I can—"

"Stop offering to pay me back and accept the fact that I like buying stuff for you. You're helping me out a lot. It's my way of thanking you."

She adjusts her glasses on her face. "Well, you helped me out a lot too. And you..." she trails off.

"What?"

"You destroyed his company."

Fuck, how did she find out? I bet Vince or Nico told her. Those two fuckers always seem to know everything. I guess they would be terrible at their jobs if they didn't, though.

"Yeah, I did. And I would do it all over again the same way. He shouldn't have treated you how he did. He deserves worse, and if you're going to ask me to apologize or undo it, I won't. Nobody messes with the people I care about and gets away with it."

"I wasn't going to say that. I was going to thank you."

"Oh, were you now?" I say with a smirk, and by the time my eyes meet hers, she's rolling her eyes.

"Don't get used to it."

"Don't worry, baby, I won't," I say as I press a kiss to her hands without thinking, and the rest of our drive is spent listening to an audiobook she put on, the weird feeling in my gut still there even after we get back to my house.

I might be fucked, but for now, I'm going to pretend this is still a mutually beneficial agreement between the two of us. Nothing more and nothing less.

No matter how easy it is being around her and how much I'm going to hate having to watch her move on in the future with someone else.

But of course, I shove those thoughts down and head straight into my shower, needing to sleep for about four days.

Chapter Twenty-Four

Dominic

— AUGUST BY FLIPTURN

I THROW ALL OF my clothes into my laundry basket as I unload my suitcase, throwing all of my small bags onto the side of my bed. I'd normally send it out, but I'm too exhausted to do that, so I'm going to do it myself.

Since we've been back, Teags and I have barely spoken. It's only been a few days, but we've avoided one another throughout the day, the two of us barely leaving our rooms besides to eat. Even then, I barely see her.

We haven't really talked about anything. Even when she cornered me in the car about destroying Gregory's company, I didn't bother elaborating on anything. She just thanked me and we got home and crashed. We both know where this is headed. After she helps me out with my parents, the two of us will go our separate ways and that will be that.

We will no longer be a present tense conversation, we'll both remain in one another's pasts and that has to be enough. I'm starting to think that isn't going to work for me, but I shove those thoughts away because it has to work for me. The two of us can't be anything else.

A soft knock at my bedroom door shakes me out of my thoughts, and in walks the girl I can't seem to stop thinking about.

"Hi," she says as she sits on the end of my bed. "Finally unpacking, huh."

"Yeah," I say as I throw a pair of pants into my hamper. "I was too exhausted to attempt it before."

"Me too," she tells me as she pushes her glasses up her face. "Can I use your washer and dryer or do you want me to wait?"

"What's mine is yours," I tell her. "I can do my laundry whenever."

"Okay," she says as she smooths her hair out. Is she nervous?

There's a few beats of awkward silence before I break it. "Is that all you came to ask me?"

"Are you avoiding me?"

Her question surprises me. "What?"

"Are you avoiding me because we had sex and now it's awkward and—"

I grab her shoulders with my hands and stop her ridiculous statements. "I'm not avoiding you. First of all, we've both barely left our rooms because of how tired we've been, so I was letting you rest."

"Oh."

"And second of all," I say as I drag my hands up and down her shoulders. "It's not awkward. Yeah, we fucked while we were on the road, but now we're home and—"

"And we're not doing that anymore."

"That was the deal we made," I remind her.

"Exactly, so everything is fine and I was just overthinking things," she says, but it sounds like she's trying to convince herself more than me.

"Everything is fine," I reiterate as I close my suitcase and leave it on the floor. "Now, let's go watch a movie and eat some breakfast, okay?"

She nods, and I grab her hand and practically drag her down the stairs, pulling her into my kitchen and sitting her down so I can make her some food. I wouldn't say I love to cook, but when there's someone else in my presence, I enjoy making a meal for them, which is exactly what I'm doing for her.

She watches me work while I make us some omelets and I'm almost done when I see her head off to the living room, probably picking some weird ass movie for us to watch while we eat.

I plate our food and grab some coffee for us before I set our plates on my coffee table, and she presses play on the movie.

"You had to pick the goriest film I've ever seen to watch while we eat breakfast, didn't you?"

"It's been a while since I've seen it," she jests as she gets up and heads to the kitchen, coming back moments later with some creamer for my coffee. She pours it for me and puts it back in the fridge, that small gesture making me feel all sorts of weird.

Fortunately, I don't have time to dive into it because I hear cars locking in my driveway.

"Are you expecting people this morning?" she asks me.

"No," I say as I head over to my window, seeing the boys walking up to my place. My heart starts to race in my chest and my body moves before my brain has time to digest what's going on, I'm shoving Teags up the stairs.

"Dom, what the—"

"Your brother is about to walk into my house," I say before her eyes bulge out of her head and she nods, heading into her room and softly shutting the door. I practically sprint back to my couch before they come in, and I switch the movie to some news channel before they all burst through my door.

"Welcome home, you son of a bitch," Tristan says as he waltzes into my living room. "It's good to see you, buddy."

"Do you feel like a changed man?" Vince asks me as he pats me on the back.

"Not at all," I smirk as I notice Harry is standing behind Vince and using him as some sort of human shield. "Harry, I'm not going to punch you."

"But I killed one of your pets," he says, his voice shaking. I can't help but laugh.

"Technically, they killed each other," I tell him. "And it sucks, but hey, that's nature for you."

The boys eye me curiously, and I feel like I'm on the spot. There's no way they know Teags is upstairs, right? Oh, fuck, what if they hear her? Or what if they go up there and accidentally walk into that room instead of the bathroom to the left of her door?

This is too fucking risky, but for some reason, I don't hate it. In fact, I like feeling like this again. When I thought I was going to be working for my parents for the rest of my life, it was as if all the emotions got drained from my body and I was living like a goddamn robot.

Now, I feel like happy-go-lucky motherfucker, and I owe all of that to the girl I'm currently stowing as a fugitive in my fucking house. She's the reason the trip went so well. She's the reason I didn't loathe myself entirely while we drove across the country. She's the reason why there's a little bit more laughter in my life than there was before.

And I shoved her away into her room like a fucking idiot.

"Why do you have two omelets, dude?" Tristan asks me as he sits on my couch. "And two cups of coffee?"

Shit.

"Pardon me for being hungry *and* exhausted after driving across the country for weeks at a time," I play it off. "I'm still a little out of it."

"Clearly," Harry says as he takes the seat farthest from me.

"How did you guys even know I was back? I don't even know where my phone is, if I'm honest."

"Ethan told us when you were getting back," Tristan says. "He also told us you gave him one of your cars, which is ridiculous because I remember you telling us you would *never* let any of us borrow one of your fancy cars."

"It was an even trade," I tell him. "And that still reigns true."

"Prick," is all Tristan says to me before he takes a sip of Teags's coffee. "When did you start drinking coffee straight? Oh, fuck, the business life has truly gotten to you."

"We have to save him," Harry says, rather dramatically might I add.

"Aw, he's growing up," Vince mocks me and Tristan high-fives him.

"Why am I friends with you guys again?"

"Because we're the only people that can deal with you," Harry tells me. "And the real reason we came over is to continue our darts tournament. It's been far too long, and if I recall, I was winning before you went on this road trip."

"Only by a few," I remind him. "I'm still sitting pretty in second place."

"It's amazing that I'm in third." Vince shakes his head. "I'm a trained fucking shot and I can't seem to figure out darts."

"You can't win them all, Vincey," Tristan reminds him.

"Yeah, well, you're in last," I remind him before he flips me off.

"I've been practicing," Tristan tells us before he gets up and heads for my basement. "You guys coming or what?"

"You two go ahead," Vince tells the other two. "I want to talk to Dom about something."

I turn to face him, curious as to why he's not being more specific.

"Business talk," he tells them.

"Boring," is all Harry says as he flips the basement door open and Tristan follows. "Don't take too long or you'll get docked on points and Tristan will be ahead of you both."

"That's fucking cheating," I remind them as they head down the stairs and out of sight. "You're not going to kill me or something, are you?"

"Where the fuck is she?" he whispers to me.

"What?"

He only rolls his eyes before he grabs me and practically shoves me up the stairs, opening the door to my room before he does a sweep of it like I've seen him do a thousand times for Bree.

"This would be a lot faster if you just told me where she is and if she's okay."

I'm about to open my mouth and tell him she's fine before he opens the door to the guest room, and there Teags is, sitting on the bed reading a book.

"Uh, hi?"

"Dude, shut the door," I say as I softly close it behind us.

"Vince, I'm fine."

"Bree is convinced you're not," he tells her as he sits on the end of her bed. "And if my girl is nervous, then I'm nervous. So, tell me you're okay, and then I can go downstairs and kick his ass in darts."

"That's a bold statement to make, but whatever."

WHAT THE FUCK IS going on?

"Just tell me you're okay so we can all stop worrying."

"I'm sorry, what?" I ask him.

"Nico was worried you were having some sort of life crisis, which you probably are. Bree has been pacing around the house wondering when she could see you. When Tristan invited me to come surprise this dumbass this morning, she wanted me to check in on you and let you know you can stay with us if you need to."

"That's not necessary," Dom tells him.

"I'd like to hear it from her."

I roll my eyes. "God, you two are incessant."

"Well, that was uncalled for," Vince says. "I'm making sure you know you have options."

"Look, I didn't get to have my coffee yet, so pardon me if this is a little too straight forward, but I'm fine. I'm choosing to be here and I chose to go across the country with Dom and help him out when we got back. This isn't a Rapunzel type of situation where I'm trapped in this house and can't leave. Everything is fine, and I am fine."

Vince really looks at me, and I know he can tell I'm still drowning in certain areas of my life. My grief is still more prominent than ever, and I don't see myself ever getting out of that feeling, but for a moment there on the road, I felt alive again. For a moment, I found myself not thinking about the constant state of drowning I was in before I left Arizona.

For a moment, I felt like myself again.

Now that I'm back, I can feel it start to seep into my bones again. I can feel the chains of grief start to hook back onto me, and I don't know how to get it to stop.

"Just don't tell Tristan I'm here and it will all be fine," I remind him.

"Okay," he says in a softer voice. "But if he hurts you, or even steps out of line once, I better be the first person you call."

"Seriously?" Dom says, offense in his tone.

"Yeah, seriously," Vince says. "And I won't even be the person you have to worry about. That's Nico."

"Oh please," I scoff. "Nico is as soft as a fucking butterfly."

"You're friends with him," Vince reminds me. "Dom isn't. And you and I both know what Nico does to people who hurt the ones closest to him."

"It's going to be fine," I tell Vince. "I'll call Bree when you guys leave and reiterate that to her, okay?"

Vince only nods before he opens my door, leaving Dom and I here by ourselves. Before either of us can say anything, Dom leaves.

Was it something I said?

But then he comes back a few moments later, my coffee in his hand, the omelet in his other.

"Here," he says as he presses a quick kiss to my forehead. "I didn't want you to go hungry."

"Thanks," I say. "And I bet you didn't want me to go uncaffeinated for the rest of the day for fear of my stabbing your eyes out while you sleep."

"Well, I wasn't worried about that, but now I kind of am."

I smile to myself. "Good. I was worried we were getting too chummy for a second."

"And that would be a bad thing? Us getting closer than we are already?" He pauses at the door, his hand gripping the knob as he looks back at me, an expression I can't place.

"Go play darts with my brother, Dom," I tell him as I hear the boys cheering through the vents. "And don't lose. That's embarrassing."

He only laughs as he softly shuts my door, joining my brother and his friends in the basement while I pick my book up and eat my lukewarm omelet.

It's still one of the best mornings I've had in a while, even as I sit and listen to Dom hang out with his buddies, loving the noise that filters through the house Dom once told me was far too quiet.

Chapter Twenty-Five

Dominic

— FAST TIMES BY SABRINA CARPENTER

AFTER THE MOST STRESSFUL few hours trying to play it cool while the boys were at my house, I'm finally in bed. Not only was I having a heart attack any time Tristan went anywhere near my stairs, but I was scared Teags was going to accidentally make a noise and the boys were going to investigate.

They always did love messing with the girls I brought back to the apartment when we were in college. We were all assholes back then, and then Tristan met Livvy. We were still assholes, but Livvy brought a new vibe to our friend group, and all of us loved her as soon as we met her.

Thankfully, I managed to escape another close call with Tristan. I feel like the worst friend in the world for lying to him, but Teags is the one who has to talk to him about all this. I'm not going to get in the middle of a West family squabble. I'm also not going to take sides, and that's probably because I'm unsure of which side I would take.

I've been tossing and turning since I laid down earlier. I'm not sure if it's all of the stress I'm feeling about the first event next week, the fact that I'm lying to my best friend and harboring his sister as a fugitive in my house, or if it's from traveling across the country for weeks.

It could also be the normal stress of simply being a fucking human being. It's probably some mixed up version of all of those things, but all

I know is after sleeping for thirteen hours last night, I'm suddenly wide awake staring at my ceiling, wishing sleep would come.

That's the thing about wishes, though, they never actually come true.

I turn onto my side, trying to get comfortable, and as I close my eyes, I suddenly find myself missing the body that slept next to me all those nights on the road. I miss feeling her press up against me so much that when I woke up she was always draped over me, her hair sticking to my arms and chest. I never bothered moving her off of me because she looked so peaceful.

That's the only time I've ever seen her look like that—truly at peace. When she wakes up, I see the switch flip behind her eyes, and I know she's remembering everything that's happened the past two years.

And for some reason, my body misses hers next to mine. My brain longs for that connection we shared, albeit a means to an end while we were on the road. It's not like I can sneak into her bed without her probably smacking me with a pillow or worse. We both agreed to keep the pact on the road, and I have to honor that.

For once, I have to be a man of my word, even though the dumbass part of my brain is screaming at me to go for it and see what she does.

When did I get so used to having her next to me while I slept? When did she cement herself into my night routine? When did everything change in my mind and she became someone I reached for instead of someone I barely knew?

I knew this trip brought us closer together, and I thought I could do what I normally do—not get attached. And fuck me for getting attached to a girl I knew I couldn't have when all is said and done. All of this is my own fault.

I shouldn't have gotten used to the way her body molded to mine. I shouldn't have gotten used to the way my name used to flow off of her lips, whether she was mad at me, annoyed, or turned on. I shouldn't have memorized the way she squinted her eyes when she didn't have her glasses on.

I shouldn't have, but I did anyway.

Fuck, I'm a selfish son of a bitch. I don't even care if I did all of those things. I don't regret a single thing about what happened between us on the road. But I know I can't keep pretending like I wish we could have had a never ending trip—that's just wishful thinking.

I last about fifteen seconds before I get out of bed, not bothering to throw a shirt on, and I swing my door open, fully prepared to softly knock on her door to see if she's awake, but I don't even get two steps out of my room.

Because she's already standing on the other side of my door.

"Can't sleep?" I ask, trying not to drool at the sight of her. She's wearing a navy pajama set, her glasses probably on her side table in her room, and her hair is tied up in a loose bun, a few strands peaking out in the front.

She's fucking gorgeous, and somehow I haven't driven her away yet. Somehow she seems to feel this... pull that I do. Is the pull for something more like a real relationship? I have no idea. I'm not even sure I'm equipped for something like that.

All I know is my head feels less shitty when she's around. My body misses her touch, and I can't seem to sleep without her next to me.

"Nope. I didn't wake you, did I? I've been pacing around here for a few minutes."

"You didn't wake me."

The two of us are quiet for a few seconds as we look between each other. She's staring at my arms and the tattoos that cover them. One thing I learned about Teags on the road is that she has some sort of thing with arms and hands. She would always stare at mine, her gaze lingering on certain tattoos and the veins that run down them.

"I'll just go—"

She goes to turn back, but I grab her by the waist before she can and carry her into my room, shutting my door with my foot as she squirms in my arms.

"Let's get into bed, Teags."

"No, it's fine, really. We agreed to it being on the road only, and now we're home, so—"

I open my covers for her and she climbs in, still protesting as she gets comfortable and I slide in next to her, my arms going around her waist and pulling her closer to me.

"Are you done, baby?"

Not a single word comes from her mouth.

"Good. How about we do whatever feels right and say fuck it to the only on the road thing?"

She shrugs against my body. "That sounds good to me."

"Glad we're on the same page."

And for some reason, when her body is against mine and I can feel the steady rise and fall of her chest, I finally relax. My shoulders fall, my jaw loosens, and I can almost feel my heart rate steady out.

Fuck.

A few minutes after we've adjusted to each other's breathing, I speak again, needing to get this off of my chest.

"I didn't mean to make it seem like I was trying to hide you earlier."

She shifts her body so now she's facing me, both of us sharing my pillow with how close we are. "My brother came over, Dom. You know, the one who still thinks I'm in Arizona? It didn't bother me that you practically shoved me up the stairs earlier on his surprise visit."

"I know, but I felt weird about it."

"Well, stop being weird. It was fine. I finished unpacking as quietly as I could and then read half of a book. It was a relatively nice day, but now, I'm trying to sleep, so if you don't mind, I'm going to do that."

And then she flips over, her hair smacking me in the face and I laugh as I pull her into my chest again. I can barely think before my eyes get heavy and I fall asleep to the sounds of her breathing, my own thoughts becoming quiet until all I can seem to think about is the girl in my bed falling asleep in my arms.

GETTING OUT OF BED while she's still asleep in my arms should be a crime, but it's been days since I worked out, and I have to run out some of this tension in my body before I explode.

I do my usual morning routine, again taking the blender outside so as to not wake Teags, before I get started on my usual route. I have to say, this is one of the only things I missed about Pennsylvania besides the boys while I was gone. Working out in shitty hotel gyms just doesn't compare to the running route I have here at home.

About halfway through my run, my phone starts to ring, and I don't look at it before I answer. I'm assuming it's Teags, even though I left her a note on the side table to help herself to breakfast if she woke up before I got back.

"Dominic." One word is really all it takes for my parents to piss me off.

"Mother," I say, knowing my father is lingering somewhere in the background. "What did I do to deserve hearing your voice so early in the morning?"

"For once, you did your job. And according to all the franchising offers we have, you've apparently done something well. I have to say, we didn't see this coming."

Oh, lovely. My father has deemed me good enough to be an employee. I wonder when he'll deem me good enough to be his son? I still have a good decade before that happens, or maybe on his deathbed he'll suddenly want to act like my father and not like I'm a business asset.

"If you're waiting for a thank you, it's not coming. I'm capable of doing my job and doing it well, regardless of what you two thought going into this excursion you made me go on."

"And it worked out well for both parties. We'll be expanding to a bunch of brand new locations, and you showed us you can be serious about the family business. Now, all you have to do is go to a few events and your job at the company will be secured. We'll call around and find a date for you for the event next week."

I stop my mother from hanging up her phone because I can't have her setting me up when Teags is coming with me. "Don't worry about that, Mother. I'll be bringing someone along."

"Oh. And who might this be?"

I don't think I've ever caught my parents so off guard. I can practically feel their anxiety through the phone. Good, they should feel like this. It's how I feel every time I conversate with them.

"My girlfriend. You'll meet her at the event." The longer I can keep my parents away from Teags, the better. I don't need them digging their claws into her, her family, her past, and anything else they might find. The longer I can put that off, the better.

But it's inevitable. My parents always find out what they need to know about people, legally or not so much. It's why they're so good at their jobs.

"Oh. What's her name? Does her family have money? What business do they run?" my father asks me.

God, these fucking questions. My parents are the most shallow people on the planet.

"You'll meet her at the event and not a second sooner. If that's all, I have to go."

I end the call before they say anything, and I know I don't have to worry about them coming over because they would have to care about me to want to drop by and see if I'm telling the truth.

And now, all I want to do is get home as soon as possible, so I turn around and as soon as I get home, I hear banging coming from my kitchen. As soon as I step into my kitchen, I see Teags fighting with my blender, trying to make a smoothie.

"This thing sucks."

"You need more orange juice," I tell her as I sneak past her to grab water from the fridge, my hands grazing her hip as I do. "Here."

She takes the juice from my hands and blends it as I stand against the counter, watching her as she makes breakfast.

Never did I think I would enjoy having someone in my house making breakfast the morning after we slept together. Normally, I would kick them out or they would leave, already having gotten what they wanted from me the night before.

But with Teags, I like seeing her fighting with my appliances as I come back from my morning run. It's nice having someone stay until the morning and not want to rush out of my presence as soon as they can.

"Our first outing as a couple is next week, so unfortunately, you can't back out of this now."

She stops the blender, pours her smoothie into a glass before handing half of it to me. "That's fine. I'm in this with you."

"Good," I say as I take a sip, positioning my body behind her before I drop my mouth to her ear, pressing a small kiss in one of her favorite spots. I already feel ten times better after the conversation with my parents. All because of her—the girl floating around my kitchen wearing one of my shirts. "You look fucking beautiful wearing that, baby."

"Dom," she says as she turns around. "Go take a shower."

"Whatever you say, fake girlfriend," I tell her as I take the smoothie and head up the stairs. "You better be ready to go shopping when I'm done."

All I hear is a groan as I head into my room, a huge, shit-eating grin on my face.

Chapter Twenty-Six

— DO I WANNA KNOW? BY ARCTIC MONKEYS

As I walk out in the only dress Dom picked out, he immediately starts laughing.

"I'm going to go back to the changing room," I say as I turn around and walk down the stupid runway back to the room. This place Dom took me too isn't busy, but I hate that he's making me model all of these. I don't know how many events I'm actually going to, so he's making me buy a bunch of dresses and shoes.

I hate that he's spending all of this money for something that's going to be short lived. It feels like a waste to me, but he keeps insisting.

"Excuse me?" he says to the attendant helping us out. "Can you find some black dresses for us? It's her favorite color."

I hate that my heart flutters at the fact that he knows that. It means nothing. He's putting this facade on to practice for what we'll have to do in front of his parents.

I sigh heavily as I turn around, my big, poofy, pink dress flowing behind me as I shiver when I pass by the huge mirror. I hate how bright I look.

After a few minutes of the attendant not coming back, I poke my head out and see Dom on his phone, scrolling on something.

"Can you help get me out of this thing?" I swear the attendant helping is trying to suffocate me with how tight she clipped this dress to my body.

"Coming, baby." I once again ignore how his chosen term of endearment makes me feel, and he closes the small curtain as he comes in. "How do I do this?"

"Take the clips off carefully and set them in the small bowl," I tell him. "And hurry before I rip this dress clean off."

"Even if it kills me, I'll make you enjoy shopping," he says under his breath as he takes the clips off. The attendant tries to come in halfway through, but Dom sends her away and promises to help me with whatever I need. She agrees as he slips her a few hundred bucks.

God, he's such a rich asshole sometimes, but I do feel a little better now that she's not going to bother us. It takes the edge off a little bit, and I'm thankful for that.

"Which one do you want to try next?" he asks me as I peruse the new dresses she brought and my eye catches on one with a huge slit and a pair of gorgeous black pumps underneath.

I grab it and step into it, not caring if he is seeing me half naked. It's not like he hasn't seen it all before.

"Can you zip me?" I say as I grab my hair and get it out of his way. I feel his hands caress my back as he trails down to the zipper. He presses a kiss to my shoulder next to the small black strap before he zips it fully, the dress fitting me like a glove.

It's tight, but not so tight where I can't breathe—which will be good for when I get nervous about being around his parents. It's scrunched in the front, and the slit goes high up my right leg, showing off my favorite part of my body. The heels make my legs even longer when I put them on, and when I walk out and see myself in the mirror, I smile.

I look really fucking hot, and I love this dress.

"Fuck," is all I hear from behind me as he steps out and takes a long, sweeping look over my body.

"I'm going to have to practice walking in heels," I say as I take a few small steps around the runway. Gregory always made me wear small, kitten heels. These stilettos are an entirely different ballgame. "If I fall on my face in front of your parents, I might die of embarrassment."

I look back at Dom, expecting him to have some stupid quip, but his mouth is slack and he's barely paying attention to anything I'm saying.

"Dom? Are you in there?" I ask as I walk toward him. "Do you think your parents will like it or is it too much?"

"Fuck my parents. You're getting the dress and the shoes."

"Perfect. Now, only a few more," I say as I step back behind the curtain. "I guess this isn't so bad after all."

"I don't want to tell you I told you so, but I did. Shopping isn't that bad, especially when you have a hot, rich man buying you pretty things."

I turn to face him as he unzips my dress for me. "I never said you were hot. Don't flatter yourself."

"Hmph," is all I hear him say as I continue trying on the darker colored dresses and shoes the attendant brought me.

About two hours and a bunch of dresses later, I've officially made it to the last one. I've picked out six different dresses in a variety of styles, as well as three pairs of shoes that I can wear interchangeably.

The last dress is beautiful though. It's a silk, cream colored dress with a cowl neckline. It drapes beautifully over my body and I like it, but I'm not sure if it will be good enough for these events.

"I don't know, maybe it's the color?" I say as I shift my stance in the mirror, trying to figure out why I'm unsure about it. "It doesn't feel right."

"You're overthinking it. You look stunning. Add it to the yes pile, and we can get the hell out of here," Dom says from behind me, his eyes still frozen on me like they have been for the past few hours.

"Fine, but please do not show me how much this is all going to cost or I won't sleep for months."

"Turn around and let me get the buttons."

"Can you unlatch my shoes first? My feet are killing me. These shoes are like small torture chambers," I say as Dom kneels in front of me, about to undo my shoes for me but all he does is run his hands up and down my calf. "Is something stuck? Oh God, am I trapped in these things?"

"Everything is fine."

"Then what are you doing?"

He looks up at me, his eyes hooded and his voice low as he speaks again. "Do you want the truth or a lie?"

"Preferably the truth."

His hand grazes my calf even lighter than before, and I swear my entire body just came alive. Every touch feels magnetized, and I already know what he's thinking about before the words even come out of his mouth.

"I'm thinking about you wearing only these heels as I fuck you. It's all I've been able to think about since you stepped out in that first black dress."

"What happened to no sex while we're back?" My voice is far too wispy for this conversation. "We're not on the road anymore, Dom."

"And what if I said I screw that stupid rule and fucked you in this dressing room?"

God, I can't really say no to that. My brain is screaming at me that this is wrong in about a thousand different ways, but for some reason, I can't seem to care. I've noticed the way he's been looking at me since we've been here. I've seen him clenching his fists as if he has to stop himself from reaching out to me.

"I'd say that sounds perfect."

And then his hands are on me, his mouth is pressing against mine, and he's reaching under my dress frantically trying to pull my underwear down before he puts them in his pocket.

"This dress is fucking beautiful on you," he says in between kisses.

"Thanks, I—"

"Take it off before I rip it to shreds."

Fuck him for bossing me around. Never mind the fact that I enjoy hearing him like this, voice filled with lust and eyes draping over my body as if he can't wait to devour me.

I somehow get all of the buttons undone in record time before his hands are around my thighs, practically holding me up in these shoes as he kisses from my mouth down to my legs. He sets me on the small ledge in here, before he drags his eyes all over my body, really taking me in as if he hasn't seen me like this before.

He looks like he's starved, his eyes full of lust as he kneels in front of me, still entirely clothed. The black compression shirt is not helping to calm me down, his muscles and tattoos are also driving me *insane*.

He starts to lean forward, his face coming toward my center, but I stop him with a heel to his chest.

"What the hell are we doing, Dom? We're in public."

"So?" he asks, a stupid smirk on his face. "I paid her a few hundred to leave us alone," he starts to inch forward toward me, my heel digging further into his chest. "As long as you can be quiet for me, I don't think we'll have a problem."

"Why don't you shove my underwear in my mouth then," I say as I get even more hot and bothered. "You should know I'm a screamer."

"Oh, baby, I know," he tells me as he slips it out of his pocket, balling them before he grabs my chin, opens my mouths, and gently puts them in my mouth. "Now be quiet or else I'll stop."

I nod, and as soon as he sees that, he throws my leg over his shoulder, and starts to devour me. I can barely sit still, but his hands steady my hips on the small ledge, his mouth warm and wet against my center. He swirls his tongue around my clit, so gently it drives me insane. He knows exactly how I like it from how much we fooled around on the road, and he doesn't let up even when I start to squirm all over the place.

"God, you taste like a fucking sin," he says before he bites the skin of my thigh. "I could do this all fucking day, but if I'm not inside of you in the next thirty seconds, I might fucking die."

I roll my eyes, noting how dramatic that sounds, but my pussy has been pulsing since his mouth was on me, and I can't wait any longer.

"Please," I say through my constraint. "Do you have a—"

"Fuuuuuuck," he shakes his head. "Not with me, no."

"It's okay," I tell him, the underwear falling from my mouth. "I'm on birth control."

"Baby, no, I'm—"

"Have you fucked anyone else besides me in the last few months?"

He shakes his head.

"I haven't either."

"I got checked before I left," he tells me, staring down at me. "Are you sure?"

"I'm sure." I trace my heel around his chest. "Please fuck me."

"I'm coming, baby," he says before he grabs my waist, scoops me up in his arms, my heels going around his back, and he centers himself before he thrusts into me, pushing us against one of the walls. "So fucking wet for me. You feel like a fucking dream," he says, brushing some of my hair out of my face.

"I need you to move," I say as I adjust to his size. "Please."

With that final plea, he does. He fucks me softer than he normally does so we're not shaking the fucking walls of this place. This angle is so different than I've felt before, and the fact that someone could walk in on us and see what we're doing turns me on more than I care to admit.

Dom is dangerous to me in more ways than one. At this moment, I *need* him, but at the same time, I *want* him. I want him like this more often. I want him with his walls down and I crave him every time I see him. We've been sleeping in the same bed pretty much since we've been back, and he's been respectful of our agreement.

Now, we're entering uncharted waters, and that scares the shit out of me.

"I need you to be quiet for me," he stares into my eyes and I nod, not wanting to say a word. "Good fucking girl."

And then he starts to move again, hitching me up in his arms for a better grip as my hands find his hair, pulling on it enough to drive him crazy, my other hand scratching the shit out of his back with my nails.

Every inch of my body is on fire, my control unraveling with every thrust, every grunt by him to remain in control as he can be. He can't go as hard as he normally does, but he knows I want him to.

"You're gripping me so tightly, baby," he whispers in my ear, his hands digging into my back as he tightens his hold on me. "God, you feel like a dream. Does it turn you on that I'm fucking you raw in public? Do you think anyone knows what a good fucking whore you're being for me in here?"

I can feel myself clench around him, his words filtering through my brain and heading right for my pussy. Dom and his dirty talk could get me off without even touching me.

"Please, I'm so close," I beg as he thrusts harder, my pleas making him go even crazier than before.

"Coat my fucking cock," he says to me, his hair falling in front of his face as he watches himself fuck me. "Just like that. Good girl, baby," he says as I fall off of the edge, his breath against my body driving me insane. I try my best to silence my moans, and I don't think I'm doing too good of a job, but I can feel his dick start to pulse inside of me as I come.

"Come inside of me," I say to him. "I want to walk out of this place with your cum dripping out of me."

"Fuck, baby, shit," he says as he lets go. I put my hand over his mouth as he moans into it, staring into my eyes as he unravels, his eyes practically rolling to the back of his head, the two of us breathing heavily as we come down from our highs.

"What fun is having rules if you can't ruin them, right?" I say and the two of us start to laugh as he sets me down, still holding onto me because I can barely feel my fucking legs. I sit on the small ledge and rip my shoes off, my feet killing me.

"You are the fucking devil, Teagen West."

"That doesn't sound like a bad thing." I bat my eyelashes at him. "Can we buy these shoes? I actually quite like them."

"I'll buy you anything you want," he says as he puts himself back together. I bend over to reach for the clothes I walked in here in, and I feel him grab my ass and spread it open. "Fuck, look at how pretty you look with my cum dripping out of you."

"I like it," I tell him as I put my bra back on. "It's our dirty little secret."

There's a flash of an emotion I can't place on his face, and as fast as I notice it, he hides it. "I'll let you change. I'll be at the checkout counter. Meet me there when you're done." Before I think he's going to fully leave, he presses a kiss to my lips, and I melt into him how I always do when his lips are on mine. "You're so fucking sexy. Don't ever forget that."

I smile at him as he leaves, and I take a few breaths to get my bearings, my emotions all over the place after the last few minutes.

What we're doing is dangerous. It's reckless. It's probably going to ruin everything, and I can't find a care in the world to tell him we should stop. I don't think he can either, but if we keep heading down this road, who knows what waits for us at the end of it.

I lie to my brain, reminding myself to stay in this moment and not worry about the future and what lies ahead, so I shove these feelings down, and walk out of the dressing room, right toward the man whose smile makes my heart skip a beat.

Fuck.

Chapter Twenty-Seven

— CAUTIOUS BY CASSIDI

Dom and I are existing in his living room, him working on something for work while I apply to some dead end jobs that make me want to stab myself with a fork. I know I have to have a plan for when this arrangement is done. I can't keep living here and mooching off of his kindness or whatever it is. I'm not really sure what to call what's going on between us anymore, but maybe that's for the best.

Friends with benefits? A mutually beneficial agreement? Who the fuck knows because I definitely don't and I'm not going to bother asking when I know he doesn't do relationships. Or I guess nobody has ever wanted him for one. At least that's the impression I'm under after all of our talks on the road.

If I wasn't so afraid I would tell him he would make a wonderful partner for the right girl. The right girl might be me, especially after what my heart has been feeling since we got home.

I've been wrestling with a lot of emotions since we got back, and part of me was happy to be feeling anything again, even if it confused the hell out of me. Dom breathed those feelings back into me and made me feel alive again. He made me feel like my stupid feelings made sense, and that I wasn't a burden like Gregory made me feel.

For the first time in a while, I feel wanted. Sexy. I feel worth the time and effort, and I don't know how to tell him I have these feelings for him, and I probably never will. We both agreed this was until he got what he needed from me and I already got what he promised me—my stuff back. I got to stick it to Gregory and even though what he did still stings, Dom made me feel like I wasn't overreacting when I was pissed that he sold all of my things.

I've never been so confused in my entire life, and with everything else so up in the air, feelings for Dom are the last thing I need to be sorting through, so maybe I'll table this until my life is back on track.

Or maybe it's not a real crush and I've been around him too much. I've been living in my own forced proximity romance novel for the past few weeks, so maybe my brain, heart, and body have simply latched on to him because of that?

A knock on the door stifles me from my spiral, and we look at one another because it could be Tristan.

"I'm going upstairs," I say as I close my laptop and head for the stairs. I hear him open the door, and the voice of my best friend filters through the house.

"Hello, Dominic. Can I talk to Teags?"

"She's not here," Dom says and I roll my eyes. I've been talking to Bree since we were at our first stop on the trip, and he knows she knows, so what is he doing? Is Tristan with her?

"Don't be stupid. Where is she?"

"Just open the door, dude," I hear Vince say, annoyed.

"Bree, she's not here. Now, please get off my property or I'll—"

"If you threaten my girl, you'll be the one leaving this property in a six foot long bag," Vince says. "And I saw her here the other day, so stop lying."

Nico holds his hand out to stop Vince from punching him in the face, I assume. "I tracked her location and I know she's here. We just want to see her, dumbass."

I step into view of them all and set my laptop on the couch. "Let them in, you idiot."

He whips his head back to me and lifts his eyebrows as if he's asking me if I'm sure about this.

"It's fine. Let them in," I say as Bree's eyes lock with mine. God, I've missed her. Phone calls really aren't the same as being in her presence. My best friend practically shoves Dom out of the way as she comes to hug me.

"I'm so glad you're home," she says into my ear.

That alone brings tears to my eyes because she's right. I'm home. Because home is wherever she exists. "Me too."

"If this one weren't holding you hostage," she says as she flips her head to stare at Dom, "then maybe we could have a never-ending sleepover."

"Maybe after this is all over, we can—"

"Teags, you're welcome to stay as long as you want. You know that," Dom says as he shuts the front door and locks it. "Does anyone want a drink or something?"

"It's like four in the afternoon," Vince says as he looks at me. "Nice to see you, psycho."

"You too, brood." I smile as I hit him on the arm.

Nico throws his arms around me, and when he pulls back, he grabs my hand and slaps it.

"What was that for?"

"For not telling me about what you two were up to and making me have to break the law to find out where you were."

"I apologized already, and it's not like you're one for having a moral code, Nico."

"That was so you never do it again. I was worried sick, Teags."

"Touch her again and the only one being slapped is you," Dom says as he comes back into the room, his gaze glued onto mine. "You okay?"

"I'm fine," I say, needing the tension in this room to lessen. "And it won't happen again, okay? I'll be home for the long haul, so you don't have to worry about that."

Nico simply nods before he takes a seat next to Vince on the couch, who's watching this all go down and already looks like he wants to leave even though he just got here.

"There's too much testosterone in here," I say under my breath before looking at my best friend. "What are you all doing here?"

"I missed you, and knowing you were sitting here at Dom's was driving me crazy."

"She also wants to know what the hell is going on between you two." Vince points between Dom and I, and Nico starts to laugh.

"Good luck getting anything out of that one," Nico says.

"Seriously?" Dom says as he slumps onto his couch. "There's nothing going on."

"Besides the fact that Teags is pretending to be your girlfriend in front of your parents so you aren't forced to marry some stupid socialite?" Bree asks him with a smile. "Or are you talking about all that transpired between you two while on the road?"

Damn. This is not what I was expecting when I heard the three of them on the porch.

"How much did you tell her?" Dom asks me.

"I'm not an idiot, you know? I wasn't born yesterday." Bree looks back and forth between the two of us and smiles. Vince and Nico are simply sitting back, huge smiles on their faces as if they're enjoying some sort of show. I should've smacked them both when I had the chance. "Do you remember what you told me at the event I threw last year?"

"Vaguely." Dom searches his brain for a recollection, but doesn't elaborate.

"We talked about your parents and how much you hated stupid events. So, when Teags told me she was helping you out with something, that was the only thing that made sense to me."

"And we didn't even have to help." Nico smiles. "But just so you two know, I would do anything illegal if you needed me to."

"Aw, how nice of you," Vince says.

"Isn't it? I think so," Nico agrees.

"So kind." Vince nods his head before he looks at Dom. "Give us an updated tour of your place."

"You were here the other day," I remind him.

"I wasn't," Nico smirks at me. "Let's go."

It's not a question, and before Dom can protest, Nico grabs him by the arm and they drag him outside, leaving Bree and I to ourselves.

As soon as I look at her, the details spill out of me. I tell her everything about Dom and I's relationship and how it's changed. I confess that I have no idea what I'm doing but my heart has somehow become tangled up in Dominic Graves and I'm not sure if I want to untangle it.

"Oh, wow," she says when I'm done. I keep pulling at the ends of my hair, terrified she's going to tell me that I'm a complete idiot, but she doesn't do that. She simply lets it all sink in and then she grabs my hand. "Vince and Nico are talking to Dom about who knows what, maybe you or maybe they're threatening him. But I figured you needed to talk it out, and I wanted to bring the boys to distract him so we could talk."

"I love you," I sigh heavily. "And I'm a fucking idiot."

"Maybe, but can I be honest?"

"Always."

"I've never seen you like this in all the years I've known you, babe." I tilt my head at her, confused as to what she means. "It's good seeing you happy. It's good seeing that light back in your eyes again. I know you were searching a lot when you were on the road. Did you find what you were looking for?"

I really think about her question because I haven't really sat down and thought about what I got from the trip. Originally, I set out to give myself a break, and I definitely feel refreshed. I'm also caught up on sleep and my reading goal.

But what did I actually come away with?

I sort of feel like myself again. I mean, I'm kind of a mess. I don't have a job, or a place to call my own, but I feel the most like myself than I've felt in years. No longer am I crying myself to sleep and being weighed down completely by grief. I'm not in an unhappy, dead-end relationship. I'm finally back with the people I love most in the world.

I found something new in someone unexpected. I'm not really sure what I feel for Dom, but I can acknowledge I do feel something for him. I guess that's what I still have to figure out. What exactly do I want from him at the end of all of this? It's going to be way too easy to fake being his girlfriend. I know that for sure. Everything with him is always so easy, and fun. I can't remember a time before now where I laughed as much as I have.

But I didn't find my brother. I still can't feel him, and that scares me the most. What if he never comes back to me through the music we used to love? What if his memory starts to fade in my mind and I forget about him? Gregory made sure all the records we shared were gone, yet another piece of my brother I won't be getting back. I didn't think I had much more to lose, but I was wrong.

That's the one thing that still worries me about all of this. Sure, I have his letter and I can still call his phone to hear his voice, but what happens when his number goes to someone else and they tell me to stop calling? What happens if I lose the letter?

And what happens if my feelings for Dom are simply because of our proximity? What if I fall back into old patterns and I can't get myself out of them this time?

Bree shakes me out of my spiral. "What are you thinking about?"

"How terrified I am about all of this."

She rubs her hand up and down my arm. "It's okay to be scared. If you're not scared, you're probably doing something wrong."

"What if he doesn't feel the same way?" I ask, self-conscious about this stupid crush I have on him. God, this is why I used to think love was stupid and embarrassing. I can't believe half of the things that are filtering through my brain, but here we are.

"Are you kidding me?" she asks as her eyebrows shoot up. "Have you seen the way he looks at you? Matter of fact, did you hear how he threatened Nico after he slapped your hand? I've never seen Dom so protective of someone before."

"Ugh." I let my head slump in between my legs. "This sucks."

"It might, but isn't it nice to feel things again?"

"I guess." Part of me is elated that Bree just said that. I know how long she spent not wanting to feel anything due to what happened with her stalker, and the PTSD and panic attacks that came with it. I watched her for years shove her feelings aside and pretend like she was fine for the sake of everyone else, and now she's finally experiencing emotions again on a semi-normal scale. It almost gives me hope for my own future. Maybe this darkness won't last forever.

She scooches closer to me. "Okay, well, switching gears off of Dom." She grabs my hand in hers. "How are *you* feeling?"

"I couldn't find him, Bree. And I can't hear him in my music."

"He'll be back, Teags. Maybe your brothers need him a little more than you do right now. You've got Dom, after all. Maybe Tobias is giving you space because you have a shoulder to lean on. Theo might not, especially since he's by himself up in Vermont."

"You're right," I tell her. "Why are you so good at this?"

"Therapy," she jokes and I laugh with her.

"If this all blows up in my face, can I move in with you?"

"Absolutely. Honestly, even if it doesn't, the offer is always on the table. You know I'd do anything for you. You're my best friend."

"You're mine too. I know I don't tell you a lot, but I love you, and I appreciate you, and I truly couldn't do life without you."

Her eyes sparkle and I feel tears start to come into mine. Fuck, I hate that I can feel things again because I basically cry at fucking everything now. I was sobbing my eyes out at one of my books the other day, and it wasn't even that serious, but it still got me.

I have emotions again. I feel alive again. I can feel my tears fall down my cheeks and even though that makes me want to jump for joy, I wish I could dial it back a smidge.

The three boys come back in and I know Bree and I are double-checking to see if they punched Dom, but he actually looks better than I imagined. Giddy, almost is how I would describe him, right now. What the fuck happened out there?

"You girls okay?" Vince asks the two of us.

"We're wonderful. In fact, we are going to go watch a movie, if that's okay with you all?"

"Watch it down here," Dom says as they walk over to us. "You all might as well stay for dinner."

"Are you sure?" Nico asks him.

"Have you got some place better to be?" Dom asks, that stupidly cute grin still on his face.

"Not really, no," Bree says. "There's no place else I'd rather be than with most of my favorite people."

"Well, if you're all staying, then I get to pick the movie," I say, grabbing the remote.

"You boys want to help me with dinner or no?"

"We might as well make ourselves useful," Vince says as he presses a kiss to Bree's forehead and heads for the kitchen, patting Dom on the back as he walks by him. But Dom is only looking at me. I swear he's going to say something, but all he does is smile and turn for the kitchen, not saying a single word.

But that one look meant something to me, and I know at some point we're going to have a long, truthful talk.

For some reason, my heart starts racing and I feel like a lovesick idiot as I sit myself next to Bree on the couch and the two of us watch our favorite show while the boys cook dinner for us before our movie night.

I really fucking missed it here, and I am so glad to be home.

Chapter Twenty-Eight

Dominic

— MOONLIGHT BY ARIANA GRANDE

I'M HALF ASLEEP BUT I bolt up, rub my eyes, and shuffle out of bed as soon as I don't feel Teags's hair on my face. Where could she have gone? My first stop is the guest room, wondering if she moved back in there. I haven't asked her about our arrangement the past few nights, but we seem to have a mutual understanding.

The only way either of us can seem to get sleep since we got back is next to one another. It's the weirdest thing I've ever experienced, and I wonder if I came on too strong. I wonder if our only on the road turned whenever we want agreement has fucked with her head as much as it has with mine.

The boys seem to think there's something serious going on with us. Nico and Vince all but cornered me when they came over. I wouldn't call it a threatening conversation, but they were pretty firm with me. I told them we were just fucking while on the road, but they didn't seem to believe me.

To be honest, as soon as the words left my mouth, I didn't really believe me either.

As soon as I head down the stairs and see her eating from a pint of ice cream, the panic in my bones stops. She turns around as soon as she hears me, and without saying a word, she grabs a spoon for me, placing it on the counter.

"Did I wake you?"

I shake my head. Her eyes stall on my arms before she continues eating, the two of us not saying a word to one another and simply enjoying the company.

Before this trip, this house felt stale. Boring. Sure, it's my home, but there was always something missing from it. I'd be crazy to say the missing piece was her, so I won't, but the energy in here feels different now that she's inhabiting my space.

"Couldn't sleep?" I ask her in between bites.

She shakes her head.

"Want to talk about it?"

"About what?"

I take another scoop. "About whatever seems to be keeping you up at night."

That earns me a shrug. "I think it's everything. I'm lying to my family. Everything that happened with Gregory is still eating at me. I miss my brother, and of course, y—" she cuts herself off before she finishes her sentence. "Forget it."

I grab her hand where she's trying to take more ice cream and I squeeze it. "You don't have to hide from me. Like I said on the road, I can be whoever you want me to be."

Her stubborn gaze finally meets mine and I'm struck with the weirdest feeling in the pit of my stomach.

"I was also thinking about you." She steals my spoon from me and grabs another bite.

"Has that crush returned or something?" I joke with her, but I notice she's not laughing or smiling.

"I don't know if I would call it that," she mumbles before I corner her on the other side of the counter. I spin her around so she's looking at me.

"What would you call it?"

"Curiosity."

"What are you curious about, baby?" I ask before I grab her hair tie and let her hair down, her long waves cascade down her body. Teags standing here in the middle of the night, in my kitchen looking like this, should be considered a fucking crime.

She's beautiful. The most beautiful person who has wanted to know the *real* me, not just the rich, playboy facade I put on.

"What are we doing, Dom?" she whispers. "Is this real or am I going crazy?"

"I don't have an answer for you," I tell her as I tuck her hair behind her ear. "I've never had someone like you. I've never felt the way that I do with you."

Her big, beautiful brown eyes latch onto the words I'm saying. I swear if I'm lucky enough to somehow have her look at me like this again in the future, I'll die a happy man.

"What do you mean by that?"

"I've never felt like anybody before, but when we were on the road, I felt like somebody to you. Not even because of the sex, but for the first time ever, you burrowed beneath my skin and I felt like I had somebody who I could tell every dark, terrifying thought to. You're terrifying, Teagen West."

"Terrifying, huh?" She smirks at me.

"The scariest thing I've ever held in my hands because now I finally understand that I have something in my life that I'm terrified of losing."

She sits with my words, the silence covering my moonlit kitchen as we look at one another.

"Can I be honest?" she whispers.

"Yeah, baby."

"I feel like too much of a mess to fall into something with you." She shakes her head to herself. "I *just* got out of a dead end relationship and part of me feels weird doing whatever we are. I still feel like my grief is suffocating me some days. I guess what I'm trying to say is I'm not doing great at this whole adulting thing."

"But?" I can tell there's one there.

She rolls her eyes at me. "But when I'm with you, I feel more like myself. I feel more alive than I have in a while, and I don't want to lose that."

"I'm not used to this either. Relationships are foreign territory to me, if that is where we are both talking about heading."

She nods. "It's weird to me too."

"So, how about we figure it out together?" I ask as I bring her into my chest, my hand brushing through her waves. "We have a few events to go to, so let's see how we feel after those, okay?"

"That sounds good to me." She lifts her head from my chest, a small smile peeking through. And before she can protest, I grab underneath her legs and sit her on top of the counter before I grab the ice cream and hold a spoonful out to her. "Thank you."

"You don't have to thank me for ice cream."

She shakes her head, her eyes shining in the low light of my kitchen. "Not for that. For being so kind to me when I showed up on your porch. For bringing me on the road with you. For being so fucking kind to me when you could have sent me right home. I feel like I have too much to thank you for and I'm going to pay you back—"

I stop her babbling with a kiss, her hands coming around my neck as she pulls me deeper into her. The first time I pressed my lips to hers, I knew she was dangerous to me, but now, I have her. I have this beautiful, magnificent girl in front of me who thinks I'm kind. She thinks I'm worth more than one night, and she's already proven that to me a few times over.

"You don't owe me a goddamn thing," I say against her lips in between kisses. "All I need is you. You in my arms, in my bed, in my fucking house." My head drops to her chest. "Just you."

"If I heard anybody else saying this to me, I think I would have thrown up or something." She laughs as I put the ice cream away. "God, you make me feel things that should be studied by science."

"Thanks?" I joke, the two of us laughing before I scoop her into my arms and bring her up the stairs, needing her wrapped around me in our bed. It feels like nothing can touch me as soon as we're comfortable, my hand in her hair and hers on my chest tracing some of the tattoos I have. "Do you want to talk about anything else?"

Her eyes meet mine and I know she knows what I'm talking about. "I have my brother's letter back, but every time I read it, I wish I had him. It doesn't feel fair. It doesn't feel *real* even though it's been two years. I wasn't ready for it. I didn't wake up that morning and prepare myself for what was going to happen, and I still feel like I'm searching for the ground to come back to my feet."

"That's completely normal, baby," I reassure her. "Grief has no time-line. Feel how you feel and every time you wake up, it might hurt a little less. Or maybe it won't, but with time and the people you have around you, we'll help you through it."

"I'll be older than him soon." She sniffles against me. "That's really been messing with my head. That in a few years, I'll be the same age as him and then I'll keep growing older but he won't."

"He would be really proud of you."

"I'm not so sure about that," she scoffs. "Even I'm not proud of who I am most days."

"Well, you should be." I grab her chin with my hand and make her look at me, fresh tears streaming down her face and onto my chest.

"Because you are magnificent. You are strong and even if you're only giving what you can, you should be proud of that. When I sit here and look at you, I'm fucking proud of you. And I know he would be too."

"Thank you," she says as I reach to grab her a tissue. "Sorry I'm—"

"Stop," I say as I wipe her tears. "If you need to cry, then cry. Your tears won't make me melt. If you want to scream, then scream into the pillow. Whatever you need, I'll be right by your side the entire time."

"I have a feeling you're going to ruin me for anyone else, Dominic Graves."

I smirk to myself as we lay back down. "Good because you've already ruined me, and I never want to go back to who I was before you walked into my life."

Chapter Twenty-Nine

Dominic

— BUT DADDY I LOVE HIM BY TAYLOR SWIFT

I'm pacing across the floor of my living room as I wait for Teags to come downstairs so we can go to this event. My heart rate has been high all fucking day, and I can't do anything to get rid of the nerves I'm feeling. It's been months since I've seen my parents in person, and I've thought of every scenario for how tonight could go, and every single one of them wasn't good.

My parents are snakes. They're always doing some sort of shady shit and I feel like the biggest idiot in the world for shoving Teags into their orbit. At the start of this, she agreed because it was a mutually beneficial agreement. Now, everything has changed, and I feel like the world's shittiest person for taking her to these things.

We haven't really used the proper relationship terms to describe one another yet, but she's all I imagine when I really think about my future. All I know is that these events are where we're testing the waters at being a couple. Part of me is excited I get to show her off in public, but my parents are taking all of the fucking fun out of this.

My phone rings and I pick it up before I even look at it.

"This is Dominic Graves."

"Is that how you answer the phone? You sound like a prick." Nico's voice filters through the line.

"How did you get my number?" I ask, an idea of how he did already forming in my head. Nico and I aren't friends even though we hang out in similar circles. He's more of an acquaintance I've come to know through Bree and Vince. "Is there a reason you're calling me?"

"Just checking in. I was going to be at the event tonight but some other business has pulled me away," he pauses. "How is she?"

"She's been calmer than I have the past few days, but other than that she's okay."

"I have to say, I really don't know what she sees in you," he jokes.

"Gee, thanks. This is really helping to calm my fucking nerves."

"You didn't let me finish," he tells me. "I really don't know what she sees in you, but you seem to make her happy. Just be careful tonight."

My eyes narrow as his words sink into my bones. "What the hell does that mean?"

"Her ex used to take her to these kinds of things and his parents were controlling and tried to stifle Teags and her voice for the entire time they were dating. Just be wary of that, buddy."

I already knew that, of course. We had a long talk last night when I kept us both up because I couldn't sleep, and she told me everything about Gregory and his stupid fucking parents. They told her what to wear, when to speak, all of it.

It killed me how they controlled her, and I promised her I would never do that. If anything, she's the one who's going to have to control me tonight. She's my tether to the ground right now, and I'm so fucking glad I have her by my side.

"You and I both know I would never do that to her. Not after the things I've seen and not after all she's told me."

"I know," he says. "I wanted to make sure we're both on the same page. I care about Teags. She's one of my closest friends and I'll always protect the people I love."

"That's understandable," I say as I hear heels clicking down my stairs. "I have to go."

"Best of luck, buddy," he says before hanging up. I don't know what parallel universe I entered into where Nico Wilder and I are buddies, but I can't say I hate it. He's got some good connections, and even though I don't know much about him, I know he's incredibly good at what he does—security, not including the illegal shit he does on the side.

My thoughts are cut off by the sexiest fucking woman on the planet. Teags is walking over to me, a smirk on her face as she comes up to me and smooths my jacket down.

"You clean up nice, Dom."

My jaw is still slack as I take her in. She's wearing black pumps, her long fucking legs driving me insane as I drag my eyes up her entire body. She's opted for the maroon dress I bought her—the corseted one or something—and part of me wants to stay home and worship her all night.

"Fuck, baby, the things you do to me," I say as grab a handful of her now curled hair. "You drive me insane."

"Good." She smiles, catching her lip in her teeth. "Can you fix my shoe for me?"

God, Teags and these fucking heels. The other day, I came home from a long workout at the gym to her walking around the house in these shoes, tiny fucking shorts, and a tank top. She told me she was practicing walking in them so she doesn't trip and fall in front of my parents and make a fool of herself.

I told her I'd catch her if she were to fall, and then she walked over to me, kissed me, slipped her tongue in my mouth, and we fucked on the floor right in my living room. This girl has made me crazy, insatiable, and I can't get enough of her. I would have brought her to our fucking bed, but she needed me right then and there and who I am to deny my girl of what she needs?

I sink to my knees, my hand tracing her leg on the way down. I take it off, massage her foot, and slip it back on, not moving to get up.

She grabs my chin with her hand. "Thanks, baby."

My head falls to her legs as I grab her hips in my hands. I press a kiss to the leg out of the slit in her dress before I get up and grab her neck.

"I'm wearing lipstick, Dom."

"I don't give a fuck," I say as I smash my lips into hers, needing to taste her. "I want to kiss you whenever I feel like it. Is that okay?"

"Of course." She smiles as she licks her finger and drags it across my lips. "And everyone will be able to tell."

"Good," I say as I grab her hand in mine. "Do you have everything?"

She waves her clutch at me before I grab my keys and we're out the door.

MY HAND IS RESTING against her thigh as we pull into the art gallery downtown. She's been grazing my hand the entire ride with her nails, and it's helped to calm some of my nerves, but as we get closer to this place, I can feel my heart rate get faster.

"It's going to be okay," she reminds me. "I know how these things go. Don't worry about me tonight, just focus on getting through it. I'll be with you the whole time."

The reassurance feels good, and her presence is helping to calm me down. "Thank you."

Those two words hold more weight than I care to admit. *Thank you for being here. Thank you for seeing past the playboy side of me and realizing I can be worth more than one night.*

I park at the valet and turn to the girl next to me.

"Whenever you want to leave, just let me know. If you ever get uncomfortable, we'll leave. If it's too much, we'll leave."

She plays with the end of her hair as she looks back at me. "This isn't my first rodeo. Now, let's put this outfit to good use, huh?"

"Let me get the door for you," I say as I shuffle out of my car, taking a big deep breath as I notice some photographers lining the staircases, and their cameras flash everywhere as they try to get pictures of some of the more high profile guests. I have no idea if my parents are here yet, but I assume they are. They always love networking at the first opportunity, and I'm sure my brother and sister are right by their side doing the exact same thing.

We stop to get a few photos, but as soon as we get inside, I feel her relax a little more into my arm. There's a lot of people in here already, and before anyone can come up and bombard us, we grab champagne from a waiter and I spot my parents immediately.

"It will be alright," she whispers to me as we make our way over. "I'm here for you."

I know she knows how much those four words mean to me, but even so, hearing her say them to me, knowing she's by my side, is something I never imagined for myself.

I can practically feel the temperature cool when we get over to them. My mother is wearing the signature colors of the business—indigo and silver. The only jewelry on her ears, neck, and fingers belong to our company. Her and my sister wouldn't be caught dead wearing something that wasn't ours. My father and brother are wearing their usual tailored suits. My father's pocket square matches my mother's dress.

Before I have a chance to say anything, they beat me to it.

"Dominic," my father says as he shakes my hand. "I have to say, I didn't think your trip would have been the success that it was, but the business thanks you for your services."

The business. It's never them. It's always about what's best for the company, not the family.

My mother comes over to me and puts the showmanship on for the cameras near us and gives me a hug. Teags's touch doesn't leave my body as I hug my mother back, putting on my fakest smile.

"I knew you'd get your act together." She smiles at me. "All it took was a little push."

"Thank you for your undying faith in me," I joke despite feeling like there's a hole in my chest.

"Well it's about time you stopped embarrassing the family," my sister jests, while her husband hangs on to her arm in the same fashion he always does. My parents set the two of them up, too, and as the first-born, my sister takes her role in the company—I mean, family—very seriously.

I ignore how annoyed that comment makes me feel before I look at Teags, and her face is as neutral as ever as she looks around at my family.

"This is Teagen We—"

I'm cut off by my brother.

"Do you realize how much money you lost me?" He pats me on the back and I can already feel my fake mask start to slip off of my face. "I had ten thousand dollars on you running off on your road trip and never coming back."

"I've never been happier to prove you wrong, Max. As I was—"

I'm cut off for a second time by my father. "You know who I saw here earlier? Felicity Brown, the heir to the gallery as soon as her parents step down. Dominic, do you need me to set up an introduction between the two of you later or do you think you can sort that out on your own?"

My mother pats his arm. "I thought I told you to set that up for him? You and I both know Dominic never goes up to—"

"That won't be necessary." Teags's voice almost sounds unrecognizable as she speaks for the first time since we got over here.

"Do you have any idea who you're talking to, young lady?"

Before I can somehow recover this conversation, Teags speaks again. "As a matter of fact, I do." Her heels click as she steps closer to them. "Do you have any idea who you're talking to?"

Neither of them answer as they stare her down, no doubt judging every single aspect of Teags and who she is, but my girl doesn't falter. In fact, I can't even tell she's nervous anymore, she just seems pissed.

"Dom has tried to introduce me since we walked into this conversation, but all you've done is undermine his abilities and make him feel less than. I know he would never go against what you're saying about him, but that doesn't mean I can't. You all act horrible to him. No wonder he hates coming to these things. He's never able to get a single word in without you talking over him or talking about how little you believe in him."

"Mind your manners, girl," my father says to her.

"I will once you all do." She smirks back at them before she grabs my hand. "Come on, baby. Let's go dance."

I let her whisk me away to the dance floor before I can even say a word, and part of me is stunned into silence as I throw my arms around her as the two of us start to sway to the music. I can't believe she did that. It doesn't feel like something I ever deserved—standing up to my parents. It never had any use, but hearing *her* say all of the things I've never been able to reminds me how I've been treated by my parents has been horrible. I knew it was, but hearing her stand up for me so quickly and easily as she just did has punched me in the gut.

I don't deserve this astonishing woman in my arms, but I'm going to fight like hell to become the man she seems to already think I am.

"I'm sorry for making a scene, but I couldn't stand there for another second and listen to them belittle you how they were."

"Why are you apologizing?" I ask her.

Her lips part in surprise. "I-I don't know. It's the first time meeting your parents and I probably fucked it all up."

I press a quick kiss to her lips. "Thank you for standing up for me. I've never had anyone do that for me before, and normally, I try to laugh it off even though what they're saying is killing me inside. Don't ever apologize for that."

"I'm sorry my parents were talking about that other girl."

"Oh, yeah." Teags rolls her eyes at me. "Who is she again?"

"She's the redhead perusing around the room talking to everyone," I tell her, seeing her eyes scan the room before they narrow on her.

"She's pretty."

"My eyes are only focused on you tonight, Teags. Fuck everyone else, including my parents."

She smiles before she leans into my chest, the two of us still dancing to the slow music, a bunch of other couples around, but the only thing I can focus on is her—us. The night may have started out terribly, but now that it's just us, I'm enjoying myself more than I ever have at one of these things.

"I didn't know you were such a good dancer," she says to me. "But before our trip across the country, I guess I didn't know much about you."

"I'm a little rusty, but I don't hate dancing at these things, especially when I have such a good partner."

"Oh, please. I practically have two left feet."

My hand finds the back of her head as I run my hand through her long, luscious curls. "I'll steady you, baby. Trust me, I won't let you fall."

Her eyes meet mine, a slight sheen to them as she looks up at me. "I trust you. I know I'm safe with you."

I could melt where I stand after hearing those words, but I don't have time to because as soon as the song ends, my father grabs me off of the dance floor and drags me away. I see my mother thread her arm into Teags's, her face pinched in confusion as my mother drags her over to the bar.

"Show is over, boy," my father says to me. "Felicity is waiting for you to go up to her, and—"

"No."

"No?"

"Teags is my date tonight, and hopefully she will be for the rest of my life, so you better get used to seeing her."

He shakes his head at me. "I always knew you were going to be the one to put your mother and I to the test. I'm disappointed you haven't proved us wrong."

"Well, when you say things like that to me, can you blame me? This isn't even what I want for my future, yet I'm doing it anyway because I've tried to win your approval my entire life. I've come to realize there's nothing I can do that will ever be enough for you."

"Do you realize how lucky you are to be a part of this family? To have your entire life planned out for the best outcome?" my father says as he drags us away from the crowd. "Some people would kill to be in the position you're in."

"Family?" I scoff at him. "We're not a fucking family. We never have been. It's always been the company over everything, and while I'm thankful I seem to have inherited your work ethic, I hope if I have kids in the future, I'm the exact opposite of how you are as a father."

He cannot keep calling himself my father. We're not a family when they weren't ever around as me and my siblings grew up. There were long nights spent at the company while we were all home being taken care of by strangers. We didn't have ice cream sundae nights, or gather at sports tournaments on the weekends. I was alone for most of my childhood, my siblings and I growing up in the same place but simultaneously growing apart as we aged.

I may have lived in that house, but not a single inch of it felt like home.

It wasn't until I got to college and met the boys where I truly felt like I fit in for the first time. For the first time ever, my parents had no say on who my friends were, or who I was able to hang out with like I did when I was in private school.

"So, you're throwing your entire future at the company away for some girl you're going to get bored with in a few weeks?"

"Don't fucking talk about her like that. You don't know me. You don't know her or the relationship we have."

He sticks his chin at me. "Enlighten me then."

"She's my girlfriend, and if you had let me speak earlier, you would know that."

"Did you get her pregnant or something? Is that what all this backlash is about?"

I roll my eyes, scoffing at his insinuation I can't just like Teags for who she is. "No, and watch yourself. You may be my father, but I won't think twice of doing something rash if you keep disrespecting her in front of me."

"Do you think it will go over well dating your friend's sister?" My eyes sharpen as I step closer to him. "Did you think we would let you bring some girl without researching her first?"

"What the fuck?" I never told them her name when they called me. "Did you have someone following me?"

He shrugs and that's all the confirmation I need. There was nobody following me on the road, I'm sure of it, but I wouldn't put it past them to have someone sitting outside my house or something.

"This family is fucked," I say as I run a hand over my face. I'm tired of catering my life to them. It's exhausting and if I keep going down this path, I'm going to be miserable for the rest of my life. That's the last thing I want. "I'm done."

I can see Teags in my future. The boys, too, unless I somehow fuck that up. I see happiness ahead for the first time in a long time and it started with a girl who showed up on my porch in the rain.

I do a quick scan of the room, and as soon as I don't see her, I leave my father and his disapproval behind me, searching for the girl who stormed into my life and changed it for the better.

Chapter Thirty

— FRANCESCA BY HOZIER

DOM'S MOTHER HAS HER hand on my bicep and it's taking everything in me not to slip from the hold she has on me, but I don't want to make things worse. I already felt like a fool for saying what I did earlier, but the way they were treating their *son* was disrespectful. I couldn't just stay quiet.

She leads us over to the open bar, and as soon as I think she's going to let go of me, she keeps me firm in her grip as we lean against the counter. My guard is up, and it has been since Dom first tried introducing me to his parents. Not only were they extremely rude, but they wouldn't let him get a single word in when he was trying to talk. They stood there and belittled him. His own fucking family.

Now, they've separated us, and I know what's coming. This is the exact same thing Gregory's parents used to do when they had something important to talk to either of us about. It was always a pull away from the crowd, or something that had us both in separate places.

One time, Gregory's mother pulled me aside to tell me the dress I was wearing was too promiscuous and if I ever wore it again, I'd be disgracing the family image. I was wearing a long sleeve dress that fell above my ankles. I was embarrassed for days and a few days after that, I came home from work and Gregory was going through my closet while on the phone with his mother, showing him all of the dresses I had and she was making sure each of them were appropriate.

I hate that I stayed silent when he was pushing me more and more into a box. I hate that I felt like I had no other option and I couldn't speak up for myself. Not this time. Not with Dom. Not only did he reassure me that my outburst earlier was okay, but he *appreciated* it. Hearing that he had never had anyone do that for him broke whatever I have left of my heart.

"Dominic has a lot of responsibilities for this family," she says, not looking at me as she takes a champagne flute from the bartender.

"So I've heard," I say as I take a sip. She might think she's intimidating to me, and maybe in a way she is, but I'm not backing down. She doesn't get to belittle her son and tell him how to live his life just because it's what they conditioned him for as a kid.

He deserves to carve his own path in life like the rest of us without his parents constantly breathing down his ear about his supposed responsibilities.

"I'd hate for a girl still grieving her dead brother to get in the way of that."

My head whips to face her, a sly smile on her face.

"So, you do know who I am."

"I know anybody my children come into contact with."

"Oh, is that what he is to you now?" I ask. "I didn't know you considered yourself his parent when you weren't around when he was growing up, or well, ever according to Dom."

She tilts her head at me. "Watch yourself, girl. Do you really think whatever you have with my son is anything more than a means to an end? If I'm correct, he's a distraction to you until you get over whatever crisis this is after dealing with the death of your brother."

I can't help the laugh that comes out of my mouth. The audacity of this woman is insane.

"If you knew your son, you would know that's not true. He's not a distraction to me." I lean closer and get into her personal space. "He's everything. If you actually got to know me through talking to me tonight and not whatever articles your guy found on the internet about me, then you would know that *your son* means the world to me."

"Interesting," she says, taking another sip, her long, pointy nails tapping against the glass. "I wonder what your brother would think about this arrangement."

And there it is. That's what I've been waiting for.

"Funny enough, that's something I've thought about myself."

She turns to me, her hand still on my bicep getting tighter around my arm, her nails digging into my skin. "You are to break things off with Dominic. He must start his life with his family and pay his dues."

"Maybe he should be the one to decide what he wants."

"And is what he wants"—she looks me up and down—"you?"

"I can't answer that for him, but I know I want him." I wait for my stomach to start flipping around how it does when I think about having romantic feelings for someone, but it never does. That sentence flowed so freely out of my mouth that I barely gave a second thought about what I was going to say to this wretched woman in front of me.

"Well, maybe I owe your brother a call then." She tightens her grip on my arm and I hold my ground, not flinching when her nails start to break my skin.

"Go ahead and call him," a familiar voice says from behind us. When my eyes meet his, all I can see is that familiar tension in his body from being around his parents. It looks about ten times worse than it did on the road after a mere phone call with them. His eyes drop to my arm, and his eyes are narrowed at his mother. "Let go of her."

"You're making a fool of yourself, Dominic," his father says as he joins us. "Even after all the money we gave you kids, you choose to act like an ungrateful brat."

"I never asked for that." He shakes his head. "If I recall, I told you to keep it so you couldn't continuously hold it over my head how I knew you would. Luckily, I'm smart with my money, even if it comes from you two."

"What does that mean?" his mother asks.

"That's none of your business. It was mine as soon as it hit my account so you have no say over it anymore." He reaches out his hand for me, and I wrestle out of his mother's hold. "Let's go, baby. We're leaving. I've had enough of this. What about you?"

"Oh, I've certainly had my fill of intriguing conversations," I say as I rub my arm, nail marks left behind from how hard his mother was holding onto me. *Bitch*.

"We could sue you for the money back, Dominic. Do not do something stupid now," his father says.

"Unless you have proof I stole it from you, there's nothing you can do. Don't worry, I checked with a lawyer when you gave it to me when I went to college."

"You talked to Mike without us?" His mother grabs her phone as if she's about to message someone.

"No." He traces his hand over my back. "I have my own lawyer who's not worried about protecting the company first before everything else. And I never signed anything stating you would need any of it back. It was a well and true gift, so try suing your own blood and see where that gets you in the tabloids. I know you'd hate to ruin the vision of our picture perfect family that you've spent years cultivating in the media."

Both of his parents are silent as they take in what he's saying.

"We're leaving," he says as he grabs my hand. We head for the door, and neither of us bother to look back at his parents. By the time we get outside, he's practically pulling me down the stairs to the valet, and I can't help the laugh that comes from my mouth.

"Oh my god, did you see their faces?" I chuckle before the valet starts to bring his car around. Before I can turn to him, he brings his lips to mine in a kiss that nearly knocks me off of my axis. "What was that for?"

"For being you," he says as he runs his hand over the divots in my skin. "I'm sorry about all this."

I shake my head at him. "Don't do that. I don't need you to apologize for other people's actions."

He smiles to himself before he kneels down and slips my heels off of my feet, gripping them in his hand as the car pulls up in front of us. Dom opens the door for me and I slide in, my aching feet already feeling better than they were now that my shoes are off.

I love that I didn't even have to tell him my feet were hurting. He somehow just knew what I needed and did it. Whatever is going on between us is getting dangerous. It's getting serious because ever since we got back from being on the road, I can't imagine my life without him.

"Let's go home," he says as he puts the car into drive.

I grab his hand in mine. "Let's."

Chapter Thirty-One

Dominic

— SPORTS CAR BY TATE MCRAE

THE ENTIRE RIDE BACK home has been silent; the only noise between us being the hum of my car engine as I speed home. Part of me is beating myself up for bringing Teags under the wrath of my fucking parents, but she held her own tonight.

My parents have had someone following me since I got back, and not only did they know who Teags was, but they threatened to give Tristan a call. That would kill me—him hearing about Teags and I before we got to tell him to his face.

He's going to kick my ass once he finds out and I'm going to let him.

To be fair, though, Teags took me by surprise. My eyes glance over to the girl in my passenger seat. Her legs are crossed, and the way she's playing with the ends of her hair makes me think she's anxious, but I don't know about what. I can't tell if my parents are the ones fucking her mind up, if it's the normal things, or if she's worried about her behavior tonight.

That's the last thing she should be worried about. My girl is a fucking powerhouse and she continues to surprise me at every turn. She stood up for me in front of my parents tonight, and that alone makes me want to hold her in my arms and never let her go. For years, I let them belittle me and treat me like shit because I thought I had to. I thought the money they gave me and continuously held over my head meant they were allowed to do that.

That's not true, though, and my parents are done treating me like I have some sort of obligation to them just because they gave me money one time. Granted, it's a lot of fucking money, but I would have rather had them be around and care about me over throwing money at me like I was a problem they wanted to go away.

Fuck them for always making me feel small. I am going to be somebody. Not just because of my last name but because I already am somebody to the girl next to me. She thinks I'm a good guy, and I'm going to work as hard as I can to keep proving her right.

I park in the garage next to my motorcycle and turn my car off, neither of us moving to get out of it. My hands hurt from how hard I was gripping the steering wheel on the drive home, and I keep seeing Teags rubbing at the spot on her arm where my mother was death-gripping her.

Tonight was enlightening to say the least, and there's not a doubt in my mind I'll be getting a call from them sooner rather than later.

"Does that hurt?" I delicately trace the ridges left on her arm.

She shakes her head.

"What did she say to you?"

"She tried to get me to say you were a distraction from my grief. She wanted me to break it off between us because you have a *duty* to fulfill for your family or some other stupid bullshit."

I sigh heavily. "I should have known this would happen. They fucking ambushed me."

"You couldn't have known." She reaches across the console and grabs my hand. "What did your father say to you?"

"He mostly asked me about you."

"What did you tell him?"

"That you were my girlfriend."

"Oh. Is that what I am?" I can tell she's fucking with me because her voice went up three octaves like it usually does when she tries to play coy with me.

"It's what I'm hoping you are even after you saw the mess of my fucking family tonight."

She bites her lip in between her teeth, and I fucking hate the silence ripping through my car, so I keep speaking.

"I don't know when you became this constant thing in my life, but if you walk out the door at the end of whatever it is we're doing, I don't think I'll survive. And if I have to crawl my way back to you through whatever depths of hell I'll be in without you by my side, I'll do it because you're worth *everything* to me, Teags."

She opens her mouth to speak, something overwhelming her because she blows out some air before it all comes tumbling out.

"I'm not a happy presence, Dom. I'm not...nice. I can be rude, and mean, and I'm still grieving my brother, and I ran away from a proposal not too long ago, and—"

"And what, Teags? Is this too fast for you?"

"No, I..." she sighs heavily. "This is so fucking embarrassing. I want you to keep talking about how you can't live without me because even though this terrifies me, I've never had someone like you before. I've never wanted to fall into something so easily with someone and that is fucking terrifying but part of me wants to do it anyway because with you everything feels like it will be alright."

I feel a slow smile spread through my face as she admits she wants me as bad as I want her. Never has anyone wanted me for more than one night, but I should have known someone would come along and prove all of the others wrong. I just never guessed it would be Teagen fucking West.

"Is that a yes?" I ask her.

"Yes, I'll be your girlfriend, you insane, wild, chaotic fucking man."

I scoff, hearing the words filter out of her mouth and through my entire fucking body. Teags is my girl, officially, and part of me wants to scream to the entire world about this magnificent woman beside me. She's all mine, and in return, I am completely hers.

"Come here, baby," I say as I grab her from her seat and she shuffles into my lap. "I have to admit, if I knew the night would end like this we could have skipped the entire middle section of the evening," I say as I run my hands all over her.

"Kiss me," she whispers as she adjusts how she's sitting. I move my seat as far back as it will go so she has more room before I smash my lips to hers. My beautiful fucking girlfriend. Mine.

"I'll have the image of this dress draped on you for the rest of my life," I tell her. "You looked ethereal tonight."

"Dom, I need you," she says before she reaches between us, hikes her dress up, and moves her thong to the side.

"Right now? Right here?"

"I can't wait." She reaches for my zipper before pausing. "Unless you're worried about messing up your priceless car."

I snake my hand up to her neck, lightly squeezing before a smile spreads through her features. "The only thing in this car that's priceless is you. So, take my cock out and sit on it, Teags."

She licks her lips before both of my hands are on her ass and the only sound besides our heavy breathing is the ripping of fabric.

"You didn't need that, did you?"

"Not right now," she tells me, grabbing my dick in her hand before she spits on it, getting it nice and ready for her sweet cunt. "And you can always buy me more, right?"

"Damn right," I say before I throw my head back, the feel of her hand on me, stroking me way too slowly driving me insane. "Baby, please."

"Please what?" I can hear the smirk in her tone before she rubs the tip against her pussy, going back and forth before she fully sits. "Fuck, that never gets old."

"I want to fuck you in every corner of this house, Teags," I tell her, moving my hips as I try to get deeper. "I think my perfect little girlfriend deserves to be worshipped properly."

She smiles before she grabs both of my hands, putting them above my head. "Don't touch. Let me take care of you and then we can talk about me."

This girl is trying to kill me. "Whatever you say, baby."

Her right hand steadies herself as the other holds onto my hands to make sure I'm being good, and then she starts sliding up and down my dick, first slowly and then she picks up her pace, her hips rolling in the sexiest fucking way I've ever felt. The fact that I can't touch her right now is driving me insane.

"God, look at how well you take care of me," I coax her.

"I hope every time you drive this car you think of what we're doing," she tells me, her hips still rolling in that same way driving me absolutely insane. Her pussy is squeezing my cock, practically strangling it as she takes what she needs from me. "God, I'm going to fucking come soon."

"Then don't stop, baby. Take what you need from your boyfriend," I praise her. "You're fucking me so well. You deserve to be rewarded, so take it and fucking soak me. Do it, baby." Her pussy squeezes and her moans are the only thing I can focus on as the sound fills my car, her hand tightening the grip she has on mine.

"Dom, shit," she says, as her legs start to shake. I keep thrusting underneath her, wanting to pull every fucking drop of her orgasm out of her. "Please don't stop."

"Whatever my perfect little girlfriend needs," I say as I keep going, her moans incoherent as I fall off of the edge with her, my own orgasm taking me by surprise. "Take it all, baby. Take every drop that I'm filling you with."

My own words come out strangled, the two of us an incoherent mess as we come down, her hand going limp as my arms come down, finding her hips as I rub my hands across them. I press a small kiss against her head as she slumps against my chest.

That is the quickest, dirtiest, and hottest way I've ever had sex. Teags continues to surprise me at every fucking turn, but whatever she wants, she gets. She's my girlfriend now, and I'm not one to not give her what she wants, especially if what she wants and needs is me.

I could fuck her on every surface of my house and not tire of her. I can't see a reality where I ever get enough of her.

"Sorry that was so quick," she says to me.

My hand is against her hair, my dick still inside of her as I laugh. "Baby, don't apologize." I press a kiss to her lips. "And I'll have my way with you as soon as we're in the shower. I need to worship you properly, girlfriend."

"Well, what are we waiting for?" She smiles at me.

"My girlfriend is fucking insatiable," I say as I open the car door, swinging us both out and carrying her up to the shower, not a care in the world as long as she's in my fucking arms.

Just like most days, she makes it so much brighter just by being around me, and what I thought was going to be a horrible night has now turned into one of the happiest I've had in a while.

It's all because of her. My girl. My *girlfriend*. The one who wants me for more than one night.

Chapter Thirty-Two

— WOULD THAT I BY HOZIER

Waking up in Dom's bed still naked, my hair a mess all over my face, is unironically one of my favorite ways I've ever woken up. I don't hear the shower running, so I can only assume he's still on his run, so I take a minute to soak in all that's happened before I start my day.

Last night was fucking amazing. Dom is my boyfriend. I'm in his bed and in his house and he's my boyfriend. I'm dating Dominic Graves, one of my brother's best friends.

I pinch the skin on my arm, to make sure this is my real life and I'm not dreaming, before I take a deep breath. I'm exhausted, but I find myself smiling as I think about what my life looks like.

I think... I think this is the first time I'm truly happy. Sure, I still have a lot of unanswered questions and grief floating through my body, but for this moment, I'm choosing to focus on happiness. Just for these few minutes as I slowly wake up, I want to feel this.

Though, I still can't feel Tobias. I miss him. I miss when my music used to feel like he was sitting right next to me, feeling the same things I was. I don't know what else I can do. I don't know how to get him back even though he's gone forever.

A few months ago, I was lost. I was fully adrift in a sea of doubt, self-hatred, compliance to a man and a family I hated, and I didn't recognize myself. This is the first time I feel like I'm on a path back to the girl I once knew. I'm not fully there yet, but maybe I can't get back. Maybe I'm on my way to a new version of who I am because of all I've experienced in the last few months. Part of me is excited to see who I become, but another part of me longs for the version of myself who my brother knew.

But he's not coming back. The only thing I can do is move forward, but moving forward without him feels like agony.

"I told you, we're not coming," I hear from downstairs. I throw one of Dom's T-shirts on before I throw some socks over my cold feet and traipse down the stairs.

He has his phone to his ear as he prepares breakfast for us, his shoulders already tense, so I throw my arms around him from behind and I feel his heart rate speed up. I have a guess at who's on the other line, and I hate that they can't even give him a full day without pissing him off.

"No," he says. I can barely hear the other side of the conversation, but all I want is for him to know that I'm here for him. Nothing more and nothing less.

"I'm done talking to you about this. Teags is my girlfriend," he pauses, a small smile coming off his face. "If you can't accept that, then we're not coming. If you can't accept that you can't sue me for the money you *gave* me and the rest of your children, then we're not coming. Stop holding it over my head when it holds no merit. I signed nothing, therefore you can't prove anything."

He hangs up, throws his phone onto the counter, and his head falls in front of him as he takes a deep breath. His hands find mine in the center of his chest, and it almost feels like he's holding onto me so he can keep standing. Before I knew him, I never knew how exhausted he truly was. Now that I've had even the tiniest glimpse into his life and the expectations on him, I can tell.

He's drained. He's who I was only a few months ago until he brought a spark back into my life and made me feel alive again. I'll never be able to thank him for that, but I can shoulder some of the weight until I can hopefully do the same for him.

"What do you need?" I whisper up at him.

"Just this," he says. "Just you."

"Okay."

I lean silently against him for a few minutes, feeling his chest rise and fall as he tries to regain his breathing and get his mind back under control. I hate that his parents still have so much control over him, but I'm proud he's finally sticking up to them.

I start to smell the pancakes burning, so I unwrap from his body and flip them all over. Some of them are burnt, but they're still edible. Dom steals the spatula from me as I'm about to check on them.

"Go sit down. I can finish these."

"Let me do it," I tell him. "You can sit or maybe get me some juice?"

"Teags—"

"Please?"

He sighs heavily, knowing he can't turn me down when I ask so nicely.

I finish breakfast, and by the time the two of us are done eating, we haven't said a word. I'm not used to this—the comfort in the silence. I'm also not used to calling someone my boyfriend and loving the way it sounds out of my mouth.

"How are you feeling?" he asks me. "Did you sleep okay?"

"I slept fine."

"Did the blender wake you?"

I shake my head.

"I told my parents to stop having me followed."

"Oh," I say. "Did they agree?" My leg starts to bounce, worry coursing through my bones at wherever this conversation is going.

"For now." He runs a hand down his face.

"I'm worried about what your mother said to me about my brother," I blurt out. "It's bad enough I've been lying about being home all this time, but to lie about us is a different level of horrible I haven't wanted to reach."

He grabs my hand with his. "I'm sorry they've made such a mess for us."

"You don't have to apologize, Dom. You didn't do this. They are the ones who are fucking this up." I wish he would look at me, but I can tell his mind is going a million miles a minute. I guess his run this morning didn't help how it usually does.

"I know, but you're my girlfriend, Teags. I want to protect you from fucking everything, but I can't seem to protect you from my stupid fucking parents. We've barely started being real and they're already making things difficult for us."

"We'll figure this out," I say as I squeeze his hand, his eyes finally finding mine. "Together."

"I'm so tired of this, baby," he says as a tear falls. "I can't keep doing this."

I get out of my chair and throw myself in his lap, my arms going around him as I feel him exhale the deepest breath he can seem to take right now. "It's okay."

His arms squeeze around me, his head on my shoulder, and I can feel the weight of everything pour out of his body as he finally lets go of all of the shit his parents have expected from him. I think he's finally understanding this is not how he's supposed to live his life, and I can only hope my presence here is helping.

"Sorry," he says when he pulls back. I wipe the stray tears off of his face, and press a long kiss to his forehead.

"Don't do that," I tell him. "No apologies necessary. Not for me, Dommy."

He laughs when I call him the nickname I'm not sure if he loves or hates, but either way, it got him to laugh. I'll take any small win I can get right now.

"Do you want to tell your brother about us?"

I nod. "I think we should. It's the right thing to do."

"He's going to be fucking pissed," he says as I run my hands through his hair. "He's going to kill me."

"I would never let that happen."

He shrugs. "I might let him get a few punches in."

"Maybe it's best if we do this in public."

"Do you think that will help?" he asks with a kiss to my collarbone.

"Maybe?" Tristan and I have a lot to talk about, but maybe after he knows about Dom and I we can somehow lay everything on the table and have a meaningful conversation. The sooner he knows, the sooner that can happen. "It might take him some time to come around, but we can handle that."

"We can handle anything," he tells me. "I just don't want to be the reason you and Tristan don't have a relationship."

"We barely have one right now," I tell him. "He and I have our own shit to sort through, but once everything is out in the open, we can all start to move forward and adjust to this next chapter."

"I'm not entirely sure what this next part looks like for me," Dom says as he pulls me in closer. "But it doesn't feel so scary now that I have you by my side."

"Likewise," I say. "Since I stepped onto that plane in Arizona, I had no idea what my life was going to look like. I can say for certain that even though the past few months have been terrifying, they've also been some of the best. That's all because of you."

He shakes his head. "I can't take all of the credit. You're the one driving your life. I just happen to be in the same car as you."

"And I'm thankful for that because the drive would be a lot lonelier if I didn't have you," I tell him. For the rest of the morning, the two of us enjoy one another's company while I try not to think about what might happen once everyone knows the truth.

Chapter Thirty-Three

— BEGIN AGAIN BY TAYLOR SWIFT

Teags: Can we talk when you have a second?

Tristan: I can call you in a few if that works?

Teags: I was thinking more of a face to face conversation? I'm in Pennsylvania.

Tristan: ???

Tristan: Since when?

Teags: I can explain when we talk. When is best for you?

Tristan: I'm working from home today. So, whenever, but preferably as soon as possible.

Tristan: You're freaking me out. Is everything okay?

Teags: Everything is fine. Can you meet me at Aroma at 3ish?

Tristan: Sure.

"I THINK I SHOULD talk to him alone first."

Dom grabs my hand in the passenger seat as we head to the coffee shop I'm meeting my brother at. I know Tristan is going to have a million questions about what the hell is going on, but he and I need to have a talk first before Dom and I's secret is thrown onto the table. Not only do I have to explain what happened with Gregroy and I, but everything that's been bugging me for the last year about Tristan and I's relationship.

"That's a good idea," he agrees, pulling into the parking lot and finding a spot. "I'll be out here, okay? Just text me when you want me to come in."

I nod, already spotting my brother's car a few spaces down. I should have known he was going to be early. He's probably been freaking out all day. I hate that I worried him, but that's also what I want to talk to him about. He's been in parent mode since Tobias died, and all I've needed from him is to be my big brother.

"Is it hard to breathe all of a sudden?" I ask as I fan myself.

Dom simply turns up the air conditioning in the car, along with one of my favorite songs.

"Just feel the air and listen to the music, Teags. It's going to be fine. Tristan *is* going to freak out. That part is absolutely going to happen, but he's also not an asshole. He'll listen to you because he cares about you. You're both adults, and you're having a conversation as such."

I nod, knowing he's right. "It's been so long since I've seen him."

The last time Tristan physically saw me, I was moving in with my short-term boyfriend across the country, and he was begging me to think my decision through. Before that, all we had done was argue I was making a stupid decision, and I was desperate to prove him wrong.

Part of me is bitter over the fact that he was right, and I hate that I have to face him and tell him about how much my life crumbled over the year I spent in Arizona. I thought that was what my life was supposed to look like. I thought love was what I was trying to find with Gregory. I thought if I could prove I could be loved that everything else would somehow fall in line and work out, but that's not true. Love isn't supposed to be hurtful. It's not supposed to be hiding tears from your partner in the shower so they don't make you feel worse about it. It's not stifling your voice to make them happy.

Love is being there for someone even through the struggles. It's about growing alongside one another, and it's messy and chaotic but it's also wonderful and beautiful. It's laughing when you probably shouldn't be. It's about being in a crowded room and only wanting to catch one person's eyes.

I was unhappy. I was drowning grief, and I lost myself alongside Gregory.

But then I came back here, unbeknownst to Tristan, and I found bits and pieces of myself that I thought I would never get back. I did that, and Dom happened to be beside me for it until his chaos mixed with mine and suddenly I wasn't alone in the darkness anymore. Sure, it wasn't pitch black before him, the light had only just started peeking through, but the simple act of him being there and reminding me I was strong helped push me out of the funk I was in.

I'm not fully out of it yet, but I'm on the way. It's been a slow, painstakingly hard journey, but slow progress is still progress, and if I have to remind myself every single day of that, I will.

Dom brings me out of my haze with a kiss to my lips, and I melt into him how I always do, a small smile coming off of my lips as soon as he pulls back.

"Text me when you want me to come in. Take your time with your brother. I'll be here if you need me, okay?"

"Okay."

I take a deep breath before I get out, sliding my phone into the pocket of my jeans before I head for the door. I spot my brother as soon as I get inside. His back is to the door, but his head turns as soon as I get into the café.

He smiles as soon as he sees me, but I can tell he's still on edge.

"What the hell are you doing back here?" he asks me as I step closer. "Can I hug you?"

I nod, and his arms are around me as fast as they can be.

"Is everything okay?"

"I'm sorry I freaked you out, but if we sit down I can explain."

"Sorry," he says. "Your messages freaked me out. I could have picked you up from the airport if I knew you were coming into town. Why didn't you tell any of us? Liv and Bree didn't know, and Mom wants to have dinner with all of us while you're in town. How long are you staying?"

"Okay, that was a lot of questions at once," I chuckle. "Just give me a second."

He puts his hands up in defense. "Sorry," he says. "I got your favorite drink from this place."

"Thanks," I say as I sip my black coffee. "Technically, it's my favorite drink at every place."

"Yeah, I know," he says as he cringes while I sip it. "I still think you're insane."

My brother starts to crack his knuckles, and I see the same rings he always wears on his fingers. He looks about the same as I last saw him. His stubble is approaching beard status, but I bet he's going to shave it soon. He never liked having it too long before, and Liv is not the biggest fan of his full beard, though she would never tell him that. His brown hair is a stark contrast to my fully black hair, which according to my mother I get from my dad's side of the family. His hair was as jet-black as mine is, and sometimes I find comfort in having a small piece of him with me even on the days I can barely remember him.

"Well, that opinion is shared by many. The first time Bree found out about my coffee order she also looked at me like I was insane."

"She's missed you a lot," he tells me, running a hand through his hair. "We all have."

"I've missed being home too," I tell him. "I missed this place more than I thought I was going to."

The two of us are quiet for a few moments as we sip our drinks, fully taking in each other's presence for the first time in a while. I have to say, the one thing I miss the most is being in the same house with all of us. It was chaotic as fuck when we were all younger, but part of me misses it. We're all spread out now. I was in Arizona. Tristan went to California for a few years until he came back here. I've only talked to Theo on the phone because he's been traveling so much for work and Tobias's bucket list. And well, we all know where Tobias is, but he's not physically here anymore.

Once upon a time, my three brothers would burst into my room, do something stupid, and then leave. I miss that. I hated it when I was younger because they were the most annoying boys on the planet sometimes. They made fun of me, and more often than not, they were terrified of me because I was a menace as a kid. I had to be. I had three older brothers who tormented me at every turn.

But they also taught me a lot at the same time. Sometimes they would come into my room just to make me laugh or to show me some new trick they learned. Other times, we would all sit on my bed and play board games, our mom having to physically separate us so we could go to sleep. Then as we got older, we all sort of went our own way. Tobias and I bonded over music. Theo and I just sort of understood one another with a simple look. Tristan and I started to butt heads at every turn.

They're still my brothers though. They're still the same kids whose height lines intersected with mine when Mom used to mark our heights on the wall, all of them making fun of me because I've always been the shortest in the family.

"Teags?"

"Sorry," I say as I grab my hair and play with the ends. "What did you say?"

"I asked how long you were staying."

"Oh." My heart rate starts to pick up. "That's kind of a complicated question. I guess I should just start from what brought me back."

"Go ahead." He smiles, trying to coax it out of me easier, but nothing about this is easy for me.

"Gregory proposed to me." He looks from my face to my hand, no ring resting on my finger as his eyes keep flicking back and forth. Surprise laces his features as the words sink into his ears, and before he can say anything I keep talking. "It happened a few months ago. I said no, obviously. I basically came home after quitting my job in Arizona to him on one knee in the entryway. It took me by surprise, and once I saw him on his knee, I realized I couldn't do it, so I left and came back here."

"You came back here months ago? Why are you just telling me now?" Concern laces his voice and I can tell he's headed right into protective mode. If he had known, he would have been there for me, I know he

would have, but back then, I couldn't deal with the weight of it all.
I couldn't look him in the eyes and tell him he was right—that I was
trying to outrun my grief and I was using Gregory as a conduit for all my
feelings.

Before I answer, I grab my phone and send off a text.

Teags: I'm ready.

Dom: On my way in.

"There's a lot of reasons why, but the point is I came back, and I found
a place to stay."

"With who? Bree would have told me if you were back," he says, and
just as he finishes his sentence, Dom grabs a chair and pulls up next to
us. "What the hell are you doing here?"

"He's here with me," I tell my brother. "I showed up on Dom's porch
and he took me in."

Tristan's eyes flash between the two of us, and part of me feels like we
ambushed him, and we didn't really talk too in depth about everything
I wanted to, but part of me wants to get this out in the open. After that,
I'll deal with however he reacts.

"W-What?"

"She showed up on my porch looking like hell." He flashes me a look
as if he's sorry, but he's right. I did look and feel like hell. "And she told
me not to tell anyone she was back, so I let her crash for a few days."

"How did she stay with you if you were on the road for weeks?" He
runs his hand over his face. "Are you telling me you were by yourself
in Dom's house for months while I thought you were still in Arizona?
What the fuck, Teags?"

I look at Dom, and he nods at me, reminding me I have the strength to do this.

"Actually, I went on the road with him. I had to get my stuff back that I left at Gregory's house, so Dom took me along."

Tristan squeezes his eyes together, his hands balled up into fists, as he absorbs all the information we're throwing at him. "Why didn't you just come to me? Matter of fact, why do I still feel like you're hiding something from me?"

"I didn't want you to rub it in my face that you were right," I tell him, my voice already straining. "I know I probably should have listened to you, but you were trying to drive my life, Tristan. I didn't need you to do that. I needed you to support me even if I was making the wrong decision, and I knew if I went to your house, I would get some sort of speech about how I should have listened to you from the start. I couldn't handle that, so I went somewhere I wouldn't have to fully explain myself."

He sighs. "I'm sorry, Sis. I just wanted to protect you and I can understand how what I was doing was too much."

"Thanks," I say as I feel Dom's foot tap mine under the table. "And Dom isn't just here because I ran to his house. He's here because he's my boyfriend."

Tristan tilts his head at the two of us, as if he didn't hear me correctly. "This guy? One of my best friends? Teags, this has to be some sort of joke or something and I'm sorry I tried to dictate your life, but—"

"She's telling the truth," Dom says as he grabs my hand in his, a smile on his face as he looks at me, my nerves calming as soon as his eyes meet mine. "She's my girlfriend."

"No."

"No?" I question my brother.

"No, you are not dating one of my best friends after you fled a proposal in Arizona mere months ago." He shakes his head at us, a long exhale coming from his mouth as he takes all of the information in. "There's no fucking way this is happening."

"Look, Tristan—"

He cuts Dom off before he can even say anything. "I don't want to hear anything out of you. That's my fucking sister! You're one of my best friends and you're dating my little sister? What the fuck is wrong with you?"

I sigh heavily, knowing this was how it was going to go. "Tristan, please listen to me—"

He shakes his head, his body practically electrified as he stands from his chair. "I-I need a minute. I just need a fucking minute."

That's all I get out of my brother before he leaves. I could run after him, but I know it's no use. He has to sort through all this on his own, and probably with Liv. If anyone can calm him down, it's her, and I assume he'll reach out in a few days wanting to talk again. He has to wrap his mind around all this, and I get that.

"I imagined this going worse than it did," I say to Dom.

"Oh, I was fully expecting him to beat the shit out of me." He smiles as he brings his lips to my knuckles. "He'll be okay."

"I know," I say, the guilt of lying still eating away at me. "I hate that I lied to him for so long."

"You were figuring yourself out, Teags," he reminds me. "It's okay. You apologized and he'll come around."

"How do you know that?"

"Because if he saw the same smile on your face when you called me your boyfriend that I did, then he'll realize for the first time in however long that you're happy. That should trump everything else as far as I'm concerned, especially since you apologized and you know you kind of fucked up."

I sigh heavily as I finish the rest of my coffee, before I grab my phone and head to a group text.

Teags: Just a heads up, Liv, my brother might be a little... tense when he gets back home.

The two of them answer almost immediately.

Bree: Oh, shit.

Liv: What's going on?

Bree: Did you tell him?

Liv: Tell him what? Teags, I didn't even know you were back until Tristan told me he was meeting you for coffee.

Liv: What the hell is going on?

Teags: I have a lot of explaining to do, but Tristan will explain, I'm sure.

Bree: Maybe the three of us can meet for coffee soon and talk? Like old times?

Liv: I'd like that. You've been missed around here, sis.

Teags: Me?

Liv: Duh. When I said you were the third biological Hart sister, I meant it.

Teags: Well, technically, you're part of the West family now.

Liv: Exactly. You are *both* my sisters, and we absolutely need to catch up.

Teags: After all this blows over, we absolutely can.

Bree: Livs, I would probably make those brownies now, so maybe by the end of Tristan's freak out, they'll be ready.

Liv: Oh, fuck. Okay.

Bree: I'm proud of you, Teags. That couldn't have been easy.

Teags: It wasn't, but I sure am glad to be home.

Liv: We are too.

Bree: The trio was incomplete without you, girl.

Teags liked two messages.

I smile to myself as Dom comes back with my cup in his hand. I didn't even realize he had stood up, but he sits across from me this time, returning the chair he stole back to the empty table.

"I refilled your coffee for you," he tells me. "I figured we could hang out here for a bit before we go home?"

"I'm okay with that," I say as I reach across the table and grab his hand. "It's nice being able to get out of the house."

"It's nice to freely hold your fucking hand in public," he tells me. "It was nice doing it on the road, but now you're mine, and I want everyone to know it."

He has a mischievous look on his face, and as he takes a big deep breath, I reach across the table and smack him on the arm.

"Don't you fucking dare, Dominic."

He lifts his hands in defense as I roll my eyes at him, secretly loving how fucking insane he is, but we've caused enough commotion in this place for one day.

Chapter Thirty-Four

Dominic

— SIX YEARS WISER BY HARRISON BOE

Teags's legs are wrapped around me as the two of us enjoy our morning on the couch until it's rudely interrupted by a swarm of annoyances entering my house without knocking.

Tristan leads the way, his face looking equally pissed off and tense as he stands in my living room. Teags gets off of me, the two of us standing up because it seems like this is headed in a terrible direction. It's only been a few days since Tristan left us hanging at the coffee shop, and I thought it would be a few weeks before we heard anything from him, but it looks like he's ready now.

I'm either about to get decked in the face a few times, or we're all going to have a civil conversation. Well, as civil as it can be with Nico, Vince, Harry, and Ethan—who is on a fucking video call.

"Okay, I have no idea what you're all doing here, but you already need to calm the fuck down," Teags says, holding her hands between her brother and I.

"It's fine, baby." The nickname slips out before I can stop it and I instantly regret not being able to control my fucking mouth.

"Oh, shit," is all Nico says, a laugh bubbling out of him. "This is going to be good."

"Tris, remember what I told you," Vince says. "You get one free punch before I protect the fucker."

"Aw, that's nice of you," I tell him.

"It's not for your sake, it's for his." My face falls as soon as he says that. "I promised Liv I wouldn't let him hurt himself too much."

"I told you that you were fucked that day you dropped your car off at my place, Dom," Ethan says, totally throwing me under the bus. "I *knew* this was going to happen."

"Your hindsight bias is showing," I tell him before he flips me off over the screen.

"I can't believe I just heard the word baby come out of Dom's mouth." Harry practically keels over from how hard that makes him laugh. "We must be living in some sort of alternate timeline."

"Ugh," Teags says as she pinches the bridge of her nose. "This is a family matter. Why the fuck are you all here?"

"Exactly why you said," Nico tells her. "It's a family matter, and we're all part of this big fucked up family in one way or another."

"And some of us wanted to see Tristan kick Dom's ass," Ethan says.

"I'm surprised it hasn't happened sooner than this." Harry says.

"Can we all take five?" I ask, still worried that Tristan hasn't said a word since he got in here. I think it's safe to say I am fucked.

"No can do," Vince says. "The first ten minutes here are fair game for Tris, and we're here to calm him down because any word out of your mouth will probably rile him back up."

"Cause you're fucking his sister," Nico says. "That's low even for you, Dommy."

Tristan steps towards me and I don't bother moving because anything he wants to throw my way is worth it if it proves to him I'm serious about his sister.

"Nico," Teags says in the scariest voice she can. "You can fuck right off back to that basement of yours."

"You don't even know what's in it." He smiles at her. "And none of you ever will."

What the fuck does that mean?

"You both are fucking freaks," Vince says to them. "And one of these days, I'm going to break into your basement just to have something to hold over your head."

"Can we get back to the matter at hand here?" I ask as I look at one of my best friends, his fists clenched and gaze trained on me. "Go ahead and punch me, Tris. If it will help, then do it."

"Don't fucking talk to me like you're the one taking the high road here."

"He speaks," Harry says, turning the volume up on his phone.

Tristan's voice almost sounds unrecognizable, and I hate that I did this to him. I hate that I would do it all over again the exact same way because Teags is the greatest thing in my life that I never saw coming. I don't regret anything I did except lying to him about it. I knew he would hate me. I knew he would want to punch me and probably never talk to me again, and I corrupted Teags anyway.

That makes me a shitty friend. These boys were my only family when my own never felt like they cared about me, and yeah, I was a fucking asshole back in college—I still am—but they accepted me. They kept me around and we've been out of college for years and they still want to hang out with me. I still want to be a part of their lives because they gave me the one thing I thought I would never have—acceptance for who I am, not the money I have.

Look how I repaid him. Look what I did when he was nothing but a friend to me.

I throw my phone onto the table, looking him dead in the eyes as if it's just us in the room.

"Do it."

And I don't flinch when he raises his fist and punches me in the jaw. My face is on fire as I slump back onto the couch, my hand goes right to my face as I feel some blood come out of my nose.

"Fuck," I say as two hands meet my face.

"Are you okay?" Teags asks me and I nod, still feeling a little disoriented, but I'll be alright. I've taken worse hits, most of them to my ego. "What the fuck is wrong with you?" she screams at her brother.

"What's wrong with you?" he asks her, his voice scratching against his throat. "That's my best friend." He looks at me. "And she's my fucking sister!"

"We are all aware of the relationships here," Nico says.

"I don't need your fucking commentary," Teags points at Nico. "As a matter of fact, if you're not my brother or my boyfriend, get the fuck out!"

"Oh, shit," is all Harry says as he scurries out of the house with Ethan still on the phone.

"Well, it was fun while it lasted," Nico says as he buttons his suit jacket. "I expect a call from you later, psycho."

"Fuck you," Teags says to him as he leaves. Vince also heads for the door, but he doesn't walk out of it. Instead, he goes full bodyguard mode, and says nothing as he stands in front of it.

"I made a promise to the Hart sisters that I would stay and make sure this all ends fine," he says as he looks at Teags. "And I'm not one to break a promise."

"Fine," she says before she heads to the kitchen. "Try not to kill one another while I get him an ice pack."

Tristan throws his hands up before he sits on the opposite end of the couch as me. Neither of us says a word before she comes back and gently rests it on my face, guiding my hand to where she thinks I need it.

"Hold it there for a bit, okay?" she whispers to me before pressing a kiss to my forehead. "You." She turns to her brother who's still moping on his end of the couch. "You're coming with me."

Then she leaves, heading for the stairs and he follows her up before I hear a door close and it's just Vince and I down here by ourselves.

"While you two were on the road and she was calling Bree, I was a lot less terrified of her." I look over at him and he hasn't moved from in front of the door. "Tonight just reignited my terror over that girl."

"She's a fucking firecracker," I say to him. "But she's mine."

"He's not going to take her from you."

I shake my head. "You don't know that."

"It'll be fine," Vince says. "Because you're a lot less of an asshole than you used to be, and he heard it from both of you and not someone else. Just ice your fucking face and they'll talk it out."

Vince might be right, but that still doesn't calm the nerves in my stomach over all this. If anyone can get Tristan to come around though, it's her. If I tried to talk to him, he would probably just disregard everything I say to him, but those two have a lot to talk about, and not all of it has to do with her and I. This conversation has been a year in the making, and I have hope that something good will come of it despite the butterflies in my stomach.

I SHUT THE DOOR to the guest room and say nothing as I look at my older brother, disappointed that *this* is how he decided to go about things. Dom thought this was going to happen at the coffee shop the other day, but I had faith my brother would take the high road and be a fucking adult. I thought he would want to talk it out and hear our side of things when the time was right.

I guess I thought too highly of the guy I've looked up to my entire life.

"Are we going to talk this out or what?" he says, his voice low and angry—at least the angriest I've ever heard him before.

I can't help but roll my eyes at him as I sit down on the bed I used to inhabit before I moved into Dom's room. "Come and sit down."

He complies and sits next to me, tension still radiating off of him. I can't tell if it's because he's still mad or if he's already regretting what he did downstairs.

"You and I are grown adults. You can't just go around punching people for me how you used to. Especially when the face you're hitting belongs to my boyfriend."

He sighs heavily as that term exits my mouth. Back when we were kids, Tristan was our biggest protector. Not only was he decently popular at the school we went to, but he was also on the baseball team. All of the sports players were treated differently than others, and whenever someone was picking on any of us—me, Theo, or Tobias—Tristan always got involved. And it wasn't always in the physical sense. One time I hit a guy in the gut for saying something stupid, and Tristan said it was him who hit the guy. He only got a day's detention but I'm sure I would have gotten expelled.

"He's one of my best friends. You're my sister. He should have seen this coming because he broke the code."

"The code?"

He nods. "You don't mess around with your friends' siblings. It's an unspoken rule, and he—"

"I'm going to stop you right there," I hold my hand up at him. "He and I aren't messing around. We're dating. Exclusive." I stop him from interrupting me again because I can already hear what's going to come out of his mouth. "Yes, we are exclusive, Tristan. I know you don't think that word and Dom's name belong in the same sentence together, but we are. He's my boyfriend and he makes me happy, so you're going to have to figure out how to deal with whatever feelings you have about it because I'm not going to switch my life up to make you comfortable."

He takes a minute to sit with what I said, and I hope it's getting through to him because I can't deal with their arguing whenever we all hangout. Just today has been a thorn in my side and it's only been half an hour. I can't imagine a whole night of this.

"You're happy?" he whispers to me.

I nod. "The definition of that word has changed for me over time, but yes. Dom makes me really fucking happy and I'm not embarassed to admit that." Bree and I have had many conversations about how much I hated talking about feelings and all the lovey-dovey stuff the books we read mention. It took me a while to realize that with the right person, you want to talk about everything and tell everyone how ridiculously fucking happy they make you. "If it helps, I feel about a thousand times better than I did a few months ago when I was in Arizona."

"I think that's what I'm the most upset about." He turns to face me. "Why didn't you tell me you were struggling? Why did you run to his house over mine? I'm your big brother, Teags, and I hate that you felt like you couldn't come to me when you were having a hard time. I mean, shit, Tobias didn't come to me when he was struggling. Theo might as well be radio silent in Vermont, and you didn't want to come to me when you were struggling. Fuck." He runs a hand through his hair. "I feel like I'm constantly failing you all because I'm finding out about all these things after the fact. I'm your older brother. I want all of you to come to me when you're struggling because I want to help, but all I've been doing is failing."

"You're not a failure, Tristan. We've had our fair share of arguments lately, and all of us are trying to navigate the strangest period of our lives. That's not a reflection of you," I tell him. "When I came back here,

I didn't want you to parent me and tell me you were right about the direction my life had taken. I needed some space to sort through all the weird and fucking confusing things I was feeling after I left Gregory. My life in general has felt like such a dead-end and I needed a minute to pretend like I had a plan and could figure something out without someone else doing it for me."

He scoffs, shaking his head as he looks at me. "Nobody knows that better than I do, Sis. God, I remember when I was your age I felt the exact same thing. You knew how I was when I was younger, always itching to get the fuck out of here, but eventually I found my way back."

Because of Tobias. What brought Tristan back here was our brother dying, and now he hasn't left, his life blooming into something beautiful alongside the love of his life. "I'm sorry I let my pride get in the way, and you were right, moving to Arizona was the stupidest decision I've ever made."

"I don't want to be right, Teags," he says as he runs his good hand through his hair. "I was trying to protect you, but Liv has reminded me that I can't control your lives just because I'm scared of something bad happening to one of you."

I assume he's talking about Theo and I, but I'm glad he realizes sometimes he has to back off and let us live. I can understand how hard it is for him, especially after all we've been through, but sometimes I need space to breathe without feeling like I'm disappointing him. "I'll try to be more open with how I'm feeling if you promise to let me make mistakes and not breathe down my neck all of the time."

"I can do that," he tells me, leaning closer so he bumps my shoulder with his. "I'm sorry for reacting how I did."

"You and Dom have your own shit to sort through, but I'm glad you at least seem like you're open to the idea of him and I."

He shivers when I say that. "I can't say it won't be an adjustment, and I hate that some of them knew before I did, but I get it. It's your life,

Teags, and as long as you're happy with him, I won't complain." I tilt my head at him. "Well, I won't complain too much."

"That's what I thought," I laugh. "And he does make me happy. Really fucking happy despite how much I still miss Tobias. Things hurt less when he's around, and I've never felt so safe with someone else before."

He smiles, a look of understanding on his face. "That's how Liv makes me feel."

The two of us sit in one another's presence, a mutual understanding between us both as our conversation sinks in and settles in our bones. When the silence starts to get loud, I head for the door, feeling Tristan following behind me as we tread down the stairs. Dom perks up as soon as he hears us.

"Is everything okay?" he asks us, and Tristan nods next to me before he goes over to him.

"I'm sorry for punching you," he says as he holds his hand out.

Dom looks from him to me, and all I do is nod, reminding him that things are okay between us. He takes Tristan's hand and they hug it out, the ice pack I gave him still on his face. "No apology necessary," Dom says as he pulls back. "I would have done the same thing in your situation."

"There's more where that came from if I hear even a word about you making my sister unhappy. Is that clear?"

"Tristan," I say as I roll my eyes. "Seriously?"

"Understood," Dom says. "Matter of fact, if that happens, you might as well just kill me because I can't live with knowing I didn't make her the happiest girl on the fucking planet."

"God, you guys are fucking dramatic," I say as I look at Vince. "Are you hearing these two?"

He shrugs. "I think I've said the same thing to my sister. Liv also has free reign if I ever fuck up with Bree."

I sigh to myself as I sit back down on the couch, wanting to get back to the book I was reading before all of these men burst in. "I really need a girls day."

"I'll tell Bree to call you later," Vince says.

"Livvy has been waiting to hear how you two even happened." Tristan looks between Dom and I. "So I'm sure you'll be getting a message from her as soon as I'm home."

"Great," I say as I grab my book. "Are we done here then? You guys almost ruined my morning."

"Let's go, West," Vince says as he opens the door, and my brother lingers before he heads out.

"I love you, Sis," he tells me. "Maybe we can all get together for dinner soon."

"Does that include *all* of us?" I ask him.

He nods. "I'll tell Mom to set another place at the table."

"Thank you," I tell him. "That would be wonderful."

"I have missed dinners at the West house." Dom smiles.

"Me too," I say with a smile as my brother leaves, shutting the door softer than he opened it when he burst in here.

"Come here, baby," Dom says as he watches me get up and practically sprint into his arms. "How are you feeling?"

"After our talk, I feel a lot better," I tell him, and my arms are still wrapped around him. "How's your face?"

"It's fine." He chuckles. "It'll take a lot more than a punch to scare me off."

"And you're fine with me still..." I trail off, unsure of how to word it. "Cohabiting your space?"

He laughs, bringing his arms around my legs and hoisting me into his arms before he carries me over to the couch. "If you're asking if I like having you here in my house, the answer is yes. It's fuck yes, I love having you here when I first wake up in the morning. If you left me to go and live somewhere else, I would crawl on my hands and knees to bring you back to where you belong." He presses a long kiss to my lips. "This is *our* home now, Teags. I can't stand this house going back to what it was before you burst into my life."

"And what was that like?"

"Cold. Sterile. It was just a house I slept in while I wasn't at work." He pulls me in closer. "You've breathed life back into this place, and call me fucking selfish, but I don't want to lose that. I don't want to lose you, baby."

"I'm not going anywhere," I whisper in his ear. "You happen to be stuck with me until—"

"Until nothing," he says. "Matter of fact." He picks us both up and grabs the keys for one of his cars. "Maybe we should go get some things to spice this place up."

I throw my head back and start to laugh at him. "All I wanted to do this morning was read my book."

"Change of plans." He sets me down on the passenger side of whichever fucking car this is. "We're going to spruce up this place."

I can't even really argue with him anymore because I'm really excited to put some of my own touches on this place. This place that I can now call my home.

Our home.

Chapter Thirty-Five

— MESS IS MINE BY VANCE JOY

"You're telling me you've been fooling around with Dom since the summer and I'm just now finding out about it?" Livvy's eyes are practically taking up half of her face as she looks between her sister and I. "You do realize by keeping this from me that you've opened yourself up to becoming a character that I kill off in the future just to get back at you?"

"I told you," Bree says as she smacks me in the arm.

I can only laugh. Being able to gossip with my two favorite girls in the world about the state of my life in the last few months is the perfect way to end the craziness that was happening between Dom and I. Now everyone knows. It's out in the open, and I thought that would scare me—everyone else being in our business—but Dom and I have been having the best time together.

"I had some things to sort through on my own," I say in defense. "If I didn't think you were going to tell my brother, you would have been one of the first people I told."

She eyes me curiously, her look softening as she smiles at me. "It's good seeing you like this, Teags."

"Like what?"

"Happy." She grabs my hand. "It's good to see your smile on your face and some pep back in your step. Every time we called you in Arizona, I could always sense there was something else going on, but I never wanted to press."

I take a drink of my coffee. "I didn't mean to worry you all."

"Girl." Bree grabs my other hand. "We're family. Let us worry about you. It's because we care, not because we're trying to always keep an eye on you."

I smile, letting that sink in before a laugh sneaks out of my mouth. "We look like we're about to cast some sort of spell."

The two of them laugh, the exact same one bubbling out of their mouths, and I forgot how much I missed their company. I feel like Arizona drained the life out of me, but just being here with these two now is helping to fill me back up.

I've said this a million times, but the Hart sisters are magical, and I'm glad we're all in the same vicinity again.

"So what has everyone been reading lately?" I ask, because the real reason we came here to talk is about what books we have been obsessed with recently. "All I did was read while we were on the road, so I have some good recommendations for you both."

"I'm sure you did a lot more of something else while on the road," Bree jokes, taking a sip of her latte.

"Can you blame me?"

They both shake their heads.

"You two were practically made for one another. I don't know how I didn't see it before," Liv tells us. "Not even how you two look together—which is hot, by the way—but I missed every sign of this happening. Bree even called it before I did."

"We both know romance, Livvy, but I spent way more time with Teags before Arizona than you did. Even at your wedding, I could tell something was up."

"Nothing even happened when he drove me home. He carried me into my house, put me to bed, and then left. That is a mere red herring in the story of Dom and I," I remind them.

"Have you figured out what you want to do in the meantime?" Bree asks, changing the subject again. "I know that question is extremely daunting, but I thought I'd ask in case we can help you figure that out."

"That was always my least favorite question in college," Liv tells us. "It feels like so much pressure trying to come up with an answer, especially when you have no fucking idea what you're doing."

I sigh, knowing the exact feeling she's talking about. "I don't know. If I was brave enough I would say something extremely crazy right now." I look at the two of them, and I can tell they're waiting for me to say it. "No way."

"Teags, what are you afraid of?" Bree asks me. "Haven't you figured out yet that you can do *anything* you set your mind to. Nothing is ever too crazy or impossible, especially when you're a Hart sister or a West sibling. It's a proven fact we're stronger than most. So, tell us what you want to do even if it scares the absolute shit out of you."

"I had this crazy idea when I was getting my business degree that I could own my own business when I was older."

Their eyes practically light up as they lean forward, wanting to hear more.

"If I was smart enough, or brave enough, I would try and open a record store here. The only one we have around here is over an hour away and it's always a trek. Plus, you never know if they have anything good. Their website is so outdated and it never reflects the actual in-store inventory. Tobias and I used to frequent it and they almost never had what we were trying to find."

"That sounds like an amazing idea," Liv tells me. "It's so very... you."

"You might be the most music oriented person I know," Bree smiles at me. "I can always trust your recommendations."

"Thanks," I say as I brush it off. "It's never going to happen, but dreaming is always fun."

"If you ever decide to do it, we'll be with you every step of the way."

"I'm phenomenal with a paint roller," Bree jokes, and then the three of us launch into an entire conversation about all of the books we've been reading, though Liv has been writing most of these days, so Bree and I practically grow her to be read list as we chat about the ones we've been devouring.

It's one of the best ways to spend an afternoon, and I'm grateful to be back in Pennsylvania and able to do this.

My phone buzzes as we start to wrap up our conversations, Vince trotting over to the table with Emerson, the two of them chatting at another table while we had time with one another. Since Vince and Bree started dating, Emerson has taken over her official bodyguard duties. He goes everywhere with Vince and Bree, and I know having him around eases all of us. None of us want a repeat of what happened in the past.

"We've got to go, angel," is all he says to her.

She sighs heavily. "I know." She turns to her sister and I. "I have a fashion show to get ready for or else I would have come to dinner tonight. Just promise me if anything happens, that you'll keep me in the loop."

"What would happen at dinner tonight?" I ask her, feeling stupid as soon as I hear the question come out of my mouth. "I think Tristan and Dom are going to be fine."

"And if they're not, Tabitha is going to ring both of their necks," Liv tells me, and I agree with her. My mom is a force of nature, and everyone who meets her loves her, but she's not afraid to tell you if you're being an idiot—which Tristan and Dom have been lately.

"We'll do this again soon," Bree says as Vince grabs her hand. "If not, I will surprise you both and drop by your houses."

"Make sure you knock first," I tell her and we all laugh.

"I did not need that picture in my mind," Vince says.

"Tristan just texted me. He and Dom are outside waiting for us," Liv tells me as I pack my bag up, throwing my notebook and random pens inside as we head for the cars. Dom and Tristan are parked in spots next to one another, the two of them leaning against their vehicles staring at one another. The tension is obviously still there, but at least they're not punching one another.

"Hi, hotshot," I say as I walk up to Dom, and I can feel Tristan's eyes rolling and I'm not even looking at him.

"Pretty girl, let's go before these two make me throw up," he says as he opens the door for Liv.

"Oh, don't be such an idiot," Liv tells him. "We'll see you two at the house."

My childhood home isn't too far from here—only about fifteen minutes—and I've been itching to talk to Dom about my pipe dream since Liv and Bree mentioned it. I don't know why I'm practically jumping out of my skin over this, but once the idea was in my mind, it just kept spinning.

"How was the coffee date?" he asks me. "Did you spill all of the beans to Liv about our little arrangement turned relationship?"

"Of course I did." I smile to myself. "It's always good hanging out with the Hart sisters."

"Good." He turns the music a little louder before I turn it back down. "Are you feeling okay?"

"I have a question for you."

He looks over at me, eyebrows pinched together as he tries to decipher what I'm about to say. "Should I be scared or terrified?"

"Neither." I smack his arm. "Have you ever had a dream about doing something else with your life?"

"Practically every day since I knew I would have to work for my parents my entire life," he scoffs at me.

"What would you do if that obligation wasn't there?"

He takes a second to think about his answer. "I'm not too sure. I mean, I love the business aspect of working for my parents, but I hate that they are holding the money they gave me over my head and being assholes. I guess if I could be more involved with creating businesses and that side of things, I'd be happy. Small businesses run the country, and being able to fund and help people and their dreams is something I'd love to do. Maybe one day," he says as he puts his hand on my thigh. "Why do you ask?"

"Liv and Bree asked me about what my next steps are looking like and I didn't have an answer. I guess part of me feels bad that I live with you and I bring in no income. All I do is sit at home, apply to random jobs I know I would hate, and read all day. The reading part is amazing, but I don't know how much longer I can handle doing almost nothing every single day, and it's not like I can walk your fish to get myself outside."

His grip tightens on my thigh. "Teags, don't worry about money. My house is already fucking paid off, so don't feel bad. I like having you under my roof and in my bed. And I want you to do whatever feels best for you, so stop applying to dumb jobs and tell me the idea that's already swirling around in your head."

"How did you—"

He tilts his head at me. "You're my girl, Teags. Do you realize how easy it is for me to read most expressions on your face?"

I can't help the butterflies that swirl in my stomach as he says that. "I want to open a record store. Not only do I love music, but it's something I'm passionate about, and I have a business degree and I think—"

"Let's do it."

I'm shocked the minute those words leave his mouth. "What?"

He turns into the driveway and parks the car. "I said let's do it."

"Are you being serious?"

He grabs my hand in his. "Of course I am. We're a team, remember, and I think it's a great idea. I can do some market research and talk to some people about investing, and even start searching for a storefront."

My head starts to spin. "Okay, I have about a thousand questions, but what about your parents? And is going into business with your significant other the best idea? What if we break up and things get awkward and weird and we hate one another?"

"Teags." He runs a hand through my hair. "Let me worry about my parents. And I might be jumping the gun a bit here, but I don't foresee us breaking up, unless you get sick of me down the road."

"I can't see that happening," I tell him. "But are you sure you want to do this? What if we fail?"

"Your dreams are my dreams." He presses a kiss to my forehead. "We're not going to fail. I'm a smart guy. You're probably the smartest and sexiest person on the planet, so we'll figure out a way to make it work."

"What does that have to do with anything?" He shrugs at me. I appreciate how nice he's being, but part of me also can't tell if he's taking this seriously. "But—"

"Let me pull some numbers and we can go from there, okay?"

I take a breath. "Okay. One step at a time. I can handle that."

"Yes you can, baby." He unbuckles his seat belt. "Because you are the strongest person I know. Now"—he gets out of the car and comes around to my side, opening my door for me—"let's go eat and enjoy some family time that doesn't make either of us want to pull our hair out."

Now *that* I can do.

— LEAVE ME AGAIN BY KELSEA BALLERINI

THE MOMENT I STEP foot into my old house, my mom's arms are around me. She looks exactly the same as when I last saw her. Her brown bob is still the same as it has always been, and part of me feels jolted back to the past as I take in the home I grew up in.

"The fact that I had to hear from your brother that you were home is the most ridiculous thing ever." She pulls away, her hands framing my face. "How are you doing? Are you hungry? Have you been eating? Do I need to kick Gregory's ass?"

I can't help but laugh. "Mom, I'm fine, and there's no need for any ass-kicking."

"I handled that part already," Dom says behind me. "As did she."

My mom starts to laugh, a snort coming out of her as she pulls him in for a hug. "I should have known the only one who could tame my wild child would be someone like you, Dominic."

He wraps his arms around my mom, throwing a wink at me as I stare at him. "She might have been the one to tame me, Tabitha. Your daughter is something special."

I feel my cheeks start to turn red, and before they keep this back and forth going, I try to get away, only to be pulled back by my mother.

"You're not going anywhere," she tells me. "Tristan and Livvy are cooking for me right now because I have about a thousand things to show you."

"Does this involve any of those classes you've been taking at the town hall?"

"No, baby," my mother says as she grabs my arm, leading me towards the staircase. "Let's go have a talk. Make yourself at home, Dominic. You know what's mine is yours."

He wraps his arm around my mom, pulling her into his side. "You're the best," he says as he heads for the kitchen. He's probably going to make himself useful with Tristan and Livvy, and I hope Liv can handle those two if they start to bicker.

Actually, I know she can. She used to run circles around all of them back when they were in college. She's told me many times how Tristan and his friends were *all* such good listeners when she asked them to do something for her. None of them dated too seriously in college except for Harry, but the minute Liv came into the picture, everyone adored her because she made it so easy to.

In a way, Liv is the glue that has brought all of us together. Obviously, Tristan and the boys would still be friends now. That wouldn't have changed, but everything else would have. Through Liv, I was able to meet Bree, the girl who I was once a huge fan of who turned into my best friend. I can't imagine not having the Hart sisters in my life, and I guess I have my brother to thank for that, since he was the one who ran into her that day on campus.

So much has changed since the day I met Liv. When she showed up for Thanksgiving dinner, I didn't know what to expect. My brother had never brought someone home before, so this was new territory for all of us. Of course, Tobias, Theo, and I made fun of him the entire time telling stories of how serious he was when we were kids. It was a great night from what I can remember of it.

Everything has changed, but as I walk through the hallways of my childhood home, it feels like nothing really has. Time stands still in here, the memories of all of us as kids floating through the rooms as if the real world doesn't exist. Tobias's room is still in the same condition he left it. None of us, not even my mother, have wanted to move things around because everything in that room was something he touched, sat on, or existed around, and none of us can seem to let that go. So it sits untouched by everything except time itself.

Before I think my mom is going to turn into his room, she drags me into my old room, shuts the door, and I see a giant box on my old desk.

"What is this?" I ask, knowing she's waiting for me to open it. My mom was never the best at hiding presents from us. She always told us at least one thing that we were getting for Christmas before December even hit.

"Open it before I scream," she says, so I do, practically destroying the box.

"What is all this?"

"I was going through some of your father's things in the basement last week and I found some more of his favorite records and cassette tapes. I thought you had them all, but I was wrong. I figured you would want them."

Tears filter into my eyes as I sort through the box. "I thought you were never going to touch Dad's old things in the basement?"

"I'm not, honey." She leans closer to me. "I've been missing him a little extra lately, and sometimes I sift through his old boxes. I know it sounds weird, but I can remember him a little better through the things he used to love. All the emotions we shared and the songs we loved help me remember those little things time has made me forget."

I shake my head. "That doesn't sound weird at all." I shove down the ache in my throat that's threatening to bubble up. I'm the same way. I like reminiscing about my brother and my father through the things they touched. Knowing I lost a bunch of those records and tapes because Gregory is an asshole makes the ache grow stronger. "Why are you giving these to me?"

"Because I know it's been hard for you kids lately. Hell, it's been tough for all of us to keep going despite what we've all been through. I wanted to give you something to hold on to when it gets a little tough. I gave Tristan his old baseball mitts that he used to use with your dad. Boy, they would play catch any chance they got, and he told me how much he appreciated it, so I thought I'd do the same for all my babies. I even told

Theo I had a few things for him whenever he's done at the old Vermont house."

I let a single tear fall from my eyes, quickly wiping it away before my mom can see it. I'm thankful for these new pieces of music that were tethered to Tobias and my father, but my heart still aches for the ones I lost, the ones they touched, and the ones Tobias and I would trade back and forth. "Thank you for this precious gift," I tell her. "I miss them both every day, and sometimes I worry I might forget them completely as time goes on."

She grabs both of my hands in hers. "If you ever need a story to kickstart that memory of yours, call me, honey. I've got thousands of things I can tell you and an infinite amount of time to chat with you about it. There is never a wrong time to call your mother."

I laugh to myself. "You know I've never been great at reaching out."

"I know, darling." She smiles. "But I am *always* here for you and I know you know that. I'm not going anywhere, and I hope you aren't either."

I shake my head. "No, Mom. I'm staying in Pennsylvania for the time being. Maybe we can sort through Dad's things together in the future? I'd love to hear some more stories about you two and life with four kids. I don't understand how you did it, especially after he was gone."

"You kids made it so easy for us." She sighs, remembering something she probably won't tell me about. "Have you heard from Theo recently? He hasn't been getting back to me as much as he used to."

"I talked to him while I was on the road with Dom," I tell her. "Though, that was a while ago. So, I guess I haven't recently spoken to him."

"I worry about him up there. There's so many memories and boxes left in that house. I hope he's found a friend to talk to."

"Or he could be busy sorting through everything?" I try to ease her mind, already knowing where it's headed based on the lived experiences we had with Tobias.

"You're probably right," she tells me. "I just miss you all sometimes. The house is quieter without you all running around and driving one another crazy."

My heart aches for my mom. Sometimes I don't know how she's still standing after all she's been through, but any piece of resilience I have in my body must come from her. "I'll be around for dinners and coffee dates more, I promise. I'm sure Dom would love to chat with you any chance he gets." The two of us laugh at that. Dom has that stupidly charismatic charm where he can talk about anything with anyone. He always did get along with my mom despite Tristan describing him much more differently than he actually is. "I'm sure when Theo gets back, he'll say the exact same thing."

"I'd love that," she tells me. "And I need all of the details of you and that man downstairs. I don't talk to you for a little bit and all of a sudden you're leaving Arizona and finding yourself an entirely new man."

"Mom, it didn't really happen like that," I tell her. "And I'd love to tell you the full story."

"Just answer me this one question before we go back downstairs."

"Okay."

"Does he make you feel like the sun hits your skin differently?"

I'm confused by her question at first, but when I really think about it, I have an answer. "Yes."

"And does he make you hear the music differently?"

"You only said one question, Mom."

She waves her hands around the air. "I know, but just answer it, for your old mother's sake."

"You're not old," I tell her. "And yes, he does."

"Good," she tells me as she sits up. "That's how your father always made me feel. I swear that man made the sun come out everywhere he went. My world was brighter when he was around, and sometimes when I feel the sun on my skin, I can feel the way your father made me feel when we were young and in love how you are."

In love. Dom and I haven't admitted that quite yet, but it is what I feel for him, at least, in my own way it is.

My stomach flips as I realize that, but my mom pulls me out of whatever spiral was about to ensue.

"Now, let's go make sure those boys are behaving." She grabs my hand as I collect the gift she gave me in my other arm. "And I need to ask Livvy about her next book."

"Of course you do." I laugh as the two of us head down the stairs, only to find the table already set and dinner practically done because of how wonderful it smells down here.

Dom locks eyes with me as soon as my mom and I turn into the room. "What do you have there, baby?"

"A gift," I say as I look at my mother. "Straight from the basement."

"Oh, wow," Livvy says as she sifts through them in my arms. "There's a ton of good stuff here."

"I'm *very* excited about some of these," I tell them all. "Though, I'm not sure where I can store all of them."

Dom smiles before he presses a quick kiss to my lips. "I'm sure we'll figure something out."

And as we all sit down for dinner, I try to take in and fully remember this moment for later. After all the big feelings and struggles I've been having, it feels good to have this small pocket of family time. I forgot how much I missed this feeling of togetherness that exists around this table, and I don't think I'll ever take a home cooked meal for granted ever again.

I'm the luckiest girl alive that I had this to come back to, and despite how terrible my life was in Arizona, I'm glad it reminded me of where

I truly belong—here at this table with these people. Though, we're still missing a few, the empty place setting there to remind us, but I'll take anyone around this table that I can get.

Those three words almost slip out as Dom and I take leftovers home, and as I crawl into bed with his arms wrapped around me, I whisper them to him as he falls asleep, knowing he probably didn't hear me, but loving the way it sounds on my lips.

Chapter Thirty-Six

— YOU ARE IN LOVE BY TAYLOR SWIFT

Teags: Can I come back home now?

Dom: Give me five more minutes.

Teags: Vince is driving Bree and I in circles around the block. He says he's going to make you pay for gas.

Dom: The rich bodyguard with his own company is going to make me pay for gas?

Teags: I'm just telling you what he said.

Dom: Tell him to park in the driveway. God, why do I ask these fuckers for favors?

Teags: Your guess is as good as mine, babe.

Dom: Get your cute ass up to the porch and I'm going to blindfold you.

I SMILE TO MYSELF as I open the door to the car.

"I can't wait to find out what he's been doing."

"Me too," I tell her as I slide out. "I'm about to be blindfolded, so I'll text you later."

"You better," she says before I shut the door and turn to see Dom waiting for me on the porch, still in that black muscle shirt and blue jean combo that he was wearing at five this morning. The smile bursting across his face has me cautiously walking up to him, my senses on high alert for whatever shenanigans he's been up to for the few hours I've been gone.

This morning he woke me up, gave me my coffee, and all but pushed me out of the house and into Bree's car. I asked him a thousand times what he was doing, but he wouldn't tell me a single thing. It's been driving me crazy all day, and nobody else knows what he's doing. I would know. I texted all of our friends and asked.

"Do I really need to be blindfolded for this?" I ask as I step closer to him.

He nods before holding it up to my face. "You and I both know how much you loved when I blindfolded you on the road." He presses a quick kiss to my cheek. "It's only for a second."

I can feel my cheeks get red, and if he notices he doesn't say anything before he grabs my arm in his and walks me into the house. We go up the stairs, and before I think we're going into our bedroom, he turns me the other way toward the room I once inhabited.

"What are we—"

"Let me take this off for you, and then you'll understand," he says as he unties it. As it falls off of my face and onto the floor, I can't help but gasp.

"What..." I trail off, trying to take in every square inch of this new space he's created. In front me is no longer a spare bedroom. Not even close. He has transformed this space into a library for all of my books and there's even an entire section and wall shelf dedicated to all of the records and cassette tapes I still had at my childhood home.

Knowing he spent most of today creating this space for me and personalizing it to fit my tastes is… everything. I even see some records I used to have up on the wall he's created to showcase what looks like my top nine favorite records at whichever moment, and I don't know how he managed to find some of these.

I'm grateful to have them back, but it still doesn't feel the same knowing Tobias and my dad never touched them with their hands.

Tears start to flood my eyes as I take in the beautiful space around me, the music and books filling up the walls reminding me of all the different lives I've lived through each medium I've found comfort in. Books will always be my favorite form of escapism, and music will always be my tether to my brother, no matter if I can't feel him through it at the current moment.

"I don't think I've ever heard you have nothing to say before." He smirks behind me. "Did I do okay? I figured you would want to rearrange your books because Liv told me everyone has their own way of organizing, and I didn't know how you liked to store your vinyls, so I—"

I cut him off as I throw myself into his arms, and tears fall down my face as I think about the greatest thing anyone has ever done for me. It's not even about him knowing I'd love something like this; it's the time, care, and effort that went into it. He bought and assembled all of these shelves for me. He put them together in this room. And he did it all because he knew it would make me happy.

"It's perfect," I say into his shoulder. "It's perfect, and you are perfect, and I can't believe you did this for me when you've already given me so much."

"Haven't you figured it out by now?" I pull back from him as he sets me down. "I would do fucking anything to see you smile at me how you are now, and that's not even the best part."

"I don't know how much more I can take," I say as I wipe a stray tear from my face.

"Go and look at those vinyls I displayed on the wall." He juts his chin out, and I'm suspicious before I take one off of the wall and see it.

Property of Tobias & Teagen West is scribbled on some masking tape on the back of the record. Tobias used to label all of his records with our names in case we ever lost one when we took it from home to college.

"But I thought Gregory sold them all?" I ask as I spin around, finding him a lot closer than I thought he was.

"He did." He grabs the record from my hands. "I found them all with that list you gave me."

"You tracked down every single one?" I ask as I peruse the shelves, and he's right. They're all here. "How?"

"I had some help." He shrugs. "It turns out Nico really *is* in the right field. He's a little too good at tracking shit down."

I can't help but burst into tears as I grab a few of the records, seeing that same tape on all of them. I thought I had lost these forever, but Dom managed to get them back for me. He did this all for me because he knew how much it meant to me—having these vinyls and tapes that my father and Tobias held in their hands much like I am now.

"Baby," he says as he pulls me in by the back of my head. "Are these good tears? Please tell me they're good or I—"

"They're the best tears I've ever felt," I say to him, my voice wispy as a few tears fall. "I can't believe you found these."

"I know what they mean to you," he says to me. "When I saw your face at his house after you found out they were gone, I knew I was going to at least try and find them. I couldn't stand that even after you had gotten out of his clutches, he still made you feel small."

"I don't give a fuck about him anymore."

He nods. "I know."

"Thank you for doing this for me," I say as I lean into his touch. "I don't know what to say."

He grabs the vinyls from my hands before he sets them down, taking one out and putting it on the new record player he bought me. God, am I dreaming? Is this a dream that I'm going to wake up from and wish I could go back to sleep just to experience a few more seconds of this?

"Will you dance with me?"

The music starts playing and I recognize it immediately. This was one of my favorite songs to listen to when I was younger. I vividly remember watching one of the home videos my parents made, and I saw them dancing to this song in the kitchen when they thought they had stopped recording for the night. It was the most beautiful display of love I had ever seen—beating out everything I've seen in movies and books since.

"Of course I will," I say as I accept his hand, the two of us swaying to the music as it fills up the room around us. There's something so magical about hearing music on vinyl. It has a different feel about it, something more ethereal about the music. Every harmony, lyric, and chord progression feels warmer than it does through my headphones or speaker.

"Can I tell you something?" he asks me as he spins me around, and there's a huge smile bursting off of my face. I can't help it. At this moment, I am the happiest I've ever been, and there's nothing embarrassing about it.

"You can tell me anything."

"I'm in love with the way you view music," he tells me. "You have this certain look on your face when you listen to it that looks like you're trying to crawl into the notes and live there. Or like you want to dissect every little thing about the song because you find it so interesting. I love how you view the world, and I know sometimes you wake up and everything feels really heavy, but I hope this room and the music that will play in it can help ease some of that for you."

"You ease that for me," I whisper to him, feeling myself get more emotional as I speak. "When I wake up in your arms, nothing bad can touch me. When I see you looking over at me like I'm the only person who exists, things feel lighter. When I'm with you, all the scary things about life don't seem so bad. I feel strong, powerful, and like I deserve to take up space when I'm with you. I've never had that before you, Dom."

"Fuck, I'm going to start crying if you keep going," he says with a laugh, but I can tell he's being truthful. His voice keeps catching in his throat.

He brings me closer, my hand now on his chest, and we keep swaying before the words tumble out of my mouth. "I love you."

He stops in his tracks, looking down at my tear-filled face as he wipes them for me. "What did you just say?"

"You're going to make me repeat it?" I chuckle, wiping my cheeks.

"Of course I am," he giggles.

"I love you, Dom. I really fucking love you."

"You love me?" he checks again.

"I do! Why the fuck do you keep asking me?" I push his shoulder with my hand.

"I'm not used to hearing that from anyone," he tells me. "But hearing those three words from your lips is my own version of heaven, so will you tell me again?"

I shriek as he picks me up and spins me around, my legs wrapping around his body as I cackle to myself. "I love you!"

"Fuck, baby, I love you too." I can hear the smile in his voice when he says that. "God, I love you so much." He smashes his lips to mine, and I kiss him back with the same fervour because this astonishing, gorgeous man inside and out, loves me. "I love how you always want to stop at yellow lights so you have the chance to hear another song. I love how music is everything to you because it explains how you feel in ways that you can't. You are music to me, Teags, and I *fucking* love you."

We pull away from one another, both of us out of breath as we take one look at each other in the state we're in and then we laugh. We laugh until our stomachs hurt and we're on the floor because we can't seem to continue standing—the love we share knocking us both off of our feet.

"I've never felt so happy in my entire life," I tell him.

"Me neither." He smiles at me. "I always thought I was immune to love, as weird as that sounds."

"What do you mean?"

He shrugs. "I don't know. I guess growing up you see love everywhere. It's in the books, the movies, and people write songs about love like it's this beautifully contagious thing. I always thought if love was like a disease, I might be immune to it. I never grew up feeling like my parents loved me, and when you go through life having people only want you for one night and nothing more, you start to believe maybe you're immune to this thing people talk about so passionately. I never really felt like I understood love and I used to worry I might be the only person on the planet to never really feel it." He looks over at me. "Until you."

I reach over to cup his face, needing him to feel every ounce of happiness and love flowing from my body towards him. "I'm glad I proved you are easy to love, and I hate that you walked through your entire life not knowing the love you deserve."

"Now I don't have to." He smirks at me. "Thanks to you."

I can't help but laugh. "God, we're so embarrassing."

He grabs my hand in his, squeezing it as we look at one another. "Oh, absolutely." He presses a kiss to my knuckles. "But I don't give a single fuck because the most beautiful girl in the entire fucking world loves me and I don't think you'll ever be able to shut me up about that."

I find a few more tears falling because my brother never got to see this version of me—the one hopelessly in love with her boyfriend. I hope wherever he is now, he can see that despite the constant struggle this past year has given me that I haven't given up yet.

"I'm the lucky one," I say. "And I'll never stop reminding myself of that."

"I love you."

I smile, letting this feeling settle into my memory so I can look back on this moment and replay it anytime the world starts to get dark. "I love you too. You've officially ruined me for anyone else."

"Good because I've been ruined for anyone else since you showed up on my porch. I'm glad you've finally caught up."

Chapter Thirty-Seven

Dominic

— CATACOMBS BY KROOKED KINGS

"You have ten minutes before I walk out of here and never come back," I tell my parents as I waltz into the conference room. Not only did they summon me here this morning, but they ruined the glow I've had over the last few days.

I'm a man in love, and I thought nothing could bring me down, only to pick up the phone this morning to my father on the other end of the line. He requested my presence at the office this morning, and the only reason I'm here is because he asked me nicely. If it were up to me, the last time I spoke to them at the art gallery would have been the last time.

"Sit down, Dominic," my mother says, so I take the seat at the opposite end of this gigantic fucking table. I grab my phone, start my timer for ten minutes, and let them speak. They were the ones who invited me here, after all. I'm not saying a damn word until they tell me why they wanted me here.

My father clears his throat, my hands tapping on the table as I watch the seconds tick down on the clock. I really don't have time for these stupid mind games, but I'll entertain them this final time.

Because I'm done after this. I'm done feeling like a puppet to my family. I'm done pretending like every holiday and birthday doesn't hurt from their absence. I'm tired of pretending we're the perfect family to everyone who sees us when in reality we couldn't be further from that.

"Alright then," I say as I move to get up.

"Sit down," my father says. "We wanted to apologize for how we acted at the gallery, but we also think your actions and our reactions were warranted."

My eyes roll of their own accord. "Not only did you belittle me the entire time, but you were also very rude to the woman I love. I don't owe you two anything, especially when you've been mostly out of my life since my childhood."

My mother's eyes roll as she stands, her arms on the table, her stance as if I'm some nobody she's trying to talk down on a deal. "Oh, quit it with that, would you? Your brother and sister never talk about this as much as you do."

"Probably because they know it would be of no use. Those two are too far gone. Your chains are already around their ankles, but not me. When I said I was done, I meant it. If you called me back here to change my mind, it's not going to work."

"Even with a few million as a signing bonus?" my father says as he slides a paper over to me. I grab it, seeing ten million dollars staring back at me, a familiar sense of déjà vu hitting me in the face. They did the same thing to me before I started college. They slid the money over to me, told me about my duty to the family, and then they outlined my entire life and future in the family business.

"I'm not taking this. I've taken your money before, and I'm sure this comes with about a million stipulations." I slide the paper back to them. "No. Now, is that all? I have other matters to attend to," I say as I stand, a little over three minutes on the clock.

"You're going to regret this, Son."

I can't help but laugh. "You don't get to call me that. You may be my parents, but I think you can agree that everything about our family is less than ordinary. I realize that you two were brought up in this"—I look around the room, searching for the proper words—"unorthodox life. And I realize maybe deep down, you thought this was best for me and my siblings. So thank you for trying to give me the life you thought was best for me, but fuck both of you for how you went about it. All I ever craved from you and my siblings was a sense of belonging, but I've come to realize that's never going to happen. You two only care about the company because it's all you've got, and I think you know that. I think you know deep down if you lost that, you would have nobody around to pick you back up. That's not the life I want for myself. That's not who I want to be, and you'll have to accept that."

The two of them sit and stare at me, not a single word uttered from their lips.

"I won't talk bad about the family to the press. I won't say anything or screw anything for all of you. I will keep the family image you've cultivated perfect, but only if you leave Teags and I, and everyone we care about, alone. If you can't agree to these terms, then I will destroy everything you've built."

I swear I can see a smile coming from my father's face.

"Fine."

"Wonderful," I say as my timer goes off. "You'll be hearing from my lawyer. As long as you sign the contract, there will be no need for me to see either of you ever again."

Neither of them says a word as I walk out the room, heading for my car as I feel my shoulders loosen, the weight of their expectations of me no longer on my shoulders. That felt good. Really good, actually. I never thought I would be capable of standing up to my parents about any of this, but after many talks with Teags, and some self reflection, I realized I couldn't live how I have been any longer.

I was tired, exhausted from the weight of carrying all their disappointment with me my entire life. It's not a physical kind of tired. It's been all mental. My parents have been draining every ounce of mental energy I've had for years. Now, they no longer have the power to do that because I was strong enough to pave my own path, to follow the road I didn't even know existed before Teags walked into my life.

Speaking of my girl, as I get into my car, I call her. She answers almost immediately.

"Hi, how did it go?"

"I'm okay. I actually feel great," I tell her, and a smile bursts off of my face as her words filter through my car. "It seems they agreed to everything. I'm going to have my lawyer send the contract with all our terms to them, and if they sign it, we'll have our answer."

"I'm so proud of you. I know that can't have been easy."

"It wasn't," I say as I turn my car on. "But it was necessary, and the fact that I already feel ten times better than I have in the past few years tells me everything I need to know."

"Are you on your way home? I thought we could talk about some more stuff for the store."

"That sounds perfect. I'll be home in twenty minutes," I say. "I even have a few thoughts on some guys I can call for some possible investors. I'll probably need to tell them part of the story of why we think this business is a good idea. I wanted to run that by you. Did you want to come to any of the meetings I set up and do that? Or did you want me to handle it?"

She takes a deep breath across the line. "I trust you. I'm not the best at the business side of this, at least not like you are. I would be honored if you shared Tobias with these guys, especially if you think that will help sell the business."

"The entire thing is because of you and him, baby. It would be an honor to carry him into these meetings with me."

"Thank you," she tells me, a sniffle across the line. "Now get your cute ass home. I want to show you how proud I am of you."

"Is that so?" I say as I pull out of the parking lot. "I'll be home in ten minutes then."

That earns me a scoff. "Drive safe, Dominic. I love you."

"I love you too."

And the entire way home, I can't wipe the stupid smile off of my face and God help me, I don't want to.

Chapter Thirty-Eight

— 5 MORE MINUTES BY SYDNEY ROSE

I WAKE WITH A weight against my chest, and I know it's not Dom because his hair isn't nuzzled against my face like it is most mornings.

I knew this was coming. I knew things were going too well for me lately. I even told Bree the other day that I haven't felt like crumbling from missing my brother as much lately. I fucking jinxed myself, but that's the thing about grief and really any emotion you can have. Sometimes it lingers and you feel it lurking, waiting for the right time to attack. Other times, you can catch it before it becomes too much. But there's times when you start to feel okay again, and you think you're fine when it will sneak up on you and remind you that you're not fine.

Today is one of those days, and part of me wishes I could stay in bed all day, but if I'm going to combat this before it becomes a spiral, I know what I have to do. I force myself out of bed and head to the beautiful space Dom created for me. The first record I grab is the last one I remember listening to with him when he was around.

The minute the needle hits the record and the music starts to play, I feel the weight start to lift, a few tears falling from my eyes as the music infiltrates my ears.

"Baby?" I hear Dom call from our bedroom before I quickly wipe my tears, hearing the door start to open. "I didn't know you were up. There's coffee downstairs for you."

"Thanks," I say.

He notices I'm off as soon as I speak. "Are you okay?"

"Just a tough morning," I tell him, the music still playing. "I really miss him."

"Come here," he says before he joins me on the floor, wrapping me up in his arms. "I can stay home today and we can hang out, okay? I'll call—"

I smack his phone out of his hands. "I'm fine. You can go to work and I'll be okay. Today is too important to cancel. Maybe I'll go over to Bree's house and try to distract myself. Or maybe my mom wants to meet up and talk," I list out a few ideas that make today not seem so daunting.

"Are you sure? I don't mind—"

"Yes, I'm sure," I say into his neck. "Plus, how else are we going to open a record store without investors?"

We are officially trying to open a business together. We've been talking over a plan to get started over the last few weeks, and every time we talk, we get more giddy and excited about this next chapter. Today he has a few meetings with some investors he's contacted, and I'm not going to let my grief stand in the way of this opportunity. Nico even said he'd invest in it, and I might actually hold him to that.

Liv and Bree are going to help with the social media marketing aspect of it. Those two are the best at that, and the store is in very capable hands. I trust them with this little idea that could, and I love having all of the people I love involved in my dream. We've been talking about branding for the store, but I don't have an official name yet, so we're taking things one step at a time.

I am really excited about this. I never thought I'd be confident enough to do it, but part of me wishes Tobias was here with me to do this. I don't think anyone would be as excited as he would be over the idea of me opening a record store where I'll be surrounded by music all day, every day.

"I know, but I can cancel if you need me."

"Dom, go to the meetings. I will be fine." I look up at him. "I just wish he was here with me."

His face falls as soon as I say that, and he squeezes me tighter, telling me he's here for me. He may not understand my grief completely, but he's here to carry me through it. I don't know how I'll ever repay him for everything he's done for me, but loving him forever sounds like a good start. "I'll be okay."

He pinches his brows, searching my face as if he doesn't believe me. "I know you will, but maybe getting out of the house isn't the worst idea in the world? And if you leave, update me, okay? I'll be worrying about you all day if you don't."

"I will," I tell him as I take my phone out. "I'll ask Bree if I can come over."

"Good." He grabs my face in his before pressing a long kiss to my lips. "I'll call you after my meetings and update you."

"Good luck, babe," I tell him as he gets up, not wanting to let go of my hand.

"I'm already the luckiest motherfucker around since I have you," he tells me. "Have a good day. I love you."

"I love you too." I smile as he leaves, shutting the door softly behind him. As soon as he's gone, my face falls. I never texted Bree. In fact, I know what I'm going to do today, and before I try to talk myself out of it, I grab the things I need, shove them into one of my bags, throw my shoes on, and walk out of the house.

As soon as I get to the cemetery, I feel uneasy. It's not even because it's a cemetery, it's because I haven't been here since I've been back. I feel like a coward. How is it that I've been back in Pennsylvania for so long and I haven't been back?

How dare I keep moving when I experienced the biggest loss of my life? How dare the world keep spinning when my world crumbled? How dare time continue to move when all I want to do is go back to when my brother was alive? God, I feel terrible. I feel like I shouldn't feel like this because it happened so long ago, but it almost feels like only minutes have passed since I got that phone call.

I spent the entire summer chasing Tobias and his presence across the country, and I still couldn't feel him. Now that I'm back, he's still not around, and my grief has somehow erupted tenfold today. Why today of all days? It's just a normal fucking Friday, but for some reason, the weight won't leave my chest.

I turn my phone off before I sit down, not wanting to be interrupted. It feels odd hearing the ping of my phone while I want to talk to my brother. I need him right now. I need his guidance, his light, anything he wants to give me to help my mind ease.

The ache won't go away this time. I had some good days here and there, but the ache still lingered. It was there, I just chose to ignore it, and now it's stronger than ever. But even on the good days, they still felt like a smoke screen. I was always waiting for something to happen, for something to remind me that he's gone. Every good day was simply a lie, at least that's what it feels like now because the bad days always came back stronger than the time before.

I wish he was still here with me. I want him, not this piece of paper. I want him, not the music we used to listen to. I want *him*, not the memories we created together.

As I walk over to where my brother's body lays beneath the dirt right next to my dad's, the tears start to fall. I don't remember my father as much as I do Tobias, and that punches the air out from my chest. Here I stand before two headstones, yet I can only see one face clearly. The other is a blur of who my father once was.

That's what sucks about being the youngest when a parent dies, you don't have as many memories as your siblings do. Even if I asked my brothers to describe our father, the picture is still fuzzy.

I wish they were both here. I wish I didn't have to say goodbye twice.

I know in the future, there's a lot more where that came from. I'll be the one that attends all the funerals, that gives all the speeches. I'll be the last one to say goodbye to everyone I love.

The grass is wet beneath me since it rained yesterday, and it's eerily quiet as I sit down, not caring if my pants get wet. All I care about is the two people in front of me.

"I miss you both so much." I say, knowing they can't hear me. "I can't believe you're missing all of the things I'm doing. I can't believe you're not by my side as I take this huge step in my life."

They're dead. They're not coming back. I'm here. I'm alive, yet it feels like something has been creeping up on my mind. Like a virus or something.

"I wish I could come see you wherever you guys are. If there was a rest stop, I'd be there in an instant." I look up at their headstones. "You know that, right? That I'd be there if I could? If I knew it wouldn't wreck the rest of us, I'd be there in an instant."

What if when I'm gone and I go wherever you go when you die, I can't see them? What if they're in some other section that I can't get into? What if they don't recognize me and the person I've become?

I have glasses now. I never had them when they were alive, so what if that is why they can't seem to find me? My hair is longer. It's darker than it used to be as I've grown older. What if all of these changes have made me unrecognizable to them?

"The noise won't stop," I whisper to nobody. "I don't know who I am without you around, Tobias. I'm opening a record store, and I wish you could see it all come together how I hope it will. It's all because of you, you know? My love of music comes from both of you, and now I'm the only one left. Why aren't you by my side for this?"

I might always be searching for him in everything I do, but his place remains the same. He will always be a plot in this cemetery. He will always be buried in the dirt me and my remaining family threw on top of him.

I unfold the letter and re-read it to myself.

Teags.

My baby sister. My only sister. You'll still have two brothers after I'm gone, but you'll always be my only sister. When you were born, I no longer had only brothers. I finally had a sister, and you were everything to me, Teags. Fuck, you were everything to all of us—Tristan, Theo, and I. I know you never needed us to protect you, but as soon as you were born, the three of us knew of nothing else. You were our sister, and the three of us knew what that meant. We knew you didn't need us or our help, but we would give it anyway.

I know you're scared you'll be the last one left, but you'll always find me where you hear the music. Can you hear the music, Teags? Not just the actual music, but do you hear it in the breeze? Do you hear it when the birds chirp and you yell at them because they wake you up?

Life is music, Teags. I need you to know that even when I'm gone, the music won't stop. Even if you feel like you've lost me, I'll always be near. Find me in the breeze, in the windchimes, in everything that brushes across your face. Find me in your favorite pair of headphones. In the speaker that lives by your bed.

Find me in the vinyls we used to share. In every stereo. And when someone plays a song we used to love, I'm right beside you there too. Even if you can't feel me, I'm always near. Turn that music up for me so I can hear it, okay?

Your big brother forever,
Tobias

Tears won't stop streaming down my face, and when I grab my speaker from my bag, the first song that I play is his favorite.

"I wish you were still here," I say as I lay down. "We still set you a place at the table, you know? It's one of our new traditions since you left."

I'm alone here, and I'm sure if someone walked by and saw me they would think I was crazy, but I'm so tired of hurting.

I'm so goddamn tired of feeling like this. I'm drained, all day, every day. The only time I feel like I have a full battery is when I'm with the people I love.

"I hope you found what you were looking for, Tobias. I hope you're okay wherever you are."

I keep crying, the tears falling into the grass as I lie on my side.

"I hope you know you could've told me. I would've understood, Tobias. I would've. I know what it feels like to be so stuck. Like living another second is the hardest thing in the world. I've felt that so many times since you left, and even before, I was good at hiding it." It was too easy for me to pretend like I was fine. Most people didn't interact with me because of how stone cold I always was, and I preferred it that way. "I wish you could've confided in me." Maybe we wouldn't be here right now. Maybe he would still be at home playing music and dreaming of traveling all over the world.

Maybe.

As the hum of the music plays, I find myself slipping into sleep, hoping I'll see a glimpse of him as I dream.

I STEP OUT OF the meeting I was just in, buzzing with excitement because every conversation I've had with these investors has gone *perfectly*. They can all see the vision Teags and I have created for this store, and I'm grateful I'm good enough at this that my presentations have translated well.

I grab my phone from my pocket, going right to my speed dial to call my fucking girl. It rings and rings and as I wait to hear her voice on the other side of it, I end up getting her voicemail.

"Baby, *please* call me back. I have the fucking best news ever and I need to tell it to you before I explode."

I end the call, swiping to the messages I've been sending her before every meeting. They've all gone unanswered.

"Dom, are you ready to lock this in?" one of the guys says to me as he pokes his head out of the room.

"Yeah," I tell him, masking my nerves. "Just give me a few minutes. I have to make a few calls."

"Understood, man. Just don't keep us waiting for too long," he jokes and I laugh back before the door closes and my face falls, my pulse getting faster. Why the fuck didn't I stay home today? I knew as soon as I saw her this morning that it looked like a hard wake up, so why the fuck did I leave?

She did say she might be going to Bree's house, so I try that route instead of jumping the gun and making crazy assumptions.

Bree answers almost immediately. "Hi, Dom. What do you need now?"

"Is Teags with you? And if she is, can you put her on the phone?" I start to pace around the hallway I'm in.

"Uhh, no, she's not," Bree's voice drops. "Is everything okay?"

"She didn't text you this morning and ask to hang out?"

"No," I hear her call for Vince as she pulls the phone from her ear. "Dom, what's going on?"

"Fuck," is all I say. "Can you give me a minute?"

"No," I hear Vince say. "What's happening?"

"I'm going to call her mom," I tell them. "I'll call you after I speak to her."

"Make it fucking quick," he tells me as I hang up, immediately calling Tabitha. Teags mentioned going over to her old house this morning too, so maybe she decided to head there instead of Bree's.

"Dominic," she says through my phone. "How is one of my son's favorite friends today?"

I smile at the sentiment behind that. "I'm doing alright. I have to make this quick, though. Have you seen Teags today? Is she with you?"

"No, I haven't seen that crazy girl since you all came over for dinner."

Fuck. Where the hell is she? "Okay," I say as I press my fist to my forehead. "Thank you."

"Is everything okay?"

"She's not answering her phone," I tell her. "But I'm sure she's fine."

"Ah," is all she says. "She does that sometimes. I call it Teags Time. Sometimes she needs a minute when her emotions get too heavy. It's how she has always been. Even when she was little, when she needed a minute, we gave it to her."

"Is that right?"

"Yes," she tells me. "Maybe give her a few hours, or if you're really worried, then I'm sure Nico can help."

I sigh heavily, realizing I have a bunch of calls to make. I'm fucking terrified that she's in a bad place right now and I'm not there to help her through it. I love the girl, for fucks sake, and I shouldn't have even left the house this morning after seeing fresh tears in her eyes when I found her in the library. "I'll call him. Thanks, Tabitha."

"No, thank *you*, Dominic. Thank you for taking care of my daughter."

"The honor is mine," I hang the phone up, calling Vince back because I'm sure Nico already knows what's going on. "I need you and Nico to pull out all the stops and find her."

"Nico is already on it," he tells me. "You're worrying us. What the hell is going on?"

"She's having a tough morning, and I should have stayed home with her, but she pushed me out of the house to go to these meetings. I've tried to reach her a bunch of times and she hasn't answered. Her phone goes straight to voicemail."

"I know. Bree just called her a few times. My girl is getting nervous."

"Yeah, me fucking too," I say as I continue to pace. "But I have to go finish out this fucking meeting."

"Then go. Nico and I will be at your place trying to retrace her steps. You better fucking tell Tristan, too, or he's going to kill you."

"I'll send a message," I say. "But I have to go."

"We'll find her. Just trust us, okay? This is what we do best."

I run a hand through my hair as all the worst things possible run through my mind. "I do trust you guys."

I hang up and open a giant thread, adding everyone I can to it before I try to steady myself. Where the fuck could my girl have gone? And why did she turn her phone off? She did the exact same thing when we were in Chicago and when I came back to an empty hotel room and no sign of her, I freaked. She had been crying all day, her eyes red and puffy when she got back and I cornered her in our hotel room.

Fuck, this trip down memory lane is not fucking helping me calm down.

> **Dom: Teags isn't answering her phone. Anyone have an idea where she would be after a tough morning?**

> **Tristan: What the fuck do you mean she isn't answering her phone?**

> **Livvy: What's going on?**

> **Bree: Her phone goes right to voicemail. Vince and Nico are trying to trace her location, but they think her phone is off.**

> **Nico: I'll start combing traffic cameras and anything else I can think of.**

Tristan: Fucking hell. Dom, I'm heading to your house.

Dom: My place seems to be the central hub. I'll be home in fifteen minutes.

Livvy: Maybe she would go to her favorite coffee shop? Tristan and I can swing by before we head to your house.

Bree: Vince and I will check out her favorite bookstore. Maybe she just turned her phone off while shopping?

Tristan: You don't think she'd go to the cabin, do you?

Livvy: Oh, shit.

Vince: I can send one of my guys to go look.

Tristan: Fuck.

Dom: I'm hoping one of you finds her and I'm overreacting for nothing.

Tristan: You better be right because if she's hurt or I find out you did something to my sister, I'm going to kill you.

Dom: Understandable.

Vince: Calm down. It's going to be fine.

Nico: Do you people have zero faith in me?

Livvy: I have complete faith in you!

Bree: Same!

Dom: Please just fucking find her.

Nico: I will.

Chapter Thirty-Nine

— AUTUMN LEAVES BY ED SHEERAN

I'M SHAKEN AWAKE BY another presence, so naturally, I kick their legs out from where they stand.

Familiar brown hair enters my vision, and when I see eyes that mirror mine staring back at me, somewhat in pain, I can't help but exhale in relief. "Theo?"

"Geez, Teags. What the fuck?"

"You snuck up on me. What else am I supposed to do? You could've been a stranger."

He only nods at me.

"What are you doing here?" I ask him as I sit up, the sun on its way to setting. *Have I been here all day?* Shit.

He rubs his head, and I should feel bad for slightly hurting him, but I don't. He's the one who snuck up on me. My brother always was one for surprise visits, but he was the last person I expected to see right now. "I could ask you the same thing."

I roll my eyes. "I mean what are you doing back home?"

"I'm looking for something," he answers. I thought he would elaborate but he doesn't.

I probably look terrible, but for once, I don't give a fuck that someone related to me is probably going to see me cry. Or know that I was crying. I'm tired of pretending like it doesn't hurt.

Because it really fucking hurts, and some part of me will always ache.

But Tobias is always with me. Even if I can't feel him, he's here. My big brother—one of them—will always be with me. The ache I'm always feeling? It's him. It's all my love that I never got to show him, never got to give to him.

That ache is music. And wherever music is, Tobias is. He told me himself.

"Are you okay?"

"No."

I know he wasn't expecting that answer, but it feels good to be honest for once. I'm not okay. I know he's not either. He looks different than he did the last time I saw him. More... weighted.

"Your face is all puffy. This is... weird. You never cry. You don't have emotions."

I roll my eyes. "Just because I don't cry doesn't mean I don't feel." I hide my tears from him. "And I do cry. A lot, it seems."

"That's refreshing," he tells me. "I was getting worried when you kept calling me and using that weird voice."

"What voice?"

"The pretend voice. Your tone gets higher when you're acting like you're okay." He pushes his elbow into my side. "You've done that since you were little. You did it when Dad died too."

I did? "I didn't know I did that."

"All of us did. We used to call your personal time Teags Time. It was code for when we knew you needed space. Nobody was allowed to disturb you during Teags Time."

"Oh." I don't really know what else to say. I didn't realize anyone paid that much attention to me, let alone my entire family. I always felt like an outsider growing up, but maybe that was my own doing. "I didn't think you all noticed I needed my space sometimes."

"You and Tristan. You two are fucking weirdos."

I laugh, a real laugh at Theo calling Tristan and I that. "Well, you and Tobias were the ones always barging in and trying to get us all to play that stupid game you guys liked."

"Capture the flag?"

I nod. "That's the one. Except the flag we used was a beach towel. I still think the teams were unfair. Tristan was never fun when we were kids."

"Well, he never really got to be one."

I turn to him. "Did any of us after Dad passed?"

He shakes his head at me. "Not really."

The two of us sit and stare at the two headstones in front of us. I notice that my music is still playing. "Heaven" by Bryan Adams is on as Theo and I stare ahead. It's not quite comfortable—the silence of the cemetery that surrounds us. It feels heavy, the air full of grief and unspoken words people never got to say.

And then I feel the breeze across my face. I hear the whistle of the wind through the air.

"Do you feel that?" I ask.

"Yeah, Teags. I do."

I smile to myself for the first time today, wanting to digest the simplest things like a small breeze or birds chirping in the distance. Life is music, you just have to listen closely enough to hear it.

"I miss them every single day," my brother admits, looking down at the grass where they're buried.

"I do too." This is the first time we're acknowledging it. Right here, sitting in front of both headstones, we're acknowledging that the two of us are in pain. We're still grieving, and we may never stop. "I'm glad you're home, Theo. We've all been worried about you up in Vermont."

"Don't worry about me. I'm not totally alone up there." He looks over at me before he scooches closer. "Can I hug you or is it not a good time?"

"I could use a hug," I tell him, my voice cracking as I speak.

And when his arms wrap around me, instead of pulling away like I normally do, I lean in. I lean in and I give my big brother a hug because he's still here. Theo and I were always pretty close, but right now, he's the one who understands my grief the most. After Tristan left, the three of us were in our house all the time before Tobias went off exploring and never came back.

"I don't know where to put it all," I admit, feeling defeated. God, it feels good to talk this all out with someone who's had the same feelings I've had for the past year.

"What do you mean?" he asks as he pulls his arms back.

I run my hand through the ends of my hair. "I've carried it, Theo. I've carried it all around with me. All the pain, guilt, and sadness have been my companions for two years, along with all of yours, Mom's, and Tristan's. It's like it all trickled down and piled on top of mine, and I don't know how to get it off." I wipe a tear from my eye. "I don't know where to put it."

After I'm done, he stands up, wipes his pants off, and reaches his hand down for me. I take it and he helps me up. He wipes some dirt off my pants before he offers me his hand again. I put my hand in his, but he swats it away.

"What?"

"You give it to me, Teags. Give some of that pain to me and let me help you carry it."

Oh, so it was a metaphor. "I don't know how to do that."

"Then we'll figure it out together. Deal?"

I nod my head. "Deal."

"No matter where I am, Teags. Call me. Text me. Especially, if you're feeling like the world is caving in." We start to walk back toward the road.

"You can't just turn your phone off and scare the shit out of all of us like this again."

All of us? "What do you mean?"

"Dom and Tristan are worried sick. So is Mom. Please fucking call someone before they put out an Amber Alert."

I stop in my tracks. "Why didn't you tell them where I was? How did you find me?"

He shrugs his shoulders. "I wasn't trying to find you. I was already headed back here when I got the message from Tristan, so I came to the first place I would have if I was you."

I might be the worst sister on the planet for freaking my brothers out how I did. I can already imagine where their heads were at.

"It's my first time here since I've been back."

"Me too. I didn't even come to visit before I left for my trip." I didn't even know he was headed back, but Theo always did prefer surprise visits. I wonder why he chose now to come back, and I wonder if this means he found what Tobias sent him searching for. "Also, Dom? Really?"

I smile to myself. "It's a long story."

"Well, tell it to me on the way home," he says. "Did you fucking walk here?"

"I needed to clear my head," I tell him. "Walks always help."

As we get into his car, I tell him about the road trip, and everything that's happened since I last saw him—not certain parts, though. I'd rather die than tell my brother about all the fun extracurricular activities we had in different hotels across the country.

Speaking about Dom makes my face light up, and when I turn my phone back on, messages and missed calls flood my notifications. I have seventeen voicemails just from Dom, and a bunch from everyone else.

I hate that I made them worry, but in a way, it feels nice having people around me that worry about me. Gregory never really did. He always let me do my own thing, unless we had an event. He never cared enough to check in with me, even though he knew about Tobias.

It's nice talking to someone who understands where I'm at. Theo knows what my grief feels like, even though it's not the exact same as his.

I send a quick message to a group chat before Theo drives me home.

> Teags: I'm okay. I'm headed home now.

> Teags: Sorry to worry you all, but don't worry, I'm still here.

Chapter Forty

— CARRY YOU HOME BY ALEX WARREN

"How much longer until an update, Vince? I could be out looking instead of you wasting my time," I say as I pace around my living room.

"Nico is running facial recognition, and about a thousand other things. He'll find something, but it takes time."

Vince is sitting on my couch, all cool and collected as I freak out in front of everyone. Bree sits next to him, both of her legs bouncing. I know she's as worried as I am, and I hate that I have no answers to soothe either of our minds.

If it were up to us two, we'd be halfway to the West cabin by now. I don't think Teags would go there, but that's where Tristan ended up when his grief overwhelmed him, and it had us all worried sick.

I knew I should have stayed home today. I knew I should have said something before I walked out the door after I saw that weird look on her face, but I brushed it off. I should know better. I should know my fucking girlfriend better.

"Dude, sit down. You're turning into Liv."

"Hey," she says, slightly offended. I've been pacing around my whole house since I found out she was missing. "He's not wrong though."

"I'm not going to calm down until we find her."

"Why don't you pet one of your fishes? That ought to calm you down," Vince says, and I see Tristan fist bump him behind Liv's head.

"Seriously? You're joking, right now? Your sister is missing, Tristan. She could be dead on the side of the road and you're making jokes?"

"Dude, obviously I'm worried, but Nico is good at his job. Vince too. They do this shit for a living, so trust that they'll find her, okay?"

A phone starts to ring, and when Vince answers it, I can only assume Nico is on the other side of the line.

"I'll be back," he says before he walks out of my front door.

"Why couldn't he take that call in front of us? Does that mean it's bad news?"

Bree stands and comes over to me and before I can tell what she's about to do, she wraps her arms around me. "She's fine, Dom. Vince always takes his calls away from relatives of whoever they're looking for. It's standard procedure."

I wrap my arms around her. "I can't lose her, Bree. I just got her."

She nods her head into my shoulder. "I know."

"Dom, I'd let go if I were you. Vince might come back and cut your arms off if he sees you touching Bree."

Liv smacks her husband. "Bree hugged him first. It was all on her terms, babe."

Bree only smiles as she leads me to one of the other couches. "Just sit here, okay? I'll go see what's going on."

After she shuts the door, Liv gets up and goes to the kitchen. She's going to bake whatever she can with the ingredients I have. I know she's stressed about this, too, she's not showing it as much as Bree and I are. When Liv gets stressed, she bakes. She knows sweets make people feel better, and she's done it for as long as I've known her.

I'm not complaining though. Her desserts are delicious.

Now, it's only Tristan and I that sit in the living room. It's not as awkward as it used to be, but there's still some weird tension filling the room.

"I've never seen you so fucked over someone before."

"I guess there's a first time for everything," I say as I run my hand through my hair.

He only looks at me from the couch, not a single muscle moving in his body besides his rapid heart rate. "You really love her, don't you?"

There's no point in lying. "Yeah, Tris, I do. More than anyone else in the whole fucking world."

And then he gets up, and just as I think he's about to punch me in the face again, he holds his hand out. I shake it, and he goes to sit back down.

That's approval if I've ever seen it.

Both of our phones buzz at the same time, and before I think Vince posted an Amber Alert for Teags, her name pops up in my messages.

Vince comes back inside and throws his phone on the table. "She was at the cemetery."

"Did you get a different text than we did?" Tristan asks him.

"What are you talking about? Nico caught Theo's license plate at the light turning out of the cemetery. She's headed back this way now."

"Theo? My brother, Theo? The one who's in Vermont right now?" Tristan asks, and he sounds as confused as I feel.

"So, she was at the cemetery?" Bree asks. "That's not the weirdest place she could be."

She was visiting Tobias. She told me once how she hadn't been back to see him since he was buried. I should've known that was the first place she would go when she was having a tough morning.

"How did she look in the video? Did she look hurt? Harmed in any way?" I ask Vince.

"I don't think so, but you couldn't really tell."

"You're really not fucking helpful." I point at him.

"I fucking found her, didn't I?"

"After she texted us that she was alright!"

He flips me off. "Whatever, man. You're the one in the relationship with her."

"Don't remind me," Tristan says as he heads to the kitchen. "That's my sister you're talking about."

"You just shook my hand in approval seconds ago."

He waves his hand at me without turning around. "Doesn't mean I want to hear about it."

I run both of my hands down my face, and as I do, my front door opens.

There she is. My beautiful girlfriend who tried to give me a fucking heart attack. Her outfit is soaked, her pants completely wet as if she was lying on the ground. There are teardrops on her shirt, or rain. Could be either with her.

Her eyes lock with mine and I can see her apology in them, but I don't fucking care. All I care about is that she's okay.

I rush her and scoop her up in my arms, her legs go around my back in an instant. My hands are up her back, practically in her hair as I cradle her to my body.

"Don't ever fucking do that again."

She pulls her head back from my shoulder, her eyes glassy. "I'm sorry. I just needed a second."

I push her head into me, needing to feel her as close as she can get. "You fucking scared me, baby."

"She just needed some Teags Time, that's all," Theo says as he pushes into my house.

I drop her to the ground as Tristan heads for his brother. There's a big fucking family reunion happening inside of my house, but I don't care. She's alright. Teags is in front of me—alive, breathing, and I couldn't be fucking happier.

Teags runs straight to Bree, and like the sun and the moon those two collide, Teags's dark hair and Bree's blonde mixing together as they hug.

"Are you okay?" Bree asks her as she brushes hair out of her face.

"Not yet, but I feel better already."

Theo hugs his brother. "Welcome home," Tristan tells him.

"Thanks, man." The two share a knowing look, and I'm so fucking happy everyone is here, right now.

This house feels like a home for once with all of these people and voices in it. That's what the West family and the Hart sisters do. They make every place, no matter where you are, feel like home.

It's just something about their presence in the world. This small family they have is full of comfort, laughter, and love, and I'm somehow lucky enough to be a part of it. I never had this growing up, but it seems these people around me are making up for lost time, and I can't thank them enough for sticking around.

"I told you all to have some faith in me," Nico says, a huge fucking smile on his face as he waltzes into my house.

"I never doubted you for a moment," I joke before reaching out to shake his hand. "In all seriousness, thank you."

"Anything for you two."

"There are sugar cookies baking in the kitchen," Liv says as she comes out, the other two girls enveloping her in a group hug. "Do not scare us ever again, Teags."

"I'm sorry," I hear her mumble.

"What are you doing back here? Are you home for good?" Tristan asks his brother.

Theo looks a lot different than the last time I saw him. His hair is a little longer, and I can see the same look in his eyes that Teags has. He looks exhausted, but he's also smiling and trying to bring the energy in the room up. I've done the exact same thing, except I masked my sadness with snarkiness. It looks like he's trying to seem okay, but I can see right through him.

He has been alone traveling across the country on whatever mission Tobias has him on. The only reason my road trip wasn't as bad as it could have been was because Teags was with me. Theo has nobody, just him and the guide his brother left for him. I can't imagine how hard it's been for him.

"No," Theo says. "I came back to look for something. I'm headed back in a few days. I have," he pauses to think of what he wants to say, "unfinished business in Vermont. I'm not quite done there yet."

"Well, I'm glad we have you for a few days." Tristan pats his brother on his back. "It's good to see you."

"You too, Tris."

I set my eyes on my girl again, and she can sense my stare, holding her arms out for me to walk right into. My arms go around her head, while Liv and Bree are next to us and still holding onto her hand together.

"I'm so fucking glad you're okay."

"I'm sorry I worried you all, but it does feel good to be home." She sets her gaze onto her brothers, and I know she probably wants to talk with them about something, so I let her go and head over to Vince and Nico.

"Do you all want to stay for dinner? I can whip up something."

"Do you have pasta?" Vince asks me and I nod. "Perfect. Leave dinner to this asshole and I."

"Aw, you're too sweet to me, princess," Nico says to Vince as they head into my kitchen, and the smell of Liv's cookies wafts into the living room.

I figure we're all already here so dinner is the least I could do to thank them for dropping everything to look for Teags. Plus, I missed this feeling of togetherness and inclusion. I want to start celebrating that more often—the fact that we all found one another and continue to choose to be a part of each other's lives. It's special, and it doesn't happen often where you find a group like the one we have here.

I'm grateful to be a part of it, and I'm grateful for the girl who looked at me and chose to love me for more than one night.

Chapter Forty-One

— AT THE BEACH, IN EVERY LIFE BY GIGI PEREZ

"Can I talk to you guys outside?" I say to my brothers as Bree hugs me for the third time. I feel like a horrible person—I didn't mean to worry everyone so much. I was just really fucking sad. I needed a minute. I needed to have a talk with my brother.

Theo and Tristan nod their heads as they head to the backyard, and I untangle from Bree and look at her face before I follow them.

"I'm sorry, Bree. I didn't mean to—"

She nods her head. "I know. Next time, send one of us a text, okay?"

"Okay," I say as I head for my brothers.

I open the sliding glass door and the two of them turn their heads to look at me as I come outside. I'm still wearing my grass and tear stained outfit. There are raindrops all over my glasses, and I can barely see them, so I take them off all together.

"I'm sorry I turned my phone off and I'm sorry I worried you all so much. It won't happen again, and I'll turn my location back on as soon as possible."

Theo's about to say something but Tristan cuts him off.

"Teags, I don't care about that," he tells me. "I just want to know you're okay."

Tears fill my eyes and before I shove them down and pretend they aren't there, I let them fall. "I'm not okay, and I haven't been since the day I rushed home and found Mom on the floor of our house in tears. I think—" I pause because I'm breathing a little too hard. All of the things I'm trying to say keep getting caught in my throat. "I think a piece of me died that day with him, and I've been searching for something to patch it back together but nothing will. I have to accept that. I have to accept that there will always be a small part of my soul missing because he's gone. I have to accept that good things can still happen and at the same time, I can be sad about Tobias missing out on them. Those two things can coexist without me feeling like I'm forgetting about him."

Theo lets me finish knowing I have more to say, but Tristan reaches his hand out and puts it on my shoulder. He always was one to comfort us—to carry us through the hard times and big feelings we were having. I'm glad he found Liv to carry him through it for once instead of just relying on himself.

"I know I'm terrible at talking to you about things and my emotions, but I'm tired of holding them inside and pretending like I'm fine. I'm hurting. We're hurting, each of us, and I don't know how to get through it without you both. I've lived my whole life surrounded by my older brothers. You've lived part of your lives without me, but I have *always* had you. And I need you right now because while I am happier than I've been, I also know this feeling I've lived with since Tobias left will always follow me. It will always follow *us*. Maybe it won't be in the same form every time, but it will always exist. I don't want to feel it alone anymore, and I know you guys understand better than anyone else can because it happened to all of us."

Both of my brothers have tears in their eyes as mine fall freely, and I no longer have a care in the world if I look weak. I need my big brothers, and I know they need me too. Through all of the terrifying thoughts, all of the searching I did for my brother, I almost forgot I still have two here who feel how I do. It's not the same feeling for any of us. We all have our own grief to sort through, but we have all lost a brother. And a father. We have all been front row at two different funerals in our lives.

I know we're not immune to being in that row again, but I really hope it's not anytime soon.

"I need you both to promise me that if it ever gets too tough and if you ever feel low and can't find a way out, you'll pick up the phone and call. Because I don't want to be sitting front row at your funerals wishing I could have done something—"

Theo and Tristan both capture me in a hug, and I fully break. All of the emotions I never felt back when Dad died, all of the emotions I buried as a kid growing up are pouring out of me as I sob in the arms of my two remaining brothers.

"It'll never come to that, Teags," Theo reassures me. "It won't."

"I don't think any of us can handle another funeral," Tristan says as we all separate. "Do you promise, Teags?"

"I do," I say as I wipe a few tears. "I can't handle setting another place at the table for one of you. I love it as a tradition, but I can't handle another placeholder. I wish he was here and not just an empty chair around the table."

I used to think death was the scariest thing life had to offer. I mean, it's kind of the whole point to living isn't it? To live means that you'll eventually die—and that fear of the unknown over what happens after all this is terrifying. You don't have the answer to what comes next until your time is up, and that scared the hell out of me.

I've come to realize that death isn't just a singular thing that happens to the person it takes. It happens to everyone who loves, cares about, or knows them. I know this pain I'm feeling over Tobias isn't singular—my entire family feels it too and there's nothing we can do to fix that.

We just have to get through it. One day at a time.

"I think we should talk about all this. It's been enough time, I think." The three of us have never actually sat down and all talked about our feelings over this, but Theo's proposal doesn't sound too bad. We're all grieving the same person in three different ways, and maybe it would be good for us all to talk and walk down memory lane together.

Memories are all we have at this point, and the three of us remember him so differently. I think us talking about him could give us all a new perspective on who Tobias West was.

"I miss him," I whisper to them. "I call his phone just to hear his voice on his voicemail box because I'm worried I'm going to forget what he sounded like."

"I still go up to the cabin sometimes," Tristan tells us. "Liv comes with me. It's hard, but it's the only place I can feel him besides our childhood home."

"I've been chasing him around the country but I still don't think he knows where I am. I'm hoping I can find him in Vermont, but all I've found so far is nostalgia."

"I don't know why Mom never sold the house." We barely used it after Dad died and it's been years since any of us have been up there. Though, I guess Tobias must have gone up at some point if he's pointing Theo in that direction.

"Do you think he's gone forever? Do you think we'll ever feel his presence again?" Theo asks us.

Tristan shakes his head. "No. I think he knows when we need him. Maybe now isn't one of those times because we have each other."

We have each other. We do, and I couldn't be more thankful for that. In the time we've all spent mourning this loss, I think we forgot the rest of us are still here.

"I hope he's not suffering still," Theo says, his voice dropping. "Wherever he is, I hope he found what he was searching for. I hope he's okay."

Tristan and I both nod our heads. I think that's all we could want out of this. Tobias seemed to be suffering silently by himself, and even though we lost him how we did, we all hope he's in a better place. I hope his pain is gone and I know every time I listen to his favorite songs he's listening to the same ones.

"We're not dying, the three of us, you know?" I say, my mind running off course.

"What?" Tristan looks at me, puzzled.

"Since he left, it felt like I was dying. I was stagnant, sad, grieving, and I ran away to Arizona to try and escape those feelings, but they came with me. And then I left and came back here only to run across the country with Dom to try and find the feeling I've been chasing for the last two years."

"What feeling was that?" Theo asks me.

"I wanted to feel alive again, and I still don't feel one hundred percent back to who I was, I don't think I ever will, but we're not dying. The three of us are not dying." Another tear falls. "We're just sad. We're sad Tobias isn't here anymore, but for me, he's music. He's in music and the wind, and any other tune life can create because that's what Tobias was for me. He was music."

The three of us sit with the memory of our brother before Tristan speaks.

"For me he was a tangent." Theo and I must look confused because he keeps going. "Whenever I called him, a simple conversation would turn into hour long calls about the most random shit." Tristan stops to laugh through his tears.

"He always did prefer calls over anything else," Theo says.

"I've never talked on the phone with someone as much as I did with him. Sometimes I still think he'll call me one day and we'll pick up where we left off about whatever topic he wanted to talk about," Tristan jokes. "But I find myself calling people more often than I used to. I crave hearing someone's voice over a simple text message. I'd like to thank him for that, no matter how much I used to hate it when he would call because I knew it would turn into an entire hour or two of conversation about anything. He used to distract me from *everything* I was supposed to be doing, but now I'd give anything for five more minutes."

"For me, he was a puzzle." Theo laughs through his tears. "I have this very vivid memory of when we were kids. I was sick and I had to stay home from school, and Tobias faked being sick too. Mom let us stay home together, but she practically sealed off his room and made us both stay in there so you two wouldn't get sick."

A faint picture of that day conjures in my mind, and I can almost see the silhouette of my two brothers, huddled on Tobias's bed laughing their heads off.

"The two of us spent the entire day doing a thousand piece puzzle he had found in the basement the night before. It took us an entire day to finish it, and he actually had gotten sick after spending the entire day with me, so that whole week, all we did was build puzzles together. I don't know why that memory of all things is the one that has stuck with me throughout all these years, but I remember that day as if it were yesterday." Theo pinches his eyes with his fingers, wiping the tears from it. I can see a faint sparkle hidden behind the sadness as if he's realized something, but he speaks before I ask him about it. "God, I really fucking miss him. This fucking bucket list he has me on has been taking a toll on me, but I also don't want it to end. I'm really dragging out this stint in Vermont because I'm worried what will happen once it's over."

Tristan throws his arm around Theo, pulling him in closer. "The three of us have already lost him, but what will never change are the memories we had when he was here. I think he knows in every life, we would choose to be with him every time."

"In every life, Tobias and I are listening to vinyls and dissecting the lyrics," I say, wiping my nose with my sleeve.

"In every life, he's a phone call and a tangent."

Theo nods to himself as he looks at the two of us. "In every life, he's a puzzle waiting to be built."

"And in every life," I say as my throat starts to close, "he's our brother."

The three of us nod through our tears, all of our arms coming around us as we hug again, the wind blowing across us as we stay linked together, all of us thinking of Tobias in our own way.

He'll always be missed, and there's nothing we can do to bring him back. All we can do is remember the good times, remember the times we grew up in the same house and laughed, argued, and cried around the same kitchen table.

That is how I'm choosing to remember my brother, and I know in every life, he'll find me even if I can't feel him.

Chapter Forty-Two

Dominic

— ISIMO BY BLEACHERS

While Teags is out talking with her brothers, and Vince and Nico are spearheading dinner, I take this moment to steal the two Hart sisters and have a talk with them.

"Should we be worried?" Bree asks me. "Are you about to say something extremely outlandish to us?"

Liv only crosses her arms at me. She knows me a little too well, and I can tell from the look on her face that she knows this isn't going to be one of my stupid conversations. "No, I don't think that's it."

"Thanks, Livvy," I say as I sit down on the ottoman in my living room, the two of them on my couch in front of me. "I, uh, I don't really know how to say this."

"Is everything alright, Dom?" Bree asks me as she twists her bracelet on her wrist. "I know today was long, but—"

"It's not about today," I say as I take a deep breath. "A few weeks ago, I basically cut myself off from my parents and their hold on me. I know it was the right decision, but part of me still feels...off. I don't really know how to explain it."

The two of them look at one another before Liv grabs Bree's hand.

"We understand the feeling," Livvy says.

"You don't even have to say anything else," Bree smiles. "I can't imagine how hard that was for you."

"It was easier than I thought it would be, if I'm being honest," I tell them, running a hand through my hair. "And I know it was the right move, but there's still this emptiness inside of me."

"That's normal," Livvy tells me. "Can I say something?"

"Of course."

"If I didn't have my sister, telling off my parents would have been a lot harder. Without Bree, my parents would have been all I had, and I don't know if I would have been able to do what was best for me if I was in that situation. I don't think I would have been strong enough."

Both Liv and Bree have gone no contact with their parents, but it took them both almost two decades of dealing with them to do it. Liv was constantly ignored by her parents as a child, and Bree was the product of all their attention. Liv cut them off when she found out they destroyed her and Tristan's relationship for no reason, and Bree cut them off when they told her very personal story for the entire world to hear. I knew they would understand all the weird and confusing feelings I'm having about my own family troubles.

Bree slaps her sister's hand. "Don't say that, Livs. You are the strongest person I know, and none of that strength comes from me."

"Some of it does," she tilts her head at her sister. "But a lot would have been different about my life," Liv turns to me. "You lost your parents and your siblings. You lost the only two other people who understood what it was like growing up in the environment you did. That's bound to be difficult, Dom. And you can accept that you did what was best for you, while still being upset at the cards you were dealt. Both of those things can exist at the same time. Not for nothing, but I'm *really* proud of you."

Livvy stands and sits next to me, leaning her head on my shoulder as her arm comes around me. Bree grabs one of my hands before she speaks.

"It's hard being a kid who's confused as to why your parents are different than other ones, but what's even harder is growing up and realizing that they never cared about what they did to you. And one of the hardest things you have to do sometimes is let go of the people who share the same blood as you because you know it's what's best."

"I've always known who they were," I tell them. "But part of me hoped they might change after I said everything I did to them."

"That's what I wanted too," Liv tells me. "And it didn't happen. It will never happen, and that realization punched me in the gut, much like it's doing to you know."

"But you know what helped the most?" Bree asks me.

"What?"

"The people in this house," she tells me. "*This* is the family Liv and I have always craved. With the West siblings, Vince and Nico, and you, Dom. We're a family because we continue to choose one another. We show up during the hard times, and we carry one another through the difficult parts because *that* is what a family does. Our versions of families growing up were skewed, but that doesn't mean that's the only family we have."

"We have all created something so beautiful, and if you ever need a reminder of what a family does, we're all only one call or text away."

A single tear falls from my eyes as I look between the two Hart sisters. "Thank you. I can confidently say I'll be taking you up on that offer."

"Good," Bree says. "Because Livvy and I know better than most how difficult losing your family can be."

"But you're never alone, Dom. Never." Livvy smiles at me. "If you ever want to come over and bake with me, I would *love* that."

I can't help but laugh. I did ask her to teach me that recipe when we were back in college. "I bet Tristan would love that."

"He would, Dom, because he loves you, even if you guys have had a rough few weeks."

"And we'll be seeing a lot of one another when the store gets off the ground," Bree tells me. "So, you're always welcome at my house. Oh!" Her eyes widen at me. "Livvy, we should invite him to do our egg-throwing tradition! Dom, it's the best."

"I can't wait to hear more." I laugh as I hear the sliding door open.

As soon as I see the West siblings walk through it, eyes red, faces puffy, and smiles on their faces, I know the talk went well, whatever it was about. Vince has taken over my kitchen with dinner preparations, and I head over to my girl as she heads for the food. I feel bad that I'm technically hosting all this and I haven't really been helping.

"How's dinner going? Can I help with—"

"No," is all I say as I slide around the counter. "Go hang out with the girls or your brothers. We've got it handled."

"Are you sure?"

I press a long kiss to her lips, my adrenaline slowly wearing off from the freak out I had the entire day, but I understand it. She needed a minute, but hopefully in the future, she comes to me when she's overwhelmed. "Yes, I'm sure."

"Well, the least I can do is set the table," she says as she takes the plates and utensils from the pile Nico made earlier.

I take a minute to really take in the atmosphere of the house I once described as sterile and quiet. Now, it's bursting with life. I hear whispers of different voices, laughter bounces off of the walls, and for the first time in a long time, I can see a future full of this. I never wanted to embrace the idea of having people over and doing family-like events because the only events I knew as a family were work things. It was a fancy night of dressing up and playing pretend for hours on end, knowing at the end of the night, I wouldn't see my parents.

Now, I can see that family is who shows up for you when you call. It's laughter and stupid jokes and dinners together to celebrate nothing. It's company when you don't think you need it. It's leaning on one another because you can no longer hold yourself up on your own. I never thought I would have a real and true family.

I guess in a way, I don't, but I have the best version of a family that one can. The group of us continues to choose one another, time and time again. Even though we didn't grow up together, we all know what it feels like to not be wanted, or to be alone, or to understand that the meaning of the word family doesn't have to mean one thing. It's not just blood or who you grew up with. It's who chooses to grow alongside you, through the good and the bad. Through tough times and through happiness. Through the worst times, they're still there for you because that's what a family is.

"You've been stirring that for way too long, Nico. There's no way that isn't done," Vince says as he turns the stove off for the sauce he made.

"How do I know when it's ready?"

"You throw it at the wall," I tell him and he laughs. "That's not a joke."

Vince only sighs as he grabs the pot and brings it to my dining room. "I prefer tasting it to a food fight, but do whatever you two want to."

"Well, it is your house, so if you want me to throw it at the wall, then so be it," he tells me before grabbing some of it out of the colander, and lightly tossing it at the wall. It sticks to it. "What does that mean?"

"It's done," I tell him as he laughs to himself. "Thank you for all you did for me today. I know you mostly did it for her, but you made today a lot less fucking scary than it could have been. I'm glad to have you in our corner."

"I'm glad you're aware enough to know it was for Teags. But you're connected to her now, and I can tell she's happy with you, so you're a part of the group I protect when I say I protect the ones closest to me."

"Thanks, man," I say as I hold my hand out to him, he shakes it, and the two of us head for the dining room where everyone else has congregated. I almost forgot that I have news to share amidst all of the chaos that happened today, and I can't think of a better place to share it than with the people I love the most in the world.

Well, minus Harry and Ethan. Harry was too busy with his girlfriend to accept my invitation to come over tonight, and Ethan is in Ohio, still shooting whatever film he's working on.

I take my spot at the head of the table, next to Teags and Tristan, and as I look around at the family around the table, I can't help but feel a pang of something in my chest. I started this year out working for my family, the unhappiest I've ever been trying to prove myself to be good enough for something I didn't even want. My family never believed in me. They saw me as a loose end, something they wanted to mold to fit all of their impossible standards.

Now, we're a few months out from the year being over and here I sit, surrounded by my favorite people on the planet and the girl I never saw coming who I love with every piece of myself. I'm no longer under the insane constraints my parents wanted me to be under. I'm happy, truly happy for the first time in a while, and I never thought I'd be here. I never thought I'd feel this again.

"Livvy, I'm sorry I caused you to stress bake in Dom's oven, but I am eyeing those cookies already. They look delicious," Teags says to her.

"I might have snuck one in the kitchen, and I can confirm they taste as good as they look," Nico says before he blocks the slap Vince was about to do against his arm. "You're too predictable, Vincey."

"You're going to spoil your appetite."

"Baby, it's okay," Bree says as she leans her head on his shoulder. "But can we eat? I am *starving*. It's been a long day."

"My bad," is all Teags says, adjusting her glasses on her face.

I reach over and grab her hand, squeezing it three times as she smiles at me. There's my girl. There's my favorite fucking smile in the entire world. "I'm sorry to tell you all, but there might be a little more of a wait before we eat. I have an announcement to make." I stand from my chair, my hand still in hers.

"If you say something insane, I'm going to punch you again," Tristan says as Livvy grabs his fisted hand on the table. He immediately relaxes into her touch, and I roll my eyes.

"Dude, seriously? Do you have zero faith in me?"

Tristan goes to speak, but Theo answers for him. "He might have faith in you, but I still need the story of how you and my sister came to be," he pauses, looking for the right word, "together."

"Any time you want to hear it, I'll give it," I tell the room. "But my announcement is exciting. Teags and I officially have investors for the record store she wants to open."

Smiles are spread all around the room, and Teags's hand falls out of mine when she realizes what I said.

"Are you serious? We're really going to do this?" Her excitement lights the entire room up.

"Say the word, Teags, and I'll call them right now and tell them we accept."

"Oh my, of course I fucking accept." She stands up, launching her arms around me in a hug as everyone celebrates. "I can't believe this."

"My meetings this morning went swimmingly and they *loved* the ideas we came up with," I say into her ear. "We're doing this, baby. Let's take your dream and fucking run with it."

"I love you," she says to me.

"I love you too," I tell her as I raise my glass. "And I want to start a new tradition with the group of us. So, before we eat, everyone raise your glass and make a toast. I'll start. To this beautifully talented woman beside me who's making every dream of mine come true," I say as I take a sip.

Teags raises hers next. "To the future. May it be the best chapter yet."

"To trying our best every day." Bree smiles. "Because just the act of trying is enough."

"To my sister, for the pasta recipe and everything in between," Vince says, a smile on his face.

"To protecting the ones we love." Nico raises his glass. "And for the ones we've lost."

Theo bashfully raises his glass. "To the past that has led us all here. May we never run too far from who we are."

Livvy smiles as she raises her glass. "To the family around this table and the ones who couldn't be here. I love you all."

"To second chances. If it weren't for those, none of us would be here," Tristan says as we all clink our glasses together and dig into dinner. I take in every inch of conversation, every smile and laugh thrown around the table, and I sit with it because I may not have known what this was like when I was younger, but I know now.

I made it out of the place that once caged me in and tried to mold me into something I'm not. I know it's not always going to be perfect—the life I want to create—and even in the joy, sadness can still exist. The one thing I'm sure of, is that if these people are by my side for the rest of my life, I have nothing to worry about.

Because there will always be laughter. There will always be chaotic dinners around a table like this one. No matter where we are, who we're with, the table will always remain the same, and everyone will always have a seat around it. We all made it through, and though we're not fully out of the darkness, the light is coming toward us.

Each of us has our own guiding light, and mine so happens to be the dark-haired girl sitting next to me, smiling to her best friend next to her as they talk about a book they read recently, or I can assume because of the amount of hand motions they're doing.

Tonight is a memory I hope to never forget. This is the very first night this house felt like a home. One filled with chaos and love, and this night will remain ingrained in the walls for years to come, and I can't wait for the other memories we all create by one another's side.

It hasn't even happened yet and already I want time to slow down. What a beautiful wish to have though.

Chapter Forty-Three

One Year Later

— GERONIMO BY SHEPPARD

"Baby?" my boyfriend's voice filters through the house as I finish buttoning the top I've chosen to wear for today. Nerves are spreading through my entire body, but just hearing his voice has started to calm me down. His hands find my body as he hugs me from behind, pressing a kiss to the back of my ear. "You look so fucking sexy."

"Do you really think it's okay?"

He nods. "Just to make sure"—he grabs my hand in his—"do a spin for me."

I roll my eyes, complying with his directions and he whistles while I spin around, pulling me close as soon as I'm done. "We can't be late to the opening of our own store."

"I know." He smiles at me, pulls me in toward his mouth by my neck, and presses a long kiss to my lips before he peppers them all over my face. "Just let me be proud of my girlfriend for a few minutes before her attention is elsewhere all day."

"Well, that is always allowed," I say as I grab his shirt and kiss him. "I'm equally excited and terrified."

"The soft launch exceeded all of our expectations, baby," he reminds me, fixing his hair in the big mirror in our closet. "It's going to be a beautiful day."

"I know, but let's head out before I freak out too much," I say as I grab my huge bags, Dom taking them from my arms before he carries them to the car, and we speed off to the store.

MY NERVES GO AWAY as soon as I'm inside of the store we created. There's always been something so soothing about music for me, and I'm thankful to have a place where I can always feel the impact my brother and his music taste had on me.

And I can't forget my father either. There's an entire cassette section of the store, where people can rent or buy them from us. Cassette players are a lost art in the era of streaming, and I love that I've gotten some messages online about people being excited we have them.

Thanks to Liv and the genius that the Hart sisters are, the social media presence the store has is beyond anything I could have done on my own. All it took was a few videos to pick up traction online, and now the account—run by my fabulous best friend—has over ten thousand followers on it. When Bree told me she wanted to run the social media, I told her no at first. She already has so much on her plate, but she convinced me to do it because that way we could spend more time together than we already do, and she genuinely loves social media despite the hardships it's given her before.

The fact that this business has a piece of everyone I love in it makes it even more special. Dom and I got this place up and running on our own—with the help of some investors. Bree and Liv helped to spread the word to their loyal readers and fans. It turns out a lot of readers are also huge music fans like I am, and our online traffic has already crashed the website twice.

Two separate times I've had to ask Nico to fix whatever was going on, and he congratulates me every time it crashes because then it gives him something to do. I didn't press about that because he's been busier than ever. It feels like every other week he's going on some sort of business trip or something, but he's been very quiet about what he's doing.

Vince even set up a security system for the store, and Dom and him got into a huge fight over payment because Vince wouldn't sell it to us at the full price, but Dom wanted to pay him properly for his services.

And everyone helped out when we were painting and getting this place ready for people to come in. Tristan and Theo helped me figure out where to put each section—vinyls, CDs, cassettes, used books, and more. This is a true family business, and I cannot believe this is my reality. I get to wake up every day and open my store, talking to people who come in about music and everything in between.

This is the dream. I am living my dream every single day, and I have myself and my boyfriend to thank for that. And Tobias, of course. Through every terrifying step of this process, I've felt his guidance through it all. It warms my heart to know there's another small piece of him present in this world. He's now been immortalized in one of Livvy's books, and now this store.

I take a deep breath as I look around at what I've created, trying to stay in the present before the chaos begins.

"I hope I'm making you proud, Tobias," I whisper into the air as I turn the music on, the soft melodies floating throughout the space. "This is all for you."

"He'd be so proud of you," my brother's voice shakes me out of my haze. "I can say for certain that this would be his favorite place to spend time in."

Theo peeks out from behind a giant flower bouquet. "And we're so proud of you, Sis."

A single tear falls from my eye as I grab the bouquets from my brothers, each of them holding one as I set them on the counter, letting their arms wrap around me.

"I'm so fucking glad you guys are here."

"Are you kidding? We wouldn't have missed this." Tristan smiles at me as he takes in the fully finished shop.

"Nothing could have kept us from being here." Theo smiles at me. The three of us look and feel so much better than we used to. It's been a hard few years for all of us, but as I take in all of us, I can't help but smile. "My girl sends her love."

"She will be missed today," I tell him.

"My baby girl," my mother's voice flows through the air as yet another bouquet is held out to me. I barely have time to say anything before she wraps me in her arms. "I am so proud of you."

"Thank you, Mom." I smile into her shoulder. "I really love this place."

"And everyone else is going to as well," she reminds me. "Tobias would love it here. Especially that all his favorites are front and center."

I smile, loving that tiny aspect of the store. There's an entire remembrance section filled with records and tapes that both Tobias and my father loved. I intend to always keep that stocked because with each purchase of anything from that section, the store donates a portion of the sales to Bree's foundation—the one that supports survivors and access to mental health resources.

"Did you all see the sign outside?" I ask them, wondering if they noticed the small detail of it. It's Tobias' handwriting from the letter he left me, and I cried my eyes out the day it was delivered.

They all shake their heads. "The line was way too fucking long. I just wanted to get inside," Tristan jokes. "The girls and the rest of the bunch are coming through the back."

"Are you serious?" I say as I peek my eyes out of the blinds. I knew the local news stations were coming to watch the ribbon cutting, but I didn't think the line would be as long as it was for the soft launch. "Holy shit."

Obviously, I was wrong. There are *so* many fucking people outside and I am so glad I bought all of the extra inventory I did because we are going to be wiped clean after today.

"Special delivery!" Bree's voice echoes through the shop as I see her, Liv, Vince, Nico, and Dom come to the register. Dom is carrying a giant box, as are Vince and Nico, and I have no idea what could be inside of it. "Livvy made enough sweet treats to feed a zoo."

"I didn't want to run out," she says as she barrels me with a hug. "Today is going to be amazing, Teags. I am *so* fucking proud of you."

"Thanks, sis," I tell her, my heart practically bursting as I look at these people around me.

"I brought some of my books too." Her smiles bursts off of her face as she unboxes her books. "I haven't signed them yet, but I figured I can sign them as people buy them. Well, if people buy them."

"They will, pretty girl," my brother says to her. "Because I'll be standing right by the section with your books and talking them up to everyone who walks by."

"That's very nice of you, my love," Livvy says as she grabs a box, and they head to the book section of the store on the other wall.

Bree skips over to me, her camera in my face as she takes videos of all of us. She's apparently vlogging the opening day of the store, and I am so excited to see what she creates from today.

"How excited are you on a scale from one to ten?"

"Probably a twenty-five," I laugh as she puts her camera down, her arms wrapping around me.

"I am so fucking proud of you," she screeches into my ear. "I cannot wait to spend day after day here and talk about books with people. God, the opportunities are endless. I can't wait to see Teags and Dom world domination."

Everyone laughs as she says that, my boyfriend coming over to me, resting his head on top of mine as he grabs my hand.

"I'm totally on board with that," he tells us all. "But we really do have to open the store soon or people are going to get restless."

"He's right," Vince says. "I saw some people lining up here at like three this morning. I thought someone was breaking in on the cameras, but when I saw sleeping bags, I knew what was going on."

Holy shit. "Are you serious?"

He nods, as does Nico.

"Well, I guess we better get out there," I say to my beautiful family around me. "But before we do, I just want to thank you all for all the hard work you've put into this with us. Dom and I could not have done this alone, and it means the world that you're all here to celebrate this insane day with us."

"We're insanely proud of you both," my mom says to me. "You two make a great team."

Dom smiles down at me. "We do, don't we, baby?"

"We absolutely do," I say before he kisses me.

"See you all out there," Tristan says from across the store, the rest of our friends shuffling outside with them, leaving Dom and I by ourselves, his lips still on mine.

"I'm so proud of you," he says against my lips. "I knew you could do it."

"Not without you," I remind him. "And I am proud of you." Not only did Dom break out of his parents' hold, but he also followed the path that was the correct one for him—the one that makes him happiest. I'm grateful to be apart of it with him because he makes me the happiest girl on the entire fucking planet.

We made a promise to them that we wouldn't ever go to the media about Dom's childhood and the real truth behind their "perfect family," if they left us alone. It's been radio silence on their end since we spoke to them, and I'm thankful Dom no longer has to worry about their opinions of him. I remind him every day that he is the most perfect man for me, and I can't imagine having anyone else by my side for this crazy new chapter of life we're on.

"Look at what we created," he says to me, the two of us looking around at our store. He grabs the small pair of scissors on the register, handing them to me. "Now, let's cut that ribbon."

I follow him out of the front entrance, applause ensuing as I take a look around at all the people here, a microphone in front of the store, the giant red ribbon held by my two brothers as Dom and I get comfortable. He steps up to it first.

"Thank you all so much for being here today to celebrate the opening of Pennsylvania's newest record store. Today would not be possible without all of the people standing beside my girlfriend and I, so thank you to every single one of you for your help and guidance," he says before he looks at me. "I'm going to hand the microphone over to the real mastermind behind this, my beautiful girlfriend, Teagen West."

Applause ensues again as I step up to the microphone. I purposefully didn't prepare anything because every time I tried to write something down, it sounded stupid. So, I'm going to speak to the people in line and the viewers at home from my heart. Whatever comes out, comes out. I just hope it's coherent.

"Thank you, baby," I say as I blow him a kiss. "Wow, I really didn't expect so many people to be here today. It's truly surpassing my expectations, so thank you for taking time out of your day to come and support the dream I've had that I never thought I'd be living." I take a deep breath before continuing. "The question I've been asked the most by people at the soft opening and in the comments online is why I chose the name I did for the store, and it's actually an easy question to answer. The store is named for my late brother, who died a few years ago. His name was Tobias, and in the last letter he wrote me, he asked me a very important question. One that I often think about when I miss him. He asked if I could hear the music even when he's not around, and I wanted to immortalize that in some way when I knew I wanted to open this store."

I fiddle with my hands before I continue. "Music was our thing, him and I. We used to dissect lyrics and anything we could when something new came out or when we found one of our Dad's old records in the basement where we definitely weren't supposed to be," I pause to laugh. "Sorry, Mom."

The crowd laughs with me as I smile at her, the brightest smile on her face as she watches me up here.

"So, it is my privilege to welcome you all to *Can You Hear The Music?* Pennsylvania's newest record store and a safe place for anyone and everyone to come and celebrate new music, music that's been out for ages, and everything in between." I take the scissors from my pocket, smiling as I look between Tristan and Theo, the two of them holding the ribbon at the perfect angle as they smile back at me. I take the scissors and cut the ribbon, applause and cheers coming from every single direction as Dom and I pose for a picture, the sign of our store in the background.

"Come on in and let's have a wonderful day," I say into the microphone as my entire family heads inside, the news crew cleaning up the wires and Vince's people making sure everyone is calm while the line starts to move inside.

Liv and Bree are welcoming people, a few customers stopping to take photos with the two of them, some people already having Livvy's books in their hands as they head over to where she stands at the front of the store. Bree is pointing out different records to people as she sifts through the section of one of her favorite artists.

Nico and Vince are at the front of the store, their heads turning back and forth how they always do as they make sure everything is safe in here. Tristan, Theo, and my mom are looking at the remembrance section, my mom probably telling another story about my father and the music he once loved to them. I see both of their faces listening intently as she speaks.

And Dom and I are behind the counter, taking in every second of a day that just seems to get crazier by the minute. I grab his hand in mine as we look at one another, huge smiles on both of our faces.

Before him, I thought love meant drowning when in a crowded room. I thought it meant I was destined to be alone forever, unsure of the road ahead of me because I lost so much of who I was trying to fit myself into a box.

Now, I know that love is swimming alongside someone, through the thick and thin. Through every bad day, I am thankful to have Dom by my side treading water with me until the current eventually sweeps us onto a different road we never saw coming.

I thought I was ruining my life when I left Arizona. I thought the worst of everything because I didn't know what I was doing or where I was headed.

Alongside Dom and this insane journey we've taken together, I've learned that the unknown is sometimes the best part. Not knowing something leads to so many roads I didn't even know were an option. It took falling apart at the seams for me to realize that once a door closes, there are so many ones that can open, and I have time to choose the wrong one. I have time to pick the wrong thing. I have time to make mistakes and be twenty different versions of myself because the real path will always wait for you. Sometimes, it just takes a few difficult moments to get to it.

I still have days where my grief feels like it's eating me alive, but now I ask the people who love to help carry me through it. Arizona was a mere chapter in my story, and despite how much I hated it when I was going through it, I wouldn't change it for the world because it might have taken me a little longer to get to where I needed to be.

Beside these people, this family, I am everything I need to be. I am alive and living in this moment, and nothing can take that away from me because I am the one driving down this road that I call life.

"And to think that day we started on that road trip I was worried about ruining both of our lives."

"What?" I ask as I turn to my boyfriend. "Are you serious?"

"I remember thinking I was either going to ruin us or we were going to get closer." His hands are around my hips and he pulls me toward him. "I'm really fucking glad it worked out for the better."

"We deserved it," I remind him. "And I think the universe knew you weren't going to ruin anything. How could you, Dom? With your big brain, sarcastic mouth, and huge heart, how could you ruin anything?"

He shrugs. "With you by my side, I don't know how I doubted anything."

"In every life, I will find you, Dominic Graves."

He smirks at me. "Is that a threat?"

"It's a promise."

"Then I'm grateful you found me in this one because I don't want to live any of the days we have left without you."

I smile back at him, my cheeks hurting already from how stupidly fucking happy I am. The rest of the day flew by. Conversations centered around music fill my store. People ask about my brother, and I tell them any story I can, his memory never forgotten. I'll never stop talking about him to anyone who will listen.

In every life, I know I feel as alive as I do now. I don't deserve anything less than what I have in this moment with this group of people, and nothing can ruin that.

Epilogue

Dominic

The Future

— ROLLERCOASTER BY BLEACHERS

"Are you seriously about to say no?"

Tristan sits across from me at the kitchen table of his house, his mom right next to him, Liv on the other side of him, the two of them looking like they want to smack him in the face.

Huh. It's probably good that I have those two on my side right now.

"I said I'm thinking about it," he says.

"Honey, you cannot be serious," Tabitha says before she grabs my hands in hers. "It would be an honor if you joined our family, Dominic."

"I can't wait to see the look on Teags's face. When are you going to do it?" Liv asks, her eyes welling up with tears. I'm way past that. As soon as I sat down and opened my mouth to make my case, I started crying. "You two are absolutely perfect together."

"Thanks, Livvy. I'm not too sure yet, but sometime soon," I say as I look back at her husband. "So? I have two out of the three of you and I would really appreciate your blessing too."

He only sighs heavily as he continues to think.

Is he serious? I really thought I was done proving myself to him after all these years, but it turns out he's as stubborn as his sister.

"Tristan West, you cannot still be thinking about this," Livvy uses her stern voice with him. "Dom is one of your best friends, and he makes your sister happy. Just give him your blessing."

"Darling, your stubbornness is showing," Tabitha tsks at him. "Just like your father, you are."

Tristan sighs heavily as he stands up from the table, coming over to where I'm sitting.

"Fine. You can marry my sister."

"Gee, don't sound so fucking thrilled about it," I joke with him before he pulls me in for a bro hug. "I love you, man."

"I love you too." He pats me on the back. "It's really fun seeing you all flustered and nervous. Maybe stop being so damn gullible and I'll stop fucking with you."

"Oh, never," I tell him as I grab my things. "I'll see you all later, okay?"

"Where the hell are you going? Aren't we going to celebrate?" I hear Tristan ask as I'm out the door.

"I have a few more people to ask," I yell before I get into my car and head for my next destination. It only takes me twenty minutes to get there, and by the time I reach where I need to be, I set my small blanket down on the ground, grab the ring box from my pocket and open it before I set it in front of Tobias and her father.

"Hello," I say. "My name is Dominic Graves, though, Tobias we met a few times back when your brother and I were in college. The first time Tristan introduced us, I remember we sat for an hour making fun of him together. I'll never forget that," I say as I laugh to myself. I clear my throat before I turn to her father. "I've been dating your daughter for a while now, and every moment with her has been nothing short of magical. Sometimes, I find myself wondering how I got lucky enough to know and be able to love your daughter. If real-life magic existed, I'm sure she'd be a part of it. Teagen has not only taught me so much about myself, but about who I can be. Before her, I never really felt like somebody. Now,

I'm certain that if I am somebody, it's because of her and all she's done for me. So, with that being said, I would love to marry her and love her forever. I know this is a bit unorthodox, but I wanted to make sure I got permission from everyone she loves and cares for, so that's why I'm here."

I adjust how I'm sitting before I lift the ring up, showing it to each headstone as if they can see it. I'd like to think they can, and I hope it's good enough. I think Teags is going to love it. It's not too flashy and big, and it's a circle-cut diamond just how she likes. Well, according to the social media posts I've seen her liking and a little help from Bree.

"This is the ring I bought. I would have gotten a bigger one but it's not her style. I'd spoil the fuck out of her if she would let me, but she always tells me to spend my money on better things. I've been trying to tell her there's nothing better for my money to be spent on than her, but that's beside the point." I get my emotions under control, my throat feeling like there's something stuck in it as I try to get these last few sentences out. "I know I'm probably not who you imagined your daughter with, but all I'm looking for is a sign or something that you both approve of me loving her forever. It would be the biggest honor of my entire life to love her as long as I'm able."

I sit for a few seconds, the wind blowing the hair out of my face as I wait. I'm not really sure how long this might take, but I'm willing to wait as long as I need to. I know her brother and her father not being here for our wedding is already going to be tough for her, but I'm hoping when I tell her I got a sign from them that they approve, it might ease her mind a little bit. Neither of us is religious, but I've never really thought that death always means someone is totally gone. I think your loved ones from beyond can show up in a lot of different ways, you just have to believe it.

I'm about to get up and walk back to my car, but just as I shift my legs, two bluebirds land on top of their headstones, both of them staring at me as they flutter around on each one.

"Huh," is all I say as I stand up, my blanket in hand. I smile down at the birds, both of them fluttering away as if they were never there in the first place. "Message received."

TEAGS HAS BEEN AT the store all day, and I change my clothes as soon as I get home, not wanting her to ask any questions about why I took the day off from the store to run errands. Well, errands in the form of everyone's blessing for me to ask her to marry me. I haven't thought much about how I'm going to propose, but knowing Teags, she doesn't want anything flashy.

After all the conversations I've had today, I am itching to ask her. In my mind, I know she's mine forever, but not knowing the answer to the most terrifying question in my life has me all riled up. I know she's going to see right through me as soon as she walks through the door. And I can't lie to her. It's practically impossible to lie to my girl.

Fuck.

I grab my phone and send her a text the minute the idea comes into my head.

> **Dom: Don't use the back door. I'm rearranging some things, so you'll have to use the front.**

> **Teags: That was great timing. I just pulled in.**

Fuck. I thought I had a few more hours to spruce this place up, but I guess this will do. All I need her to say is yes. I can focus on the showmanship and showing her off how I want to when we plan the wedding.

I hear her car door shut, and I get ready in the doorway, the flowers I picked up on my way home in my hand, the ring in my back pocket.

She walks inside, and my beautiful girlfriend looks at me as if I'm crazy. God, I get to see her look at me like that forever. I could not be more excited to see her, kiss her, and spend every fucking day with her going forward. *If she says yes...*

She will, right? No, she will. She's as obsessed with me as I am with her. It's going to be fine.

"Baby? What did you do?" she asks me as she smirks, setting her purse and things down on the entry table.

"Why do you assume I've done something? I can't just get you flowers because I love you?" She eyes me skeptically before she brings the flowers to her nose, smiling as soon as she has them in her hands, and before I know it, I'm grabbing her free hand in mine. "Baby..."

"What the hell are you doing?" she asks me as I get down on one knee. "Oh, fuck. I'm having déjà vu."

I laugh, my eyes already tearing up as I think about spending the rest of my life with this powerhouse of a woman in front of me. "Teags, this spot marks the beginning of the adventure we've shared over the past few years. Right here was where our journey down this road began, you clutching your bags with a pissed off expression on your face, me in my pajamas about to embark on what I thought was the beginning of the end for me."

"Well, rightfully so," she jokes, and there are tears in her eyes too. "I was struggling."

"I know, baby," I remind her, squeezing her hand one time before I keep going. "I thought I had everything I needed in life. I thought I was headed for a career and down a road I was going to be unhappy on for the rest of my life. That night you showed up on my porch changed *everything* for me. You showed me how easy it was to love me. You taught me how to be strong even when my voice wants to shake. And you are the reason the word happiness has a definition in my life."

"Fuck," she says as she wipes her tears. "Sorry. I'm totally ruining this moment."

"You could never ruin anything," I tell her, a small laugh bubbling through my body. "I had everything I wanted before you. I was content as I could have been. I had everything I wanted and nothing that I needed because I thought I would survive without it. Now, all I need is you because I cannot live without waking up to your beautiful face in the morning. I cannot live without seeing you smile at me. It's all I want. Some days, the only thing I want is to see you smile, and as soon as it happens, nothing can top that. I fucking love you, Teagen West." I pop the ring box open, tears streaming down my face as I ask her the most important question I'll ever ask another person. "Will you do me the honor of making me your husband?"

"Yes," she whispers before I close the box and spin her around in my arms, never wanting to let go of this girl and this beautiful moment we're sharing, just the two of us in our home. "I love you so much, baby. I have to say, this is not how I imagined this evening to go."

"I asked your family for their blessing earlier, and I knew I wasn't going to be able to wait," I tell her as I slip the ring onto her finger. It fits perfectly.

"My family? Like Tristan and my mom?"

"And Tobias and your dad," I tell her. "I had to ask everyone, Teags. I wouldn't have been able to ask without knowing they gave me their blessing too."

She tilts her head at me, tears in her eyes as her arms go around my neck. "This is beautiful, Dom. It's perfect."

"It's only beautiful because you're the one who's wearing it," I remind her, pressing another ten kisses to her face as I bask in the happiness coursing through my veins. "I love you so much."

She laughs, the two of us giddy as we take in this moment with one another. "I love you too. Now"—she grabs my shirt—"can we go take a shower and celebrate just us before I call Bree and scream at her?"

"Of course we can, baby," I tell her. "Or we could take another trip and elope in Vegas this time?"

She smacks my arm as we head up the stairs. I'm not sure what kind of luck I have in this life to be able to say this woman is going to be mine forever, but I'll be counting my lucky stars that she said yes to being mine.

Wherever we seem to end up, I know the journey with her is going to be worth every fucking second because the two of us are just getting started.

Acknowledgements

Being an author would not be possible without the amazing people I have around me.

Lexi—For everything. From starting out as my right-hand girl to *literally* being in business with me. It is an honor every time I get to call you my PA, but it's always even sweeter calling you my best friend. I am so grateful for your love for my stories and everything you do to get them from draft one to the final product seen here. There are never enough words to tell you how much you mean to me. I love you forever and ever, babe. To the damn moon and Saturn.

Hannah—For the beautiful designs. Your mind never fails to blow every design out of the water. I love telling everyone who will listen that you designed the covers and the beautiful insides of every book I write. My words would not shine without the designs you make, and I *love* you so damn much. Here's to so many more beautiful covers and words and years of friendship.

My Beta readers—Liana, Holly, Sara, Samantha, & Shannon. I cannot thank you all enough. This story would not be what it is today without all of your beautiful suggestions to make my story shine even brighter. I am so thankful for you all. I was terrified to share this story with anyone after having it all to myself for a year, but those fears were eased as soon as I saw all of your comments and suggestions. *Thank you* never seems like enough.

Josh—For everything. But especially for loving me throughout a time of immense confusion, doubt, worry, and sadness. The dark is always less scary when you're by my side in it, guiding me through it. I can't wait to love you forever, even when you're sick of me asking if you still like me. I'd say it won't happen again, but we both know that would be a lie.

Alyssa—For all the years. And for basically yelling at me when I told you Teags was getting a book. You'll always be my favorite person to blab all of my story ideas to, and yes, you can always come over and steal books and art prints from me.

Kristen—For all of the edits! I am so grateful for you! You made editing way less of a feat and your feedback was *perfect*. I am so grateful for everything you did to make this story shine at its brightest.

Ember Literary PR—For making arcs and marketing so easy to manage! I absolutely adore your entire team, and I am so grateful for you guys streamlining this process and taking some of the weight off of my shoulders. You're the best!

Shannon Carse—For everything, really. It's hard to believe a job led me to you, but I will always be thankful to that place for bringing us together. Here's to many more signings, chaos, and crazy book ideas in our future. I love you so much.

E. Salvador—For the support. And honestly, everything in between. I am convinced some cosmic force knew we needed to find one another. I can't wait to yap with you about our book ideas forever in eight minute long staggered voice notes. I adore you and our friendship so much!

Loretta & Sarah—For the laughs. When things feel crappy, I can always count on you guys for a meme, a funny video, or a good rant session. I adore you both so much, and I am grateful the universe brought me to you two! Here's to more laughs, memes, and crash outs together.

My therapist—For everything! I genuinely never fathomed what being in control of my own life felt like until I started working and talking with you. I never imagined what my life looked like into my twenties because I never imagined being here, but now, I have less worry. Less fears about the future. You'll never read this, but I still need to thank you for everything.

My agent—For believing in my stories! I never thought I'd have an agent, let alone someone like you to champion my stories! I cannot wait to see where this partnership takes us.

To the music—Thank you for understanding my brain and feelings in a way I never thought it would be. Music has always been a huge part of my life and now my writing process, and I am grateful to be alive and be able to hear stories told through the medium of music. It's a huge part of Teags and Tobias's stories as well, and being able to share that part of them while feeling so connected to music in my own way was *very* special. Whenever I feel down, I know I will always be thankful for the music, no matter what way I hear it.

And finally, to myself—I know I do this every time, but I have to. I used to write in my journal, terrified that everyone would see the parts of me that I don't like. I would judge my every move and criticize myself for feeling so much, or for saying something stupid. Now, I take pieces of myself, or my mind, or my life—and my confusion about it—and I write about them for the world to read and consume. More than once, someone has felt seen through the stories I love to write, and I'm really damn proud of that. So, dear reader—if you're still here—thank you. Thank you for making my dreams a reality. I'll never take any word, period, or sentence I write for granted. I'm still in awe sometimes I get to call myself an author, and it's all because of *you*.

Also by Emily Tudor

The Grand Mountain Series:

Replaying the Game

Redefining the Rules

Reconsidering the Facts

Reconciling With the Rival

Rewriting the Story

The Hart Sisters:

The Road Not Taken

The Road Less Traveled By

About the Author

Emily Tudor creates characters and stories about platonic and romantic love for anyone and everyone. She lives in the state of New York and loves listening to music and creating stories. She loves Marvel movies, the song *mirrorball* by Taylor Swift and buying too many books when she already has many to be read at home.

You can find her on social media at:
@authoremilytudor
www.authoremilytudor.com